REDISCOVERY

L. S. SILVERTHORNE

He was her last hope at a deep space career.

She was his last hope.

A First Contact Mission from Hell…

"Of all the fueling stations in all the solar systems, she had to be on FS-314." **Captain Quinn Sayre** must sign a third medtech aboard ship or abort his grim recovery mission to the Rim. The only medtech available in the whole damned quadrant is space shy ex-girlfriend, Tarateal Roberts—who hates him more than deep space travel.

"Right now, she'd settle for canceling Sayre out of her life." **Class One Medtech Tarateal Roberts** would rather shove Sayre out an airlock than sign aboard his ship, but this mission is her last chance to save her failing career. And get home to Earth, away from Sayre, the Rim, and a murder investigation.

"All Gage's hatred could be tied up into a neat little bow around Sayre's neck." **Agent Kenrick Gage,** Sayre's former military commander, shows up to usurp command of the mission contract and prove that Sayre killed his son and destroyed his ship.

ACKNOWLEDGMENTS

For my brother JEFF, for answering all of my medical questions and providing all the smart aleck responses I've come to know and expect [and love] from you. Scumbag.

For my dear friend PATRICIA DUFFY NOVAK. (an amazingly talented writer in her own right), for all your support and encouragement.

For DEAN WESLEY SMITH, a writing god, for helping me kick all of those negative voices out of my office and for helping me step over the obstacles and tiger pits in my way. You've helped me more than you'll ever know and I thank you for that.

ISABEL'S TEARS

LANDFALL

PACIFIC BLUE TATTOO

Haunted Portraits series:

BEAUTY: CAPTURED AND FRAMED

FORTHCOMING!

Writing as Lisa Silverthorne

Paranormal Romance & Romantic Suspense

A Game of Lost Souls series:

*The Divine Newlyweds Show, Book Nine (**Nov 2021**)*

The Celestial Couples Show, Book Ten

The Enochian Apocalypse Show, Book Eleven

The Angelic Anniversary Hour, Book Twelve

A Game of Lost Souls—Angelic Hearts:

Muriel's Spark

Kesien's Fire

Anahera's Flame

Azrael's Embers

ONE

A KISS BLOWN to him from a snowy magtape image. Soft hands waving. Larena.

Quinn Sayre leaned back in the desk chair and covered his bloodshot eyes, the image still too painful to watch. His chest tightened as he reached out to the *Magellan*'s composite wall and steadied himself. The ship smelled of amara and recycled air.

On the screen, Larena kicked up rose-colored surf, dotting the screen with little rosy spheres. She used to say the water looked like pink champagne against the Sancian beaches' patina finish. Sand mixed with oxidized copper flakes, giving it a creamy mint cast. Her iridescent teal suit glistened in the sun's ruddy glow, auburn hair like burnished copper. She reminded him of a butterfly flitting across the minty sand.

Out of the cocoon and already dying.

A lump lodged beneath his Adam's apple, anxiety roiling through his stomach, tightening his muscles.

I'll be with you in a little while. Those words haunted him now. How many times had he told her that? Now, she was dead. How could it have happened?

He sloshed the blue-green amara around in his glass before he tossed down the last swig. Some of the amara spilled onto his blue sweatshirt.

Deceased: remains unrecoverable. That's how the official report read.

But without a body, how could they be sure?

Sayre ground his teeth together, eyes narrowing. As long as she fit neatly into one of their categories, the bureaucrats were satisfied. Dead, no body. That was the end of it—next case. They'd be sure to advise him of any changes.

As if he'd sit back and wait for their next response.

Nearra was a dangerous place, the suits told him, said he should be thankful his wife survived as long as she did. Surviving a two-year First Contact mission would have qualified her for immediate retirement and pension. Six more months and it would've been over. She'd have been with him aboard the *Magellan*.

Now, he was alone with this antique magtape viewer she'd always wanted. She never even got to see it.

He reached over and poured himself another glass of amara as Larena began singing an old Irish ballad. Her voice, sounding like a worn wind chime, ached through him. Anguish trembled through his stomach as he pressed the cobalt glass against his mouth and grimaced. Drinking amara was like swallowing crushed glass, but the calm it produced made up for the momentary pain.

In moments, the ache in his gut melted into warmth and he imagined her beside him in the baked sand. His breath caught and he closed his eyes, almost smelling the tang of chlorine salt mixing with Larena's jasmine-vanilla scent, feeling the silky warmth of her skin.

The comm panel in his desk lit green and a soft chime resonated in his ear, almost in harmony with Larena's gravelly alto voice and fake brogue. Wiping his eyes, he punched the mute button and Larena's voice dissolved.

For a moment, he felt paralyzed.

Staring at her frozen smile, he couldn't recall the sound of her voice and that terrified him. Would everything about her fade like that eventually? He tried to hold onto the echo, the melody. *May the road rise up to meet you.* How many times had she sang those words?

Why couldn't he feel them now, vibrating in his ears, brushing across his chest?

Again, the comm's tinny chime sounded through the room. He poked the flashing button, making sure the video feed was off.

"Sayre here."

"You asked to be notified a half hour out from the fueling station." Sanji Shahir's tight-lipped Indian accent rolled out through the speaker, the rich tones soothing despite the news.

Sanji. Always punctual, always diligent. For once, Quinn wished his communications specialist hadn't been on time. Sanji knew how much he dreaded the refuel. It meant the last stop before facing reality: Larena lived only in the digital world now.

He rubbed his eyes again, the guilt gnawing at him as he remembered that final string of messages they'd exchanged, his rushed responses that he'd wished he'd deleted before sending. Had the argument caused her to be reckless? He winced and took another grating sip of amara.

Had her death been his fault?

He'd gone over the details a hundred times since that first government transmission. What went wrong? He sighed, tears stinging his eyes. None of it made sense anymore. But he still had one thing left to do: bring her home.

It was the last thing he could ever do for Larena.

"Quinn, are you there?"

He hesitated, the amara fogging his thinking. Before Larena's disappearance, he'd hated this alien swill, but now, he'd grown a taste for it.

"I'm here," he answered finally, his voice soft and sleepy. "Are we ready to pick up our third medtech?"

"Yes. Taka says you know this one?"

"I—used to."

He rubbed his face. Government contract rules demanded that three medical technicians accompany any mission to the Rim. Over the past six weeks, he'd tried three base hospitals, two pathology outposts, and four fueling stations, but none of them had medtechs interested or up for reassignment. He thought his luck had finally run out until he'd contacted Fueling Station 314. FS-314 had the most hostile weather of any station he'd ever encountered, but perched on the edge of the system, it was the last stop before the Rim.

Prime real estate. Usually packed with people trying to get home. Or get lost.

He sighed. Of all the fueling stations in all the solar systems, she had to be on FS-314. How could he have known that Tarateal Roberts, his ex-girlfriend, would be the only medtech up for reassignment in the whole damned quadrant?

"What do you mean *used to?*" Sanji asked.

Quinn smiled at the irony. Roberts was the only class one medtech available—anywhere. He'd loved her once; he admitted that now. It was a messy breakup and he knew the feelings of hatred were mutual.

Maybe the past few years had mellowed her attitude a bit? Mellowed, as in maybe she no longer wanted to rip his face off and shove him out an airlock?

The deep space exploration he'd craved terrified her and the security of Earth that she yearned for scared him to death. In a heated argument heard by the entire flight school and half the Medical Sciences Academy, he finally told her he wouldn't be chained to Earth for the rest of his life. Crying, she'd told him to go to hell (amongst the other insults she'd hurled at him). They hadn't spoken since.

"An old girlfriend, Sanj. She's the class one medtech—and my last chance. Let's just say she won't be very happy to see me."

"Then she doesn't know you hold her contract?" asked Sanji.

Quinn smiled. Not if he could help it.

"No, Sanj. I can't believe she even accepted this assignment. It's not her style. But if she knew the *Magellan* was my ship, she'd have refused. I couldn't take that chance. It's already been six weeks..."

Quinn glanced at the cactus wilting in a blue ceramic pot on his desk. Larena sent him the cactus halfway through her First Contact mission. Told him that by the time the flowers bloomed, she'd be back. Now, it was dying. He shook his head. Married to a botanist and he couldn't even grow a cactus. Larena always told him that he was good with people, not plants—that's why she'd given him the cactus. Even he couldn't kill a cactus, she'd said.

She was wrong. About a lot of things.

"Do you want Sheryl to handle the landing?"

Good question. He scratched his jaw, feeling thick, black stubble trying to become a beard. What if Roberts was waiting on the tarmac for the *Magellan*'s arrival? If she even heard a whisper of his name, she'd be a memory. She had an aunt at the Assignment Bureau who'd spring her. But without Roberts, the government wouldn't give him Rim clearance. He had to make sure Roberts was aboard.

"Affirmative. I'll be up there as soon as I've shaved and changed clothes." And sobered up with a hot shower.

"I will contact the fueling station with our ETA and get an update on our medtech."

"Good man, Sanji. Sayre out."

"Quinn?"

He paused. "Is there more?"

"Yes. It's about the crew." Sanji hesitated.

"I'm listening."

"There seems to be a few...personality problems. With the new crew members."

Quinn bristled. He'd flown this ship with Sanji Shahir and Taka Yawakani, his senior medtech, since he'd been *asked to leave* the service. Sheryl Hannaford, his navigator, came later, but stayed despite him. The other medtechs seemed to come and go with the contracts. He never understood why his engineer, Jim Winston, disembarked three weeks ago. It'd been a scramble to find a new one, too. Luckily for him Kuruk requested a contract with the *Magellan* or else he'd have bigger problems than medtechs. Vardissians were a newly discovered humanoid species eager to collaborate with humans. They had photographic memories and extreme patience—a perfect fit for his crew.

"What sort of personality problems?"

"Kuruk and Sheryl seem to disagree on everything from flight patterns to drive maintenance. And Dale Park is—a bit overeager."

"Tell anyone with a grievance to stow it until we have a full crew. Otherwise, we'll all be stranded on FS-314 without a credit in our pockets. And it's a long walk back to civilization. Sayre out."

Quinn rose unsteadily from the desk and stretched. For a long time, he gazed at Larena's frozen image.

Maybe the reports were wrong? Maybe—somehow—it was all a mistake?

But the ache in his chest told him otherwise. It wasn't a rescue mission—his head knew that already. It was his heart that couldn't quite grasp the search and recovery mission.

He set the amara bottle on the table and started to sit down, but his comm chimed again. With wavering steps, he made it back to the desk and pressed the comm button.

"Sayre."

"I've just been informed by the station that Class One Medtech Tarateal Roberts is meeting us at the runway," Sanji said.

"Glad to hear she hasn't bailed on us yet and run home to Earth." First piece of good news he'd had in weeks.

"May I make a personal observation, Quinn?"

"Always, Sanji."

There was a pause. "They seemed anxious to get rid of her."

Quinn frowned. "Why do you say that?"

Sanji seemed at a loss for words, and now Quinn wished he hadn't turned off his video feed. Sanji was an excellent judge of character and whenever he had a problem with someone, Quinn paid close attention.

"I heard voices in the background, joking that she wasn't leaving soon enough. It sounds peculiar. What if she is incompetent?"

"I don't care if she can't—grow a—a cactus," Quinn said with a growl. "We need three medtechs and right now, I'll take anybody— even Tarateal Roberts."

"It seems as if she was a problem they wished to be rid of, Quinn. Can't we get a medtech elsewhere?"

"Sanj, you saw what happened whenever the Rim came up. No one wants to go out there—not even me, now. But I have to go. They don't. I'm lucky to have even gotten Park. Hell, I've got shoes older than him."

"Quick medical treatment could be life or death out there," Sanji continued. "What if she cannot perform procedures correctly?"

"Time's running out and problem or not, Roberts is our last chance." He gazed at the video screen again. His last chance to bring Larena home. "Still, I appreciate you telling me this, Sanji. Especially right now." He rubbed his drooping eyelids, the amara finally taking effect.

"I am very sorry about Larena. And I understand how heavily this contract is weighing on you. If I can do anything else—"

"Just watch my back. I admit, I'm not myself. I'm a little distracted."

"May I start by suggesting a few cups of coffee?"

He smiled. "I'll get right on that. I want to be sharp when I talk to Roberts again. Sayre out."

Switching off his comm panel, Quinn gazed at Larena's grinning face and those luminous blue eyes that she'd always complained were too wide set for her nose. She never knew how beautiful they were and how much he hurt when he couldn't look into them. Now, he could only look *at* them. His hand trembled as he reached down and shut off the video. With a flash, Larena's face went dark.

AFTER TWO CUPS OF COFFEE, Quinn changed into a grey flight suit. He ran a hand through his disheveled hair, trying to smooth out the curly locks. What if there *was* something wrong with Roberts' performance? Of course, that had to be it. No medtech with any skill would be at a fueling station—especially a last-chance rock like 314. Back when they were both in training on Earth and her satellite training station, Salice Minor, Roberts had flatly refused to venture even beyond the shipping lanes.

How'd she end up out here?

Sanji's gut feelings had always panned out before. Quinn had known the man since flight school and Sanji knew him better than anyone. Sanji wasn't the type to toss out a careless comment about another human being. Not unless he meant it. Was signing Roberts aboard endangering his crew? He had to make sure she was at least competent.

Quinn pressed the door release and the door softly whirred open. The narrow hallway was empty until Taka Yawakani emerged from one of the cubicles. Her glossy black hair swung in a bob beneath her chin as she walked with short, brisk steps. The yellow flight suit bagged around her small frame. She wore a white T-shirt underneath the flight suit that was unzipped to her navel.

"Quinn, you look tired," she said with a brief smile, and paused outside his compartment door. She smelled like soap. Her mahogany eyes softened.

"Hi, Taka." He ignored her comment. He wasn't tired—he was exhausted. "Are all the medical supplies stowed?"

Taka nodded. She gazed at him for a moment. "I'm very sorry about Larena. We'll do what we can to help you bring her home. We won't let you down."

He smiled. "Thanks. I just hope we get our clearance. We're running out of time."

Her eyes widened. "What if we don't?"

"I'll go anyway."

His words sounded hollow. He knew he and his crew would be arrested long before they ever reached Nearra if they violated regulations. Even failure to file a flight plan and personnel roster would send the military crawling all over them. He'd been arrested before and had no desire to go through interrogations and trials again. The *Augustine* disaster was enough for him.

"With or without the amara?"

His face flushed. "Amara?"

She shook her head. "Don't think I didn't notice, Quinn. I've seen the signs: glazed expression, constricted pupils, exaggerated calm, and slowed responses."

"It's just whisky with a little kick."

"Kick." She clucked at him and laid a hand on his arm. "Look, I know how hard this has been for you, but that stuff will kill you. That's why it's illegal."

He sighed and looked away. Didn't she know how badly he needed it? He had too many ghosts from his past roiling around him and not enough fight without it. With Larena gone...it was too much.

"They can take your flight certification. Do you want that?" She shook his arm. "Do you?"

Wincing, he gazed at her again. Of course, he didn't.

"Lose that and you'll never reach Nearra," said Taka. "A third medtech will be the least of your worries."

"I know, I know," he said, and pulled away from her.

"Amara possession could even land you a stint in a penal colony, Quinn. Then you'd wind up unemployable and on the streets. Is that what you want? Wasn't the Augustine affair bad enough for you?"

"All right, all right! I get your point." He ran his fingers through his dark hair. "I'll cut back on the stuff."

"No, you'll stop," she ordered, and crossed her arms, her gaze hardening. "You'll stop or I'll be forced to turn you in, Quinn. I can't fly in good conscience with an amara-fogged pilot. At the very least,

I'll disembark on FS-314 and you'll be looking for two medtechs instead of one."

He knew she was right. "Message received. I'll do what I can. You know I'd never fly like this."

"I know you wouldn't," she said, and her gaze softened. "I've been part of your crew since the Augustine, Quinn. We've been through a lot together and I'll be there through this one, too, but only if you give up the amara."

He sighed. "I give you my word that I'll do my best to kick it."

"That'll do for now," she said, offering a wary smile. "Now, I need to finish vaccine rounds before we land. Have you seen Park? He's missing a couple of vaccinations."

Quinn shook his head. "Haven't seen him."

"You weren't kidding about taking any medtech, were you? He's barely twenty and on his first assignment."

"He was the only medtech willing to come out here," Quinn said with a shrug. "He's hungry for deep space experience."

Taka rolled her eyes. "And he needs it, too. I don't think he even understands basic first aid procedures, much less a trauma situation. My word, Quinn—he's a bloody intern! What were you thinking?"

Only that Larena was lost. He couldn't think beyond that. He squeezed Taka's arm. "Good thing I've got you aboard."

"Damn right you are," she said, and poked a finger at him. "Remember that the next time you reach for the amara. We'll discuss that before we lift off FS-314. And be warned. Any of that stuff I find gets jettisoned."

She hurried past him down the hallway and toward the infirmary. He lingered a moment outside his compartment then hurried up the hallway toward Navigation.

When he first bought this ship (out of a small inheritance his dad had left him) he regretted buying the cheapest model available. His dad had always told him that if he was only going to buy once, he'd better get exactly what he wanted. As usual, Quinn hadn't listened. He'd convinced himself he could live with anything.

Natural lighting had been too expensive, so he'd opted for standard. After two weeks of the harsh glare, Larena demanded that he make improvements. Grudgingly, he'd shelled out the credits for natural lighting along with better-equipped quarters, mess, and infirmary. But the hallways and quarters were still cramped. He turned sideways to allow Dale Park to pass him.

"Captain Sayre," said the sandy-haired young man.

With slowed responses, Quinn turned toward Park. "What's up, Dale?"

"Ms. Hannaford said to remind you about the autopilot," he said with a polite smile. "I was just coming to get you."

Quinn gazed at Dale's close-cropped sandy hair, not a single strand out of place. He wore a blue flight suit that Quinn could almost swear had been pressed. His black chukkas gleamed brighter than the natural lighting. The grads got younger and younger every year. Records indicated he was twenty, but this kid looked about seventeen. He looked like the poster boy for government service, all polished and squeaky clean. Still, he looked vaguely familiar. Quinn stared at Park's class four rating pin that gleamed black and new gold on his collar. With a class one already dead, Quinn hoped this contract didn't send the kid home in a box.

He winced. Like poor Matt Gage. What had he been thinking to sign this kid aboard?

"I was just on my way up to Nav. I'll take care of it. Thanks, kid."

"No problem, sir."

Quinn turned toward Navigation, but stopped. "Park?"

"Yes, sir?"

"Taka's looking for you. She was headed to the infirmary."

"Thanks, sir." Park whistled as he hurried toward the infirmary. The shrill notes reverberated through the passageway, hurting Quinn's amara-fogged head.

He hurried toward Nav. The *Magellan* would slip out of autopilot in less than ten minutes. Sheryl would be sullen and silent if he shoved another unexpected duty on her this week. She'd been a good sport to put up with him this long. They all were. He hoped to put that behind him now. Once on the ground, he'd deal with the medtech situation personally. He couldn't hide his identity from Roberts any longer.

The amara he'd deal with later.

TWO

"I NEED BANDAGES OVER HERE! NOW!"

Tarateal Roberts held down the writhing runway steward, trying to keep his severely burned arm still. She'd already neutralized the acrid white sludge clinging to his arm. The burn needed immediate attention. So where in blazes were the other medtechs?

The man's face contorted in agony and he screamed. She pressed harder on his torso, feeling the sickbed creak beneath him. He outweighed her by at least sixty pounds. She couldn't hold him if he fought. The sour smell of sludge mixed with the man's sweat-laden clothes and she turned her head.

Interns and medtechs rushed past her station in the brightly lit, twelve-bed infirmary, walls as white as sludge, and ignored her patient. And ignored her.

Glancing around the room, she saw two other curtains closed. There were only three injuries. Why was everyone suddenly too busy to assist?

The steward groaned, his whole body shaking from pain.

"Hang in there, Bennett," she said with a smile, and smoothed the hair out of his eyes. "You're going to be okay." She slipped a blanket across him to keep him warm.

Medtechs Raul Hernandez and Stewart Anderson slipped past her station, laughing about some sports score.

"Raul, Stew, I need some help here!"

Hernandez stared at her for a moment, casting a smirk at Anderson. "Help with a sludge burn? You're kidding, right?"

"Supplies, smart guy! I need supplies. Whoever was assigned to this station didn't restock it."

Bennett shouted again and she fought to hold him on the table.

"C'mon, I can't hold him much longer."

"Can't help you, Roberts," said Anderson, snickering under his breath, and followed Hernandez out of the infirmary.

"Good luck on your next commission!" shouted Hernandez.

She heard them laughing in the hallway.

A service intern with a stack of forms in his hands rushed past her station.

"Wes, I need supplies here!"

The young man ignored her, moving behind a desk to collect some reports. He started past her again, but Tarateal stuck out her leg, catching the intern in the shins. He stumbled and papers went flying.

"Hey! What'd you do that for?" The young man struggled to his feet and scrambled for the papers.

"Now that I've got your attention, I need supplies and I need them now!" She nodded toward the supply room, shaking dark blond hair out of her eyes. "Get some bandages and some blankets over here. I've got a man on the verge of shock! Get to it!"

Mumbling to himself, the young man rushed over to the supply room at the end of a short hallway.

"I can't stand the pain! Can't stand it!" Bennett clutched the sleeve of her white scrubs with his left hand.

Tarateal gripped his torso tighter as the man began to thrash. "Help's coming. Hang on."

In a few moments, the intern rushed back to her station, a tray in his hands. He set it on the table beside her.

"Now, hold him down so I can strap him in," she replied.

The young man complied, allowing her to slip straps around Bennett's ankles and chest. When she'd secured his good arm, she sighed in relief.

"Thanks, Wes," she said with a relieved sigh. She nodded toward the forms littering the floor. "I think you dropped something."

"Yeah, thanks for nothing," he muttered, and stooped to pick up the forms. "Now I know why everyone's glad you're leaving."

"What was that?" She glared at him.

His face paled. "Nothing, ma'am. I've gotta turn in these forms." He made a hasty retreat toward the hallway.

That was one more thing about this place she wouldn't miss. She turned back to her patient.

Quickly, she irrigated the burn. Fumbling with the cap on the tube, she opened it and spread a thin sheen of clear protective gel across the sludge burns. Almost instantly, the gel's local anesthetic took effect and Bennett relaxed. He was stabilizing. When he settled back against the pillow, exhausted from fighting the pain, she injected him with painkiller and went to work on bandaging the wounds.

Using forceps, she lifted a translucent strip of synthetic skin out of its packaging and covered the wound. The synthetic skin would insulate the wound while it healed. In a couple of weeks, Bennett would be back clearing more runways of that nasty white sludge they had the nerve to call *snow* here.

When Bennett's eyes closed, Tarateal covered him with a blanket. She leaned against the cabinet, snapping off her gloves. This was the last time she'd ever have to work in the station clinic. No more sludge burns and hangovers. No more Hernandez and Anderson. A deep space contract mission was a big step, but after years of medtech experience, she was finally ready.

She watched Bennett's vitals for some time, making sure he was stable before she signed him over to the next shift.

How she'd gathered the courage to accept a deep space contract, she'd never know. The *Magellan* mission was the only way to get the other medtechs off her back. It'd been the shortest contract mission available.

No deep space experience necessary, the listing had read. Boy, was she qualified for that!

If a short run to the Rim would get her back home to Earth, then she'd do it. She sighed. She'd even walk barefoot through FS-314's *snow* to get home. With a hospital job back on Earth, she'd be okay. Safe and sound back in Washington State.

She started when she glanced at her watch. The *Magellan* had arrived ten minutes ago! She was late. A quick change of clothes and a stop at her storage locker, then it was goodbye fueling station.

BENNETT WAS STILL stable when Tarateal signed off her shift. In the locker room, she changed into a white T-shirt and navy blue flight suit. She took the lift down to the basement and retrieved her duffel bags from a storage locker. The well-lit tunnels, smelling like apples and recirculated air, were nearly empty. She mumbled a quick goodbye to a couple of medtechs in scrubs and ran with both duffel bags toward the Visitors' Pavilion. The *Magellan*'s captain was probably wondering why she hadn't met the ship.

She followed the bright yellow stripe down the tunnel until it veered right. From there, she followed it to a yellow door marked *Visitors' Pavilion*. Setting down one of the duffel bags, Tarateal thrust open the door. How had she ever managed to reduce her life down to two duffel bags? Holding the door open with her foot, she retrieved the other bag and plunged into the waiting room.

Sludge ran like paint down the windows, coating everything in a caustic film. She groaned, dropping her bags beside the windows that faced the landing area. Of all days for sludge to fall, it had to be today. She glanced up at a flight schedule screen on the wall. The

Magellan's liftoff time had been pushed back at least an hour. If this sludge started to fall again, the station could delay them for days.

Groaning, she slumped against the wall. She wanted off this rock today. She couldn't face Hernandez and Anderson if she didn't leave today.

Through the streaks of glass, she watched the stewards steaming away the ooze from the tarmac beneath mist-filled hangars where ships huddled out of the storm. Bennett would be back at the job soon enough. She'd seen to that. Gazing at those glistening outbound ships made her smile. They reminded her of the ones from those old magnetic tapes in the museums. She wondered which ship was the *Magellan.*

The sludge had stopped falling, but the oozing continued long afterward. It was beginning to harden on the runways. As soon as the stewards removed the debris and clearance was given, the *Magellan* would depart for the Rim.

The Rim. It sounded like the end of the world.

She gazed up at the familiar sky. FS-314 was as far out in space as she'd ever ventured. What would the Rim of known space feel like? Would it be as lonely and barren as this place?

She'd heard bits and pieces about the *Magellan's* commission in the clinic lounge. Something about a rediscovery mission and a government First Contact team that lost half its crew. The *Magellan* needed another medtech. Everybody had been talking about it. Because of the danger, government rules required three medtechs for all deep space missions. The third medtech aboard ship was considered a fail-safe in the event of a catastrophic accident. Odds were high that one of three medtechs would survive.

She shuddered. Whatever contract the *Magellan* had negotiated was dangerous.

Tarateal turned away from the window. It wasn't exactly the Rim that frightened her—it was the dying part. She was twenty-seven, still young enough to do whatever she wanted. Was a rediscovery mission worth risking her own life? Let the government go in and reestablish contact with their own team. No one knew if this team was even still alive. Communication had been lost for some time, so the whole mission might be nothing more than a coroner's run. She leaned against the curved window of the waiting room and glanced over at the four empty rows of orange chairs. Not once since she'd been on this station had even one row of those chairs been filled by passengers. No one spent much time here, unless they were delayed —or desperate.

In the corner of the room, the soda machine buzzed, its purple and teal panel flickering. The smell of burned coffee tanged the air, the coffee machine's touchscreen panel dark. She sighed. Vending machines were broken again. For the third time this month. She was tired of warm sodas and recycled coffee grounds shipped out here from Earth. Even the station's meals were unsold government surplus. Just once she'd like something better than other people's leftovers.

She snapped her navy suit's neck flap tighter and removed a safety helmet from a shelf on the wall. She thrust the helmet over her head and a twinge of excitement quivered in her stomach. Old coffee and warm sodas didn't matter now. She wouldn't miss them or the clinic. Hopefully, this contract would be her ticket home to Earth— and fresh coffee for starters. Going home. It was all she'd dreamed of for years. She adjusted her sleeves, being careful that no skin was exposed, and fastened her wrist straps. The *snow* could burn bare skin in seconds.

Quickly, she slid on black, tight-fitting gloves, her thoughts drifting to the Rim and the alien races she might encounter, races she'd seen only virtually in her medical interactives. For once, she could be there instead of simulating contact. With actual contact experience, she might bypass any more bedpan shifts at places like this. Although, she'd never heard of anyone dying while cleaning a bedpan. Reaching inside her helmet, Tarateal whisked away the wisps of dark blond hair clinging to her cheeks.

The green canvas duffel bags at her feet made her smile. No more snow sludge to burn her skin and no more rain dust to scour her clothes to rags. Other than the weather and the coffee, this fueling station was actually one of the safest places to be stationed—besides Earth. But three years on this rock was enough. Throughout her career, she'd only been injured badly once and she had no desire to tempt fate a second time. She'd been twenty-two, fresh out of the Medical Sciences Academy, and on her way to her first commission on Lunar Colony.

When everything collided.

She turned back to the window, squinting at the misty spray scattering rainbows across the greyness of the runways.

Twenty-two. The year everything fell apart. Her mother warned her about turning twenty-two. *Some of the biggest decisions in your life will happen the year you graduate,* her mother had once said. *Those choices will change your life.*

For years, Tarateal dreaded that day. Looking back now, she had good reason. She and her boyfriend, Quinn, had parted enemies just days before her graduation. Then her mother died soon after Tarateal graduated from the academy on Salice Minor. Later that year, the shuttle accident happened on Lunar Colony—she'd almost died. Ever since that accident, she'd been haunted by the thought of space travel and vowed to avoid it. That was as close to dying as she ever wanted to come.

The thick ooze finally trickled off to heavy droplets that splattered against the domed roof of the Visitors' Pavilion. Relieved, Tarateal trudged out of the waiting room and out onto the hardening, ankle-deep sludge to find the *Magellan.*

A pale sun hung high in the sky, craggy ground covered white. Behind the Visitors' Pavilion stood the flat, star-shaped clinic building. The clinic's white walls seemed to fade away whenever a snowstorm erupted. To her right, runways stretched across the whitened landscape like arteries. Hangars dotted the horizon, a white haze surrounding them. If she squinted, the transparent hangars reminded her of those antique snow globes with the chunky squares of snow fluttering around an ice skater or some quaint cottage.

All around her, sludge clung to the rocks and ground, molding itself to the terrain. What she wouldn't give to see a forest of Douglas firs on the horizon. She licked her lips. Or a fresh-brewed mocha back home in her favorite Washington State coffeehouse.

The sludge had hardened on the runway, ready to be chipped away. Abruptly, three runway stewards waddled out of the misty hangar and across the congealing ooze, their faded yellow boots quivering around their legs. The first steward, a scrawny, balding man, halted in midstride when he saw Tarateal. His mouth slowly widened beneath his bulbous nose and he thumped one of the other stewards on the shoulder. This steward, a dark, stout woman with a double chin and wind-burned cheeks glanced up at Tarateal.

"Is that her?"

Tarateal squinted at them.

The third steward nodded. "Yeah, that's the one."

"Must be too well-paid to turn down all those contracts."

Tarateal frowned. Not this medtech. Maybe by back-world standards she was well-paid, but on Earth, she couldn't afford even an efficiency.

"Isn't she the one signed aboard the *Magellan*?" When the balding steward realized that Tarateal could hear him, he stopped talking. His face reddened as he thrust a spiked rake into the muck. "How's Bennett," he asked without looking at her.

"Bennett suffered third-degree burns on his right forearm, but he's resting comfortably. He should be back at work in about a week." She glanced around the runways. "Where's the *Magellan* docked?"

One of the stewards pointed at the sleek silver ship two runways over. "That's her. The man pacing the runway is the captain. He's been looking for you."

"You mean, the fool without a protective suit," the other steward replied. "Refused the one I offered him."

Great, Tarateal thought, *the man doesn't have enough sense to get out of the sludge and he's heading this mission.* Her stomach tightened. *I feel much safer now.*

With the crunch of sludge reverberating inside her helmet, she walked slowly toward the ship. A restless, wiry man with close-cropped sable hair stalked the sludge-covered runway. His eyes looked hollow and shadowed. He seemed as if he hadn't slept in some time. He looked so familiar.

Suddenly, the realization hit her.

Quinn Sayre.

Anger flushed her face as she stormed toward him.

"Why are you here, Sayre?" She glared at him, her jaw tight, her voice strained.

How she'd hated him over the years—his carelessness, his callousness, dumping her for the Rim. But the worst was finding that bitch Larena Neville hooking up with him not two days after the breakup. She hadn't seen him since. And didn't want to either. She'd been so in love with him and their breakup had taken a long time to get over. She didn't want to dredge all of that up again. She couldn't.

Sayre whirled around, honey hazel eyes wide. For a moment, she remembered starlit walks through the botanical garden and snuggling through old magtape showings in the museum. Dinner and ale at the Silver Orca Pub. Those eyes still churned with fire, vaguely reminiscent of that fiery young man who'd once vowed to take the Rim by storm. She'd loved him more than her own dreams, but not enough to conquer her fears. She used to admire his assertiveness and how he'd always managed to get what he wanted out of life. She'd simply waited for life to find her.

But seeing him over her so quickly hurt more than those good memories.

A boyish smile cracked the moody, tired mask and he looked more charming than brooding. A ghost of the young man she once knew. He seemed exhausted, his tanned skin lined a little too deeply around his mouth and eyes. With his drooping features and short steps, he looked almost—strung-out.

"Roberts," he said quickly. "It's—been a long time."

"Not long enough! How dare you not tell me up front that you held my contract? How dare you!"

He held out his hands. "If you'd seen my name, would you have accepted this contract mission?"

"Not a chance! And I have no intention of doing so now."

He took hold of her arm and for an instant, she saw the desperation in his eyes. "It's too late for that. You've already accepted this assignment."

"Let go of me, Sayre," she said in a low voice. "There's no way I'm stepping one foot aboard your ship."

He'd aged since she'd last seen him. Probably had traveled half the universe by now and gotten into a lot of trouble in the process. That was just like him. Always the tough guy, pretending he was indestructible. That always made her crazy. Somewhere beneath that haggard mask was a man she'd once loved. Why'd he have to come back now? Now that she'd finally gotten over him and had a chance to go home.

"In forty-five minutes, we're bound for the Rim. I have a signed contract from you, Roberts."

"I'm not going anywhere with you. Now, let go of my arm!"

He glared at her, his eyes narrowing. "If you're not aboard this ship in forty-five minutes, I'll have you arrested."

Her hand slammed against his cheek. He let go of her arm, grabbing his face.

"No, I've got forty-five minutes to get out of this contract, Sayre. Have a good life and stay out of mine!"

She turned to leave, but he rushed in front of her.

"Wait! Don't you realize how valuable contact experience is to potential employers?" His voice took on a recruiter's edge. "After this mission, you'd have your pick of reassignments—including Earth."

Surprised by his desperation, she took a step back from him. "Don't worry about me, Sayre. I'll get home without contact experience."

He sighed and his gaze fell to the hardened sludge at his feet. "Roberts...how many class one medtechs do you know—without deep space experience—working back on Earth?"

She opened her mouth to respond, but nothing came out. He was right. Medtechs without galactic experience ended up in nursing homes and morgues back on Earth.

"No company on Earth would hire a class one without that experience," he said, shaking his head. "That's what they pay all their personnel for—experience. Any bonehead can go out and get a degree, but a medtech with solid experience is more valuable than fresh produce."

That's when she noticed the wedding ring on his finger. For an instant, the universe imploded and then expanded. Her lungs constricted. He'd married that bitch!

"Leave me alone, Sayre!" She brushed past him. Her boots crackled across the sludge as she dashed toward the ridge.

"Roberts, wait!"

"Hey!" the female steward called to her. "The trams will be out in a minute or two. Until the sludge shatters, it's dangerous out there."

Tarateal didn't break stride toward the station administration building. He was married! She felt sick inside.

She'd wasted so many years crying over him. At least he hadn't made smart remarks about her assignment here. On Salice Minor, he would have.

So, what if she'd stayed in one place? She liked familiar places. She liked knowing what to expect every day and not having to worry about getting killed. No, she'd done the responsible thing. She'd played it safe. She'd protected her life—she sighed—preserved it like the magtapes in the museums. And it was just as pristine and singular as it had been years ago when she met Sayre.

Now, he was married! What was he doing here?

Already, the sludge had stiffened, the smacking of her boots turning hollow. The sky and flat terrain beyond the ridge looked whitewashed—so sterile and safe. It reminded her of her first commission at a lunar hospital. Back then, she'd needed the safety of those walls and floors—she couldn't help herself. She'd vowed that as soon as she'd built up some courage, she'd put in for a commission farther out. But when a First Contact team commission to Nomas Major came up, she passed on it. Later, when she was ready, she'd go. Later turned into years.

She'd board one of those mythical ships from the magtapes and experience what she saw in the interactives. All of that was so long ago and right now, she missed those magtapes and how they'd once made her feel invincible. All of it floated around the networks, free to view, but she loved seeing the actual tapes in the museum.

She sighed. With someone she loved.

The ridge looked smooth, all the rocky crevices caulked with snow and molded into softness. No sharp edges to slip on and no loose rocks to dislodge. With tear-filled eyes, she crested it, her boots hugging the hardened snow, and stared at the building below. Covered in sludge, it looked more like an igloo than an administration building. She glided down the hillside and onto level ground.

There had to be a way to sign off on this mission.

When she entered the building, her boots clicked across the shiny tiled floor. She moved toward an alcove with a cluster of computers. The walls glimmered clinic white, reflecting Tarateal's tired face in the glossy surface. Laying a hand to her face, she noticed the lines beginning beneath her eyes and brushing softly across her cheeks. She ran her fingers across the two grey strands of hair in front of her right ear, remembering her anxiety at finding them. They didn't even show against her dark blond hair, but she knew they were there.

She moved to the reception desk. A young man with blond hair and a dark uniform looked up from his control panel.

"May I assist you?"

"Tarateal Roberts, Class One Medtech. I need to speak with someone about a contract commission I recently accepted."

The young man looked down and began keying in some

information, his fingers flashing across the clear surface. "Are you on leave?"

"No," she answered with a sigh. "I'm due to ship out in less than forty-five minutes, so I need to speak to someone right away."

"What is the nature of your visit?"

"I want out of this contract!" She cringed at the shrillness of her voice. She was beginning to sound as desperate as Sayre.

The young man looked up, a surprised look on his face. "I'll see who's available, Ms. Roberts. Please wait here."

As the young man rose from his desk, Tarateal wandered over to the computers in the alcove. If she could get out of this contract, she'd be away from here—and Sayre—in a couple of taps.

She removed her helmet and studied the virtual keyboard projection beside the touchscreen. She wanted a cancel or delete button to all of her mistakes. Press backspace and become twenty-two again. And lose her edge, her experience? She smiled, her index finger brushing across the touchscreen.

Right now, she'd just settle for canceling Sayre out of her life.

If only she knew at twenty-two what she knew now. Maybe things would have turned out differently? But she didn't even know who she was at twenty-seven, much less the person she'd been at twenty-two. She frowned. And she'd never know if she kept making the same stupid mistakes. Walking that same infinite loop. Always trying to prove Sayre was wrong about her. She despised him for that. Why did she even care what he thought? She'd prove him wrong. Somehow.

Removing her ID card from her sleeve pocket, she tapped it against the screen. Why hadn't anyone told her that Sayre was in command of this mission? He sounded so desperate. Was there something else about this mission, some sort of emergency that no one had mentioned?

Reaching out, she tapped through the job listings until she found the *Magellan* contract and accessed its listing. Sayre needed another medtech for the voyage and the risk factor was labeled high risk. The probability of fatalities was high. Her fingers turned cold. She didn't want to die on some flight of fancy that Sayre had dreamed up. Besides, he was married.

No, she *had* to get out of this commission.

She closed the window. There had to be other commissions out there.

After paging through lists of available commissions, she found nothing closer to Earth than reassignment on FS-314. How could that be? She felt the emptiness expand inside her. FS-314 for three more years? How could she stay now? She'd packed all her bags and told everyone she was leaving.

Artificial light streamed through the building windows. She imagined how the sludge would be cracking about now. The pocked ridge would have already broken through the layer of sludge and the stewards would be readying the *Magellan* for takeoff.

What would she tell the station staff now? In less than thirty minutes, they'd be coming to the Pavilion to see her off. How would she explain not being aboard?

"Ms. Roberts," called the receptionist.

She put away her ID card and hurried back to the desk. Standing there was an older, dark-haired woman waiting patiently. "I'm Commission Assignment Officer Nancy Callahan."

"I hope you can help me," said Tarateal.

"This way, please."

Tarateal followed the woman down the hallway and into a small, beige office. The woman motioned Tarateal into a seat in front of the desk as she sat down behind it.

"Now then," said Callahan. "I'm told that you want to be released from a commission?"

"Yes, ma'am," said Tarateal, leaning forward. "It's a contract assignment."

The woman frowned and keyed in a few commands on her tablet. "That's a tough one. May I have your ID please?"

Tarateal handed her the card. The woman tapped it against the screen and returned it.

"Approximately one month ago, you accepted this contract with the *Magellan*, contract held by Captain Quinn Sayre."

She bristled at Sayre's name. "At the time that I signed aboard, I was not told who held the contract."

The woman studied Tarateal for a moment. "Is there a problem with Captain Sayre? Something that would prevent you from serving out your commission?"

"A personal one, I'm afraid."

The woman smiled. "Is it something that you're willing to sacrifice your class one status for?"

A cold chill rolled across her shoulders. "What do you mean?"

"Because this is a contract commission, you're allowed to decline the mission up to thirty minutes prior to departure, but—there's a substantial penalty."

Tarateal's eyes widened. "What—sort of penalty?"

"Demotion. You would be downgraded to a class three medtech if you signed off on this commission."

Class three? She shuddered. That would mean a massive pay cut, fewer benefits, less choice of assignments. A class three was a step above an academy graduate. There had to be another way. There had to be.

"I would advise against signing off, Ms. Roberts. I'm sure it must have taken you several years and a lot of work to reach class one status. To throw that away on a personal disagreement with the *Magellan*'s captain is unfair to you."

Tarateal sighed. The woman was right. Dejected, Tarateal rose from the chair.

"Thank you for your time and the information. I need to think it over."

"You're quite welcome," said the woman, seeing her out of the office. "Good luck with whatever you decide."

Not looking back, Tarateal headed out of the office and out of the building.

When she crested the ridge, a tram had paused to pick up passengers, so she scrambled aboard. The slow-moving craft rolled roughly over the terrain, sludge cracking and popping beneath it.

Finally, the tram lurched to a stop near the runways and Tarateal slipped out of her seat. Sayre walked across the tarmac, carrying a case of supplies toward his ship. His short, dark hair curled just above the collar of his black jacket. Damn him, he was still as attractive as ever. He set the crate on a conveyor when he saw her approaching. She groaned, feeling her body stiffen. There was no way to avoid him.

"Roberts!" he called, anger in his eyes. "I'm not through talking to you yet."

She knew that look.

"Not now, Sayre," she said, brushing past. "Besides, you had your chance back on Salice Minor. And you blew it!"

She dashed across the cleared runway, past the passenger shuttle, and into the Visitors' Pavilion to retrieve her bags. She was young. She had time to work back up to a class one again.

The whole deep space idea was stupid anyway, she thought, and hefted the bags.

She was going back to her quarters and wait for a safer commission, one suited to a class three. She didn't relish the thought of spending weeks fighting with Sayre and rehashing old arguments. She'd had her fill of that a long time ago.

As she started out the door, Hernandez and Anderson stopped in front of the Pavilion, their backs to the door. She pulled back toward the threshold.

Hernandez, dark-haired and wearing a red hazard suit, stood beside Anderson, a taller, blond man with a beard and loose-fitting brown scrubs. He wore a black fake-leather jacket over his scrubs.

"Think she's aboard?" asked Hernandez.

Anderson shrugged and thrust his hands into his pockets. "She better be. This is her last chance at a career."

"I heard she could still walk—it being contract work and all."

"If she's stupid enough to pass this up," said Anderson, his voice rising, "then she gets what she deserves."

Hernandez shushed him. "You mean demotion?"

"Damn right," said Anderson, his voice softer. "They won't keep paying her at class one status for faux experience. Not even here. She's had three years to get some deep space experience and she's turned everything down."

"You'd think she'd have taken something—at least a two-week contract."

"The Board won't put up with it anymore," Anderson continued. "They'll have her cleaning out bedpans at class three and half her salary if she walks away from this contract. They certainly wouldn't let her sign up here for another three years."

The nylon handles on Tarateal's duffel bags bit into her palms as she gazed out at Sayre.

Sayre, looking dejected, thrust his hands in his jacket pockets and leaned against the ship as he watched the supplies loading into the rear of the vessel. He signaled to a tall, lanky Indian man with bushy black hair and gentle brown eyes.

"Sanj, we're lifting off in ten minutes. Oasis-Station Theta's on our way out of the system. We'll hit them up for additional personnel."

"On our way?" The other man stopped checking off supplies on his datapad, his mouth hanging open. "Quinn, that's quite a deviation from our flight trajectory."

"We don't have a choice, Sanji," he snapped. "Just see to it."

The man called Sanji stood there for a moment, the datapad dangling from his fingers, and then resumed checking in the supplies.

The Rim. Tarateal shivered. It was the end of the world.

The thought of being shipwrecked on some uncharted, hostile world with her life draining away terrified her. Almost as much as spending several weeks fighting with Sayre.

She glanced at Anderson and Hernandez, anger swelling in her stomach. The thought of another tour on someplace like FS-314 with recycled coffee and *friends* like these made her ill. Dammit, she was a good medtech and after she came back from the Rim, she'd be one of the highest paid in the system. They'd kill to have her back here.

Bedpans. She scowled. *Not this tour, boys.* She let the door to the Pavilion slam behind her.

Startled, Hernandez snapped his gaze toward her and his eyes widened. "Roberts!"

Anderson turned and his cheeks flushed. Quickly, he shuffled out of her way.

"Guess this is goodbye," she said with a smile. "Take care of yourselves. Seeya in the holos."

She made her heavy duffel bags look weightless as she moved toward the *Magellan*. Sayre's mouth gaped.

"I thought you signed off on me," he said, confusion in his eyes.

When she didn't answer, his gaze fell to the ground. Desperation tightened his pale, stubbled features.

"I lied," she said flatly. "Where do I stow my bags?"

The tension left his face and his shoulders relaxed. For an instant, he reminded her of that boyish, insatiable maniac she used to love, but the gold wedding ring gleaming up at her made her look away.

Smiling, he pointed to the ship's belly where Sanji conveyed supplies into the hold, a young woman beside him.

"Hand them off to Yawakani. She'll have someone stow them in the infirmary for you."

Sayre paused for a moment, sighed, and then glanced away from her face. Tarateal saw his eyes turn glassy as he stared into the distance.

"Regs are strict about medtechs," he said in a softer tone. "We couldn't have gone without you. Thank you."

There was an awkward moment of silence between them.

"Hope you're up to the challenge, Roberts. There's a billion ways to die in the Rim." His voice ached, his words like a requiem, and

Tarateal wondered what hid behind those hazel chameleon's eyes. He wasn't telling her something.

"I can hold my own, Sayre."

"Better get aboard." Sayre motioned to the lithe woman with dark hair and chestnut, almond-shaped eyes by the conveyor. "Taka Yawakani is my senior medtech. She'll show you to your quarters. If you need anything, anything at all, just ask Sanji. Or me."

A stocky flight maintenance steward stepped up to Sayre. "Sayre, we're ready to run pre-flight checks and engine diagnostics on your order." The man laid a hand against his thick neck, the grime on his face making his grey eyes look glassy.

"Not enough time," Sayre answered. "We're lifting off in less than ten minutes."

"But regulations insist on a scan. What do I tell your engineer?"

Sayre motioned toward the ship. "Remind Kuruk that the engines were scanned on Thessario and passed with zero defects. It's not necessary. Besides, if that sludge starts falling again, we won't get out of here for days."

The steward sighed. "You're the boss. I'll tell your man to just do a test-fire. That's enough for clearance off the station, but I'd recommend an engine scan."

Sayre shook his head and the steward walked away.

Tarateal glanced back at Anderson and Hernandez gawking at her from the edge of the runway.

Let the games begin, she thought as she turned toward Taka Yawakani, who took one of her bags.

Taka was wirier than she appeared. Tarateal saw well-defined muscles beneath the thin fabric of her canary-colored sleeves. She had a nice smile and her eyes gleamed like polished topaz.

"This way," said Yawakani, who took long strides toward the ramp leading into the *Magellan*. "The *Magellan's* infirmary is state-of-the-art. And we have a full crew. We should be fine."

"What have I gotten myself into," Tarateal mumbled under her breath as she ascended the ramp, Taka behind her.

"A murder investigation," said Taka.

Tarateal stopped on the ramp. "What?"

"We're trying to find out why four class one government employees died on Nearra."

Four class ones? She looked back at FS-314 and wondered how many ways she could die out in the Rim.

THREE

QUINN'S SMILE was grim as he glanced up at the pale sun. He was going to the Rim. All his life, he'd dreamed of discovering worlds and sentient species. But not like this. He shook his head.

Not with Larena dead.

He'd tried to understand why she didn't wait for him to come with her on this First Contact opportunity. Why she'd insisted on going alone. Two years away from him after they'd just gotten married. But all of that seemed so pointless now.

At first, she messaged him every day, but with the passing months came shorter, less frequent messages until all he had were memories and an empty inbox.

He sighed. He needed a drink.

Brittle, putty-colored sludge chunks littered the tarmac and he kicked at them, waiting for Kuruk to finish the engine test-fire. He pulled his jacket tighter around him. The wind had picked up, carrying the caustic smell of fuel and sludge across the scorched, blackened runway. How could Roberts have stayed on this dead station for three years? He coughed and moved away from his ship. At least she hadn't signed off on him.

Maybe his luck was starting to change?

Someone shouted his name.

Didn't sound like Kuruk. Quinn frowned. The blasted maintenance crew probably wanted to throw another regulation in his way. Hadn't he gone enough rounds with them and Roberts for one day? Quinn hurried around the nose of the *Magellan*.

"Sayre!"

Had he forgotten essential supplies or was Park fighting with Sheryl again? Expecting to see Sanji frantically pacing the runway, Quinn was surprised to see another red-faced ghost from his past. He stiffened and nearly snapped a salute. Old habits died hard.

Former Commander Kenrick Gage glowered at him, shoulders squared and deep-set grey eyes dull. The lanky man stood six-foot-four to Quinn's five-foot-eleven" frame. His thick brown hair bristled grey into a military haircut. The man had aged a lot in five years.

"Sir...it's been a long time, I—"

"Just shut up and listen, Sayre!" Gage poked Quinn in the chest. "I didn't come here to wax poetic over the glory days. There weren't any!"

Flashes of that night aboard the *Augustine* surged over Quinn— the lost communiqué, the privateers' plasma fire erupting through the buckling hull, and the desperate scramble through exploding darkness to reach a life-pod. In moments, Quinn's first commission had gone up in flames. Gage lost his son and his ship in that ambush and Quinn had taken the blame for it. Poor kid had been only days away from a shore leave that would never come. A short trial later, Quinn was dishonorably discharged from the military. Gage wanted the death penalty, but the jury recommended discharge. Gage hated him. It seemed like a lifetime ago, much longer than five years.

Sayre swallowed back a sigh and faced his former commander. "What can I do for you, sir?"

"Do for me, Sayre?" The hatred still burned hot in those grey eyes, as fiery and malicious as it had that night in the life-pod. If anything, Gage's fury had deepened, rekindled by this meeting. Quinn felt like he was being interrogated all over again. "You've done quite enough. Now, I've come to do something to you."

Quinn frowned. Whatever it was, he'd take it. For Sanji, he'd accept whatever revenge this man sought.

"I'm no longer a ship's commander, Sayre, but I've built up a lot of seniority as a government agent. When they posted this assignment, I called in every favor ever owed to me to get it."

He poked Quinn in the chest again. Quinn took a step back, gritting his teeth.

For Sanji, he told himself.

"You're a dangerous screwup, Sayre. You always have been. Now, I've got the chance to let you finally prove it to the government. And I'm here to make sure this delicate situation is handled properly."

"You damned right it's a delicate situation," Quinn said with a snarl. "My wife's dead! I'm going there to recover her body. It's the only reason I took this contract."

A satisfying smile puckered Gage's tired face. The man was enjoying his pain. Quinn remembered the kind, patient commander who went out of his way for even the greenest ensigns, treating them like sons and daughters. Quinn had revered him once, but he despised the bitter man who emerged from the life-pod that night.

"That's the only reason they gave you the contract, Sayre. Don't ever forget that. You step out of line once, deviate from regulations even a millimeter, and I'll have your ship and you in chains."

Quinn bristled. He'd die before he'd let anyone take his ship.

"Quinn?"

He glanced up at Sanji, who stood in the threshold of the open hatch. Gage's shoulders sagged as he paced toward the cargo conveyor.

"What?" Quinn snapped, unable to hold back the edge in his tone.

"Kuruk says the engine test-fire has been completed. We've got liftoff clearance."

"Thanks, Sanj," he answered in a softer voice.

"Surely even you realize that this situation has moved beyond search and recovery," said Gage finally, the anger in his voice softening. "We've lost contact with the team, and now their whole mission is in jeopardy. I'm here to reestablish contact and oversee this contract." He turned around and smiled menacingly. "Any questions?"

Quinn clenched his hand into a fist. No, he'd come this far. He'd endure Roberts and Gage both if that's what it took. He'd find out what happened to Larena if he had to drag every bad memory from his past on a string behind him.

"Just one." Quinn's eyes narrowed. "How do I get you off my ship?"

"Stand down from this mission," said Gage without hesitation. "Confess to the authorities that you're a privateer and that you helped destroy the Augustine that night."

"That'd be so easy, wouldn't it?" He took a step toward Gage. "Then all your hatred could be tied up into a neat little bow around my neck. You're way off base, commander. I'm no privateer and I didn't help *anyone* destroy that ship."

"I'm still amazed that they awarded a screwup like you this contract," Gage said, and shook his head.

Quinn wanted to laugh. It was so obvious to even the medtechs he'd tried to hire. They couldn't get away from him fast enough. "We both know why the government's letting me go in."

Gage frowned, but said nothing.

"If this thing blows wide open, then the government can say I went psycho over my wife's death. They can blame me for everything. It's the perfect setup, commander, and you know that's why I got that contract." Quinn pointed toward Sanji, who was lowering a passenger ramp from the hatch. "Sanji will show you to suitable quarters," he said, turning away. "I'll be in Nav. Sanj, give Kuruk the word. We're lifting off. Now."

He started toward the ramp, but Gage grabbed his arm.

"I'll prove you were working for privateers that night," he said, his voice a low growl. "I've known it for five years and before this contract is finished, the government will have proof."

Quinn jerked away, his anger unchecked. "How does that night on the Augustine have anything to do with Nearra?"

Gage's lips twisted into a snarl. "A scout ship tracked the privateer's escape trajectory to the Rim. They only had enough fuel to reach Nearra." Scowling, he turned toward his duffel bags lying on the tarmac.

A cold chill rushed over Quinn, filling the hollowness in his gut. Privateers in the Rim? He shivered. What had Larena encountered on Nearra?

FOUR

ONCE SHE GOT past the *Magellan's* rocky takeoff and the small ship had stopped shimmying, Tarateal was able to pry her grip from the sides of the restraint harness. Rising unsteadily from the chair, she moved toward the portal in her chamber. The cold darkness shimmered white with stars, a handful of red and blue glimmers dotting the fabric of space. Even with all those promises of life, she felt like the only person in the universe. She didn't like what she'd left behind, but feared what awaited her and the *Magellan* out in the Rim.

She thrust her hands to her face and began to tremble. What was she doing here? Why wasn't she back on FS-314 treating burns and hangovers?

She turned away from the portal and leaned against the grey composite wall. It was cold against her back. She knew why; she had to prove to herself that she could compete with the best of them. Most of all, she wanted to show Sayre she was tough enough to endure this Rim that fascinated him so much. The stinging image of his wedding ring burned through her again and she crossed her arms.

So, what if he was married! She wanted no part of him.

Still, she couldn't help but wonder why he'd looked her up after all this time. Talk about desperate!

The chamber's soft lighting made her drowsy as she sat down at the small white table across from the single bunk. What made Sayre desperate enough to sign her aboard his ship? Her stomach twisted into a knot. She gazed at the datapad inset in the top of the table. Sliding back the clear protective cover, she flicked it on. The screen blanked a moment and then the Government Satellite Network login screen appeared.

The chime on her chamber door buzzed softly in the silence.

"Come in," she called.

The door slid open and Taka Yawakani stood in the doorway. She smiled. "I was heading down to the galley for some dinner. Would you like to join me?"

Tarateal returned her smile. "Thanks, I'd love to. I was going to do some research, but I can do that later." She rose from the chair and moved to the doorway.

Taka led the way down the short corridor to the galley, one of the larger compartments on the ship. Tarateal stepped gingerly inside. Four small tables were arranged around a narrow galley in the back. All of the tables were empty.

"Everything here is self-serve," said Taka. "Quinn stocks the best rations available, but they're still rations. We have a few specialty items now and then. Quinn's good at trading for luxury items."

Tarateal made a face. "I hope the rations here are better than the garbage the government ships out to FS-314."

"They are," Taka said, and led her into the galley. "Quinn refuses to buy government surplus rations."

"Thank God for that," said Tarateal. "Hope that includes the coffee."

The galley was small with beige storage and food compartments on one side. Chairs padded in a dark blue fabric were bright against the ivory walls. Not exactly cheerful, but pleasant enough. Apparently, Sayre had some taste after all.

Taka opened the nearest storage compartment. "Quinn deals with some freighter captain who shuttles Kenyan coffee out to him in exchange for transporting delicate cargo now and then."

"Delicate cargo?" Tarateal raised an eyebrow.

"Breakables, perishables. Only government-approved cargo. Quinn isn't a privateer."

Taka removed a supper tray containing meal rations and set it on the counter. On the largest pouch, she pulled the self-heating tab. In moments, the scent of simmering tomato sauce filled the galley.

Tarateal reached into the compartment, found a tray labeled Swiss steak, and removed it. She pulled the ration's self-heat tab and waited for it to heat.

"Ever since takeoff, I've heard the word *privateer* whispered in the corridors," said Tarateal. "What's wrong with being a privateer? They're perfectly legal."

"Until they cross the line into piracy," Taka said, and pulled a carton of juice out of a compartment. She moved toward the nearest table.

"Where's the coffee?" Tarateal asked.

Taka pointed toward the galley. "Third compartment down. You'll find spare mess kits in the fourth compartment."

Finding the coffee dispenser and cups, Tarateal inserted an insulated cup and waited for the steaming coffee to fill it. She drank in the rich scent as it flowed into the cup. It didn't smell stale or recycled. She passed over a carton of milk, grabbing some sugar packets instead, and hurried over to the table with her tray and mess kit.

This was already better than the fueling station, she mused.

She sat across from Taka, who had opened a small grey case containing a set of eating utensils.

"We're each responsible for our own mess kits, so try not to lose that one."

Tarateal nodded and eagerly tore open the sugar packets. After she'd dumped them into the steamy coffee, she swirled it around in the cup and took a slow sip. She didn't know Kenyan from Brazilian; she just knew when it tasted fresh. It was a sip of heaven. With this cup, she could have skipped dinner entirely. After a few more sips, she turned to the Swiss steak and green beans.

"You didn't answer my question," said Tarateal, opening her mess kit. "What's so terrible about privateers?"

Taka frowned. "You were on that fueling station a long time, weren't you? In the last five years, lots of privateers have become pirates. They attack, board ships, and steal information or cargo, leaving the ship disabled and calling for help while they slip away. Most of the time, they don't leave witnesses."

Taka took a bite of what looked like chicken in tomato sauce.

"Why doesn't the government outlaw privateering and arrest these people?" Tarateal asked, and savored another sip of coffee.

"The government says it doesn't want to risk its fragile contract arrangements with civilians. That without that civilian service, they'd exhaust precious cash reserves. I think it's because the government can't patrol the space lanes."

Tarateal took a bite of Swiss steak. It was hot, that's all she cared about. She cut up the steak and ate a few more bites.

"So, what's being done about the problem?"

"All civvies require licensing now with contract commissions, making them temporary government agents," said Taka. "As government employees, we're bound by more stringent rules and the penalties for breach of contract are much harsher. So, any privateer with a contract who's convicted on piracy charges gets a mandatory sentence of life at hard labor. Some have even gotten the death penalty."

A sandy-haired young man sauntered into the galley. He stopped at the table and smiled at Taka. "Good evening, ma'am," he said to Taka, and plopped down at the table.

Taka sighed. "Taka or Yawakani will do, Dale. This isn't the military."

"Yes, ma'am, Taka." His cheerful face turned to Tarateal. "I don't think we've had the chance to meet, ma'am," he said, and extended his hand. "I'm Class Four Medtech Dale Park!"

His voice was loud and boisterous. She exchanged a perplexed smile with Taka, who rolled her eyes.

"Class One Medtech Tarateal Roberts," she said, and shook his hand. "And I don't go by ma'am either."

He nodded, the smile never leaving his face.

"Is this your first commission, Dale?"

"Yes, ma'am, eh, Tarateal! Captain Sayre signed me on about two weeks ago."

Tarateal suppressed a laugh. "Done much field work, Dale?"

He laid a hand to his chest. "Me personally or as a medtech?"

"Either one," said Tarateal, leaning back in her chair.

"I've been through deep space training sims about four times and I've read all the v-journals." He grinned. "What about you?"

Obviously annoyed by the overeager young man, Taka hunched over her dinner and tuned him out.

"Enough to know my way around. On FS-314, we didn't have a lot of runway stewards dying in the hangars from refueling wounds."

Tarateal heard Taka snicker, but she didn't look up from her meal.

Dale opened his mouth to chatter again, but Kuruk entered the galley.

"Cool, there's Kuruk! He promised to explain how the engines work. Seeya later, Taka! Nice meeting you, Tarateal." He stumbled up from the chair, his chukka boots nearly tangling his long legs, and hurried toward Kuruk in the galley.

"That kid will make me crazy by the time we reach Nearra," said Taka with a sigh.

Tarateal heard him prattling away in the galley at poor Kuruk. He was Vardissian, but his skin was a light blue and mottled grey. His thick grey hair reminded her of dreadlocks. He had no facial hair, not even eyebrows. Each of his hands had what appeared to be two thumbs and four fingers. His eyes seemed lower on his face than human eyes and they were rounder and wider, almost owl-like despite their pale blue color. He looked calm despite Dale Park's incessant banter. The engineer calmly fixed his supper and sat down at a table near the door. Dale turned a chair around and plopped down. Tarateal watched as Kuruk took a bite of food and then explained in a gravelly voice about plasma engines.

After finishing her meal, Taka separated the ration wrappings into their appropriate recycle bins and returned with a cup of coffee. Tarateal followed Taka's example and then refilled her own cup.

"So, why did Sayre come all the way to FS-314 for me?" Tarateal asked. "I had to be his last choice."

"You were his last hope. Sanji said you and Quinn know each other well."

Tarateal stared into her coffee. "Sayre and I were once—how should I put this—insignificant others."

Taka laughed. "We all end up there eventually, don't we?" She set down her coffee cup.

"We met in school on Salice Minor."

"Sanji only told me a little about you, just that you and Sayre used to date. So, you were with him in his flight school days?"

"I had the unfortunate pleasure," said Tarateal, leaning her elbows on the table. "After we broke up, he transferred to Ramantra to finish school. He didn't want us running into each other on Salice Minor after our rather—colorful parting. I couldn't have been happier about it."

Taka lowered her voice. "Quinn has some serious trouble in his life right now, Tarateal. Trouble you don't want to get mixed up in, believe me."

Tarateal felt her mouth go dry and a thousand thoughts scrambled through her brain...trouble with the authorities, credit problems, privateer problems? She took another sip of her coffee and set down the cup. "What kind of trouble?"

"I think you know his wife is dead."

"What? Dead? He's going there to claim her body, isn't he?

Now, Tarateal felt sorry for Sayre. If he was desperate enough to sign his ex-girlfriend aboard ship for a mission like this, then it had to be bad.

"There's not a body yet, but it's been a little over six weeks."

"Six weeks? Why'd he wait so long to go out there?"

Taka made a sour face. "Because it took that long for him to gain the necessary clearances and approvals."

"What was his wife doing out in the Rim?"

Dale's loud voice shrieked out a high-pitched laugh and he pounded the table. She glanced over at them. Kuruk seemed happy enough, still talking about plasma engines. Her gaze drifted back to Taka.

"Larena was part of a deep space—"

"Wait a minute. Larena? Larena Neville?"

Taka nodded.

Tarateal's stomach clenched and hot anger rose to her cheeks. *So, he did marry that bitch.*

She remembered Larena's smug smile giggling at her from the pub's entrance. That night on Salice Minor, Larena Neville looked delighted by the public breakup. Tarateal had always blamed it on Larena. She despised that woman! Even now, the question nagged at her.

Did Sayre cheat on her? Did Larena steal him from her?

"I won't even ask," said Taka with a wary grin as she held up her hand.

"So, what was Larena Neville doing out in the Rim?" Tarateal asked, trying to sound nonchalant.

"She was part of a deep space First Contact mission, one of a dozen government scouts. She's a—was a botanist specializing in the gene-splicing of plant species. She was researching some process she called *artificial targeted selection.*"

Artificial targeted selection? Tarateal shook her head. That's how the little bitch grabbed Sayre, too. Nothing like a few *artificial* anatomical enhancements to wag Sayre's tongue. She'd swear that woman had been half silicone.

"Something about cross-species gene-splicing to protect plant species on the verge of extinction. Forcing them to adapt to the conditions killing them off. Earth wouldn't let her use it there until she'd proven it in the field."

"So, she was doing research."

Taka nodded. "It was research, but this mission was considered highly dangerous for a researcher."

Tarateal stared into her cup a moment. "What kind of First Contact mission was this?"

Raising her cup to her lips, Taka took a long draught. She cast a disgusted glance at Dale. "Larena volunteered for a two-year mission to a Rim planet called Nearra." Taka leaned forward. Her dark eyes looked intense.

"Two years?" Tarateal gaped at her. Two years on some uncharted world? Larena was so much like Sayre. He feared nothing and Larena didn't seem to fear anything either. Apparently, Tarateal had been much too boring for Sayre, too predictable. No wonder she found Larena on his arm so soon. Those two had been cut from the same cloth.

"I know two years is a long time," said Taka with a shrug, "but this place is supposed to be a botanist's dream. Cataloguing plant and animal life never seen before and making contact with a sentient race."

"How did Sayre feel about it?"

Taka smiled. "He was adamantly opposed to it, of course. They'd just gotten married a couple of months ago, but Larena never considered anyone's feelings but her own. She drove him crazy with her wild decisions and he was always powerless to stop her."

"Did they have a good marriage?" She wanted to kick herself for asking that. It was none of her business.

"What is this, an interview for the Satellite News?" Taka asked with a smile.

"Come on, answer the question or I'll start streaming this to the networks."

Taka laughed and fiddled with her empty coffee cup. "In some ways, yes. At first anyway. She was never really there for him when he needed her to be. Like the time he contracted Arcturian Fever, or when his father died, or when he was discharged from the military. She always had some excuse and he always forgave her. He was always the one apologizing."

Sayre apologizing? He *had* changed. So Larena had been a little too much like him. Back then, Tarateal couldn't compete with Larena's shapely build and ability to twist men around her finger.

"So, what happened on Nearra?" she asked.

"No one knows. Nothing adds up," said Taka.

"What do you mean?" she asked with a frown.

"Larena only had about six months left there. And she was fine—no trouble of any kind reported. Then Quinn couldn't get through for days at a time. After two agonizing weeks of waiting, the official communiqués began to arrive, informing him that she was missing. Then presumed dead."

A shiver trickled down Tarateal's spine. "How did it happen? What was her commander's explanation for all of this?"

"The government lost contact with the team about that time. A magnetic storm in that sector is being blamed for the communications breach. Quinn's afraid the government will label the mission a failure and order a pullout before he can get there. Then he'll never lay her to rest."

"How's he taking all of this?" If she knew Sayre, it would be badly. He never handled bad news well.

Taka shook her head. "Quinn hasn't been himself since the news. It took so long to get clearance, and the three-medtech rule slowed him down a lot. No one wanted to go out to the Rim."

"Why not?"

"Because of Quinn." Taka's mahogany gaze turned hard.

"Sayre? He graduated number one in his class. He's an excellent pilot." The intensity of her voice surprised her. She leaned back in her chair. Why did she care? She had no interest in what people thought about Sayre. Right?

Taka nodded her agreement. "He's one of the best pilots I know." Her voice fell to a whisper. "When he's not stoked to the gills with amara."

Pressing a hand to her mouth, Tarateal tried to hide her shock. She'd seen a couple of former medtechs wasting away from the stuff on FS-314. They were zombies.

"I know. I didn't believe it myself until I saw him with the bottle," said Taka. She sighed. "He loved Larena—much more than she loved him. I'm convinced of that. She loved him in her own way, I suppose, but she didn't want to be with him. At his side. She didn't want to make any compromises to be with him either and he can't face that."

That was a familiar story. Tarateal slumped in her chair. She hadn't wanted to compromise for him either. But why should she give up anything? He sure hadn't offered to give up anything for her.

"I'm trying to get him off the amara," Taka whispered, "but it isn't easy. Once he recovers her body, I hope he'll give it up. Until then, as senior medtech, I've got a fight on my hands."

"Does Sayre think there's a chance his wife's still alive?"

"Probably," said Taka, setting down her cup. "Somewhere in the back of his mind, I suppose. Until he sees the body. The search is the one thing keeping his hand off the amara at the moment."

"You don't think she's alive, do you?"

Taka was silent for a moment. "No. Not with Derek Faxon leading that team."

"Derek Faxon?" Tarateal asked with a frown.

"I served under him for a few months as a medtech. I barely got out alive. He was brought up on charges for excessive force and unwarranted attacks on civilians. They demoted him and moved him to a scouting rotation."

"Why the hell did they let him lead *any* mission?" The man sounded like a lunatic.

"Punitive assignment. And with Larena Sayre's quest to preserve every ecosystem, they were bound to clash. Her with her unsanctioned experiments and him with his slash-and-burn tactics. Bad match."

"Does Sayre know all this?"

"Quinn doesn't have a clue about what he's walking into," said Taka, shaking her head. "And don't think I didn't try to tell him."

Dale's shrill voice rose again.

"Dale, keep it down, please!" Taka shouted.

A sheepish look slid across Dale's face. "Sorry, ma'am. I didn't realize I was so loud." He turned back to Kuruk and lowered his voice.

"That kid doesn't know anything about medical procedures," said Taka, irritation in her voice. "But if he knows what's good for him, he'll stay out of my way." She rose from her chair and moved into the galley for more coffee.

Tarateal followed. "What will I be doing aboard ship, Taka?"

Taka reached out and touched her arm. "Maintaining the medical equipment and the health of the crew. In case—something happens to me. Dale's too clueless to be reliable, if you ask me. You're our failsafe. Quinn's, too. Somebody has to make sure he doesn't get himself killed out there."

A tall man with thick greying hair entered the galley. He stepped up to the compartments and Taka's posture stiffened.

"Good evening, Commander Gage," said Taka. "You look more rested than you did on liftoff. Are your quarters acceptable?"

"They'll do, Ms. Yawakani," he said in a formal, austere voice. "Have I missed mess?"

"No, sir," Taka answered, casting a sideways glance at Tarateal. "All the rations are located in this first bin." She pointed to the nearest bin. "You should find a mess kit and drinks without any trouble. It's all self-serve. If you need anything at all, sir, please ask."

The man nodded his thanks and hurriedly retrieved a meal without even reading the label. He quickly slipped past them and filled a cup with coffee. With heavy steps, he left the galley and moved to a table farthest from Dale and Kuruk and hunched over his food, head down.

"Who's that?" Tarateal asked.

"He was my first commander. And Quinn's. He's a government agent assigned to oversee Quinn's contract. I think he's just gathering evidence to have Quinn arrested again."

Again? She glanced at the pale man. His eyes looked tired. No, weary. And haunted. "Arrested for what?"

"Privateering. Privateers destroyed Gage's ship and killed his son, but he blames Quinn for it. Had him dishonorably discharged over the incident. He won't quit until Quinn is executed on privateering charges."

"What have I gotten myself into?" Tarateal asked with a groan.

"A class reunion," Taka snapped. "One I don't care to attend. Just hope we can get off Nearra without dying or without Gage arresting Quinn."

Tarateal and Taka leaned against the counter, watching Dale terrorize poor Kuruk, who took all of Dale's incessant banter without a whimper. Gage ate in silence, keeping his back to the others. Finally, Tarateal yawned and straightened up.

"Glad I had the chance to interrogate you, Taka," she said with a grin.

She stood up and stretched then started to leave, but Sayre sauntered through the doorway bound for the galley.

"How you settling in, Roberts?" he asked, not breaking his stride.

"Don't worry about me, I'm doing just fine," she replied, and crossed her arms.

He pulled out a ration and set it on the counter to heat while he got a cup of coffee. He smirked at her over the brim of his cup as he took a quick sip.

"I expected to find you cowering under your bunk about now. The unknown isn't exactly your strong suit, Roberts."

She felt the slow burn begin in her cheeks as she glared at him and leaned against the counter again. She'd taken this shit on FS-314, but she wouldn't take it here. From Sayre.

"I'm through being scared, Sayre."

"Until we reach Nearra?" he asked. "On Salice Minor, you were even afraid of the carnival rides." He laughed. "Remember that reverse thrust ride—Shooting Star? I had to peel you off the floor after that one was over." His laugh deepened. "Your face was white for days!"

Reaching into one of the bins, Tarateal grabbed a container of milk. She opened the cap and smirked at him.

"Let's see how long *your* face stays white, Sayre," she said, and emptied the milk container on his head. It drenched his black hair and ran in rivulets down his face. She shook the container, making sure she'd gotten every drop. "Need sugar with that coffee?"

"No, no," he said in a small voice. "I'm good, thanks."

Taka tried to hold back her laughter, but it spilled out when Dale Park let out a belly laugh.

"Thanks for supper, Taka," Tarateal said, setting the empty container beside Sayre's milk-soaked dinner. "Think I'll read for a while and turn in."

"See you in the infirmary at 0800," said Taka with a grin.

"We'll have to do this again sometime, Roberts," Sayre called, his tone facetious. "Good to see you again."

She hurried into the hallway, snickering, but her mood quickly darkened. There were too many things about this mission that weren't funny. They worried her. Was Sayre chasing a ghost? And would his obsession lead her and the rest of the crew to their deaths out there?

She pressed the door release on her compartment door and the rush of air startled her. This was going to be a long trip. And like it or not, she had to stay at Sayre's side.

FIVE

NEARRA WAS A SWIRLING, azure sphere in the *Magellan's* view screen. It looked serene, bluer even than Earth, but Quinn knew that Nearra was a difficult landing. Solar wind shears, a phenomenon unique to Nearra, could suddenly slam a ship into a downward spiral, turning a well-executed landing into flaming wreckage.

Quinn swiveled around in his chair and glanced over at navigator Sheryl Hannaford. She had her head down, calculating trajectories and reading data gathered from Nearra. Her brown hair was thrust into a tight ponytail, accentuating her high cheekbones and long face. A thick band of bangs brushed just above her full eyebrows. Her lips were a little too plump for her angular face and heavy brows, making her look hard and sulking at times.

Sheryl had studied at all the best schools, taken all the right courses, and apprenticed with all the right ships, yet she had missed the cut for aerospace service by two places. That's how she ended up in the private sector and for that, Quinn was thankful. She was a damned good navigator and made him look like a better pilot. Still, she was a confirmed cynic, did everything the old way, and kept to herself, definitely not a people person, but she was a loyal crew member. He was grateful to have her aboard.

"Sheryl, do you have those trajectories yet?"

She nodded, her gaze still on the computer screen. Her short fingers thumped across the control pads. "Almost. I'm still monitoring the wind speeds for those solar wind shears I've heard so much about." She glanced up at him. "I'm adding the data to your flight plan now. You should have course corrections in a few moments."

"Let's hope we don't learn firsthand about this phenomenon."

Sanji stepped over to Quinn's console with a steaming cup of coffee. His coarse ebony hair lay in unruly waves across his forehead.

"Then you will need this to clear your mind," he said, and handed Quinn the coffee.

Quinn frowned. Sanji wanted to make sure all traces of amara were out of his system. Especially with Gage aboard. That was a complication Quinn hadn't expected. Sanji was a good friend, always looking out for him. The man had missed his calling. He spoke more languages than Quinn could name and could translate even the most primitive scrawlings, but his gift lay in interpreting people. He knew exactly what they needed and when.

It was too bad Sanji didn't have the education to back his experience. The *Augustine* disaster had taken a lot out of Sanji, with contracting Arcturian Fever on top of that. Despite his commission aboard the *Augustine*, the government wouldn't award Sanji anything higher than class four status. A perpetual intern. Lots of people were punished for the *Augustine*. When Quinn first bought the *Magellan*, he had to do a lot of maneuvering to get Sanji back from his family's farm.

Quinn gratefully accepted the cup. After a long sip, he set the cup in a nearby holder and watched the new data scroll across his screen. The *Magellan's* navigational system snatched up the data and made slight corrections to the *Magellan's* course and approach vector. A yellow light on the panel blinked at him, warning that autopilot was about to terminate. He moved his hand to the stick and pressed his restraint activator. The harness descended around him.

"Sanji, tell the rest of the crew to prepare for landing. I want restraints on now. Ask Taka to check on Roberts and Park." He sighed. "And Gage."

"Right."

Sanji made the announcement and Quinn tuned him out when he saw a yellow light flash in the upper right-hand corner of his screen.

"Sheryl? Why the flashing light?"

"A caution light. The conditions are right for solar wind shears, Quinn. If you get the red light, back off and abort a punch-through. In fact, you may want to think twice about landing unless the indicator is green."

"It's still flashing yellow."

She frowned for a moment. "I'd wait it out for a bit. But the conditions change so quickly. My advice: if you get a break, go for it."

"How long until you attempt a landing?" Sanji asked, and slid his lanky frame into the chair beside him. Quinn heard the whirr of Sanji's restraint harness lowering, followed by a sharp snap.

"I'll give it another twenty minutes and decide," Quinn mumbled. "Any response from the surface?"

Sanji shook his head. "Only dead air, Quinn."

The yellow light in the corner of his screen pulsed more quickly now.

"Conditions are starting to erode," Sheryl announced. "We may have to back off into a stable orbit and wait for another opportunity. No matter what, it's going to be a rough landing."

Quinn's grip on the stick tightened. With the flick of a few levers, he manually adjusted his speed and angle of descent, not trusting the *Magellan* to do it for him. As they got closer, Nearra's glowing surface became more luminous and the blue tinge to the atmosphere looked like a colored lens had slid across the planet. Larena must have been so anxious when this blue beauty came into view. Colors were her most cherished memories of deep space travel. She had babbled about the ruby leaves on Denias and the purple sunsets on Kalaf. Her arrival here must have been a special memory.

His thoughts drifted to Roberts and he wondered if she was watching their descent from underneath a bed in the infirmary. He smiled. Larena would have sat on the nose if it had been possible.

The comm light on his control panel winked at him.

"Quinn," growled Kuruk. "You'll have to delay landing. There's a problem with the engines."

"What kind of problem, Kuruk?"

The Vardissian clicked his teeth together and sighed. It was bad. Quinn gripped the edge of his chair.

"The main engine is overheating. I need to investigate further."

"Damn. I'll be right there." He turned to Sheryl. "Drop us back into a stable orbit while I investigate Kuruk's problem."

"Good luck, Quinn," said Sheryl as she reactivated the *Magellan's* autopilot.

"If you don't hear from me or Kuruk in about fifteen minutes, then it's safe to proceed."

"Affirmative. I'll wait thirty minutes just in case and retry the landing."

Quinn nodded and hurried into the narrow corridor. He rushed into the cargo lift that stood beside the galley and veered left out of the lift, into the engine room.

He wanted to kick himself! It'd been foolish to leave FS-314 without those engine checks—even he knew that now. But dammit, he had to lift off. If there was any chance at all that Larena was still alive, he had to take it. He knew he was just fooling himself, but time meant everything.

His stomach clenched. But this time, he'd endangered his crew and that was wrong.

Kuruk's dusty blue skin had paled almost pearly white as he hunched his lanky frame over a computer screen. The Vardissian was at least a head taller than Quinn. Thick, ropelike locks of grey hair lay heavy against his head, brushing his temples. His cerulean eyes looked avian, narrowing as he clicked his teeth.

"What's up, Kuruk?" Quinn asked.

The long silence made Quinn anxious. Finally, Kuruk looked up. "Conduits might be damaged," he answered quietly, his tone and words formal. "The system is unstable. I am detecting fluctuations in energy conduction. But none of these readings makes any sense." Quinn speculated Kuruk's politeness came from growing up the son of an ambassador to Earth.

"That could cause the whole damned engine to fry!"

Kuruk nodded stiffly, the gesture still unnatural for him. "It could. I was about to analyze the conduits when I called you."

"I'll do it. You monitor that reservoir."

Kuruk held up a slender, two-thumbed hand. "Wait, Quinn. I am not through with the preliminary check. Allow me two minutes. The instability could increase."

"In two minutes, that instability could frag the engines," said Quinn, grabbing the technician's tool belt from the wall.

Strapping on the belt, he hurried toward the access panel. He knew these engines like the back of his hand. He pressed the release lever and carefully removed the panel. Kuruk's clicking intensified behind him. He knew Kuruk was annoyed, but he also knew the Vardissian would say nothing further on the subject. Kuruk had already voiced his opinion, leaving the decision to him.

On first glance, everything looked normal. No scorch marks, turbines spinning normally. Quinn grabbed a flashlight and the structural scanner and scanned the main engine. Everything looked normal; no sign of energy buildup. He slipped through the opening and crouched to scan the conduit. Everything was functioning properly. He poked his head out of the panel to gaze at the indicator grid. All the numbers looked right.

He ducked back in and crawled toward the cramped confines of the engine housing. He scanned again. Toward the turbines, he noticed a fluctuation in the energy levels. He rubbed his chin. What could cause that? The valves—that had to be the problem. He needed to clear the conduit and reset the valves.

"Found your problem, Kuruk," he shouted over his shoulder. "It'll take just a sec to fix it. Hang tight. Close the reservoir valves. I need to clear the conduit before I reset."

He avoided the turbine brushes, not wanting to get an unnecessary shock, and reached down to a small shielded panel. He entered his personal key code and sent the keystrokes that would jettison plasma from the conduit. With the conduit clear, he wouldn't risk a buildup of energy that could discharge right here in the access tube.

When a green light on the panel winked at him, indicating the conduit was clear, he started the adjustments. It would take a few moments to reset the valves.

The ship jolted as the shrill squeal of an alarm shrieked through the engine room.

"Quinn, get out of there! Plasma surge imminent!"

Thrown backward, Quinn stumbled and grabbed for a handhold. His hand hit one of the turbine brushes. A burst of energy blasted up his arm, rolled across his body in a razor-sharp wave, and slammed into his feet. Everything went dark.

SIX

PAIN SURGED through nerves and muscles, evolving into numbness that quickly spiraled away into darkness. Abruptly, a voice filled the void of senselessness that rose from the darkness to merge again with pain.

"Get Yawakani!"

"Kuruk, what happened?"

"Sayre's hurt—hurry!"

The voices were swallowed up by the pain arcing through limbs and organs. In moments, the darkness rose up and away, replaced by a red haze as pain vibrated and pulsed in throbbing moments of agony. A frantic voice pierced the fog.

"Sayre, it's me, Roberts. It's Tarateal! Can you hear me? Sayre! If you can hear my voice, squeeze my hand."

"He's flatlining!"

The red haze lightened. Sayre? The redness swirled and danced. His name. Scenes from his past coalesced in a mist, ghosts slipping softly toward him. The air sparkled as shapes bled through the vapor, consciousness trickling back then fading.

"Clear!"

His whole body jerked, convulsing. Darkness ebbed and flowed with the scarlet cloud of pain, reality just a wave rolling out toward open sea.

Sea...Larena loved the sea.

"Still no pulse."

"Give me three hundred joules. Clear!"

Again, the world shook.

For a fleeting moment, he felt his feet touch solid ground and he saw the loamy banks of a misty swamp around him. In the distance lay the wreckage of a ship, the First Contact ship. Larena stood beside it, her face lifted toward the sky. With longing, he reached out to the vision. Larena. Auburn hair flowing. Blue eyes twinkling. Hands reaching. He felt her silky skin against his fingertips and the soft whisper of *dearest* against his ear.

She was against him. Pulse racing. Hands caressing. Voice singing *may the road rise up to meet you.* It had been so long since he'd held her.

She flitted out of his reach.

Beside him stood Roberts, wheaten hair in ringlets around her face. Big blue eyes vibrant in the mist. His fingers ran through her soft tresses. Strong, beautiful, and stable—he missed her.

Consciousness was ripped out of oblivion and then thrust back into his body.

Sayre—his name was Sayre. A chill snaked over him. He shivered, his whole body jolting as icy fingers brushed across his spine.

Quinn Sayre...he was Quinn Sayre.

"Sayre!" an urgent, disembodied voice shouted.

The pressure of a hand gripping his sank through the fog. He was aware of the sensation now. His body felt familiar again. Slowly, he worked his fingers, drawing them toward his palm until they touched the gripping hand.

"That's good, Sayre."

Shapes and images intensified until he made out Roberts' burgundy sleeve draped across his line of sight.

"He's back in sinus rhythm."

Abruptly, the worried face and fearful blue eyes of Tarateal Roberts wavered in and out of focus. Laying a hand on his bare chest, she removed two silver disks.

"Welcome back," she said with an exhausted smile. She handed the silver disks to Taka, who stowed them in a small black case. Her pale face was slowly regaining its color. "We thought we'd lost you."

He tried to talk, but only a squeak came out. "Larena?"

"Easy, Sayre," said Roberts, pressing gently against his shoulders. "Don't try to talk. Just nod yes or blink your eyes no. Do you remember anything?"

With effort, he closed his eyes and then opened them. What an idiot he must look like, sprawled across the engine room floor with a structural scanner welded to his hand. It all happened so fast...the alarm, the shouting. The last thing he remembered was trying to adjust the plasma conduit.

Kuruk and Roberts lifted him up from the floor, placing him on a gurney. He felt straps being stretched across his chest and legs.

"I've seen a few people survive such a blast," Taka whispered to Roberts. "Only a handful came away breathing though. He was very lucky."

Sheryl's voice sputtered through the engine room. "What's the story, Kuruk? Do we drop back or punch through?"

Kuruk pressed the comm button. "I have rerouted to the auxiliary engine. Proceed with caution."

"Affirmative, Kuruk. How's Quinn?"

Kuruk glanced over at Quinn. "He is alive and conscious. They are taking him to the infirmary."

"Thanks for the heads-up."

Quinn regretted not being at the helm for the landing. It would be tough, but he knew Sheryl could land this ship as well as he could. Probably better.

"I'll attempt punch-through and landing in ten minutes," said Sheryl, her voice unwavering. "Everyone, prepare."

Roberts wheeled him out of the engine room and into the cargo lift.

FROM THE INFIRMARY PORTALS, Quinn gazed out at Nearra's swirling blue mist. Moisture streaked and vibrated across the portals as he felt the *Magellan's* bulky nose nudge through the vapor. Black, muddy water covered with a thin, blue film. Gnarled brush dotted the edge of the black water. Mist hung above brown, shriveled foliage.

A massive thunderhead glided into view on the murky horizon. The ominous sight made Quinn think back to his childhood. On Earth in the Midwest Biosphere—Tornado Alley—that's where he'd grown up. Back then, the radars could only pinpoint where tornadoes might form, not alert before they developed like now. If they were close, he and his sister would rush to one end of the biosphere to watch. This slate grey obelisk looked no different from those Oklahoma wall clouds.

The *Magellan* pitched and Quinn reached out for the stick that wasn't there. Roberts gave him a peculiar look as she ran a quick medical scan. She seemed to have mellowed considerably. Maybe she'd work out after all?

He felt the ship level out and adjust its altitude with the sudden rush of wind speed. A fierce gust of wind rushed over the hull with an ominous moan. Another one sent the *Magellan* rocking.

"We're flying into a damned tornado," Quinn muttered, trying to unfasten his restraints. He had to get up there. He had to.

Foliage rushed past the portals.

"Sayre, no!" Roberts cried. She refastened his straps and then plopped down in a restraint harness beside his sickbed.

"Approaching base camp landing strip," Sheryl announced over the comm. "Lock into your restraint harnesses now. This isn't my idea of a landing strip, but it's all we've got."

Relieved, Quinn laid back against the bunk, but a sharp surge of air slammed against the *Magellan*'s nose. Not now! They were so close to the landing strip.

Again, air smashed into the nose, plunging the *Magellan* toward the dark bog below.

A siren shrieked through the ship as emergency red lighting filled the halls.

"Dammit," Sheryl growled. Her voice echoed through the deathly silent ship. "Auxiliary engine has gone off-line. Looks like we're in for a rough one. Prepare for emergency landing. Repeat, we're in for a hard landing."

Quinn felt the craft's rotation increase as Sanji's grave tone crackled through the comm, outlining emergency procedures. Quinn could feel Sheryl trying to pull out of the spin, but the wind sent the ship reeling faster every time she moved the stick. He felt trees gouging the hull and he feared it would breach.

Suddenly, he felt it.

That moment all pilots feared the most. He felt the *Magellan* go out of Sheryl's control, snapping off treetops and scattering branches.

He fought to stay conscious, but felt himself slipping beneath the red haze of lighting and wail of the siren. He slumped against the bunk, hearing Roberts and Taka shouting. One final time, he felt the nose drop, but then his consciousness spiraled away.

SEVEN

TARATEAL PRESSED a cool cloth against the side of Sayre's face. His left eye had swelled shut and his cheek had been sliced open. One of the worst cases aboard the *Magellan*, but most of that was from his accident in the engine room.

They'd gotten everyone off the ship and moved into the makeshift infirmary at the First Contact team's base camp. The six-bed space had been built with materials from the planet, a greyish blue wood-framed structure with woven mat shutters on the windows. The box structure smelled musty from the nearby waterways surrounding the camp.

While Sayre was still unconscious, she carefully closed the gash with microsutures and applied a tissue rejuvenant to remove all but the faintest of scarring. He had a mild concussion and a few cracked ribs, but he'd recover.

It was the slight alteration of his vital signs that worried her. Nothing critical and barely out of the normal ranges, but disturbing nonetheless. He was stable and for that, in these primitive conditions, she was grateful. But he hadn't regained consciousness since the crash. On FS-314, she had treated an assortment of minor injuries, but never anything like this before.

The whole incident terrified her. She'd never seen anything like it —not even her near-fatal shuttle accident on Lunar Colony. Once, she had gathered the courage to watch the news footage of the accident where she'd almost died. Seeing it made her fear space travel. But the *Magellan* had narrowly averted a deadly crash that could have killed them all. When Sanji Shahir had announced emergency crash procedures, she clung to her chair, fear cold and sharp in her stomach.

It would be worse than Lunar Colony, she'd told herself.

For weeks after that crash, she'd struggled with the broken bones, but the fear and the flashbacks lingered for months. Injured and alone in an unfamiliar place, having to rely on strangers for every need, and the nearest medical facility a world away...she shuddered. She couldn't think about that right now.

She reached up to the wall to turn on the medscanner, but caught herself. This was a back-world planet with a handful of solar-powered generators. The camp's commander, Commander Faxon, asked them to conserve energy consumption as much as possible. Until the *Magellan*'s critical systems were operational, she'd have to rely on the hand scanner. Kuruk said he'd have communications and the infirmary equipment online in a few hours.

Kuruk was such a peculiar person, but Taka assured her that Kuruk would not quit until the *Magellan*'s engines were repaired. He finished whatever he started. She had no choice but to leave the medical systems in Kuruk's hands. She'd only treated a handful of Vardissians and worried about her limited knowledge of their physiology. She hoped he didn't get seriously injured out here.

She gazed around at the crude infirmary. It was barely functional as a triage unit, much less an infirmary, with its lack of stabilizing equipment and minimal supplies, but at least there were beds for her patients. Six beds in all, three facing three, allowing only a narrow walkway between them.

In the farthest bed, Dale Park lay on his back resting comfortably, that indelible smile on his face. He broke three ribs because the bonehead didn't secure his restraint harness. In the bed between Sayre and Park lay Comm Specialist Shahir. He injured his left hand while investigating damage to the cargo hold. A crate shifted and fell on him. He would be fine tomorrow, but for now, she wanted to keep him under observation. Sayre, who lay in the closest bed, had sustained the most damage.

A heavy, rattan-like shade covered the open window and most of the far wall. The walls had been whitewashed long ago, but the thin paint had faded and worn away. Mud-stained handwoven throws covered the wood planked floor. Blue-black swamp mud smeared the throws' muted sand and mahogany hues. The building looked like a makeshift lean-to hastily thrown up by someone desperate for shelter.

Maybe the First Contact team felt marooned here, shipwrecked? Especially with their communications down. The government provided them with enough supplies for six months and a few furnishings. After that, they were stranded and on their own for another six months until a supply ship landed. Still, equipment wore out and things broke.

Nothing lasted forever and that included people.

Sayre groaned and his puffy lids rolled open.

"At last," Tarateal muttered, and pulled the cloth away. She placed a small sensor on his right thumb and read the results on a hand scanner. "Everything appears to be in order. How do you feel?"

"Like somebody hit me with the *Magellan.*"

She smiled. "With the amount of energy that pumped through your body, it's no wonder. I don't know how you survived that accident, but here you are."

"Will I have any complications from this?" Sayre asked, rubbing his forehead.

She hadn't a clue, but she wouldn't tell him that. "Miraculously, there are no residual effects reflected on the scanner. Other than a slight change in your normal vital signs readings, you survived with minor injuries." She winked at him. "Something you can tell your grandkids."

She cringed, wanting to kick herself for saying that. His wife was dead and now she'd opened her mouth and said something stupid. Sadness glazed his eyes.

"I'm sorry," she said, and laid a hand on his arm. "I didn't mean to...Taka told me about your wife."

"Forget it," he snapped, and averted his gaze. "Now you know why I needed a medtech so desperately."

"Do you think there's a chance she's still alive?"

He glared at her. "Of course, there's a chance! When there's no body, there's always a chance. Tomorrow morning, I start my search and I won't quit until I find one. Either way, I will lay Larena to rest."

"Commander Faxon is anxious to speak with you," Tarateal replied, changing the subject. "He'll visit you first thing tomorrow morning to discuss your wife."

Sayre nodded and rolled onto his side. He winced at the effort, face taut, eyes squeezed shut. When he settled into a comfortable position, he lay still and she left him to rest.

Lying beneath that blanket, his hair tousled, he looked more like the old Sayre. Her Sayre. She smiled. Sometimes, in those moments of misty greyness before dawn, she still missed him, remembering his touch against her back, the warmth of his breath against her neck. In those fleeting moments, his steady presence beside her, she'd felt like she had it all. But then the sunlight would stream through the window and his eyes would open. He'd kiss her, rise from the bed, and leave for class. With every stretch, every footstep, they moved farther and farther away until the distance was too great.

She sighed. They were worlds apart now. The distance was too far. Just too far.

She stepped out back and onto the loading ramp, metal planks forming an overhang. She unfastened the neck of her FS-314 flight suit and plopped down on the steps to gaze out at the moors.

The Nearran moors steamed. Blue-black mud gurgled. Above

her, a grey creature screeched and scampered down a tree trunk. Brush crunched. Something trilled. She gazed out into the haze settling around the compound. Like dropping a veil. It flowed around her like water and she felt the moisture bead across her cheeks. She wrinkled her nose.

The air smelled musty like a fishing wharf. Like fall afternoons on the Washington coast. Her parents moved there to avoid the biospheres back east. She sighed, remembering the smell of the ocean, the scent of fir trees that framed the mountains. This marshland wasn't an ocean, but there was something comforting about being near water. Beyond the edge of the muddy bank, bare trees, black and thin, dotted the blue-black water. Out the corner of her eye, the prow of a small wooden boat appeared.

Hollow echo of oars slapped the thick water and thwacked the side of the boat. Faces, brushed black and white with paint, floated like apparitions through the mist.

Tarateal scrambled to her feet, mesmerized.

"They look quite formidable, do they not?"

She wheeled around. Commander Derek Faxon stood in the doorway of the compound's infirmary. Shoulders squared, posture stiff, Faxon was about five-foot-ten. He pointed toward the boat quickly disappearing into the greying mist. His small blue eyes gleamed, chin sharpening as he smiled. His thinning brown hair greyed at the temples and across his high forehead, hairline receding.

"Who are they?" Tarateal asked.

"The Shikari's, a race native to this world. Frankly, I am surprised to see them so close to our camp."

"Your team made first contact with them?"

Faxon nodded, the smile fading from his wide face. "This is a very dangerous world and making that first contact was a great sacrifice. Since we've been on Nearra, there have been a few lives lost, good men and women. Like everything else here, the Shikari's are dangerous."

Tarateal shuddered. She didn't want to die alone on this alien world or at alien hands. The thought terrified her.

"Is she out there alive somewhere?" Tarateal asked.

"Who?"

"Larena Sayre?"

"No," said Faxon, stiffening. "She died trying to locate one of the Shikari priests. Much of these moors is unmapped and considered dangerous. She took an unmapped route and was never seen again. The Shikari's reported that she died on their sacred grounds and was buried there."

Tarateal pictured statues and ruins of ancient structures. "Have you searched these grounds? For her body?"

"Not yet. These sacred places are well-hidden sanctuaries deep in the Nearran moors. Only the Shikari's know how to reach these havens and they have never trusted my team enough to take us there."

"Have you questioned any of the natives?" Tarateal asked.

He sighed, looking annoyed at her barrage of questions as he leaned against the door frame. "I wish it were that simple, Ms. Roberts." There was irritation beneath his words. He spoke to her as if she were a child, and she gritted her teeth. "Unfortunately, the Shikari priests must trust you enough to lower their masks. Only then will they allow you to speak with them."

Tarateal gazed out at the moors again. The boat had completely disappeared, not even the echo of oars remaining. The hair on her neck bristled. "Must you speak with a priest?"

"They are the only ones permitted to give voice to those beyond the Shikari tribe. Their gods would be angry if the others spoke for them in place of their priests who are trained in such matters."

Tarateal brushed the hair off her forehead then rubbed her eyes. "Poor Sayre," she said with a moan. "He'll never find his wife's body out there."

"Searching for a body in all this," said Faxon, gesturing at the vast network of waterways stretching into the distance. "It's an impossible task. It's a shame he came all this way for nothing. And to lose his engine on approach." Faxon shook his head. "The man's luck has run out, I'm afraid. He's probably at his wit's end."

Not quite, Tarateal thought.

Anyone who counted Sayre out was pushing their own luck. She'd seen him beaten so many times, yet he'd kept going, eventually coming up the victor. He'd lived through worse than this, including the accident in the engine room. He'd survive this, too.

Unlike her, Sayre was a survivor.

He'd handle this just as he'd handled everything else that happened to him. She only wanted to gain the necessary experience to get back to Earth. She couldn't help but accomplish that goal here. If that meant doing whatever she could to help Sayre recover his wife's body, then so be it. She'd help him put her to rest. Like everyone else, Sayre had written her off once. Now was her chance to prove them all wrong.

She wouldn't be written off again.

"He's got a clear head and a lot of luck left," she answered, her tone bordering on defiance, "and we're going to help him pay his last respects. Can you provide us with maps of the areas you've explored, including what you know of the Shikari territory?"

"Of course," said Faxon, his voice smooth. "Whatever you need for your search. I will have one of my engineers assist in the repair of your ship. We should have you up and running within a day or two. I will place one of my boats at your disposal."

"Thank you, Commander Faxon. We appreciate your help. Sayre's crew has a rediscovery mission to complete. That will mean compiling data on plant and animal life-forms here as well as creating an inventory of events to date."

"We have all the records Sayre's crew will require. Your rediscovery mission will be a short one." He turned to walk down the steps of the loading dock. "We will have your ship repaired very soon. No worries about being stranded. You won't be here long, I promise."

Something about his words made her uneasy as he strode down the steps and across the darkening compound. Behind the infirmary were six structures arranged in a half-moon. Cabins most likely. One structure stood in the middle of the compound. Must be the mess, she decided. Near the dock stood two buildings. Judging from the crates and tools stacked near the door of the larger building, it was a storage area. A light suddenly flicked on in the smaller building near the dock. She could see a man's shadow at the window. No doubt Faxon's office. He seemed so anxious for the *Magellan* to leave.

She wanted to know why.

THE NEXT MORNING, Sayre pulled himself out of the sickbed and dressed in tan trousers and a heavy blue mesh shirt. He wasn't well enough to be on his feet yet, but he seemed his old stubborn self. He looked pale and unsteady, his left eye blackened. He held his arm against his rib cage and leaned against the wall as he studied the maps Faxon had provided.

Tarateal stood nearby as Sayre questioned Faxon about his wife—in case Faxon gave him trouble.

"So, she set out for one of these Shikari temples alone in a native boat? God, that's so typical of Larena. Didn't anyone try to stop her? Knowing how dangerous the moors were and knowing you were down to six crew members, you just let her go?"

Faxon shook his head, his eyes narrowing. "I tried to talk her out of it. I warned her that trying to make vocal contact with their priests was too dangerous, but you know Larena. She never heard a word I said. She'd long ago made up her mind that she was going and nothing I said made any difference, Sayre. We watched her boat drift out into the moor channels and that was it. She never returned. She was killed not twenty-four hours later."

Sayre winced. "Was she armed? Did she have a guide?"

Faxon leaned against the wall. "Sorry, Sayre. She left alone. She felt that going alone would be less frightening to the Shikari's, but they feared her like they feared all of us. That's why they killed her. But without a body..."

This statement made Sayre straighten up, the determination returning to his sad hazel eyes. Tarateal frowned, wondering if Faxon was just playing into Sayre's grief.

"May I have the use of one of your boats?"

"I've already arranged use of my personal craft for Ms. Roberts."

Sayre frowned. "It's not for Roberts, it's for me."

"You can't seriously consider going out there alone in your condition. Especially after what happened to your wife. That is most unwise, Sayre."

With painful steps, Sayre moved slowly to the bed and pulled on a tan jacket. "I can and will. This is my problem. I won't ask my crew to risk their lives like this. They've done enough of that getting me here."

Tarateal felt her stomach flutter. He couldn't go out there alone in his condition. There was no telling how the accident had affected him, and not knowing the natives or the area, he could die a million ways before nightfall.

Hadn't he learned anything from his wife's death?

"Sayre," said Tarateal, stepping toward the bed. "I'm going with you."

"Out of the question. I'm going alone. This is my problem—"

She waved him off. "I've heard all of that already. Enough machismo, Sayre! You and I both know that at least one medtech must accompany every mission." She smiled curtly at him. "It's in the manual. Look it up."

His face pinched with anger. "Don't pull that reg crap on me, Roberts!" He cast a sideways glance at Gage seated by the door and sighed.

"Sayre, you're not well yet and it's foolish to go out there alone," said Tarateal, her voice louder than she'd expected. "Even you know that, but you're too damned stubborn to admit it. Now, I came all this way to get contact experience and you're not taking that chance away from me. I'm going! Any questions?"

He suppressed a smile. "None here, Roberts. Will you take care of the supplies? I'll take a look at this boat."

"Right away," she answered, and hurried outside to gather supplies from the *Magellan*.

From the supply room, she collected rations, fire starters, and canteens. She also removed the main medical field kit from the infirmary. As she walked toward the door, she noticed a collection of hazard masks hanging on the wall. She plucked two off their hangers, slid them into her field pack, and hurried back to Nearra's infirmary.

When she returned, Sayre had assembled his crew members in the room. Faxon was nowhere around. Commander Gage sat within earshot, but he had his back to Sayre.

"Glad you're back," said Sayre, motioning her inside. "Close the door and join us."

She shut the door and hurried over to the bunk area. Dale Park sat on the bed, his leg propped up. Sanji leaned against one of the bunks beside Sayre, Sheryl on the other side of him. Kuruk faced Sayre, his posture stiff, and Yawakani sat on a bunk, her arms crossed and her expression wary. Tarateal stepped around to stand on Sayre's other side.

"All the gear's ready. What's up?" she asked, handing him a small field pack and canteen. She hefted her pack onto her shoulder.

"A meeting," said Sanji in a soft voice.

"All right, folks, here's the situation," Sayre began. "You all know my wife—died here. My main reason for accepting this government contract was to recover her body. I'm asking for your cooperation in this because I'm going to be asking a lot from you."

"More than just agreeing to come out here?" Park asked with a smile.

"Yes, Dale, more than that." He cleared his throat and nonchalantly laid a hand against his chest. Tarateal knew his ribs still hurt him. He wasn't hiding anything. "We have a rediscovery mission to complete. That means logging the First Contact team's data and doing a reevaluation of some of that data-gathering. We'll need to verify specimen samples of new plant species and v-logs of unknown sentient species."

"What you're asking is for us to take over the rediscovery mission while you, uh—search," said Sheryl Hannaford.

Sayre sighed and bowed his head. "I don't like to ask so much from you, but there's no other way." Rising from the bunk, he began to pace. His steps were slow and a bit unsteady. Tarateal cringed. "Government won't let us lift off without completing this mission," he continued. "But I'll make sure that all of you get a big bonus. Somehow, I don't know, but I will pay you back for this. You have my word."

At last, Gage got to his feet and stepped over to Sayre. "I've heard enough!" He pointed a finger at Sayre. "I told you on the tarmac that your contract was about the rediscovery mission, not your wife." His voice was cold and sharp. "You've got two days, Sayre, to search for the body. After that, I'll consider any shirking of responsibility to your contract a violation of regulations."

Gage turned and left the infirmary. Sayre just stood there with his jaw clenched.

Sanji moved over to him. "I will do whatever I can to complete our rediscovery mission. No bonus expected or required, Quinn."

"Thanks, Sanj."

"I require no bonus, Captain," said Kuruk.

Sayre turned around and gazed over at Kuruk. "Thanks, Kuruk. I want you to concentrate on the *Magellan*. I want those engines online as soon as possible."

"None of us wants a bonus, Quinn," said Taka. "We've been together a lot of years and most of us knew Larena. I wouldn't have this any other way. Forget the bonus."

"No bonus, Quinn," said Sheryl. "This is an incredible opportunity and that's payment enough for me. Do what you need to do. We'll worry about the data—and Gage."

"Yeah," said Park. "Do what you have to do. We'll handle the rest."

"Thank you," said Sayre, his voice cracking. "This means everything to me."

Tarateal crossed her arms. "Forget it, Sayre. I want the bonus."

Sayre sighed as the room fell silent. "Name your price, Roberts," he said in a weary voice.

"I will," she said, holding back a grin. "I want the best damned reference a class one can get."

He laughed, his voice thin. "You've got it, now c'mon, we've got a boat to catch." He moved toward the back door.

Sanji grabbed Tarateal's sleeve. "Watch out for him. He is in great pain and thinking only with his heart."

She patted Sanji's hand. "Don't worry," she answered. "I'll do whatever it takes to bring him back alive."

"Quinn is the best friend I've ever had. He's done so much for me. If it hadn't been for him, I'd be back on my father's farm in Jammu still dreaming of space travel."

"I understand, Sanji," she said, almost sad. Why hadn't Sayre been like that with her? "I'll do my best."

"Roberts!" Sayre shouted from the loading dock. "Get a move on it! I don't want to lose the daylight."

"Unless I kill him myself," Tarateal said through gritted teeth, and hurried out the door.

WHEN SHE REACHED the loading dock, Faxon and one of the First Contact team members waited for them. The blond-haired man stood beside Faxon, his gaze darting from the storage building to the horizon. He seemed nervous and his hand hovered near a plasma pistol in his belt. Why did he need to be armed here—in camp? Sayre didn't seem to notice. He squinted at Faxon. "Is the boat ready yet?"

Faxon looked meek and out of shape standing beside Sayre, who was lean and wiry and muscled in all the right places. Sayre looked like an athlete, full head of thick black hair, only his eyes giving away pain.

"Of course," said Faxon, pointing to a boat at the end of the pier.

A dark-haired woman was finishing what looked like maintenance checks on the boat's engines.

"I must insist that you keep in close contact with the compound while you're gone. We don't want anything to happen to you out there. It's bad enough that four of our team have been lost over these past six months."

"How many did you arrive with?" Tarateal asked.

"Eight and myself," said Faxon. He folded his hands in front of him. "I'm down to four team members now. We don't want any more deaths."

Tarateal cringed. She wouldn't let Sayre or herself die out in those moors. They were coming back—with answers.

Sayre motioned her onto the loading dock and down the muddy stairs. They sloshed across the damp, mucky ground until they reached the sagging dock. A bird warbled. Insects buzzed. The water purled. A line of fuzzy blue mold gripped the boards at water level. Thin, spongy spires clung to the underside of the boards, the smell reminding her of spoiled mushrooms.

As they approached the craft, the woman closed the engine housing in the back of the boat and clambered onto the pier. She made eye contact with the blond man as she passed them. Tarateal watched her walk toward the storage building.

What was that look between them about?

She paused on the pier, waiting for Sayre to give the word. He seemed to be deep in thought, his gaze on the horizon for some time. Finally, he snapped out of his reverie and nodded to her. She climbed into the boat. Visibly struggling against the sore ribs and muscle aches, Sayre lowered himself into the boat and reached for the steering wheel, but she pushed his hands away.

"I'll pilot. You navigate."

He started to protest, but the pain in his side made him stagger and he relented. Reluctantly, he settled back into the padded seat in the stern and set his pack onto the boat's dank bottom.

"Here, Sayre," said Faxon, handing him a small datapad. "All known routes have been recorded. I've tagged routes that your wife frequented. If you explore additional, unrecorded passages, please mark them and we'll upload them to our system. Until this planet gets sat-mapped, this is all the data we have."

Sayre nodded, studying the grid. He paged through the various map screens, touching locations on the Nearran chart with his finger to access the maps. He had to be wondering where she'd taken her last breath. His face looked taut, his eyes full of pain.

She glanced up to see Sanji hurrying across the compound. Faxon stepped up to the boat and reached for the mooring line as Sanji dropped down on his haunches on the rickety dock.

He handed Sayre a wrist comm. "You forgot this," he said in a thin voice, cradling his left hand. "We expect you to contact us frequently, but this will report your position and condition."

"Sounds fair, Sanj," said Sayre, forcing a weary smile. "Don't worry about me so much. I'm fine. I've got Roberts along, remember?"

Sanji cast a peculiar look at Faxon and the hard-looking man with his hand on the plasma gun. "How long do you expect to be gone?"

Sayre shook his head. "Until I find some answers."

"We'll keep Gage busy with plants and animals," Sanji said with a wink.

"Keep us informed, Captain," said Faxon. He released the mooring line. "While you're gone, I will gather up Larena's things and have them placed in your quarters. I'm certain you'll want to examine them."

Tarateal saw Sayre wince at the prospect, his attention on the maps wavering. He obviously didn't want to think about going through his dead wife's belongings. She couldn't blame him.

She switched on the motor and the boat purred away from the dock. She gave the wheel a gentle turn until the boat glided through the thick muck toward a small channel to the left of the dock.

"This is insane," she said. "You know that, don't you?"

"As insane as Larena's death."

She nodded and eased the boat toward a long stretch of blue blackness that led deep into the Nearran wilds. This place was dangerous; her death wasn't so hard to believe now.

Didn't Sayre see that?

Maybe he wasn't even reacting to the planet's dangers? Maybe it was the contact team itself?

As she glanced back at the compound, she noticed Faxon and the blond man enter the storage building. Faxon's behavior seemed peculiar. After six weeks of radio blackout, Faxon should have been grateful to the *Magellan* for assisting them. Instead, he seemed almost annoyed by their presence. Was Faxon hoping they'd been forgotten?

What was Faxon hiding?

EIGHT

THE WATER WAS an oily swath slithering across the land. On all sides of the murky causeway, green gauzelike vines clung to towering trees. Massive trunks rose like monoliths around them. The hollow thump of something gnawing on wood echoed across the gurgling water.

Quinn frowned. Not even Larena could have found beauty in this muck.

He studied the map Faxon had given him, noting causeways that had been explored and those labeled too dangerous. His skin crawled and he felt moisture collect in the corners of his eyes.

Had Larena taken one of these routes to her death? There was no way to tell.

Maybe Roberts was right? Maybe this was insane, but he had to go through with it. He couldn't live with himself knowing he didn't do everything to find her. And he had to see the body, to accept that she was really gone.

Thinking about all the ways she could have died out here was more than he could stand. He had to know. Sighing, he let the datapad rest against his knee. Without Larena, he didn't know if he could live with himself. Gage would make certain he was arrested before they left this place anyway. Even if he was acquitted, his contract days were finished. No one would hire a suspected privateer. Accusations had a funny way of turning into convictions.

Roberts kept quiet as she gazed at the surroundings, the motor chugging softly. She seemed to keep to herself almost as much as he did. Her curly, dark blond hair tumbled around her shoulders, not the harsh, taut ponytail like he remembered from FS-314, and those blue eyes were still luminous.

He'd mistaken her steadfast loyalty for timidness. He saw that now.

What else had he misread?

After everything that happened on Salice Minor, he'd expected a much different reaction from her. He'd expected some anger, especially after he'd pulled that dirty trick on her at the fueling station—not telling her who held the contract—and a lot of bitter indifference. But here she was out here risking her life to find the body of a woman she blamed for their breakup.

Roberts didn't know that Larena chased him relentlessly on Salice Minor that last semester (when he'd been with Roberts). Yeah, she was the hottest woman he'd ever seen, but he wasn't a cheater. Days after the breakup, she contacted him. She was a rebound hookup. She followed him to Ramantra when he did the right thing and transferred to another campus. He'd never meant to flaunt that in Roberts' face.

Larena finished college after his first commission on Ramantra and they became a long-distance relationship when he was assigned to the *Augustine*. And the years of chaos that followed. When he bought the *Magellan*, she moved in with him. They got married shortly before the First Contact mission.

He'd never meant to hurt Roberts. Just knowing how much she still despised him hurt more than he'd expected.

Of all his crew, only Sanji or Taka would have offered to accompany him out here, yet Roberts had diligently volunteered without a whine or a whimper. He'd expected nothing but complaints and excuses—her being a stick in the mud—something the old Roberts was famous for, but she'd silently offered her expertise and strength. Larena wouldn't have taken this risk for someone else.

He sighed. Or him. He knew that now.

Larena reminded him of a butterfly: beautiful, constantly in motion, but short-lived. And that stick in the mud was becoming a handhold. Holding him up.

He ran his fingers across an image on the datapad, of Larena standing beside a group of Shikari's, some of them small like children. She never saw danger in anything she desired, not even in the Shikari's and their children. Larena couldn't have children, but never seemed to miss them. Frankly, she'd never had time for them and neither had he. It had always been just the two of them. He twisted his wedding band around and around. Now, it was just him. The melody of "May the Road Rise up to Meet You" rose to his lips and he hummed softly, remembering Larena's charming smile and affinity with everyone she met.

"What are you humming?" Roberts asked as she opened up the throttle, sending the boat gliding at a full clip. The boat skimmed faster over the water.

"Is this the beginning of a conversation?" he asked with a smile.

"Who knew?" Roberts said with a shrug. "Actually, you're the only person here and I thought it'd be rude if I didn't at least make small talk."

He rolled his eyes. "It's something Larena used to sing. 'May The Road Rise up to Meet You.'" He gazed out at the blue grasses fanning across the marshy banks and leafless trees. Something that looked like a bird screeched overhead. The sky seemed darker than it had earlier.

"That's an Irish blessing," said Roberts. "May the road rise up to meet you. May the wind be always at your back." She leaned against the boat and let her arms fall against her side, a wistful look in her eyes. "May the sun shine warm upon your face—"

"And the rains fall soft upon your fields. Until we meet again..." His voice trailed off.

It would be an eternity, he realized. She was dead. He felt the moisture rise in his eyes again, the realization sinking in at last. Quickly, he thrust the grid back to his face and studied the tributaries leading toward the Shikari homelands, the GIS map layer marked with a red X. He felt a vibration in the boat against the water when it rocked to the right.

"Take the right fork," he muttered.

There wasn't an exact route marked, so he was just going by his gut, despite the constant amara burn. He was used to it by now.

They traveled for a long time in silence. The water seemed to hum louder against the boat as they drew closer to Shikari lands. He wondered if they'd find the camp before nightfall. In the flickers of light through the trees, the sky had taken on a charcoal cast that was deepening. He pointed at the sky.

"The sky looks bad," he said. "Think the weather's going to kick up?"

Roberts squinted and scanned the horizon. "I don't know," she said, casting an uneasy glance at him. "It doesn't look good."

A distant rumble roiled across the moors, shrouding it in stillness. Chitters and chirrs died away to whispers then silence.

Quinn rose from the seat and moved beside Roberts.

"I don't like this, Sayre," Roberts said, uneasiness in her voice, her fingers gripping the stick.

Her gaze flicked from sky to treetops.

"Neither do I," said Quinn as the rumble of thunder deepened.

A ball of blue fire crackled up from the clouds, blooming then dissipating into feathery strands against the horizon.

Another bloom of electric blue filled the sky and careened across the cloud tops, the sound like shattering glass. Roberts grabbed hold of his arm and gripped it tightly, but her other hand remained on the wheel.

Quinn laid a hand against hers and squeezed.

"We're okay," he said softly. "But we need to get out of this storm. Let's move into that smaller channel up ahead on your left."

She nodded and nudged the boat toward the channel.

A red blossom of light crackled overhead, the thunderclap sharp.

He felt the energy pulse across the channel. His hair stood on end. This was too dangerous. They had to get off the water. Now.

Roberts cast a brave glance at him, but he saw the glint of fear in her eyes. She didn't say a word though. He offered her a smile and squeezed her hand again.

Flashes of blue and red exploded on the horizon, the wind rising.

"Sayre, look!" Roberts cried, and pointed at the shoreline.

Ahead, on a path near the water stood two stone columns.

The darkness grew thick and charged around them. Every time the sky flashed, he caught the dark outline of a small structure beyond the columns. It was barely an afterimage as the rain surged against the moors, the roar deafening.

The boat rocked, nearly pitching them into the water.

"Hold onto it, Roberts!" he shouted above the squall.

"I'm going toward the columns!" she yelled, veering left.

Fiery swells lit the treetops as the boat thumped against land. Quinn grabbed his field pack and struggled out of the boat. Every stretch and every turn made his chest ache. He fought the rising wind and pounding rain to tie down the boat. Roberts jumped out and grabbed another mooring line, tying off on another tree.

Quinn grabbed her arm. "This way!" he shouted.

With her field pack on her shoulder, Roberts followed him into the trees. Ahead stood four more columns and a small stone structure. In the distance, he saw several more buildings, some with crumbling walls, others intact. He pulled her inside the nearest structure that had a roof overhead and a heavy door.

Inside, the rain scent mixed with the smell of moss and dirt. Darkness hung damp and heavy in the structure, making him uneasy. He fumbled through his field pack for a glow stick. With a quick snap, the glow stick cast clear blue light through the small structure.

It looked like an abandoned storage place. What might have been a fire pit gouged out the center of the floor. Blue flecks glittered across several grass mats that covered the floor and framed the fire pit. A rail with wooden pegs ran around the entire length of the walls.

Must be part of the Shikari lands, he realized.

Maybe a place where they hung crops to dry or salted meat? But why had it been abandoned? All of the buildings in the area were overgrown and falling down, but it looked like someone had recently stayed here.

Roberts grabbed hold of the heavy wooden door and latched it shut. Winded, she set down her pack and leaned against the wall.

"You okay, Roberts?" he asked, laying a hand against her back.

She turned her gaze to him and nodded. Her eyes were so luminous, her wheaten hair curling around her face. He reached out and smoothed the soaked curls off her cheek, unable to look away. There was a glimmer of vulnerability in her eyes, a depth of spirit that he'd never seen in Larena's eyes. It was something he'd loved about Roberts once.

And missed.

"I'm fine," she answered softly, and then turned away from him to her field pack.

"How are those ribs?" she asked.

"Sore," he answered, "but I'm okay."

Outside, the storm pounded full force across the moors. Rain pelted the stone building, making him smile. He loved a good thunderstorm. Roberts sat down and leaned against the wall. She gazed at the ceiling.

"The rain doesn't sound so hostile in here," she said, and pulled a glow stick from her pack.

Slowly, he slid down beside her, his chest hurting. "I could listen to that all night," he replied.

She smiled and shook her hand through her soaked hair. "Me, too. I love the rain."

Larena hated the rain. Too messy. "Bet you never thought you'd end up with me out in the Rim, did you, Roberts?"

"The thought never crossed my mind," she replied.

Ouch. He deserved that. She'd gotten over him a long time ago. "I'm sure it didn't."

She frowned. "What's that supposed to mean?"

"Nothing, I—"

"I didn't spend the last five years pining over you, Sayre, if that's what you're thinking. I'm so over you!"

He set his jaw. "It was an ugly breakup, Roberts, and I'm sorry if I hurt you. But that was years ago."

Her blue eyes sizzled. "It was a lifetime ago, okay! Let's just forget it."

She turned her gaze toward the rattan shade fluttering against the window.

He let the subject drop. He got to his feet and paced around the building, the soft thrum of rain pattering against stone. He sighed. It was going to be a long day.

"I wonder why these buildings are abandoned," he said aloud as he examined the long-extinguished fire pit.

"Do you think they're Shikari dwellings?" Roberts asked. Her gaze was steady, the anger gone.

He shook his head. "Don't know. Most likely, but they look recently abandoned." He lifted the corner of a woven mat. "I mean, these grass mats are still in good shape. There's still some ash left in this fire pit."

Roberts rose from the floor and moved over to the fire pit, shining her glow stick into it. "I suppose some of the First Contact team could have used these as a halfway point."

He frowned. And most likely drove the Shikari's out of them. He glanced up at Roberts. In her eyes shined the same suspicion.

"Sayre," said Roberts, holding out her arms. "Do you think Faxon did this?" She stared uncertainly at him.

With the toe of his boot, Quinn nudged one of the mats. There were burn marks on them and not just from the fire pit. Looked more like laser fire. He studied the walls, finding scorch marks in the stones. A chill danced down his spine.

He nodded. "I think Faxon's been lying about a lot of things."

AFTER AN HOUR OR SO, the rain stopped falling. In the silence, he and Roberts gathered their field packs and went back to the boat. After backtracking to the main channel, they continued deeper into Shikari lands.

Soon, the moors darkened, the vegetation increasing. Powder blue vines clinging with fuzzy blue growths draped across the tributary, creating a canopy overhead that darkened into an eerie, mist-trapped corridor. As the tributary widened, Quinn saw the small, lithe bodies of Shikari's, their faces painted black, skin washed grey as they flitted back and forth.

"Sayre, look!" Roberts said in a hushed voice.

The Shikari's danced across the banks, chattering in high-pitched syllables. As the boat drew closer, the voices faded to silence.

When the boat nudged the soft ground, Roberts cut the motor and jumped out, beaching the prow firmly into the blue-black silt. She tied off on a thick clump of jagged brush and waited for him to climb out. Like dragonflies, the Shikari's silently darted around her for a moment and then around him. They poked at his clothes, tugged at his backpack. Rough, handlike appendages stroked down his arms and across his chest. The silence was unnerving.

"I wish they'd say something," he said finally.

Roberts nodded. "Even something harsh would be welcome. Not that we could understand it anyway."

Some Shikari's wore black paint dotted across their cheeks and the bridge of their noses. Their fierce, bronzed faces looked almost equine, a thick bronze sheen of short, silky hair covering their bodies. Some of the Shikari's had jagged streaks of cream across their chests. Quinn had never seen anything like them.

Long, diamond-shaped faces, tapering at the chin, cheekbones jutting out in sharp points, and bright, dark eyes watching him warily. Long, flat noses wrinkled, reptilian eyes unblinking. Some of the Shikari's crouched on all fours, huge ochre eyes staring blankly. One scratched at the ground with its foot, the appendage cleaved with only two toes. Their hands cleaved in threes, one appendage resembling what almost looked like a thumb.

He sensed pride, not fear or hostility. Abruptly, the line of prancing Shikari's parted and what looked like a priest approached them. Its mask, painted black and red, had a gaping mouth, huge angry eyes, and long snout with flaring nostrils. It reminded Quinn of a dragon.

"Can you understand me?" Quinn asked the nearest Shikari.

The creature's ears pressed flat against its head and it stared.

"Faxon said that only their priests talked," Roberts warned. "Don't get them angry."

He ignored her and pulled a holo of Larena from his pocket. He held the holoimage up to a Shikari, who scrambled away from him. Only the priest remained. With thick fingers, the priest snatched the holoimage from his hand. It gazed at the image for a moment and then threw it into the swamp.

"Hey!"

Roberts grabbed his arm before he could react. "Let it go, Sayre," she said in a low voice. "If you don't want to be thrown in after it, I suggest you stand still."

"Since when are you an expert in alien relations," he answered.

He forced his anger back under his tongue as the priest thrust a hand toward his pack. As much as he hated to admit it, Roberts was right. Where had she picked up this attitude? He'd never seen it on her before.

The priest clawed at the pack until Quinn deflected its reach. Unshaken, the priest grabbed his arm and pulled him toward the boat. Firmly, the creature pressed his hand against the side of the boat and then gestured at the land behind him.

Quinn shook his head. "I don't understand you."

The creature snorted, threw back its head, and gestured toward the water. Again, it pressed Quinn's hand against the boat and then against his pack.

"Sorry," he said, shaking his head. "I don't understand you. I'm looking for a woman. Her name is Larena."

Once again, the priest threw back its head and pointed to the water.

"The holo, Sayre," said Roberts. "It's pointing to where the holo landed. See?"

"What's that got to do with my pack?"

"Maybe he wants you to sleep in the water?" she said with a grin.

He glared at her. "Cute, Roberts. You should have your own show."

"Seriously," she replied, the smile fading. "Maybe they're inviting us to camp here tonight?"

Quinn gazed into the blank gold eyes and patted his pack. He threw back his head, mimicking the Shikari priest's gesture. Immediately, the tribe darted up the bank and disappeared into the foggy marsh grasses. The priest turned and followed, leaving Quinn and Roberts standing on the bank.

"Nice going, Sayre. You scared them away."

"I think they want us to follow," he said, stumbling up the bank behind them.

Roberts hesitated and then fell in behind him.

The Shikari's led them to a dry stretch of tall grass near a rocky pit. He scanned the area for some sort of structure, but found no buildings. Not even a shed. Only a fire burned in the pit and a small, blackened pot perched over the flames. The Shikari priest clawed at his pack until he finally set it on the ground and yanked out his bedroll. This seemed to satisfy the priest, who abruptly left him alone, moving toward a hollowed-out tree trunk on the other side of the fire pit.

"He seems anxious for you to go to sleep, Sayre." Roberts nudged him with her elbow as she set down her pack. "Maybe you're on the menu tonight?"

"Stick to medicine instead of comedy, Roberts," Sayre replied with a growl.

"No sense of humor," she muttered, and laid out her bedroll. "You haven't changed a bit."

He looked away, gazing out at the blue sky that washed amethyst as the pale sun sank into the marsh. Firelight flickered through the chirring grasses, casting shadows into the misting moors. Insects clicked and scritched near the slap of water against mud. Something spicy rose on the wind, the scent reminding him of curry. Larena's favorite spice. It made him sick. He sighed and the cool breeze rising off the moors made him shiver. He couldn't leave here without finding her body—he couldn't.

"Tell me about your wife."

He glanced over at Roberts. She wore only a thin pair of black leggings and a white T-shirt as she folded her flight suit. She slid her lean frame into her bedroll, looking more like the passionate medtech student he'd fallen for on Salice Minor. Wavy, wheat-colored hair framed her oval face and warm smile. When he had first seen her standing outside the door of the magtape viewing room in the Cultural Technologies Museum, he'd fallen hard for her. He thought she was everything he'd ever wanted, until the Rim came up.

"What do you want to know?" he asked finally.

"What she did in her spare time, what books she read, the kind of perfume she wore. Things like that."

"Romance novels."

"I've never thought of Larena Neville as a romantic."

He shrugged. Neither had he. "Larena read several a week when she'd finished with her botany v-journals. She never wore the same perfume for more than a month, but the last one I remember was Spring Rain."

"Spring Rain? Mmm, what's that? Sounds nice."

Roberts's face looked softer now, softer than Larena's chiseled lines. Girlish to Larena's siren-like beauty. There was a realness, a vulnerability about Roberts that had always been absent from Larena.

Larena never seemed to need anyone for very long. Something in Roberts' eyes told him that she longed to be needed. Larena never seemed to need him except for those rare occasions when she felt lonely. She loved him, but in her own way—and sometimes he wondered even about that.

If he'd gone missing on Nearra, would she have come here to search for him? Or recover his body? He sighed, already knowing the answer. Larena would have quietly mourned him as she went on with her life, but she wouldn't have come to Nearra to find him. It hurt, but he knew it was true.

"Spring Rain was something Larena had mixed specially for her. Had it engineered to perfectly complement her own biochemistry. She says it smells like spring rain through eucalyptus, kancha, and jasmine." He smiled. Everything about Larena was spring and jasmine—short-lived and intense.

Roberts' eyes turned sad. "Look, I know how much you must miss her. And I know this must be really hard on you, searching for a body and all. I'll do what I can to help, okay?"

"Why?" he asked. "You don't even know me anymore. Why would you do this for me? Someone you hate?"

She plucked a blade of grass and twirled it around her fingers. "Because I'm tired of patching up sludge burns and treating flu. I'm tired of stale mochas and warm sodas, but mostly, I want to go home. I don't want to die out here, but I'm tired of being treated like an intern. And I'm tired of running from that night on Salice Minor."

He cringed at the horrible timing. Him asking for them to take a break and then the nasty argument/breakup on the steps of the flight school. And two days later, she sees him with Larena. He hadn't meant for that to happen. Now, every time she thought about her academy days, she'd feel the pain of that breakup. He regretted how everything happened that night and he wished he'd told her in a gentler way. Had waited before hooking up with Larena. But he couldn't change that now. In her eyes, he still saw the hurt. Even though a long time had passed, that night still brought her pain. He felt terrible.

"I'm so tired of feeling like I know half as much as other class ones." She threw down the blade of grass. "I'm tired of feeling fresh out of school—without any experience except bedpan shifts. I want to grow old, Sayre. I want to see you grow old, too—not flitting around the Rim like some testosterone-pumped magtape star trying to be eighteen forever. It's no good."

How different these two women were. Larena never wanted a wrinkle and she never wanted to grow old. He sighed. She went to all the latest spas, tried all the newest treatments, fighting even the slightest hint of aging. She wanted to be eighteen forever.

He just wanted to be content.

"How long have you been in contract work?" Roberts asked.

He rubbed his chin. He didn't know if she knew about his discharge from the military. He certainly wouldn't volunteer that information. "A few years. I started out taking any contract offered, but lately, I've been playing it safe."

"Me, too," she said, plucking another blade of blue grass. "My whole life."

Two Shikari's tromped through the grass until they reached the small plateau outside their camp. One set a bowl in front of him and the other Shikari set a bowl on the ground beside Roberts. They turned silently and walked away. Roberts swept hers up and sniffed the contents.

"Smells like some kind of spiced grain."

It reminded him of rice. He poked his finger at the round granules floating in a spicy broth. Roberts pressed the bowl to her lips and tasted. Quinn followed her example. It tasted rich and warm, the grain filling. Roberts finished her meal quickly and settled deeper into her bedroll.

"Sleep well, Sayre," she said, rolling over.

He laid back in his bedroll, watching the indigo blackness brighten with cold white stars and knowing Larena could no longer see them. The sky looked so different, and for the first time in his life, the Rim scared him. A sick feeling quivered in his stomach and he wondered if she'd collapsed somewhere out in the damp moor mist, longing for a death that finally came.

He shuddered.

Had she been held captive in some dank shack and tortured to death? Or was she buried deep in the cold, unmarked ground, never to be found. He understood Roberts' apprehension now. And he respected it.

He slid a small flask out of his boot and tossed down two razor-sharp shots of amara. Pain ripped down his throat as he swallowed quickly. It burned his stomach. When the amara kicked in, his weary eyes closed, squeezing out tears as he fell into an exhausted, amara-fogged asleep.

GHOSTS. From his past. Lingered on the edge of his dream.

Guys he barely recognized from the military, women he knew before Larena and Roberts...strange places he knew yet had lost somewhere in the silvery, misty layers of his memory. His mom used to say that everyone's life leaves behind an impression in the world and those impressions were most visible in the dreamtime.

Here. In this translucent hall of memory, layered with dreams and sensations, he felt those impressions. They felt so real, so vivid. This was unlike any dream he'd ever had before.

His footsteps made no sound as he walked down a long hallway, the floor pearlescent, so bright, so intense. Perhaps the Shikari's had put something in those grains? Was that why he was having such an intense dream? But deep in the pit of his stomach, he knew it was something else.

Something more revealing than he dared hope for.

Ahead, the translucent entrance of the old shuttle terminal where they first met materialized and there stood Larena. His first impression of her. Eighteen-year-old auburn hair glistened, teenage porcelain-smooth face, the wrinkles of living absent. He preferred her older. Much older. Her father had just gotten her a job with the government offices on Salice Minor. Then later—Ramantra where she'd work and go to school.

She smiled and flitted toward him. "Quinn! Oh, Quinn! It's been so long!" Throwing ghost arms around his neck, she pressed ghost lips against his and they felt moist. Surprised by the sensations that weren't supposed to be there, he felt them all. His chest ached. He didn't want this to be a dream. It had been so long.

He kissed her urgently. Six weeks she'd been gone from the universe. Six weeks of loss, heartache, of hiding the pain from his crew, and tempering it with amara. Suddenly, her eyes turned cruel and she playfully pushed him away, grinning.

"You're so old, dearest," she said in a soft voice.

He nodded, the tears burning his eyes. He was twenty-eight. To her, that would have been ancient back then. He felt the years in those tears, the weeks flooding away, the hours of amara-fogged mourning. Of not knowing. His chest ached.

He reached for her.

"Larena," he choked out. "I miss you."

"Plenty of time for that, dearest. When will your first commission start? Will it last more than six months? I want to get married and go off to school." She leaned against him, hands on his waist, legs rubbing against his. "You look tired."

He'd forgotten how she'd been at eighteen. Had she ever been this infatuated with him? She hadn't understood him back then. She'd hated age and anything that looked worn and beaten—like he looked now.

The clean scent of her perfume washed over him. Surprised, he took a step back. Spring Rain? Spring and jasmine. Eventually, she'd come back to this fragrance. He smiled. It would stay with her like eighteen.

"I *am* tired, Larena," he said, and collapsed onto a shuttle track that wound its way into the distant amber sun setting on the horizon. "I've come to Nearra to search for your body."

She sank down beside him and slipped her arm in his, nuzzling her face into his neck. "Silly boy, I'm right here. There is no Nearra."

Her heady scent wrapped around his brain, making him feel light-headed. He thrust his arms around her, drawing her closer. "I can't believe I've lost you," he said with a moan. "They say you're dead, Larena. Oh, God—" He laid his head against her shoulder and cried.

She stroked velvet fingers through his tousled hair, silent and uncertain what to say. She never knew how to take his moods, and later, this would drive her out of his arms until he was happy again. She never understood the darker emotions. They annoyed her. At eighteen, though, these moods had fascinated her.

A shadow fell over him and he raised his head. There stood the Shikari priest, forbidding mask casting a long shadow across him. He stifled a cry of surprise and scrambled back from the native. He tried to pull Larena back too, but she giggled and scurried off toward the shuttle terminal. Dissolving into the mist along with the terminal.

"I knew I you find here," said the priest. "Your language—difficult for us. Been time long since I speak it. Patience."

The sound of the priest's voice startled him. "Thought you only talked to people you trusted."

"Here I talk—safe. I remember now words."

"I'm glad this is a dream," Quinn muttered.

"Dream?" The Shikari cocked its head.

"Yeah, you know, where your body's asleep and your mind's running wild."

"This not a dream, Quinn Sayre."

He frowned. "Of course, it's a dream. I just saw Larena and held her in my arms. And you're talking to me." He sighed. He was arguing with a figment in his dream.

"No, you far moved beyond dreamscape. You walk the astralscape. Where there are no masks."

"What are you talking about? This is all a simple dream."

The Shikari priest shook its head. "All lives have echoes. And what has passed resonates here."

His stomach clenched. "You mean whatever has died?"

"It just the past, Quinn Sayre. Ghosts from your past. Their echoes here stir." The Shikari leaned closer to him, reaching out the cleaved hand to his arms. Abruptly, it jerked back its arm.

"What is it?" he demanded.

"You walk here because of injury. And something else don't I recognize. Your body—energy force bad altered—or you not could to be here with me."

The accident in the engine room?

He thought back to something Roberts said. Something about the only aftereffect was a slight change in his vital signs. "I did have an accident a few days ago," he mumbled, scratching his head.

"No. Something else." The Shikari reached toward its left temple and pressed. It pulled something free with its hand and dropped it into his hands.

"What is it?"

"I not know, but it from came your people. It see is hard. Remember look for to it soon."

"I'll try," said Quinn, not understanding.

The words were jumbled, in the wrong order, and it hurt his brain trying to process it. And the thing in his hand was smoky and formless. He couldn't tell what it was.

He thought for a moment, processing the jumbled words. "If I'm here because of this—" he said, holding out the formless smoke in his palm. "Then how did you get here?"

"*Loahn*. Gift from Chiriga to Shikari, allowing our eye souls wander to. On astral, eye souls safe from shadow souls that Faxon into our lands released. Many Shikari's die. Evil. Evil!"

He stared at the priest. What was it talking about? None of this made sense. But he'd long suspected that Faxon was up to no good here. "Are you saying that Faxon is hurting your tribe?"

The priest snapped its head back. "Your skin turns grey. Your eye soul wearies, Quinn Sayre. Return to your body. I more learn and we again talk, but only here. Faxon no longer has eye soul and his shadow soul reach us cannot here. Only do here I trust you."

The priest turned to leave, but Quinn grabbed its arm. "Wait," he cried. "Do you know what happened to my wife? Larena?"

"Go back to your body, Quinn Sayre."

Abruptly, the priest disappeared into the greyness, leaving Quinn standing in the dissolving translucence. He felt the weariness bend him at the knees and he was falling back into his body, darkness covering his eyes with sleep.

"SAYRE? YOU AWAKE YET?"

Slowly, he rolled over, feeling the stiff ache in his muscles and the pounding in his head. Like the amara feedback he awoke to after a night of watching Larena on his datapad. His mouth felt like sandpaper and his dry eyes burned with grit. When Roberts saw his face, she gasped and dropped down beside him, a hand on his forehead.

"You look terrible! Must have been the grain. Your skin is grey!" She rubbed his hands together in hers until the grey began to recede. "You look like a corpse."

"Good," he mumbled through taut lips, "because I feel like one."

She reached into her medical kit and retrieved a syringe and needle. Before he could protest, she gently pressed the needle to his shoulder.

"What the hell was that?"

"Relax. It'll give you some energy and get this blood flowing." She patted him on the shoulder and left him to dress.

After he'd put on his clothes, he sat down beside Roberts, the field pack on his shoulder. He plopped it down and dug out the rations.

"Hungry?" he asked.

She nodded. "Surprisingly yes. After that grain concoction, I didn't think I'd ever be hungry again. Talk about filling. I slept better than I have in weeks." She squinted at him. "From the looks of you, I'd say you slept about an hour tops."

"No, I slept fine. I fell asleep the moment I laid down." He sighed. But he felt exhausted. Had that dream been real somehow? Had he really held Larena in his arms and talked with that priest?

The roar of rocket engines suddenly seared the solitude of the moors. A small craft ripped across the misty ground from somewhere to the south and slashed across the sky, leaving slate grey smoke in its wake.

"What the hell was that?" Quinn shouted.

"Do you think that Kuruk fixed the *Magellan's* engines already?" Roberts asked, scanning the horizon.

He shook his head. "Not a chance. Those engines were fragged. And as far as I know, Faxon has no ship. I remember Larena saying that when her tour was over, a ship would be called in to retrieve them."

"Maybe it was the supply ship?"

"Out this far in the moors? Not likely. Besides, they haven't had operable communications for weeks, remember?"

Or had they?

"Something weird is going on here," she said, a wary look in her eyes.

Stiffly, he rose from the ground and gathered his gear. "We'd better get back to camp and see if Faxon has more visitors."

Roberts collected her things and hurried behind him as he staggered toward the Shikari fire pit.

NINE

SNAPPING ON SAYRE'S DATAPAD, Kenrick Gage collapsed into a chair and glanced back at the mess he'd made of Sayre's quarters on the *Magellan*. He hoped to make an even bigger mess of the man's life.

Clothing hung out of compartments. Discs and papers littered the floor. A stack of magtapes had slid off a shelf and onto the bed, scattering tapes all over the blanket. Gage shoved some papers off the table and entered his access code, overriding all of Sayre's passwords. Somewhere in this room or on Sayre's computer lay evidence that would convict him on privateering charges. At last, Sayre would be arrested for the destruction of the *Augustine*—and Matt's murder. He'd waited so long for this resolution.

Gage rubbed his eyes as he scrolled through file listings. What had the privateers offered Sayre? What made him sell out? That question had haunted Gage for five years.

Of all the new recruits, Sayre had been the least likely suspect. He had been a personable young man, easygoing and doing more than the job required. Matt idolized him, too, following Sayre around during downtime and playing poker with him. Sayre, three years older than Matt, had taken the boy under his wing. Like he'd taken Ensign Shahir and the Indian's unfortunate lack of schooling in tow. Shahir, the oldest ensign aboard ship, had no chance of promotion given his background, but Sayre had befriended him and Matt, helping both get through drills and procedures.

Until he sold out the ship to privateers.

Sayre strung poor Matt along, pretending to be the boy's friend. Gage gritted his teeth. He'd make Sayre pay for that and for what happened to his son. Poor Matt—he didn't deserve to die. Gage's eyes stung. Why hadn't he kept a better watch on his son's whereabouts that night? Why couldn't he have been the one sitting with Matt when he died?

That one detail had been held back from the news reports. He'd watched the *Augustine*'s logs, garbled and nearly beyond repair from the explosions, until his eyes were bleary with tears, but he couldn't identify the recruit who stayed with Matt in the engine room that night.

Why couldn't it have been him?

"What happened in here?"

Gage jerked his gaze to the doorway. Sanji Shahir hurried into the room, anger in his dark eyes.

"Just a little research, Shahir."

Shahir stiffened, his lips flattening into an angry line. "You have no authority to rifle through Quinn's private quarters. I must ask you to leave."

Gage slid out of the chair and moved toward Shahir, who held his ground. Gage folded his arms against his chest. It wasn't the man's fault. Shahir was just being loyal. Too bad. Sayre was slime.

"Look, Shahir, I'm investigating a potentially volatile situation, and like it or not, Sayre's right in the middle of it."

"I respect you, sir, as my former commander," said Shahir, squaring his shoulders, "but Quinn did not do what you accuse him of. I would stake my life on it."

"And you were lucky to escape with your life. As I recall, you were half-dead when they brought you into that life-pod."

"When *Quinn* brought me into that life-pod," Shahir corrected him.

Couldn't fault this man for his loyalty.

"All right, when Sayre brought you aboard." Gage began to pace. "But you were unconscious! You had no idea what transpired. I'm sure Sayre twisted around the trial findings for you and made himself look good."

Shahir leaned against the wall and his gaze fell to the floor. "I didn't get out of hospital for three weeks and Quinn would tell me nothing the entire time. I had to ask Taka to find out he had been discharged from the military."

"Then I'll make it all clear for you, Shahir," said Gage, still pacing. "Scan records placed Sayre at the comm board within ten minutes of the message that transmitted our location to the privateer vessel. His access code was still active."

Shahir's face paled. "I was in hospital during the trial...I never got to testify. But I swear to you, Commander, Quinn Sayre was not at the comm board that night."

He took a deep breath. "I was."

"No!" Gage poked him in the chest with his index finger. "Don't you dare lie for him. Sayre killed Matt and destroyed the Augustine. Covering for him after all this time won't change that...and it won't save his hide this time."

"I do not lie!" Shahir lurched forward, his white teeth bared. "But that night, Quinn lied." Shahir turned away, his hands pressed against the wall. He struck it with his fist. "I didn't report to detox before leaving Negaff station. A week later, I got sick. I asked Taka to examine me and a blood test revealed Arcturian Fever."

"Arcturian Fever! Dammit, man, you could have infected the entire crew." Gage's eyes narrowed.

"I know." Shahir turned to look at him. "It was stupid of me, but if I had told you, you would have set me ashore at the next port."

Gage crossed his arms. "Exactly right, Mister. Skipping detox can be grounds for dismissal."

"I begged Taka to keep it quiet." Shahir's voice turned shrill. "I couldn't go back to Jammu, I couldn't! The night the *Augustine* was destroyed, I had comm board duty. I collapsed from the fever and Quinn found me. He called Taka, who treated me while he took over my comm duty, but not until he had gotten me to the infirmary."

Gage shook his head. "I didn't see Yawakani testify on Sayre's behalf."

"Quinn made her promise not to testify, so my name would stay out of the proceedings."

"You're not making sense, Shahir. What does Yawakani have to do with comm duty that night?"

"Don't you understand, sir? Even though Quinn entered his name on the duty roster for comm duty, the comm board was unmanned for a half hour. He was with Taka, trying to get me stabilized. He wasn't there when that message was sent."

"Scans don't lie! A combat neural implant was detected at the comm board within five minutes of the transmission of our location." Gage began to pace again.

"Combat implant!" Shahir turned him around. "What are you talking about?"

Gage cursed under his breath. He hadn't meant to reveal that—especially to a class four like Shahir. Not even Sayre knew he carried around some experimental government hardware in his head.

"It was a government project," Gage began. He dropped down in a chair. "Sayre had no idea that the shuttle accident that put him and some of the other new recruits in hospital was staged."

Shahir followed, his mouth gaping. "How can this be?"

"The government needed live subjects to test combat implants. Shortly after the accident and the installations were complete, the project lost funding and got scrubbed. But no one worried about the implants. They would never be activated, so none of the subjects was ever told."

"That does not prove anything," said Shahir.

"Two of those test subjects were stationed aboard the Augustine. Sayre was the only one who survived the Augustine's destruction. And with his access code still active, it had to be Sayre at the comm board that night. It had to."

Shahir started to speak when someone knocked on Sayre's door. He moved to the door and pressed the release. Gage squinted at the sandy-haired young man in the threshold. That annoying chatterbox medtech, Dale Park. Didn't the academies train these youngsters to keep their mouths closed anymore?

"What is it, son?" asked Gage. "We're very busy right now."

The young man pointed at Shahir. "Kuruk sent me to tell you that he successfully linked to the compound's computer system."

"Thanks for the info, son. Now, back to your post." Gage reached over and pressed the door close button.

Park nodded stiffly and turned away from the door as it closed in his face. That young man looked vaguely familiar, but at his age, they all looked like kids. Probably reminded him of a long-ago ensign. With that feathery blond hair, he reminded Gage a bit of Matt.

He sighed. Would Matt's memory ever stop being painful?

"Commander, what if you are wrong about Quinn? What if you've been chasing the wrong man for five years?"

"But I'm not, Shahir," he said, and rose from the chair.

"Then let me prove it." Shahir grabbed his arm. Gage started to pull away, but Shahir's pleading gaze made him stop.

"Why are you so certain this man is innocent?" It made no sense.

Shahir bowed his head. "I was sick that night and abandoned my post. Quinn took the blame for my mistake and it cost him his military career. It is time that I own up to my mistake. Quinn has paid enough."

Sayre wasn't noble. He was a criminal. Gage had the scan log and Sayre's active access code to prove it. At Sayre's trial, the panel had ruled the evidence inconclusive on the charge of treason and privateering. But the suspicion was enough to get him dishonorably discharged.

"Your son was like a brother to Quinn."

Gage recoiled, his chest knotting. No, he wouldn't listen to those lies. He stared into Shahir's desperate gaze. The Indian believed what he said. He owed Shahir the chance to try.

And Matt.

"All right, Shahir," said Gage. "Prove to me that Sayre didn't transmit the Augustine's location to the privateers. I'm going to do everything I can to prove that he did."

Gage waved Shahir away and returned to Sayre's datapad. He tried to ignore the hiss of the door closing and Shahir's determined departure. A part of him feared that Shahir would succeed.

TEN

AS TARATEAL GUIDED the boat against the dock, three of the First Contact team members rushed toward a boat near the vine-covered storage building. Blue vines littered the ground from where they'd been torn away from the door. Team members hurriedly loaded wooden crates into the boat and then ran for more. Faxon's white powerboat glistened with blue-black mud, swamp grass clinging to its hull and plexi-shield. It had come in hard and fast from the moors, even though she never heard even the whisper of a motor out there.

Team members rushed back and forth from the supply building, stacking unmarked crates on the bank. Nothing about the crates left any clue to what lay inside. When Tarateal saw Faxon saunter out of a cabin across from the dock, she climbed out of the boat ahead of Sayre and raced down the creaking dock toward him.

"What's going on?" she shouted. "Are you pulling out?"

He smiled that *you're-so-naive* smile and folded his arms behind his back, brown First Contact coveralls taut across his thick middle.

"Not hardly," he said. "We're preparing to go into the moors to do more research. That's what we do here. Research, remember?"

Sayre stepped up. His lean face seemed thinner than yesterday, eyes hollow, and congeniality fading. He made Tarateal uneasy; she didn't know what he'd do next. His wife had been gone so long now that he was losing his perspective. She knew he almost dreaded finding her now, knowing she was dead, but his temper wouldn't outlast Faxon's smug, vague answers. She saw the tension in Sayre's clenched fingers and she feared he'd lunge at the man. Faxon had done nothing to help their search except send them out into dangerous landscapes to search for a woman's body. A woman that shouldn't be dead.

What sort of commander let that happen? Especially out in the Rim. Sayre would fight to the death for any one of his crew members, yet Faxon seemed content to let them wander off.

"All right, Faxon," Sayre said, his speech slightly slurred. "I want to know what happened to my wife! Dammit, I want answers! Now!"

She wondered how he'd been drinking without her seeing it. Must have hidden it in his pack, she decided.

"Captain, calm yourself," said Faxon in his best business transaction voice. "Perhaps I was too hasty in letting you wander off like that, but I have enough to worry over with my own crew. I don't need more neophytes getting into trouble."

Tarateal nodded. Of course, he'd been too hasty—and just plain careless. And attributing deaths to headstrong team members didn't excuse him from negligence either. Even though she suspected that he'd caused Larena's death. Regardless, the government would simply attribute it to this hostile world and that would be the end of it. Faxon was winning and she couldn't let that happen. It was time to make some noise.

"Why don't you tell Sayre what really happened to his wife instead of making him piece it together like some puzzle?" She glared at Faxon, disgusted by his condescending attitude.

"At least have the decency to tell me how she died!" shouted Sayre. He moved closer. "I have the right to know, dammit—I'm her husband!"

Faxon stepped back from Sayre and leaned against the stacks of crates. Tarateal wanted to slam her fist into his face.

"As I've already explained to Ms. Roberts and Mr. Shahir, your wife refused to listen to my warnings and went out in that ridiculous rowboat to find the Shikari's. Alone."

"Rowboat!" Sayre went ballistic.

Roberts grabbed his arm before he could swing at Faxon. "You let her go out there alone? In a rowboat? A ROW boat!"

"Larena did whatever she wanted, Sayre!" He eyed Sayre warily, keeping his distance. "You of all people should know that."

"But you're in charge! You could have stopped her." He glared at Faxon. "It was your job to protect her!"

Faxon seemed unaffected by Sayre's tirade. "I told her not to go alone," he said matter-of-factly. "That the Shikari's were violent around those they didn't trust. I warned her that they killed whatever they feared, but she ignored my protests. That's the last we saw of her until the empty boat floated back into camp. She's dead, Sayre. Let her go."

Tarateal stiffened. Faxon had changed his story. And he was lying.

The Shikari's did not trust easily, that was obvious, but they were not violent. If they had been, she and Sayre would have already been dead. Besides, none of the Shikari's carried weapons—not even a hunting knife. She'd seen that much herself. And those deserted buildings in the moors—had Faxon and his team driven them out? Or sent them into hiding? Faxon didn't know that they'd found the Shikari's.

It had been easy with Sayre reading the map.

She studied Faxon's granite expression and unruffled demeanor while he lounged innocently against those crates. She wanted to wipe that annoying smirk off his pudgy face. Faxon was stringing poor Sayre along with guilt and ambiguity. Why?

She ran a fingernail down one of the crates and gently tugged on the lid. She squinted at the traces of sparkling blue dust that clung to her skin. Like the flecks she'd seen in that stone structure.

Faxon leaned forward, anger sparking in his blue eyes, and slapped his hand against the lid.

Startled, Tarateal took a step back.

"This is sensitive research equipment, Ms. Roberts. Please do not touch it. If Veider has to recalibrate those instruments again, he'll explode."

Another lie. People didn't bang on sensitive equipment.

"All right," she snapped. "Lighten up. I didn't harm anything. You're the one jostling it around."

She studied his expression, noting the flush in his broad face. At last, the facade wavered. What was in those crates that he didn't want her to see?

"Dammit, Faxon!" Sayre shouted, and lunged at him, but Tarateal grabbed him around the waist and pulled him back. "I want some answers! Maybe this satisfied the official inquiry, but it doesn't work with me. She was your top botanist! How can you be so indifferent about this? Didn't you even try to find her?"

She waited until Sayre regained control before she released him. She smelled the stale, chemical stench of amara. It nearly took her breath. He swayed and nearly fell.

Faxon's eyes narrowed. "Of course, I looked! Larena was the best and I couldn't afford to lose her, but we have to go on now. You have to go on now. Sober up, Sayre. Accept that she's gone and go on with your life."

She bristled. Like that was so easy.

Faxon moved away from the crates and walked toward his office. Sayre lunged at him again, but she yanked him backward.

"That's not the way, Sayre," she said in a low voice.

"I'll be working on reports for the next few days," announced Faxon, not turning around. "I won't be available if you require anything else." He paused in the threshold. "Oh, and my team helped your engineer complete repairs to your ship. You can leave Nearra any time now." He snapped the door closed behind him.

Sayre ground his teeth together as he watched the team members loading crates.

She clenched her hand into a fist. To be dismissed like some first-year trainee was intolerable. And that announcement sounded more like a warning. Faxon was trying to get rid of them now. Patience had been replaced by anxiousness, even his faux compassion replaced by condescension. What was he hiding? Why had he lied about the Shikari's and Larena?

She feared the answers to those questions.

As she watched the rest of the First Contact team restacking crates on the floor of the boat, one of the men tried to start the engine. It gurgled and clicked, but refused to start. The two men stacking crates climbed aboard to help, also bringing the dark-haired woman on board.

Tarateal seized the opportunity.

Slowly, she edged against the crates, finding the one with a loose board on top. She slid her hand inside and scooped out a small handful of powder. Thrusting her hand into her pocket, she moved away from the crates.

Sayre gave her a strange look, but she looked away, back at the boat.

As the woman closed the housing, a clump of blue vines in her hand, the engine started. In moments, it purred softly above the sound of something warbling in the trees. The men returned to the crates, the woman monitoring the engine.

Tarateal backed away toward the path that led through the half-moon ring of cabins and to the landing strip. Sayre ambled behind her with amara-fogged steps.

"Roberts!" Sayre called. "Where you going?"

"To the *Magellan*."

She rushed ahead of him toward the ship. When she reached the landing strip, she stopped in midstride. The same grey-blue vines that had covered the storage shed and been pulled from the boat engine were everywhere. Grey-blue vines, their feathery leaves tipped silver, covered the strip and had even encased the *Magellan*.

Sayre staggered to a stop behind her.

"What the hell?"

"I don't know, Sayre," she said with a shrug. "I've never seen anything like it."

"Kudzu," Sayre mumbled.

Tarateal squinted at him.

"Kudzu. It's a vine native to earth. If you fell asleep in a field of the stuff, it'd grow over you by the time you woke up. This stuff always fascinated Larena."

Sayre walked past her and fumbled through the leaves for the hatch release. When he found it, he yanked it hard, breaking away large skeins of the strange vein.

"I'll get Park to take care of this—mess. If you want me, I'll be in my quarters."

TARATEAL HURRIED to the infirmary's lab with the powder she'd taken from the crates. Carefully, she emptied her pocket into a container. Even through the container, the blue powder sparkled. Among the granules, she found bits of grey-blue leaves. After clearing out the leaf debris, she sent a small sample through the analyzer and waited anxiously for a readout. As the analysis report scrolled across the screen, one of the chemicals stood out. She shuddered at the long name.

The drug trade and the junkies called it Visiondust.

She'd read stories about this drug. It sent chemical signals to the brain, accessing memory and emotions—and a steady euphoria rushing through the body. People who used it said it was an incredible trip down memory lane. And it was highly addictive. Sometimes, people who got hooked on Visiondust became catatonic zombies, unreachable from the outside world. More than a few promising careers had been obliterated by this junk. Several years ago, it was the most popular street drug around, until the government burned the last supply source to the ground. That was nearly four years ago.

She slid the sample out of the analyzer tray and sighed. So, Faxon found a source for the drug on Nearra. He'd turned a First Contact into a drug harvest. Now she knew what happened to Larena. She must have discovered Faxon's drug-running operation and Faxon killed her for it. Remembering how the Shikari's had reacted to Sayre's holo of Larena terrified her now. That priest must have seen Faxon throw her body into the moors. Maybe that's why it threw the holo into the water like that? It made sense now. The priest tried to show Sayre that it did know what happened to Larena. Too bad Tarateal couldn't prove it. Still, she had to tell Sayre.

Later, she decided.

Sanji was no doubt sobering him up and persuading him to get some sleep. After he'd slept and eaten, she'd gently break the news about the Visiondust—and her suspicions about Larena's fate.

QUINN SAT on the edge of the bed, his disheveled quarters darkened. He groaned and rubbed his eyes, feeling the amara sensation slip away. Sleep pulled at him and depression set in again along with the ache in his chest. He was getting nowhere with Faxon. And the amara hadn't helped his temper any. All he needed now was a run-in with Gage.

Carrying a flask of amara in his pocket embarrassed him, but he couldn't get through the day without it. He was thankful that Roberts hadn't discovered it in the Shikari camp or on the boat. It was out of hand, even he knew that, but it was the only thing getting him through this. The stomach pain was getting worse, but he couldn't stop now. Not yet.

There was a knock at his door.

"Enter."

Sanji stepped into the room, concern bleeding through the typically pleasant expression. Sanji stepped over Quinn's belongings scattered across the floor.

"Are you all right?" Sanji asked, and sat down at the table across from the bed. "Tarateal said you were ill."

"I'm fine," he answered. Stretching stiffly, he rose from the bed. He plopped down at the table and reached for the triangular bottle of amara. Sanji grabbed his arm.

"No more, Quinn. This stuff is killing you."

He pulled his arm away. "Don't tell me what to do."

Sanji sighed and for the first time, Quinn saw anger in those dark eyes. "Taka says that your stomach can't take any more amara. If you start to bleed internally, you could die."

He shrugged. He was used to the stomachache by now. It was nothing new.

"No big deal, is it? It gets you through the nights, right? But every morning when you wake up with a hangover, you will still be without her. Will you drink this liquor until it kills you? Is that what you want?"

"Stop nagging, Sanji. I'm not in the mood for it." He reached for the bottle and pulled it toward him.

"As your friend, I cannot. I understand how much you miss your wife. All of us feel terrible about it and want so much to help you. You are fogged half the time, Quinn, and no longer can we look the other way. If you are bent on killing yourself, we do not want to be witness to it. Unless you give up the amara, we will be forced to turn you in to Gage. I mean it, Quinn."

Sighing, he shoved the bottle away. "All right, all right."

Sanji snatched the bottle away. The Indian moved to his ration dispensary and retrieved two cups of coffee. Sanji handed one to him and he gratefully accepted it.

"So, who redecorated the place?" he asked, nodding toward the mess.

"Commander Gage. I'm sorry. I tried to stop him. I'll help you clean up."

He waved Sanji away. "Tomorrow." He had nothing to hide from Gage.

Sanji was silent for a long while.

"What happened while we were gone?" Quinn asked finally.

"Nothing. Why do you ask?"

"Because suddenly the camp has gone wild, and now Faxon is treating us like irritants."

Sanji set down his cup. "I do not trust Faxon."

He leaned forward, eager to hear what Sanji thought. "Why do you say that?"

He'd had his own suspicions, the changing stories, the abrupt attitude shift, but he wanted to hear Sanji's reasons. He wasn't sure if the amara had colored his observations.

For a moment, Sanji seemed at a loss for words. His friend was an accurate judge of character and whenever the man had a problem with someone, Quinn paid close attention.

"His attitude is much too casual for someone who has lost seven of his eleven team members."

"Seven? Are you sure?"

Sanji nodded. "I checked the official logs. Your wife was the sixth."

Faxon *had* lied to them. There hadn't been a reason to check the team roster when Faxon so willingly offered up the information. He'd probably been counting on that.

"Faxon said he'd lost four of his eight team members."

"It would appear that several team members died out here, much more than four. Gage downloaded records from their station computer without Faxon knowing it. Until today, Faxon seemed concerned only for our comfort. Perhaps he knows that we have accessed his files?"

"All Faxon seems concerned with is hastening our departure."

"He has provided little to no help with your search," said Sanji with a scowl. "To send you out alone without a guide makes me wonder if he has set us up to fail. As if he does not want us to find Larena."

"Wonder if it has anything to do with those crates. Roberts seemed pretty damned interested in them. I saw her stick something in her pocket, but honestly, Sanj, I was so full of amara that I barely noticed."

Sanji stood, stretched, and moved toward the door. "Get some rest, Quinn."

"I will," he said, rising from the chair. He collapsed onto the bed and stretched out.

When the comm specialist left, Quinn settled himself under the sheets and closed his eyes. Maybe he could steal back some of the sleep taken from him at the Shikari camp?

TARATEAL PERUSED hundreds of screens at the research carrel when Taka sauntered into the infirmary carrying a tray of cultures taken from Nearra. Taka paused by the carrel, leaning over Tarateal's shoulder.

"Case study?" she asked.

Tarateal shook her head. "Something I found around the camp."

Taka looked more closely, her short, burgundy fingernail tracing across the diagrams on screen. "Looks like some sort of pharmaceutical—in pure form no less." She squinted at the printout, lurching forward. "Wait a minute, that's an odd configuration." Frowning, she stared at her. "Tarateal, what is this?"

Tarateal gazed at Taka's suddenly stern eyes. "Visiondust," she muttered. "Pure stuff. Source unknown."

"You found it here? In raw form?"

Had she found it in raw form or had it been somehow—

processed? Did Faxon have some sort of processing facility on Nearra, hidden out in the moors somewhere?

"I—I don't know that yet, but I intend to find out. I remember reading in a v-journal that Visiondust was refined from some sort of plant—chirigus casandras, but it's extinct in most systems." Then she remembered the boat. "Has Faxon's boat left dock yet?" She scrambled up from the chair.

"About fifteen minutes ago."

Defeated, Tarateal slumped against the chair. Faxon had to be moving those crates where they could be safely shipped off-world— without any of the *Magellan's* crew seeing their contents. Still, she wondered where the Visiondust had come from.

"People would pay a tidy sum for Visiondust," Taka remarked, and wandered over to the equipment cabinet. She retrieved a hand scanner.

Tarateal frowned and turned away from the screen. "What's the hand scanner for?"

Taka leaned her head against the cabinet, her features drooping. "Sanji asked me to give Quinn another once-over. He's going down fast, Tarateal. Sanji's terribly worried. Between his out-of-control behavior and that amara, I don't know if there'll be much left of him if he does find his wife. I've never seen him like this before. Good thing Sheryl's aboard or we might not lift off alive."

"He can't help it. Losing someone that close to you hurts. Probably the worst thing that's ever happened to him."

Tarateal remembered when her mother died. If only she could have done something. Or at least been there with her. She'd been on Salice Minor when the call came. Two months after her breakup with Sayre. She never even got the chance to tell her they'd broken up.

"That and the Augustine disaster," said Taka. "When he got his private scout ship, he seemed fine. All of the bad stuff seemed behind him and nothing ever got to him. I've seen him roughed up, shot up, and held up, and he took it all without batting an eyelash. But this—"

Taka sighed. "When the government sent him that official message, he just curled up inside himself and refused to come out again. We don't know how to help him. It's like he's got a death wish or something."

"He's got to pull it together," said Tarateal. "Especially if she isn't coming back. Gage is poised and ready to destroy him."

Taka ran her index finger across the scanner grid. "Quinn won't rely on anyone else like he relied on her, that's for sure. He never could live his life with her because she was always off pursuing something else. Even so, he feels lost."

"Do you think that accident in the engine room contributed to his personality change?"

She shrugged. "Maybe. He seems a little more withdrawn than he has been," said Taka as she removed a small canvas bag from the cabinet. "Otherwise, nothing that I've observed." She started toward the door, but Tarateal stopped her.

"Let me take care of this one. Please, Taka."

"Sanji asked me to—"

"I know," she answered, and tucked a datapad under her arm as she stood up. "But I've got some things I need to discuss with him— difficult things. This would be a good way to approach him."

"Difficult things?" Taka's eyes were wide with apprehension.

Tarateal nodded. "Larena's not coming back, and if we're not careful, there'll be more deaths."

Taka's mouth gaped. "Why do you say that?"

"You and I both know the legal status of Visiondust. That stuff can cripple whole colonies, leaving them ripe for privateers to pillage. If Faxon is running drugs, then he isn't going to let an unexpected visit from a rediscovery team destroy his operation."

"But even if we all died out here, the ship's disappearance would still be noticed. Especially with Gage aboard."

"Of course," Tarateal said, frowning. "There'd be a barrage of unanswered questions about the ship, but only Faxon would be there to answer them."

Taka's face brightened. "No, the government would send in a reconnaissance team to investigate our disappearance. That's why Gage is aboard—to make sure everything goes well. They'd still nail him."

Tarateal shook her head. "Faxon couldn't risk such an investigation. Govs are too thorough and he knows it. He's nervous enough about Gage's presence. No, Faxon would have no choice but to kill us and destroy the ship, saying we crashed on departure. That way, there wouldn't be an investigation."

Taka thought for a moment. "You may be right," she said, and reached for her comm unit. "I'll have Sanji contact home base, to make sure that someone knows the *Magellan* made it safely to Nearra." Taka pushed the scanner and bag into Tarateal's hands. "And reconfirm our ship's roster."

"Before we left, Sheryl told me she hadn't had any trouble sending messages, but there seemed to be a problem receiving them," said Tarateal. "A couple of messages arrived last night, but since morning, nothing."

Taka nodded. "Funny thing about that. Government detects a magnetic storm in the area, but it's miraculously gone when we arrive. And for some unknown reason, no one can receive messages. He's probably jamming transmissions. Faxon has told so many lies."

"We just need to catch him in the big one." Tarateal took the equipment and shuffled toward the door. "Thanks, Taka. I owe you for this."

"Just take good care of Quinn," she called. "Go easy on him if you can."

ELEVEN

QUINN WALKED out of his body, slipping far and away. At first, he thought he was dreaming when the dark spiral appeared near the center of his dimly lit dreamscape. But then he felt drawn toward it, the pull on his limbs almost painful. Finally, he gave in to the force and tumbled into the spiral. He pitched and reeled until he rolled out onto a translucent patch of ground. Beneath his feet, thick clouds swirled gently against the translucent ground, making it hazy. He walked for a long time over the frosted ribbon until he finally realized that he was in the strange place he'd been before—in the Shikari camp.

Where he'd held Larena in his arms again.

Ahead, mist rose, squall of wind whipping. Critters chattered. Insects clicked. The Nearran moors—he recognized them, now. Blue-black water undulated against the edge of the frosty ground, rainbows reflecting off the murky surface. Smears of blue-black mud swirled across the smooth edge. On the horizon, a rowboat rocked toward him and he waited for it.

He listened, almost hearing the echo of oars slapping against the edge of the boat. Wood creaked. A creature called. The boat nudged the ground with a groan. He reached out for it.

Empty.

That emptiness reverberated through his legs, vibrated into his torso, and squeezed his lungs. He laid his hands against the boat, tilting it toward him. There on the seat lay his holoimage of Larena. He snatched it from the seat and pressed it against his chest.

Feeling a presence behind him, he turned.

The Shikari priest stood motionless. It wore a turquoise and green mask, diagonal stripes broken only by hollow, downturned eyes, and a fierce mouth. It wore a frayed cream robe, the fabric thickly woven.

"You come to the astralscape again. Why?"

Quinn held out the holo. "Please, I've got to find her!"

The priest plucked the holo from his hands and flung it into the moors.

"No!"

He leaped into the murk after it. Mud sucked at his calves and clamped onto his feet. He fought the sticky muck and sifted through the water for the holoimage. When he felt something solid in the mud, he yanked it out.

A hand.

He screamed.

A woman rose from the water, hair plastered blue-black against her pale face, wedding ring encrusted blue-black. Moor grass clung to her face and brown coveralls, blue fuzzy patches of mold clinging to the sleeves and torso. Blue eyes smiled at him. Larena. His heart wrenched. Another ghost.

"Dearest," she cooed. "Is that you?"

"Larena?"

"He knew I followed him there, dearest. He had to silence me somehow." She turned her head, revealing a blackened scorch mark on her shoulder. The black burn marks bled outward across her neck and onto her chin, fanning around her shoulder in a brushed, charred circle. Part of her beautiful auburn hair above where her ear had been was burned away.

He clutched her hand, pressing it against the side of his face. Her skin was as cold as her wedding ring.

"Larena," he moaned. "I was so sure you were alive. I was so sure."

"Listen to me, dearest, he'll tell them that the Shikari's did this to me, but they didn't."

"Of course, not—"

"Listen to me. I don't even know what it was I saw, but he killed me for it anyway. Dearest, he's exploiting the Shikari's. They're forced to harvest some sort of pollen for him and it's terribly dangerous. Many of them die in the harvest while he sits back and watches."

Quinn frowned. "Where is this place?"

Larena's gaze fell to the Shikari priest. "Peetrek knows. He will remember this journey and he will take you there. I can't remember for you because I only live in your memory now. I've left my imprint on Nearra. Trust Peetrek. He can save them. Faxon must be stopped."

"I didn't come here to stop Faxon!" Quinn shouted. "I came here to save you!"

She shook her head. "I was lost some time ago, dearest. Please, Quinn. Faxon must be stopped." She leaned forward and kissed him on the cheek. Then she walked slowly back into the murky water.

"Larena! Don't go...please!" He ran after her.

Peetrek pulled him out of the mud and back onto the polymer.

"You speak only to a vision of Larena's eye soul. There be will others. You must be strong enough to let them go." His grip tightened on Quinn's shoulder. "They help can you understand what's happened here. That's all."

Tears streaked down Quinn's face as he watched the water ripple where Larena had been. "How can I stop Faxon?"

"He not does understand our ways," said Peetrek, his voice hollow behind the mask. "We protect Chiriga. He exploit. He does understand not them, so he destroys—forcing help us to. If they die, we die."

Quinn rubbed his forehead, the images and words swimming through his brain. His stomach ached. "You're talking about things I don't understand, Peetrek."

"The Shikari's endure not much more. Your wife know this, but she alone. Faxon killed her to keep your people knowing from what he has here found."

"What has he found?"

Peetrek shook his head. "Your eye soul wander too far. It not was meant to be here. That thing in your head here you brings—accident only part of it. Your body suffers, Quinn Sayre. Return. In time, grow you will stronger. Return."

He rubbed his temple and finally nodded. Thing in his head? What did Peetrek mean by that?

Quinn's body sank through the frosty ground until he was tumbling into blackness toward his body.

<hr>

HE OPENED HIS EYES, nausea rising in his throat. Roberts stood over him, syringe in hand, blue eyes fearful. Grim-faced, she ran a hand scanner across his bare torso. Behind her stood Taka and Gage.

"Sayre?" said Roberts, exasperated. She held up her hand. "How many fingers?"

"Five," he snapped, and pushed away the scanner. "And I'm fine. What the hell's the scanner for?"

Roberts frowned. "Sanji was worried about you. In case you haven't noticed, you've been acting like a wild man."

He looked away, ignoring her comments. Sickness rose in his throat again and he swallowed hard, forcing it to recede.

"If you don't lay off the amara, you're going to wake up in a body bag, Sayre. I don't think you want to end up there, do you?"

"Amara?" said Gage from the doorway. "Did she say amara?"

"I don't think so, sir," said Taka. "She said tomorrow."

Quinn shook his head. That's all he needed, Gage busting him for possession of amara. Then he remembered the dream. He'd had that same dream again. About the Shikari priest—and Larena. He grabbed Roberts's arm.

"Roberts, I had the strangest dream! I've had them ever since my accident."

"Dream?" She sat down on the bed beside him. "What dream, Sayre?"

He started to reply, but felt Gage's weighty stare from the doorway. Roberts picked up on his apprehension.

"He's all right, Taka. I think I jumped the gun a little when I saw the grey skin. I'll give him a vitasup and he'll be fine."

Taka gave her a wary look and shuffled into the hallway, leading Gage and Sanji away. Quinn found himself alone with Roberts.

"Is that better?" Roberts asked.

He nodded, his face flushing. "It's bad enough that you'll think I'm crazy, but I can't have Taka telling the whole crew I am."

Roberts laid her hand on his arm, her touch comforting. "Tell me about this dream."

He settled back against his pillow. "Twice now, I've seen that Shikari priest in my dreams. He says he can only speak to me in some astral place because I can only be trusted there. And Larena's there, too."

"Sounds like a grief dream, Sayre."

"No! Peetrek says that my accident caused a change in my body—"

"We've already confirmed that." She let the hand scanner rest in her lap.

"Let me finish. Peetrek said my accident allows me to venture beyond the dreamscape when I sleep." He touched a hand to his temple. "And he says there's something here, in my head."

She scanned him again and smiled. "Nothing registers in that head of yours either, not even a brain."

"I'm serious, Roberts."

Roberts rose from the bed and paced around the table. "Maybe you are, Sayre, but you've got to admit, it all sounds pretty crazy."

He rose up on his elbows. "I know that, but—I think he's right. He said imprints of people I knew are drawing me to this astralscape. I've seen Larena at eighteen and Larena here on Nearra."

She shook her head, pausing in front of him, and he saw the worried look flash in her eyes. She did think he was crazy.

"Please," he insisted, taking hold of her arms. Her skin was so soft. He'd forgotten how soft. "Hear me out. Larena told me how Faxon killed her—a laser blast to the head. Then he dumped her body in the swamp."

The realization hit him. Larena was dead.

He began to shake. "Dear God, Roberts. Larena's dead." His voice fell to a whisper. "She's really dead."

From somewhere deep inside, the sobs bubbled up into raw agony. Sorrow heaved in his chest, breath falling away as his rage mixed with anguish. He drew ragged air into his burning lungs and choked.

Beneath his cheek, he felt the steady rise and fall of breath. Roberts. She held him, a hand gently stroking the side of his face.

"It's okay to grieve for her," said Roberts in a soft voice, and brushed the hair out of his face. "We're going to get Faxon for everyone he's killed."

His skin burned at her touch, every nerve, every memory sparking a fever that trembled through him. God, she was beautiful! He wanted her back in his life again.

He pulled away as his aching stomach lurched and he scrambled up from the bed. He lunged into the bathroom as his stomach emptied. He barely reached the head.

"Are you okay, Sayre?" Roberts called.

He retched again. When his stomach finally calmed, he pulled himself out of the floor and moved to the sink. He washed his face and rinsed his mouth. On shaky legs, he went out to face Roberts.

He took a deep breath and sat down beside her on the bed.

"Are you all right?" she asked, her eyes glassy and wide.

He nodded.

"Tell me about this dream of yours."

He cleared his throat. "Peetrek says Faxon is using the Shikari's to harvest some kind of pollen. From a plant critical to their survival on Nearra. He called it—a Chiriga."

The color drained from Roberts' face. She gripped his arms for a moment as she tried to find her voice. "Chiriga? Sayre...remember I slipped something out of that crate by the dock?"

"Barely."

"It was a sparkling blue powder. Putting it through the analyzer revealed that it's pure Visiondust. The source is an extinct species of plant—chirigus casandras."

All he could do was stare at her, knowing the shocked look on her face mirrored his own expression. It hadn't been a dream after all. Peetrek had told him the truth on the astralscape. And when Peetrek said his body was suffering, he was right.

"We've got to go after Faxon," Sayre said finally. "If he's harvesting Visiondust, he's got to be stopped. I'm guessing that Faxon takes a midnight jaunt out on the moors tonight or tomorrow. Care for a late evening boat ride?"

"Are you up for that?" Worry shined in her eyes.

He nodded.

"I'll meet you near the dock with field packs," she said with a smile.

"Don't tell Sanji about this or Gage will find out. I think my two days are up." He paused for a moment. "Look, tell Taka but no one else. Have Taka tell Sanji and the others in the morning—if we're not back. If I know Sheryl, she'll contact the contract bureau as soon as she hears about it."

Roberts reached into her medical kit and retrieved a syringe.

"What is that?" he asked.

"A supplement," she said, and pressed the needle into his arm. "That should help minimize whatever damage the amara's done. Get some good sleep, Sayre. I'll see you later."

He tried to speak, but his eyes were closing. Roberts tricked him, dammit! That shot was a sedative. He slumped against his pillow.

TWELVE

JUST BEFORE MIDNIGHT, Quinn and Roberts slipped out of the *Magellan*, through the tangle of veins that had covered the compound again, and down to the dock. He and Roberts slipped into Faxon's spare boat and lay side by side in the bottom until long past midnight, but Faxon never showed. His private boat was still moored at the end of the dock.

Quinn gazed over at Roberts, whose shoulder was pressed firmly against his arm. In the indigo moonglow, he traced the outline of her lips and the sprinkle of freckles across her small nose. The confidence in her expression was so attractive. Why hadn't he ever seen that side of her before? They had been good for each other back then.

Until he brought up going out to the Rim.

The night whispered and buzzed, but nothing stirred across the water. He glanced at his watch: 1:44 A.M. He'd been so sure that Faxon would go out there tonight. All the crates that stood on the dock yesterday had disappeared from the dock. Faxon left no trace of them either.

Roberts yawned.

"Tired of waiting on Faxon?"

She smiled. "Just this boat."

He returned her smile. He never realized how much he'd missed her over the years until now. He could always talk to her; Larena never wanted to talk about unpleasantness. She never wanted to hear anything but the good. The unpleasantness was too ugly for her, too much clutter. Larena hated clutter. But Roberts—he watched her twist a curly strand of hair around her index finger—she knew how to deal with clutter.

"Sayre, I think I finally understand your fascination with the Rim."

"What?" Did he hear that right?

She nodded, still twisting her hair. "I know, strange stuff coming from me, but I can't stop thinking about the Shikari's. We could learn so much from them—new medicines, mythologies, new ways of looking at things. I feel their wisdom, Sayre. I feel it."

He knew that wisdom well.

"They know so much and we know so little about them. Why isn't Faxon gathering data instead of moving crates? The Shikari's are a First Contact team's dream. He acts as if they're his enemy."

She was right. Faxon did treat them like the enemy. Peetrek had already told him as much. Now, Roberts seemed so much like the woman he first loved on Salice Minor. How could he have let her go? How could he have chosen the edge of space over her? He started to reach out to her, but stopped himself.

What was he doing? His wife was lying dead out here and he was thinking about Tarateal Roberts.

"Roberts, they're not coming," he said, sitting up. "Let's call it a night."

Roberts stretched and sat up as he scanned the camp and the horizon for any sign of Faxon. Nothing. Finally, he stepped out of the boat and waited for Roberts to stiffly climb onto the dock. He walked beside her in the moonlight, longing to take her in his arms. Feeling guilty, he shoved his hands in his pockets as he walked beside her toward the *Magellan.*

She stopped on the path and turned to him. "Is it everything you ever wanted, Sayre?" A touch of sadness brimmed her eyes.

"What do you mean?"

She waved an arm toward the ship. "The trips to the Rim, the alien worlds...Larena Neville?"

He bowed his head. How could he answer that? He loved Larena more than she'd ever loved him. He knew that when she took this assignment—hell, he'd always known it. He just never wanted to believe it. So many times, she'd hurt him and so many times he'd forgiven her. He'd even forgiven her for coming out here.

"I don't know." He sighed. "I thought it was at one time, but now I stand here as empty as this camp." He ran a hand through his hair. "I remember that first year we were married and I ache all over. As always, I expected too much. It all changes so quickly. Now, it's gone."

Roberts reached out and took his hands.

"I wish things had been different."

He slid his hands out of her grasp and enfolded her in his arms. It was time he faced reality. Larena was dead.

"But they aren't," he whispered against her hair that smelled of ripe peaches. "It's time I dealt with that."

He let go of Roberts and moved toward the ship. Those damned vines had already covered it over again, engulfing several buildings in Faxon's camp.

"Remind me to have Sanji and Dale clean off these vines again."

Roberts nodded as he pressed his thumb to the ship's main hatch.

WHEN QUINN REACHED HIS QUARTERS, he pulled out the box of Larena's things. He'd been avoiding this chore. He sat down in the floor and with shaking hands, he lifted the lid. Her datapad lay on top of a jumble of items. His eyes misted. All he could do was take out the datapad and close the box. He couldn't face the rest right now.

He couldn't.

He stumbled up from the floor, datapad in hand, and dropped down on his bunk. He turned it on and scanned through the files until he found her messaging folder. Paging through the entries, he saw several messages he'd sent her, all of them unread.

Unread?

He stared at the dates, realizing that they'd arrived well before Larena had disappeared. His chest tightened. Why hadn't she read his messages?

That's when he saw all the messages from Ian Veider. He gritted his teeth and touched one of the messages. It scrolled across the screen.

*RECEIVED from GSN Satellite by GSN-Server * * *12 <gsn1227.earth.gov>*

    Bounced to Base Station Nearra at 16:38 GAT
    DATE: 20 December 2151 16:42 GAT
    TO: Ian Veider <veider@bsn.gov>
    FROM: Larena Neville Sayre <neville@bsn.gov>
    SUBJECT: Us
    MESSAGE ID <A12389344I2GSNBSA>

IAN,

YOU KNOW I LOVE YOU. Why do you doubt me? I know I said I would do it sooner, but I can't. He's going through some rough times

*right now. As soon as the mission is completed, I swear to you I will
ask him for a divorce.*

*I'LL MEET you in your quarters after meal and we can watch the sun
rise over the moors.*

I LOVE YOU,

LARENA

RAGE AND SHOCK ripped through Quinn. For a moment he
couldn't breathe. Finally, he sucked in a breath.

She was cheating on him!

He remembered the nervous blond man that worked beside
Faxon and his anger burned. No wonder the guy was so nervous.

He read response after response from Larena and Veider, her
telling him that she loved him and that she would ask for a divorce.
Every message cut through him, his anger swelling. He kicked over a
chair and threw a canteen at the wall.

He ripped open the compartment at the foot of his bed and
pulled out a bottle of amara. He'd risked his life to find her and all
along, she wanted a divorce. Damn her. Damn her!

With a yank, he released the pressure cap and pressed the bottle
to his lips. The amara cut him all the way down, ripping at his
stomach, but he kept drinking. How could she cheat on him like this?
How! He glared at the wedding ring on his hand. Finally, he jerked it
off his finger and heaved it against the wall.

Just then, his datapad beeped.

As he moved toward the unit, he felt the amara kick in and soften his fury. He called up his inbox and found an official government transmission awaiting him. He hesitated. There was only one thing they could be sending him this night.

Funny how the magnetic storm had suddenly cleared up with their arrival, he thought with a scowl. His fingers trembled as he opened the message.

*RECEIVED from GSN Satellite by GSN-Server * * *5 <gsn5.earth.gov>*

>*Bounced to PSV Magellan <gsn5.magellan.psv> at 1:58 GAT*
>*DATE: 28 March 2152 2:02 GAT*
>*TO: Quinn Sayre <sayre@gsn5.magellan.psv>*
>*FROM: Aaron T. Carlson <acarlson@earth.gov>*
>*SUBJECT: Official Notification*
>*MESSAGE ID <A12389344412GSNBSA>*

MR. SAYRE, we regret to inform you that, due to overwhelming evidence, your wife, Larena Neville Sayre, has been declared legally dead. Reasonable attempts to locate your wife have failed and no new evidence exists to suggest that she was not killed as the result of hostile alien environment as reported by Commander Derek Faxon. It is our sad duty to close this case and establish a date of death. Death certificate will soon follow.

REGRETTABLY,

AARON T. CARLSON
>*Bureau of Deep Space Affairs*
>*United Countries of Earth*
>*acarlson@earth.gov*

. . .

QUINN TOSSED down another swig of amara that sliced down his throat in a burning wave. Holding his stomach, he collapsed onto his bunk and tried to blot Larena from his memory.

Dammit, why did he come here! Why?

The amara slid down, softer now, and he kept drinking. His senses dulled until her memory no longer tormented him.

He awoke late in the morning, Larena's datapad against his cheek and an empty bottle of amara in his hand. He dropped the bottle on the floor and slowly sat up, the pounding in his head making him sick. He staggered to the bathroom and wet down his stubbled face. Glancing in the mirror, he saw a deathly pale face, red-eyed and shadowed. His stomach churned from last night's drinking. The anger that coursed through him had cooled to numbness. Nausea pressed up into his throat and he gagged. He fell to his knees and hung over the head.

He threw up blood.

After a quick shower, he brushed his teeth. And felt better. He moved unsteadily back to the bunk and flipped on Larena's datapad to search for more information. He still wanted to find out why she died. He couldn't believe she'd been cheating on him all this time. It just hadn't fully registered yet.

For hours, he scanned through files, most of them empty. He found a number of text files that Larena had been forming into an article. She kept referring to a delicate, complex Nearran plant that was slowly dying out. Larena noted that its genetic makeup closely resembled that of a fast-growing, thriving earth vine. She described a splicing of those two genetic makeups, producing a heartier species that would do well on Nearra. He thought about the vines that covered the buildings in the camp that had already shrouded the *Magellan* twice.

Toward the end of the article, he found an embedded document. He tried to open the file and it popped up on the screen. The document accused Faxon of destroying the delicate environmental balance. She indicated that the kudzu hybrid would slow him down. She feared that he'd do something drastic when he realized what she had done.

Quinn shut off the datapad and lay back against his bunk. For the first time in several months, things were clear. She'd interfered with Faxon's plans and he'd killed her for it. Would Faxon do the same thing to him and his crew? After all, they were a long way from the shipping lanes. His stomach clenched as he thought about what could happen to them alone out here. Other than Gage, there were no government personnel to back them up. He and his crew were on their own against Faxon and it was his job to stop the man before he killed anyone else. When Faxon went out into the moors, following those mysterious crates, Quinn would be there to follow him.

Quinn punched his comm button.

"This is Sheryl, Quinn."

"Sheryl, I'd like you to uplink with the nearest government agency and describe our situation."

A heavy sigh hissed through the comm. "Quinn, I'd like nothing better than to send a message, but something has been interfering with outgoing transmissions all day."

Quinn frowned. "What kind of interference?"

"I'm not sure. Whenever I try to transmit a message, it gets bounced, saying a satlink is down."

"Have Sanji try to track down the source of the problem. Send that message as soon as you can. Sayre out."

He moved toward his gear piled in the corner and shifted it toward the door. Then he hit the comm button again. "Roberts, this is Sayre. Want to go on a date?"

"Sayre, you're delirious," Roberts snapped.

"A little moonlight cruise through the moors. We can take in a few sights, spy on a few bad guys, and be home by morning."

"How can I resist an offer like that," she said with a laugh. "When?"

"Get your gear together," he said. "After dark, I'll meet you at the dock."

"See you there," she answered, and the connection cleared.

Quinn grabbed Larena's datapad and his field pack and set them by the door. He'd just grab some sleep first.

THIRTEEN

TARATEAL MET Sayre just after the compound lights had blacked out for the night. She crouched beside him in the boat, a scanner in her hand, his warm, earthy scent burning through her. She'd forgotten how good he smelled. Not in an aftershavy kind of way, just warm and buttery, a touch of wood smoke.

Earlier, Sayre attached a small sensor to the edge of Faxon's boat so they could follow him. She glanced over at Sayre, his gaze trained on the dock. He seemed more rested and alert than he had in days. His face was clean-shaven, but weakness clung to his eyes. Still, she wondered if he'd slammed any amara. Not smelling it on his breath was a good sign.

It seemed like hours since the lights had gone out. Just as she was beginning to think that spying on Faxon was a wasted effort, a door creaked open in the evening stillness. Whispers whistled in the silence, growing more tangible as boots clacked softly against the dock boards.

A boat pitched as someone climbed aboard. Then another. And another.

She counted four people. Faxon's entire team must have slipped back into camp unseen.

The mooring rope thumped against the dock and then there was no sound. She imagined they'd allowed the boat to drift away from the dock. An eternity passed and then she heard the *ka-chunk, ka-chunk* of the motor engaging. It purred off into the distance.

Sayre turned toward her and tapped the hand scanner. She pressed the test button and a red grid flashed on the view screen, a green dot blinking. She nodded at him and he smiled. He seemed to listen for more movement, but only the gentle creak of their boat floating away from the dock trickled into the night. He popped up from the boat and scanned the horizon. She followed.

The dock and compound were deserted. No distant lights gleamed from the *Magellan*. Even they retired early.

"Keep me posted on Faxon's position," said Sayre as he engaged the motor.

Tarateal nodded and swiveled around in one of the chairs.

The boat slid through the dark waters and entered the moors.

The sky was black velvet, with rough white and blue spheres poking through the haziness. Mist rose around them, hanging like veils. The air felt cool, sharp. It heightened her senses.

The low-pitched pule of some animal reverberated from a strip of brush framing the bank to her right.

Something squawked, fluttering out of the foliage. It zipped across the water's onyx surface.

Musty water scent mixed with the smell of grass and algae.

Something jumped out of the water and splashed off to the left.

She tried to shut out the night sounds, concentrating instead on the course that Faxon's boat had taken. But tonight, she was distracted.

"The first causeway to the left will dead-end into wilderness," she directed. "Avoid it. Take the next one."

"Where'd you get that scanner, Roberts?" Sayre asked. "I expected my heart rate and blood pressure to appear in the left-hand corner."

"Kuruk loaned it to me," said Tarateal. "It scans the terrain and maps it in relation to the target that I'm scanning. Kuruk said his father used it to launch missiles."

"There's good news," Sayre mumbled. "Can it show us the way back to the compound?"

"I stored the coordinates displayed for Faxon's boat when it was still docked, so we'll find out."

The night hummed and chirred around them. Skimming across this causeway made Tarateal feel alive tonight. All of her senses felt heightened as she took in the moor's strangeness. Sayre kept quiet. She wondered if he felt the same excitement.

"Were you ever married?" Sayre asked suddenly.

She glanced over at him, a smile on her face. He was so attractive in the mist, the moonlight in his hair. His hazel eyes burned like embers. She longed to touch his face, feel every curve of his chin, sip from his lips. Feel him against her skin like back on Salice Minor.

She shook her head and clenched her teeth. What was she thinking! No, she was so over him. Sayre was ancient history.

"Engaged once," she answered. "To a sweet man stationed on Salice Minor, but like you, he had plans for deep space. I couldn't move that far out into the universe. He's married now, two kids, a parrot, and two crellens. Connor never did get past Lunar Colony though."

Sayre laughed and reached down to set the autopilot. "What is it about deep space that frightens you so much?"

The emptiness, she thought. So huge and heavy that it might suck out her soul. Like being set adrift in an ocean.

She had visions of dying slowly in some slimy back-room tavern on some ore-refining plant out in the Rim. Grim-faced, sex-starved miners drooling over her fever-ridden body as she died of some hideous alien disease.

"Never seeing the world I grew up on again. Breathing recycled air for the rest of my life. Being trapped in some space suit and never feeling again." She sighed. "Dying alone."

She expected him to laugh at her silliness, like he had so many times on Salice Minor, but he didn't. Instead, he hung his head, a hand brushing through that thick sable hair. How she longed to run her hands through his hair again, explore every facet of his body, rediscover his fire. The thing she'd loved most about him.

"I hate the loneliness most," he said. "I used to lie in bed at night, knowing Larena was a million miles away, and feel empty. Now, she's gone forever. She died alone out here, Roberts. Somebody should have been with her—to hold her hand. Something."

Tarateal reached out and took his hand.

He squeezed, drawing her close. "Govs sent me a message earlier, before the interference kicked in again," he said, his voice shaky. "Said she'd been officially declared dead."

"I'm so sorry," she said in a soft voice, and stroked his fingers, noticing that his wedding ring was gone. She hated Larena Neville, but the woman hadn't deserved to die.

He was silent for a long time, looking away. Finally, he spoke. "She was cheating on me," he said softly.

Tarateal stared at him in disbelief. "What? Are you sure?"

He nodded, closing his eyes.

"She hadn't read my messages for weeks before she disappeared. I found love letters to Ian Veider that she'd written, promising him that she'd get divorced." He laughed bitterly and shook his head. "And here I am risking my life to find her body."

"God, Quinn—I didn't know."

"Neither did I until last night," he said, grimacing. "I tried to stay away from the amara, but couldn't. Sanji asked me to—he's a good friend. He doesn't know how much I appreciate him."

"Isn't that...well—justice?" she replied, knowing she was rubbing salt in his wound, but she couldn't help the hurt she still felt.

"Justice?" he snapped.

"The cheater got cheated on," she said with a smirk.

He didn't crack a smile, his face hard now, eyes distant. "Tarateal, I may be a bastard, but I never cheated on you. Ever."

She dropped down in front of him. "Two days after we broke up, you were with Larena. Two days, Sayre!"

"But not a moment before. I told her I was in a relationship, but she still chased after me that entire semester, Roberts. And I never texted or tagged Larena before that either. I didn't cheat on you, Tarateal. I swear it."

Something broke inside her, flushing away the hard, sharp edges of the anger and resentment that she'd carried all these years. She'd been so sure he'd cheated on her. So sure!

He gazed into her eyes now, hazel eyes a mixture of hurt and indignation. A shiver snaked down her spine, warmth spreading through her stomach. That look had melted her years ago. She saw it in the wounded look in his eyes. Felt it in his unblinking stare.

It was the truth.

"It's okay—I believe you," she said, laying her hand on his shoulder, squeezing.

He relaxed, the corners of his mouth quirking into a smile. "You've always gotten me through the bad stuff, Tarateal. This time's no different. Thank you."

Moonlight pooled in his watery eyes. His smile widened, trying to cover up his emotions again. His vulnerability.

"Y'know, I've been so wrong about you," he said. "Thought you'd be terrified to set foot outside the ship, and here you are in a boat chasing ghosts through uncharted, alien moors. I'm impressed. You're holding up better than I am."

Something about his strong jaw, those sad hazel eyes, and that boyish smile trying to cover his pain drew her toward him.

She couldn't help herself. She forgot about Larena and Salice Minor as her lips pressed against his. He kissed back with a passion that startled her. His hands slid around her waist, across her body, over her breasts, the intensity and urgency sharp.

Aching.

He caressed her neck with his kisses, his hot breath growing heavy, lips velvet against her bare skin. At last, she raked her fingers through his dark waves of hair and felt his hands slide underneath her shirt, cupping her breasts. She wanted to lose herself in his fire. She unzipped his flight suit and slipped her hands inside, across his smooth chest.

"I think I'm falling for you again, Tarateal," he whispered, his voice husky.

Her body churned with need. To touch him, to feel his breath against her skin, his body against hers. Underneath all her hurt and anger, she'd never stopped loving him.

Her clothes fell to the floor of the boat beside his flight suit as his arms enfolded her against him, drawing her down. Her body shuddered, his hands explored every curve, traveling over her stomach, stroking her thighs, delving deeper. She trembled at his touch, her own hands sliding across his chest and thighs, holding him closer.

He sipped her skin and breasts as he rolled on top of her. Their hips met, the rocking of his body against hers stoking the desire she felt for him. She moved with him as the fire built wild and furious between them.

The moors burned, the alien world and ghosts from their past falling away, surging and ebbing as one, desire reaching flashpoint. His body shuddered against hers and she gasped, overwhelmed. At last, he collapsed against her, his chest heaving, and nuzzled against her neck, his short black hair drenched.

She wrapped her arms around him and held him tightly against her, pressing her face against his shoulder.

For a long time, they lay together, entwined and content. She didn't care if they ever found Faxon's boat. Because now, just for a little while, she was in his arms again and everything was okay.

Finally, he sat up and reached for his clothes. He leaned over and kissed her as she dressed. Reluctantly, he returned to the wheel. She moved toward him and slid her arms around his waist, laying her head against his shoulders.

"I've missed you, Quinn," she whispered in his ear, and nibbled on his earlobe.

"And I nearly missed you," he answered, his words shuddering down her spine.

———

THE BOAT CRAWLED along the causeways, underneath low-hanging branches that dragged thorny vines and snapping night creatures. The craft slid silently through tall grasses and haunted woods. He sat beside her, an arm around her waist, and she held his hand, feeling a familiar warmth from so long ago. Still, the green light of her scanner winked in the darkness, showing the way to Faxon's boat.

Wherever that was in this tangle of water and darkness.

As the blackness turned steely grey, they caught up to Faxon's boat. The mooring line had been attached to a tree, no dock, no buildings in sight. Sayre cut the motor and steered the boat into a clump of bushes. Tarateal tied off the line at the base of the thorny foliage.

"Where do you think we are?" Tarateal asked in a half-whisper, and crouched as she slid the scanner into her field jacket.

Sayre shrugged. "Hard to say. If Faxon's running drugs, then this is either his shipping or processing station."

She tugged on his sleeve and winked. "Let's find out."

Once they stepped onto the grasslands, she found a well-traveled path winding through the swampy soil. The muddy ground, smelling of mildew, sucked at her feet as she hurried down the path. The land, dotted with massive trees, sloped into a hillside and she climbed it, not waiting for Sayre. As she reached the top, she ducked back again. Her mouth twisted into a painful grimace. Sayre frowned.

"What is it?" he asked, a hand on her arm.

"Look," she whispered, and rose to look again.

He peered over the top of the hillside. Below, several wire pens sprawled across the grasslands. Four and five Shikari's lay curled up in each of those pens.

"What the hell's Faxon doing?"

Beyond the pens was a lean-to where stiff grey bags stacked to the ceiling. She knew what was in those bags. Visiondust.

"He's making these poor people harvest Visiondust, Sayre. And he's treating them like animals."

The Shikari's' bronze skin had turned ashen. She recognized that hue, remembering when she saw it on Sayre. Across the compound, Faxon's team led a detail of Shikari's into the camp. They staggered down the dirt road toward their pens, limbs drooping, faces haggard. One of the First Contact team members, the blond one called Veider, led them toward a vacant pen, laser rifle slung across his shoulder. Another of the team members held open the door.

"Where's the rest?" the dark-haired woman demanded.

"Kyle's bringing them back soon. They're almost finished."

"Didn't he take them toward the water, looking for some secret worship spot?"

The man pointed toward Tarateal and Sayre. "Yeah, over that way, I think. Faxon doesn't know for sure where it is. He thinks the savages are leading him on a wild goose chase."

The woman laughed. "That won't last for long, Ian. Faxon'll put a stop to that nonsense right away."

"Hey, what about those two?" The woman pointed to the hillside, startling Tarateal and Sayre.

"They've escaped!" Veider shouted, and raised his rifle.

Laser fire scoured the hillside as Tarateal ran, Sayre beside her, the First Contact team shouting.

Grass snapped against her calves. Mud splattered. Creatures screeched.

She dodged left.

A laser blast burned the grass.

She wheeled right, throwing herself to the ground as laser fire ripped across the moors.

Water filled her boots. Lungs burned. Side ached.

Sayre was a step or two in front now. He veered right, toward a line of brush.

She followed.

Light exploded in front of her as pain arced in ribbons that sliced through her chest and into her groin. She shrieked, agony blazing into her arms and stomach.

She stumbled, losing control.

"Roberts!" Frantic, Sayre fell down beside her.

The scent of burned fabric made her sick. Smoke rose from her uniform. She struggled up from the muddy ground, but her legs collapsed.

Sayre slid his arms beneath her body and carried her into the waterlogged moors.

Before long, she felt the roughness of the boat at her back. The grey sky had lightened to a soft putty color. This world's pale sun would rise soon.

His desperate face hovered over her, medical supplies littering the bottom of the boat.

"It's bad, Roberts," he said, glassy-eyed. He loosened her shirt.

From the pain, she realized quickly that the blast had struck her in the back. Every breath was agony. With every beat of her heart came a surge of pain. She sucked in a breath of air and gasped.

"Damn," she said, her voice weak. Tears welled in her eyes. "I went through—a lot to get here—and now it's gone. I threw it all away."

"Don't you dare quit on me, Roberts!" he cried, taking hold of her hand. With his other hand, he caressed her cheek, smoothing hair from her face. "Don't you see? You had it in you all the time." His voice cracked. "It just took a little longer to bring it out, that's all."

She gripped his hand. "Don't leave me now, Sayre. Don't let me die alone."

"You stay with me!" he shouted. "You're not dying on me now."

Tears slipped down his face. "I'm not going anywhere and neither are you, you hear me? Roberts!"

Her eyelids drooped and she fought to stay conscious. Her chest hurt so much.

"Stay with me, Roberts," he said through gritted teeth. "I'll stay if you do. Who's going to keep me from being arrested as a privateer? Or from getting my fool head shot off? Talk to me, Roberts."

"I wish we could go back," she said, struggling to form words. "And change everything." She groaned.

"I miss those nights at the Silver Orca, drinking black cherry ale and laughing ourselves silly. God, I miss us, Tarateal."

She squeezed his hand. The Silver Orca. He hadn't forgotten after all these years. Even time hadn't taken that away. He slid his arms around her and pulled her into his lap, cradling her against him, the boat on autonav back to the dock. His closeness felt reassuring. He held her so tightly. She was losing herself in his touch. But he was starting to feel so far away. She held on, but her hands were too weak.

Feeling his steady breathing and seeing his tears made her realize, as the air began to sparkle, that Quinn Sayre still loved her.

THE BREATH LEFT her body as Quinn lifted her out of the boat. He felt her heart stop beating when his feet touched the compound pathway. Shouting for Taka, he burst into the *Magellan*'s infirmary and laid Roberts' charred body onto the table.

"Taka!" he shouted again. "Ta-ka!"

Half-dressed and bleary-eyed, Taka staggered into the infirmary. She let out a cry when she saw Roberts' lifeless body, Quinn covered in her blood. His hands shook as he pointed to the laser wound.

He watched helplessly as Taka tried to revive her.

With every compression against Tarateal's chest, Quinn felt his heart sink into his feet. In moments, Dale Park burst into the infirmary and went to work beside Taka.

"No response," Park replied, his tone clinical. "Still in fibrillation."

"Induce adrenaline. Defib to 220." Taka pressed two silver discs against Tarateal's chest. "Clear!"

Over and over, he watched dead limbs shudder and go limp. Every jolt tore through him. She looked like a rag doll. His stomach burned, the fire making him sick.

"Come on, Taka!" he shouted, gripping her arm. "Don't give up on her now. Please!"

"Quinn, there's no response—"

"Don't quit now," he said in a half-whisper.

She nodded and reached over to recharge the defibrillator. "Charging. Upping to 260." She took hold of the discs and pressed them to Tarateal's chest. "Clear."

Again, Tarateal's body shuddered against the charge.

"I've got a pulse!" Park shouted.

Quinn's body went slack, the relief overwhelming. "Thank you," he choked out.

Taka laid a hand on his shoulder. "Leave us now, Quinn. There's a lot of work to be done. We have to close the wound and treat the burns. I'm going to keep her sedated for the day, let her build up some strength. The best thing you can do for her is to get some sleep."

Feeling drained and sick, he sank into a chair. He'd almost lost her again. He couldn't look at her unconscious body on that table. Only a few short hours ago, he'd held her in his arms and made love to her. It was his fault she'd been shot. Why hadn't he kept a better watch? He covered his eyes, not wanting Taka to see his pain. He gripped the arm of the chair. He wouldn't risk Tarateal's life a second time. He rose from the chair and laid his hand against Tarateal's cheek.

"Sleep well, kiddo," he whispered in her ear, and headed out of the infirmary.

When her condition was stable, he'd head out into the moors alone and finish this thing with Faxon. Once and for all. Faxon had taken a lot from him. It was time he returned the favor.

FOURTEEN

ICY BLOOMS OF LIGHT. Hanging. Spiraled away into silence. Like a feather's touch, Tarateal's consciousness blossomed. Thoughts. Working through punctures of light. Became clear.

She remembered.

Bits of childhood. Fragments of adulthood. Twinges of something in between. She felt submerged. In darkness. Cold pierces of light ached. She wanted to push away the lights, to coil tightly inside herself. Block them out—couldn't. Sensations. Harsh.

Raw skin. Fiery eyes. Dry mouth. Aching muscles.

She squeezed her eyelids together, fighting for memories. Anything. Nothing touched her but icy air. She shivered, at last feeling the shape of her hands, her feet. She felt the cold on the tip of her nose, the weariness in exerted muscles, the beating of her heart. Her chest rose. She laid her hand against bare skin. It rose again. Fell.

Then she realized it. She wasn't dead. Pain throbbed through her chest, but she was happy to feel the pain. She was still alive!

"Sayre?" she muttered in a thin voice, trying to sit up. "Sayre?"

A dull ache rose in her chest. She winced, rubbing at the bandage across her torso. Her skin felt like it was stretched too thin. It burned. Struggling, she lowered herself back against the bed. The room was familiar at last. It was the infirmary.

"Tarateal!"

Taka rushed over to the bed, smiling at her. She took Tarateal's pulse and scanned her vital signs.

"I expected to wake up dead," said Tarateal with a weak but wry smile. "What happened?"

"Quinn brought you in half-dead, but Dale and I were able to resuscitate you." She paused to study her readings. "Everything looks fine." Taka moved to the IV drip and recorded the fluid intake. "I've never seen Quinn so scared in my whole life."

Tarateal smiled, remembering Sayre's touch against her skin, his lips sipping her neck.

Taka stared at her for a moment. "Just what happened between you two last night?"

"Sorry, that's classified information, Yawakani," she said with a wink.

"Fair enough," Taka answered. She moved to the cabinet and retrieved a bag of antibiotics. Removing the empty bag, she hung the antibiotics and started the drip.

"So how long before I'm out of this sickbed?" Tarateal asked.

Taka shook her head. "You'll be here for quite some time, I'm afraid. Your moors traveling days are over, Tarateal."

"No," Tarateal cried, grabbing Taka's arm. "You don't understand. He'll go out there alone now—and get himself killed. It took me years and a trip to the edge of the world to find him again. I'll be damned if I lose him to some drug-runners."

"I know you're scared, Tarateal, but don't worry about Quinn. He isn't a loose cannon. He won't do anything crazy like going out there alone. With Gage watching his every step, he'll be careful." Taka gently pressed Tarateal's hands against the mattress. "Besides, he's got me and Sanji nagging him. He'll be okay."

She hoped so. She couldn't lose him a second time.

"Where is he?" she asked.

"I'll call him." Taka leaned over to the comm unit at her elbow and called Sayre's quarters. Tarateal barely heard Sanji's voice through the link, saying Sayre was out at the docks. "Tell Quinn that Tarateal is awake and asking for him."

"I'll go tell him, Taka. I'm sure he will come right down when he finds out. He made me promise to come get him the moment she regained consciousness."

"Will do, Sanji. Yawakani out."

Taka injected something into Tarateal's IV line, and a warm grogginess settled over her like a thick blanket.

"Your timing reeks," Tarateal muttered, her tongue feeling thick.

"Sorry, it was time for your pain medication," she said, and patted Tarateal's arm. "That wound needs to heal and you need your rest."

As she tossed the syringe into the waste disposal, Sayre hurried into the infirmary, handsome face lined with stubble, bright hazel eyes burning. His dark hair lay in tousled waves against his forehead, cropped short over his ears. Wavy hair hung just at his collar. The worry was etched deep into his face, his eyes rimmed red.

He looked exhausted. He'd no doubt been up all night.

"Tarateal!" Sayre cried, and took hold of her hand. He leaned over her, kissing her gently on the lips. He was all smiles as he sat down on the edge of the bed, still holding her hand, and brushed the hair off her forehead. "I thought I'd lost you."

"Not if you tried," she said, reaching out and cupping his stubbled chin. She was too weak though and her hand fell away.

He sighed. "I'm so sorry I did this to you. I didn't use very good judgment out there. I didn't mean for you to get hurt like this."

"It's okay. Was my choice." It was getting harder to form words. And her eyelids felt so heavy.

"As captain of this mission, your safety was my responsibility."

"Sayre, no—not your fault." Her eyes were closing.

He sighed and rubbed her shoulder, but she saw the guilt shining in his eyes. Nothing she said would convince him it hadn't been his fault. She tried to speak, but the words wouldn't come. The painkiller enveloped her like a warm blanket and she fell asleep.

FIFTEEN

QUINN NURSED his pale ale and stared at the dark portal above Sanji's head. Nearra's moons hadn't risen yet. When he'd signed Roberts aboard, he thought a few bottles of ale would be a good peace offering. Now, she was lying half-dead in the infirmary.

And it was his fault.

Sanji sipped fruit juice and waited. He seemed uneasy and Quinn quickly realized that he hadn't stopped in for a social call.

"What's on your mind, Sanji?" he asked finally, and set down his glass. "Just say it, don't stew over it."

"I have been unable to find the downed link. Our communications are still being blocked. I am trying other ways to get messages out."

"Good, keep at it," said Quinn. "I know you'll find a way." He was quiet for a moment and then gazed at Sanji. "But that's not what's got you so riled. Talk to me, Sanji."

"Our rediscovery mission is being accomplished as planned. We have gathered a lot of data on the First Contact team, but—" Sanji sighed. "At some point, we must interact with all species reported by Faxon's team."

"No," Quinn snapped, and rose unsteadily from the chair, bottle in hand. He wandered over to his desk. "Totally out of the question."

Sanji set down his glass. Quinn saw that Sanji was fighting not to show his exasperation. "Sheryl wants to take Taka and Dale out into the moors tomorrow."

"It's too dangerous, Sanji." He stared at the shriveled cactus on his desk, the green darkening to mud brown at the top of the cactus. The rough landing hadn't helped any either. After repotting it and giving it a little emergency care, the cactus was beyond saving. Like everything else in his life. He laid a hand against the pot. Despite Larena's betrayal, he just didn't have the heart to throw it out.

"Quinn, we need that data."

He whirled around. "Don't you get it? I don't care about the damned data! Roberts almost died out there, Sanji! Look how that's nearly crippled our efforts. Who knows when she'll be on her feet again?" He shook his head, guilt rising in his throat. He'd been so reckless out there and now Tarateal was paying for it. "I can't risk any more people here. It—" he sighed. "It's just not worth it anymore."

"But if we go well-armed and in larger groups, then we will be fine. And with more people, we can do our analyses more quickly."

"No, Sanji!"

His voice sounded harsher than he'd intended. He closed his eyes for a moment and rubbed them with thumb and forefinger, trying to calm himself. "Look—it isn't just the expertise. You're...one of the best friends I've ever had. Don't you get it? You could die out there."

Sanji rose from his chair and stepped in front of Quinn. He looked shaken. "Five years ago, when I got out of hospital, no military vessel would accept my commission. I had to return home to Jammu and my father's farm. I thought my life was over. The whole time, it never occurred to me to fight back. I didn't even try."

"I know that was hard, Sanj—"

"Let me finish!"

Surprised by his tone, Quinn simply nodded for him to continue.

"I lost my certification when I went home, but you told me not to worry about that. You would help me get it back again. I never thought it possible until the day you comm'ed from port with a job offer."

Quinn smiled and set down his ale. "I even maneuvered us into some regular government contracts, so we'd all get a few extra government benefits, too."

"I remember," Sanji continued, "but it's always been left up to you, Quinn. For years, you've taken care of all of us. Now, it is our turn to repay you."

"But it's too dangerous right now. You'll have to give me more time. To find out about Larena, I mean."

Sanji sighed again. "You will never understand debt, my friend. It has a way of catching up to you unless you pay it. All debts aside, you must realize that the data on the Shikari's has to be gathered so we can leave this place. You know that only complete mission data properly submitted will mark this mission finished. Without it, we won't get paid."

Quinn slapped a hand against the desk. "Damn, I forgot about collecting data on the Shikari's." He drummed his fingers on the desk for a few moments then picked up his glass and drank deeply. "All right, all right, I'll let you know when it's safe. Until then, no one goes out into the moors without my permission. No one." He wanted to tell his friend about what Faxon had done—and Larena—but decided against it. For now, Sanji didn't need to know all that.

"It will be done, Quinn," said Sanji. "I only hope that you will have the good judgment to follow your own rules. It is not the mission data that I worry over either."

Quinn reached into his desk drawer and retrieved a bottle of pills. For his stomach. He tossed a couple down with a swig of ale. Then he slid a bottle of amara from a compartment in his desk. He set it on the desktop and dropped into his desk chair.

"No!" Sanji shouted, and moved toward the desk. "I will not let you keep doing this to yourself." He grabbed hold of the bottle, but Quinn clutched the base.

"Let go, Sanji," Quinn growled.

"I swear to you, Quinn, I will report this to Gage."

"No need."

Quinn jerked his gaze to the doorway.

Gage stood in the threshold, delight in his eyes. He motioned to the open door. "I started to knock, but the door was ajar." He stepped toward the desk and his gaze fell to the bottle of amara Quinn and Sanji held. "No amount of amara is going to erase the faces of the Augustine crew, Sayre. It won't wipe out your guilt either." He snatched the bottle from Quinn's hands. "I'm placing you under arrest for the possession of an illegal substance. That's enough to get you into interrogation when we return."

Quinn dropped his head into his hands. He was so tired of fighting the whole world.

"Care to confess now or wait for the interrogators back on Earth?"

"I had nothing to do with destroying the Augustine! How many times do I have to say it?"

Gage grabbed him by the collar and jerked him out of the chair. Gage's eyes burned like hot ash. "You killed my son! He was barely twenty-one years old."

Quinn tried to get to his feet, but Gage's grip was fierce.

Rage narrowed Quinn's eyes. How dare Gage accuse him of killing Matt? Quinn grabbed Gage's arms and broke his hold.

"Matt was like a brother to me!"

He winced, remembering the young man's screams that night and how he'd tried to pull the instrument panel off Matt's legs. He wanted to die himself that night and erase the horrible memories of that attack. After five years, he still carried them with him like a lodestone.

"Liar!"

"No!" He caught Gage's stare and held it. "You were in the life-pod. You weren't there! I was with Matt when he died."

"Stop lying, Sayre!" Gage shook Quinn. "You've been lying for five years. Tell the truth!"

"All right!" He shoved Gage away and scrambled to his feet. He turned toward the wall and held his burning stomach. "I'll tell you the truth. I'll tell you every last miserable detail that happened that night." He faced Gage and pointed a finger at him. "But I want you to listen and keep your mouth shut until I'm finished."

The anger left Gage's face. He set the amara bottle on the table. "Talk, Sayre. I've waited so long to hear your confession."

"You assigned me to the engine room that night with Matt. When we knocked off our shifts, we were going to play poker with Duffy and Harker. An hour before our shift was up, Taka called me on the comm, pleading with me to help her." His gaze fell to Sanji. "Sanji was sick, she'd said. Said he hadn't gone through detox because he'd gone someplace he shouldn't and gotten sick. He had raging Arcturian Fever and needed to be stabilized."

Gage opened his mouth to protest, but Quinn pointed a finger at him. "You promised me my full say, sir."

Grudgingly, Gage didn't utter a word, but he glared at Quinn.

"Matt said he'd cover for me in the engine room, so I hurried down to the comm room. Sanji was lying on the floor convulsing and Taka was kneeling beside him. I held him still while she sedated him. Then I changed the duty roster, adding my name and deleting Sanji's. I logged Sanji out and logged myself into the console and then carried Sanji down to the infirmary. Thirty minutes later, we were under attack." Quinn sucked in a breath and began to pace. "Then Matt sent an urgent message to the infirmary, begging for my help. I went to help him."

"No," Gage muttered.

"Yes!" Quinn shot back. "I left Sanji with Taka and went to the engine room. It was on fire. The others were dead. I put out the fires and when I got to Matt, he was pinned under an instrument panel." Quinn's voice choked. "I tried for twenty minutes to free him, but those bastard privateers kept blasting the engine room. Finally, I managed to free his torso, but not his legs."

Quinn slammed his hand against the wall. "Why couldn't I free his legs?"

He bit his lip against the anguish, but he couldn't stop the tears from running down his face. He quickly wiped them away.

"Blood started trickling out Matt's ears and mouth—that's when we both knew he wasn't going to make it." His voice fell away to almost a whisper. "But I couldn't leave him like that. I sat there in the crumbling engine room and held his hand until he died. God, I miss Matt."

Defeated, Quinn dropped down at the table and pressed his face into his hands to hide the tears still welling in his eyes. He grabbed hold of the amara bottle. "After that, Taka was shrieking my name in the hallway," he mumbled in a gravelly voice. "I kicked into autopilot and helped her get Sanji to the life-pod."

Sanji reached out and squeezed Quinn's shoulder. "Forgive my stupidity, Quinn. I caused you so much grief."

"Forget it, Sanj," he mumbled, waving him off. "That was five years ago. They got their whipping boy and I played the part for them. Let it go."

"I cannot let it go! You took the blame for me. I abandoned my post, not you—me!" He turned to Gage. "There is your confession, sir. For the last time, Quinn did not call the privateers and he did not kill your son."

Gage hesitated and then moved toward the table, tears streaking down his face. Sanji stepped back as Gage stood behind Quinn. At last, Gage laid a hand on Quinn's shoulder. Quinn closed his eyes.

"The ship's disaster log recorded someone trying to save Matt, but the disc was badly damaged. The sound was too garbled to recreate and the video was grainy and burned, but someone sat with Matt while he died. That information was held back and never released to the public. Why didn't you tell the tribunal, Sayre?"

Quinn turned to face Gage. "I tried, sir, several times, but you would never let me finish a sentence."

The silence in the room was palpable. Finally, Gage spoke.

"It's not proof of your innocence," said Gage, taking the amara bottle, "but it's enough for me to take you seriously."

"Am I still under arrest?" Sayre asked.

Gage nodded. "Until I find out exactly what happened...you're confined to quarters." He moved toward the door.

"Wait!"

Gage halted in the threshold.

"Why would you come all this way to the Rim if you were just investigating me and the Augustine disaster? Tell me why you're here."

Gage's shoulders slumped. "Because Derek Faxon may be involved in privateering—and drug-running activities. As far back as five years ago. Data from the Augustine's computers was stolen that night—before its destruction."

Quinn frowned. "What kind of data?"

"Data from the Rim. My ship had returned from the Rim shortly before you and the other recruits came aboard."

Stunned, Quinn could only stare at him. The man slipped into the hallway without another word.

"Are you all right?" Sanji asked.

Nodding, Quinn rose shakily from the chair and poured himself some coffee. "I'm fine. For the first time in five years, I think he heard me."

"I hope so, Quinn," said Sanji. He moved toward the doorway. "I hope so."

FOR A LONG TIME, Quinn lay on his bunk and stared at the ceiling. The whole thing was crumbling around him and he couldn't stop it. While Yawakani and Park studied the First Contact team's impact on Nearra, Hannaford and Shahir studied the compound and the team's records. Kuruk occupied his time with ship's repairs and testing the plasma engines. But now, Quinn was confined to quarters.

His crew had silently fallen into the rediscovery tasks without any direction from him. They knew what to do. For that, he was grateful. They'd done just as he had requested; they'd left him the time alone he needed to search for Larena, knowing Roberts would be there if he got into trouble.

Now, Roberts wasn't able to help him. Even worse, it was his fault she'd been shot. She wouldn't be there to help him anymore. He had to be the one to deal with Faxon and the Shikari's. If he told Sanji, the man would insist on coming with him, and Quinn refused to endanger his best friend. He wouldn't risk Sanji's life—or anyone else's—out here. Not after what happened to Roberts. No, he'd go after Faxon alone. He just had to get past Gage without being seen.

He glanced down at the box beside his bed. Larena's belongings. Something about opening that box again made him feel queasy. Until now, he'd avoided it, but he knew that eventually he'd have to open it. Even though she didn't love him anymore, the loss still hurt. The box flaps rasped open.

Taking a deep breath, he looked inside.

A text reader with a stack of modules, holos of their wedding and the day he christened the *Magellan*. A Sancian beach globe filled with rose-colored water and mint green sand. He picked it up and shook it, watching the colors blend and separate, Larena's voice singing in his memory. There were several discs of e-notes from him. Along with her messages wanting a divorce. He cringed.

At the bottom of the box was Larena's burgundy e-planner. He slid it out of the box and switched it on. At first, he scanned the whole thing, but then he settled back on his bunk and viewed the last six months' worth of entries.

Many of the entries were blank. Faxon had no doubt erased most of them. Still, his eyes crossed at the volumes of intact data scrolling past. Information on Shikari genetics and physiology, botanical and anthropological terminology hurting his head. In several places, she'd hand-drawn sketches into her notes. He pressed on the highlighted keywords and studied what was displayed.

Toward the end of Larena's final entry, he saw the words *may the road* flashing on the touch screen. He frowned and smashed his thumb against it, hoping it might provide a map. A question box appeared underneath the highlighted words, *May the road?*

A password! His heart hammered against his chest.

Quinn spoke softly into the microphone, "Rise up to meet you."

Another question box appeared, *may the wind?*

"Be always at your back," he answered.

Again, another question box appeared, *may the sun?*

"Shine warm upon your face."

The screen went blank and a one-page entry scrolled onto the screen as Larena's voice filtered out from the speaker.

"Quinn, I knew you would decipher those passwords. Faxon knows that I know his secret. I found the slave labor camp Faxon has hidden in the moors. He has taken a number of Shikari's hostage to farm Chiriga pollen. Shikari's and Chirigas are both dying, and soon the whole planet will die. He doesn't understand the balance here. Gases excreted from the Chirigas bond with the lethal moor gases and render them harmless. Without the Chirigas, the air will become poisonous. I've got to try one more time to stop this. Beware of overharvested areas. They are pockets of poison now. The Shikari's refuse to tell Faxon about the Chiriga breeding grounds. They are sacred and if the Chirigas die, this planet will turn lethal. If I die before Faxon is stopped, promise me you will not let Faxon succeed. Visiondust will sell high on the market, but its sale will kill several species. And a planet."

He cringed, her voice a razor. For six months, he'd longed to hear her voice, but not like this, not through this thing. Knowing she'd wanted a divorce.

"Whatever you do, don't reveal the location of the Chiriga breeding grounds. If you can, take footage of the slave camp and the breeding grounds and send it to Earth's Deep Space Exploration Bureau. That and the mention of Visiondust will be enough to shut Faxon down. Hurry, Quinn. I don't know if it's already too late.

Faxon's first shipment has not yet gone out. He is expecting a privateer ship to arrive soon, one to smuggle out the Visiondust. Peetrek will help you. Only in Haven will he speak frankly with you. He will help you defeat Faxon. Stop Faxon, Quinn. Stop him."

A document popped up on the screen, describing this place called Haven. His first instinct was to bolt out into the moors to find these places, but he willed himself to read the document. It was important or Larena wouldn't have included it.

In Larena's words, Haven was the Shikari place of gathering. A place where the dead began their journey to the afterlife after leaving their shadow soul behind.

For a dying Shikari, the last rites were a cleansing ritual, Larena had explained. It purged the shadow soul from the body, allowing the eye soul to journey to the afterlife. For the living, Haven was a place for the eye soul to wander and see the world through different eyes.

According to the document, Shikari priests had strange powers and could invoke powerful curses and blessings through Haven. Such as *Ekan'da*, or blind death. *Ekan'da* blinded the eye soul of a dying man, allowing his shadow soul to consume him.

Quinn didn't buy into this mythology crap, but this curse business made him uncomfortable. He shut off the e-planner. He had work to do.

He bolted up from his bunk. Moving to his flight chest, he repacked his field pack. From his desk, he retrieved a digital camera and slid it into his pack. His stomach pills sat on top of the desk. He threw those into the pack along with a canteen. He set the pack beside the door and entered the hallway. The infirmary was down the hall on his right.

Inside, Taka was studying some of the mission findings. Roberts lay in the corner bed, steady click of the monitor showing her vital signs. All the IVs had been removed.

"How's Roberts?" he asked in a quiet voice.

"Quinn, you're supposed to be in your quarters," Taka cried, her voice low.

"I came to check on Roberts," he replied, and moved over to the bed.

She was asleep.

He sat down beside her and brushed a wisp of wheaten hair off her bruised forehead.

"She's doing fine, Quinn. All her vitals are good and stable. In a few minutes, Sanji and I will be moving her to her own bunk. She'll be more comfortable there."

"Glad to hear she's on the mend," he said to Taka, and then turned his gaze back to Tarateal. "Hang in there, kiddo," he said, stroking her hair. "I'll have you out of this nightmare in no time. When this is all over, you and I need to have a talk because I'm not letting you walk out of my life again." He leaned down and kissed her on the lips. With a sigh, he rose from the bed and turned back to Taka.

"Take good care of her, okay? If you need me, I'll be under arrest in my quarters." He cast a wry smile at her and then hurried out of the infirmary. He ducked back into his quarters and snatched the e-planner from his bunk. Quickly, he tucked it into his jacket pocket and pulled on the blue jacket. Then he shouldered his field pack and waited, making sure no one would come down to check on him. Only when he was certain it was safe did he slip out of his quarters again.

The hallway was empty. None of the crew—including Gage— saw him access the airlock.

He scrambled across the runway, down the dark compound pathway, and onto the creaking dock. The air was crisp. A chilly breeze brushed across his face as he creaked down the dock boards and climbed into one of the boats. He glanced behind him, making sure no one had come after him. The camp looked deserted. It didn't take long to start the craft and head out into the fog-laden moors.

Using Larena's e-planner, he accessed her maps. A winding course ambled through the moors toward Faxon's slave camp. Along the route, only one other point was marked: Haven. He remembered Larena's message about Peetrek speaking at Haven. He would stop here before he went back to the slave camp and recorded evidence.

AFTER WINDING through dark channels and beneath forbidding trees, Quinn's boat edged toward a hazy inlet. Broken stone columns rose from the tall blue grass of a small island that emerged from the mist.

He eased the boat toward the island, the boat's soft gold lights ecrie in the fog. A moss-covered structure nestled in the line of trees ahead. After shutting down the motor, he climbed out of the boat and tied it to one of the ruined columns. He sank to his ankles in blue-black mud as he trudged forward with a blue glow stick in hand.

The structure looked ominous and faintly reminded him of temple ruins he'd seen as holos. The grainy stone was pocked and blackened, blue moss clinging to the toppled pieces strewn across the mud. The pathway looked like it had once been a walkway leading into a temple or oracle. He imagined torches and columns framing a cobbled walkway into a dimly lit temple.

When he reached the structure, he gazed inside, glow stick held out in front of him. A narrow entryway led into smoky darkness. The floor was a solid slab of smooth rock, and his steps echoed as he moved deeper into the structure, muddy footprints marking his path.

Abruptly, the entryway led him into a low-ceilinged chamber, no windows, and no door. Quinn fished in his pack for a small lantern. He turned it on and set it on the floor. The lantern cast a warm glow through the room, softened by the blue glow stick.

There on the wall, he saw a large, shiny black square. At first, he'd thought it was a door, but it was unlike anything he'd ever seen before. It sparkled and rippled as if filled with water. It reminded him of the moors. He peered more closely at the glistening square. Reaching out, he ran his fingers across the slick, glasslike surface. Cool to the touch, it parted like water at his fingertips. Feeling a gentle tug, he stepped forward through the square and into darkness.

TRANSLUCENCE WAVERED in sheets around him, gleaming. Indigo blackness hung heavy behind the translucence, peppered with stars. In the distance gleaming blue and gold lines pulsated like live neon in the blackness. At his feet, a slate-like blackness, barely visible, etched its way across the nothingness. He felt energy vibrating around him until his skin began to tingle. Larena had called this Haven...a place where the eye soul wandered.

Whatever that meant.

He felt drawn toward the buzzing, shifting geometric lines ahead, but when he saw the vestibule of stars in front of him, he balked. To reach those lines, he'd have to pass through here. And for some reason, that frightened him.

"The astralscape calls to you again, Quinn Sayre, but this time you fight it."

Peetrek.

Smiling, Quinn whirled around to face the thin Shikari. He wore a round mask in russet and gold tones. The mask seemed pleasant this time.

"Peetrek, Larena told me to seek you here." He'd been asleep all those times before, but this time, he was wide awake. How was this possible?

"With my help, she hid here many times from Faxon."

"Do you know what happened to Larena?"

Peetrek jerked his head up, the heavy mask swaying.

Quinn's stomach fluttered. His body stiffened as he gathered the courage to ask. "How did Larena die?"

Peetrek swept a hand through the blackness, leaving a white afterglow behind. In that stretch of lightness, the last few days of Larena's life played before him.

Bloodied and burned, she clung to the edge of her boat, clothing torn, auburn hair flat and tangled. Her blue eyes were swollen, cheeks bruised, fingernails broken and bleeding. He saw her enter Haven and collapse on the floor, but she never made it to the inner chamber with the black square.

Faxon and two team members trudged into the building, laser weapons in hand. Larena fought them, but she was no match for their strength. They dragged her outside and in the half-light of looming dusk, Faxon pressed a laser pistol to her head and fired. Larena's body shuddered and lurched forward, collapsing in the mud. Faxon and the others heaved her body into the moors and slipped away in their craft.

Quinn's body jolted, his nerves screaming. Agony scraped his throat raw and his fingers turned to ice. Muscles and limbs locked like seized bearings. The sharp, burning ache in his chest spread through his body, building into a shriek of misery that reverberated across the astralscape.

Grid lines rippled, dimming then readjusting. The vestibule contracted and then expanded. Even the darkness beneath his feet wavered for an instant. Peetrek bowed his head, a hand to his thin chest. Quinn thrust his hands over his eyes and turned away.

"All the astral feels your pain, Quinn Sayre. It spills even through the vestibule into Nearra. But there is other pain. That why Larena here you sent. Your former commander."

"You know about Gage?"

Peetrek snapped his head up. "Faxon has hurt many people. Your Commander Gage. Chirigas. And Shikari's."

"The slave camp!"

Peetrek nodded. "Faxon work us day and night. Offer food and water for pollen. He will soon enough have a shipment away to send. Ship here now. We stop him. You stop them. Make the pollen stay here."

It was some time before Quinn could compose himself. When he finally turned back to face Peetrek, his anger surfaced. "You have my word, Peetrek. I'll do my best to stop him. I'll finish what Larena started." He felt the tug on him from the onyx square in the distance. It was trying to pull him back, but this place held him transfixed.

Did Peetrek have some sort of magic over this world—and him?

Quinn nodded toward the onyx square. "I feel something pulling me back, Peetrek. How is it that I'm here? Some sort of magic?"

Peetrek's head jerked up. "It is Shikari way, but there more other powerful magics here. There no much time. Just know Faxon stirs them up. Unleash their curse."

The Shikari turned and walked slowly away from the vestibule.

"Peetrek, wait—"

"There more no time, Quinn Sayre. I see you soon."

Peetrek disappeared into the darkness.

Then Quinn was alone in the silence. He called out to Larena until she finally appeared next to the image of Haven's columns. She stood inside the threshold, and when she noticed him, she rushed out.

"Quinn!" she shouted, and rushed toward him. He remained distant this time.

Her soft rain and jasmine scent wafted toward him.

"You cheated on me," he snapped, his voice hard. He ached at the thought. Her betrayal hurt so much worse now. "Why the divorce? Why didn't you have the decency to at least tell me?"

She bowed her head. "You found the file I hid in my e-planner."

He nodded. "I also found your messages to Veider and mine unopened. Why?" His jaw was tight. "Why the divorce?"

"There isn't time now, dearest. You have to stop Faxon. He killed me, Quinn. But not before I found the slave camp. Three times, the Chirigas killed my colleagues. They were supposed to kill me, too, but I escaped. I didn't know Faxon knew about Haven, but he did."

Quinn gritted his teeth. "I won't let Faxon get that pollen off this planet."

"There is another part to this, Quinn. You must save the Shikari's as well. Only they know how to care for the Chirigas, and without those plants, the planet will die. Faxon holds their priest hostage at the camp, forcing the Shikari's to work."

"Peetrek?" But he'd just talked to Peetrek.

She nodded. "Many die trying to harvest pollen Faxon's way. I tried to capture Faxon's operation on optics, but failed. Quinn, you must capture this on optics and send it to the authorities. It's the only way to stop Faxon from killing any more people."

Her gaze fell to his left hand. She took hold of it gently and stroked his ring finger, the indentation of his wedding band still there.

"What went wrong, Quinn?" she asked, staring into his eyes. "We both wanted the same things."

He'd always thought so, but now he realized that he'd spent their whole marriage trying to keep her happy. Deep down, he'd always known that she'd never stay with him. She got bored too quickly. He sighed, wishing he could go back to Salice Minor and fix things with Tarateal. Erase so many years of pain.

"What went wrong?" He smiled hollowly at her. "I didn't follow my heart. And I've spent years trying to convince myself that I had."

Larena's eyes widened. She let go of his hand. "There's someone else?"

Quinn laughed bitterly. Typical Larena, always blameless. "There's always been someone else. I've just been too stupid to realize it."

"Who is she?" Larena demanded, crossing her arms.

"Tarateal Roberts," he said, his thoughts warm with memories. "We met on Salice Minor and dated for two years until I nearly flunked out of flight school. Then we broke up and days later, you followed me to the shuttle station, and Roberts—met you later that evening."

"Do you—love her?" Larena's eyes were stark, a mixture of anger and anxiousness.

"Does it matter?" he asked. "You wanted a divorce, remember? I'm not your problem anymore. Besides, you died nearly two months ago. They've declared you legally dead."

Larena's hands snapped to her hips and she stepped away from Quinn. "I fell in love with Ian on Nearra. I needed a change, Quinn."

Her words wounded. He glared at her. "And I found what I lost. You were my lover, but you were never my best friend, Larena. You never cared enough to be my friend. And now, I'm not sure you ever loved me."

Larena turned away, her form slowly dissolving. "I did love you once, Quinn. Miss me a little, won't you?"

Her form dispersed into a ball of light that streaked across the sky toward the horizon. It pulsed like a shooting star and disappeared into the darkness.

He thought about Sanji's term *debt* and it made sense to him now. It was time he paid his, but first, the breeding grounds. He had to document the Chiriga breeding grounds and Faxon's slave labor camp—before anyone else died out here.

Quinn turned and plodded away from the vestibule of stars. He felt his way through the darkness until he found the shiny blackness of Haven's onyx doorway. His fingers slipped through and he plunged forward.

SIXTEEN

LONG AFTER MIDNIGHT, an explosion rolled out from the *Magellan*'s engine room, engulfing half the ship in flames. Thrown out of her bunk, the room collapsed around Tarateal. When the smoke cleared, she lay wedged between her bunk and a ruptured bulkhead.

The bunk had prevented her from being crushed.

The air clouded with smoke as the chemical extinguishing unit sprayed white chemicals everywhere. She gagged, the acidic smell burning her lungs. Her chest ached, the pain throbbing through her ribcage. Taka had helped her down to her quarters only three hours ago, and Tarateal was still groggy from the pain medication. The synthskin and tissue rejuvenants had closed up the wound, but she feared it had broken open again. She struggled to brush away the powder and stumble to her feet.

She tried the door release, but it didn't respond.

Cold panic gripped her for a moment and she backed away. What if everyone else was dead? What if she was alone here—with no way to contact the outside world?

Part of her wanted to hide under the bunk until it all went away.

To wait for someone else to handle it, but the ominous, lingering moments of silence mounted. A chill danced down her spine. What if she was the crew's only hope of survival? What if they needed immediate medical attention?

Her throat tightened. What if Quinn needed her?

"Deep breaths," she muttered, and took as deep a breath as her wound allowed. She held it for a moment and exhaled, the first wave of panic washing away.

She was a medtech. She was trained to save lives. Okay, so maybe treating hangovers and sludge burns hadn't prepared her for this accident, but she had the skills to save lives.

And she would use them.

Bracing her body against the wall, she threw the door's manual release lever. Using her shoulder and all her strength, she shoved open the door. The pain was horrible and her chest felt like it would tear open. Bathed in dim red light, she laid her head against the wall, waiting for the sharp edges of pain to soften. Finally, she felt strong enough to stand. As she stepped into the corridor, she felt the warm stickiness of blood on her shirt.

The hallway had folded in on itself, walls leaning, equipment and debris scattered everywhere. Acrid smoke hung in the red emergency-lit corridor.

Coughing, she covered her mouth and worked her way through the wreckage.

Outside the infirmary, she found Taka Yawakani lying face down. A heavy sheen of white powder from the chemical extinguishing units clung to her hair and clothes. Tarateal pressed her hand to Taka's neck. She smiled. There was a pulse.

Gently, Tarateal checked for broken bones. A muffled groan touched her ears.

"Taka?"

"What happened?" she asked in a weak voice, and slowly rolled onto her back.

"Not sure," said Tarateal. "Tell me what hurts."

"My left ankle," she answered, gritting her teeth. "I think it's broken." Taka's gaze fell to Tarateal's shirt. "You're bleeding!"

She shrugged it off. "It'll be okay. Here, let me help you up."

Reluctantly, Taka accepted her help and struggled to her feet. Tarateal bit her lip against the pain as she steered Taka toward a handhold.

"I'm going forward," said Tarateal. "Stay here until I see how the others are, okay?"

Taka nodded, her face a mask of pain. "I'm not going anywhere."

Crouching, Tarateal moved through the hallway, weaving around fallen bulkheads and through holes until she reached the command area. Sheryl Hannaford lay across the console impaled through the chest with a metal rod. Sanji Shahir lay moaning beside the ruptured instrument panels. The pilot's station had been obliterated, nothing left of the instruments. She went to Sheryl first, checking for an unlikely pulse. None. Sheryl was gone. Next, she turned her attention to Sanji.

"Sanji, it's Roberts! I'm here to help you. Just hang on, okay."

When she reached Sanji, she saw the gash across his cheek. Shrapnel from the instrument panels had cut him up badly, but he seemed to have been thrown clear of the blast that had killed Sheryl Hannaford.

"You're going to be okay," she said, smiling at him. "I know you're in pain, but if you can hang on just a little longer, I'll get you some help, okay? I need to account for the entire crew."

He nodded, his eyes closing. "Sheryl is dead, isn't she?"

Sighing, Tarateal bowed her head. "Yes. I'm sorry."

His jaw tightened and he turned away, his eyes glistening.

"I'll be back," she said, patting him on the shoulder, and turned toward the hallway again.

She shouted for Park, Gage, and Kuruk, but feared that Kuruk had been closest to the explosion and would never be found. Gage's quarters were next to the command area. He'd probably perished too.

"Someone! Anyone—answer me!"

In a short time, Dale's thin voice called down the main corridor. He staggered into the command center, his face contorted in sorrow as he set down the medical bag.

"Roberts," he moaned. "I can't find anyone! They must have all died."

Fighting down her panic, she summoned a flicker of courage. She moved stiffly toward him and laid her hands on his arms.

"Dale, you're hurt," she said, and eased him down on a chair, noting a small gash across his forehead.

He could have a concussion. She rummaged through the bag for the hand scanner and ran it across the wound. He was fine. Must have been farthest from the blast. After bandaging his head, she propped him up against an intact bulkhead.

"Sheryl's dead," she said, pointing where the navigation station had once been.

"Oh, God!" Dale cried, his gaze darting toward her.

"But Sanji's okay. He's cut up and badly bruised, but he's still with us."

Dale's eyes widened. "Sanji's alive? That's a relief!" He gazed around the wreckage. "Pretty miraculous considering the engine room is below us."

Tarateal nodded. "Stay with him, Dale. I've got to find a gurney or a transport board, something to get him out of here."

"Sure," said Dale in a weary voice.

She fought her own pain and exhaustion to move toward the hallway in search of a gurney. She would need one to get Sanji out of there. She'd check on Taka first and try to get into the infirmary. When she reached Taka, she helped her through the maze of red destruction and into the infirmary.

The infirmary walls were intact. She helped Taka into the nearest sickbed and grabbed a transport board. Dale would have to help her get Shahir into the infirmary. As she emerged in the command area, she heard the voice in the hallway behind her.

"Shahir? Yawakani!"

From the sharp clicks and heavy tones, she realized it was Kuruk. Dale's face paled.

"In the command center, Kuruk!" she shouted.

Kuruk's skin had turned grey, sharply curved ears drooping. He looked weak, but otherwise in good shape. "Roberts," he clicked. "What happened?"

"Don't know," she answered, and held onto his arm, steadying him. "I thought you'd been killed."

"Only one thing—could cause this damage," he answered, searching for the correct words. "Someone—tampered."

She shivered. Had someone sabotaged their ship? But who would do such a thing? Could Faxon have done it somehow? But he was out of the compound, she realized. How was that possible? Somehow, he'd had a hand in this. She was certain of it.

"Who, Kuruk? Who?"

His ice blue eyes narrowed and she thought she heard him hiss. "Faxon's engineers. Said they'd help. I...I see their kind of help." He glanced around, the anger leaving his face that now drooped into sorrow. "Did anyone—die?"

"So far, just Sheryl Hannaford. Gage is still missing. I'm so glad you're here. I need to get Sanji down to the infirmary on this transport board."

He nodded. "I will help." He cocked his head and studied her for a moment. "They said you were scared of everything, but I see you as very brave, Roberts."

She smiled. "Thank you. I'll get Dale down to the infirmary."

"I'm fine, Ms. Roberts. I'll help Kuruk carry Sanji," said Dale, moving unsteadily toward Sanji.

"Someone!" came a shout from the corridor. "I need—help! Someone, please!"

Tarateal hurried into the corridor and saw Gage slumped against a bulkhead, clutching his side. His flight suit was torn and soaked with blood.

"Commander Gage! Let me help you, sir."

With difficulty, she bent down and slid her arm around his waist. Rising unsteadily from the ground, she helped Gage into the infirmary.

She cleared off one of the sickbeds and laid Gage down. Shortly, Kuruk and Dale carried in Sanji. Kuruk cleaned off another bed and eased Sanji onto it while Tarateal applied pressure to Gage's wound. In a few moments, it stopped bleeding. Then she fumbled through the smashed medicine cabinet until she found a vial of painkiller. Quickly, she injected Gage and microsutured the wound.

"I will return to the engine room now," Kuruk announced. "There is much to investigate." He paused in the threshold. "I will also make the proper arrangements for Sheryl Hannaford."

Tarateal sighed. That meant cremation. It was better than burying her here in this horrible place.

"Thanks, Kuruk," she said with a weary smile.

He nodded and slipped into the dark hallway.

"I can't believe Kuruk's alive," said Dale. "The engine room practically imploded! How could anyone survive that?"

She shrugged. "Must have been his Vardissian physiology." She glanced over at Commander Gage. The man cast his scrutinizing gaze at the young medtech.

"What about Captain Sayre?" Dale asked, changing the subject. "I checked his quarters. It's obliterated."

Tarateal felt terror snake through her. Oh my God! Sayre! Where was Sayre?

"I don't know, Dale. But I'll find out. Sanji needs medical attention. Take care of him, will you?" Her heart pounded against her chest. She was unable to even think about the possibility that he was—

No, he was all right.

Dale nodded and grabbed the medical kit.

Ducking under a fallen composite panel, Tarateal bit back her pain and made her way through the dim red lighting toward Sayre's quarters. His quarters were halfway to the galley. He was all right, she kept chanting to herself.

She fumbled for the access panel and snapped the manual release lever. It took some effort to shove open the door, but she managed.

"Sayre!" she called. The red wash of light gave his quarters an empty feeling and she hated the silence. "Sayre, are you in here?"

No response.

"Quinn, answer me, please!"

She walked through the room, stepping around the overturned desk and table, chairs strewn everywhere. All of his magtapes were shattered and littering the floor. Then her foot kicked a small pot. She reached down and picked it up, yelping when something sharp pricked her thumb.

Then she remembered. Sayre's cactus.

One last time, she called out to him, but the only response that greeted her was the echo of her own voice. Painfully, she worked her way back through the debris toward the infirmary.

Taka was sitting up in the sickbed when she returned. Tarateal clambered inside, setting down the cactus.

"Did you find him?" Dale asked anxiously.

Sadly, she shook her head. "His quarters were destroyed," she said. "Let's check the airlock records? Maybe he wasn't aboard?" Hope trembled through her. That was it. Sayre simply hadn't been there. She had to keep telling herself that until she knew for certain.

"Good idea, Roberts," said Gage. "If I know Sayre, he slipped out to look for his wife again, despite being confined to quarters."

"I'm surprised you're not blaming him for the explosion," Tarateal said, an edge in her tone. Taka told her more than enough about the things Gage had already accused Sayre of doing.

Gage shook his head. "No man who cared about his crew would destroy his own ship. Sayre cares a lot about this crew. I've seen that." He cast a scrutinizing gaze around the room. "No," he said slowly, "it was someone else."

Park swept Tarateal's handheld scanner off the table and perused the airlock access records, Tarateal watching over his shoulder until he found Sayre's access code. "Yep, he left the *Magellan* three hours before the explosion."

She grinned, feeling a wave of relief rush over her. Maybe he was safe out there? She gazed at the cactus, tinged brown at the edge of one small pink bud. Didn't look too hopeless. It would probably survive long enough to bloom.

"He wasn't aboard. Then he must be safe."

Unless he'd gone after Faxon alone.

She moved over to Sanji's bedside and sat down. Dale had removed the shrapnel and bandaged his wounds. He would be okay in a couple of days. Sanji tried to sit up, but she eased him back against the bed. "Sanji, did Sayre tell you where he was going?" she asked.

He thought for a moment, his brow furrowing. "Not that I recall. Perhaps he went out to collect more samples?"

Tarateal laughed. "Don't kid yourself, Sanji. You and I both know he's gone after Faxon, but it's a big planet out there."

"I'm sorry," Sanji said, shaking his head. "He never mentioned to me that he was leaving."

Tarateal sighed. If Sayre wasn't back by tomorrow morning, she'd go out there after him. There was no choice. Besides, she needed another day to rest.

"I'm sure he'll return soon, Sanji." She smiled reassuringly at him and gently patted his arm. "Get some rest."

As she moved toward Taka, the comm unit chimed. Tarateal snapped toward the panel. Only the audio feed remained intact. She fought back the urge to shout Quinn's name. "This is the *Magellan*. Identify yourself."

"Uh,...this is Derek Faxon."

"Kuruk!"

She heard the footsteps in the corridor and Kuruk rushed inside. He'd heard the chime. Tarateal pointed to the comm panel and he stepped closer, his ears flattening.

Slowly, she punched the respond button. "What do you want, Faxon?" Tarateal asked, her tone crisp.

"What the hell happened over there? There are scorch marks on the runway and some of the foliage is burning."

Kuruk's eyes narrowed. "Until I can get into the engine room and investigate," said Kuruk, a growl in his voice, "I cannot say for sure, but I suspect an overload occurred."

"We saw the fire from the moors and hurried back as soon as we could. Do you need help? Medical assistance?"

"Everything is under control. Kuruk and I will assess the situation tomorrow. Sanji Shahir will contact you with the results."

There was a long pause. "Was anyone killed?"

The Vardissian shook his head. Tarateal nodded her understanding to him. If Faxon had anything to do with the explosion, she wanted him to know that his attempt to kill them had failed miserably.

"Negative, Commander. We're all fine here."

There was a pause. "Keep me informed then. Faxon out." She read the trace of disappointment in his voice.

"*Magellan* out," she said, and cleared the connection.

THE NEXT MORNING, Kuruk and a shaky Sanji Shahir analyzed the remains of the engine room. Tarateal assisted them, handing them tools, and watching the monitoring equipment. Earlier, she'd applied more tissue rejuvenant and synthskin to her wound. It was healing nicely despite yesterday's exertion.

Kuruk lay flat on the rubble-strewn floor, studying the blackened hunk of what used to be an engine. With a scanner, he evaluated the remnants of the plasma channels. Sanji scanned the reservoir and the massive rupture, hoping to find the cause. Finally, Kuruk growled, a long string of clicks following, as he plucked something from the charred wreckage.

"What is it, Kuruk?" Tarateal asked.

Kuruk held out the melted device, his ears flattening. "An overload device—with a timer. The engines could not handle the strain."

"I saw a few of these in Jammu," said Sanji, who frowned as he touched the broken four-pronged edge. "It created such a strain that it ruptured the reservoir, producing a tremendous discharge of plasma. We are lucky to have survived."

"So, this was deliberate," said Tarateal.

Kuruk nodded. "The only way it could have gotten here was by Faxon's engineers. I left them alone only a short time and I should not have."

"It's not your fault, Kuruk," said Tarateal. "I don't know why Faxon thinks he can just kill an entire rediscovery team and get away with it. I wonder what else they sabotaged."

When Sanji gave her a fearful look, Tarateal realized that there might be traps all over the ship.

Taka's scream reverberated through the corridor as the whole ship shuddered.

Tarateal, flanked by Kuruk and Sanji, rushed down to the infirmary.

Sobs echoed from the storage room off the infirmary. She and the others hurried into the storage room to find Taka kneeling among the remains of the computer and their supplies. Tears streaked her face as she struggled to stand. Debris cluttered the floor where the computer had once been. Dale was off to one side, sweeping up debris. He cast a quick look over his shoulder, but kept cleaning.

"So, Faxon's trying to erase any remaining evidence we have on him," said Tarateal.

"It just exploded," Taka mumbled as Kuruk helped her up. "I was cleaning up the infirmary and heard the explosion. All our data backups, all the samples—everything is gone!" She stared at Tarateal, terror in her dark eyes. She wrung her hands and rocked gently back and forth. "What's happening out here? Why do they want to kill us? Why?"

Tarateal knew why—thanks to her analysis and carefully tucking away the Visiondust sample. "It's about the drugs," she blurted out.

"What are you talking about?" Sanji shouted. "Why hasn't anyone told us about this?"

Dale moved closer.

"It's in my logs. For now, our backup computer is still online. Kuruk, will you go over everything and see if you can find any more detonators?"

Kuruk nodded.

"Roberts, what about these drugs?" Sanji asked.

"A few nights ago, Sayre and I found Faxon carrying crates to his boats. In one of those crates, I found a strange blue powder. After doing a few tests on it, I discovered that it was Visiondust."

"Visiondust!" Sanji shouted.

Tarateal nodded. "Faxon's harvesting it somewhere out in the moors. They're holding Shikari's hostage out there, making them harvest the drug." She touched the bloodstain on her shirt. "Apparently, Sayre and I were closer to their processing camp than we realized."

"Faxon can't be allowed to export that stuff," said Gage. He rose from his sickbed and hobbled over to Tarateal. "We can't let this drug back on the market again."

"Are you sure about all of this?" Dale asked. He moved toward the others, his face pale.

Tarateal nodded and went to the specimen cabinet. She dug through the disheveled containers until she located the Visiondust sample. She thrust it into Sanji's hands. "Take this and seal it into a security capsule along with the lab report. That will be our ace in the hole. Launch it as soon as we can get a working satlink."

"I will take care of it," said Sanji.

"Do you need any help with that, Sanji?" Dale asked, hurrying in behind him.

Gage raised an eyebrow as he watched Dale and Sanji. Tarateal wanted to know what Gage was thinking.

Sanji muttered a quick no and slipped into the hallway with the container. Dale started after him, but Gage limped forward.

"We need your help in here, Park," he announced in a gruff voice.

Park hesitated, but then went back to his cleanup efforts.

Tarateal helped Taka over to a bed. She was trembling, fear shining in her eyes. Her broken ankle was still wrapped in a fibrous cast, making her steps clumsy. Tarateal sat down beside her and gripped her arms.

"Listen to me, Taka, we're going to survive this thing. Okay? Do you hear me?"

"How? Sheryl's dead!" she cried. "Quinn may be dead, too! Then they'll pick the rest of us off one by one—"

Tarateal shook her. "No, they won't! Listen to me! We're going to survive this thing, do you understand me? We're going to get out of here alive!"

At last, Taka's gaze met Tarateal's and she nodded.

"We need you right now, Taka. You're our senior medtech and we have lots of injured people. Somebody needs to take charge in here, okay?

"Yes—yes, of course." Taka took a deep breath and rose from the sickbed. "Dale, let's get this place back together."

At last, Taka's military training kicked in and she seemed to move by instinct.

Slowly, the infirmary began to look like an infirmary again.

WHEN THE NEXT MORNING ARRIVED, Sayre hadn't returned from the moors. Now, Tarateal feared he was in serious trouble. She kept quiet about her impending excursion into the moors. They'd try to stop her, but she had to rescue Sayre.

He had a way of diving headfirst into an empty pool.

She wished that he'd look first, but knew that it just wasn't in Sayre's nature. The man acted before he thought. Always had. She feared that some of Faxon's team had gotten to him. Maybe he was lying in one of those wire pens, being worked to death like the Shikari's?

She shuddered. She had to find him.

She packed her field pack and continued with the *Magellan* cleanup throughout the day. While Kuruk and Sanji tried to bring the auxiliary engine online, she helped Taka and Dale in the command center. When everyone finally retired for the night, Tarateal geared up in her quarters. She found the two contaminant masks kicked into a corner and thrust one into her jacket pocket along with a couple of glow sticks. She waited there for two hours and then slipped into the silent hallway toward the airlock. Sanji was waiting for her.

"You're going after him?" Sanji asked.

"He's in trouble, Sanji, I just know it. You know how he is."

Sanji nodded. "Quinn never thinks about the consequences. That usually gets him into trouble."

"Like now." She laid a hand on his shoulder. "Look, I know you're frightened for him and I know you want to come with me, but I'm going alone. They need you here. If the worst should happen—" She shook her head. "No, I'll be fine. I'll bring him back safe, Sanji."

Sighing, Sanji bowed his head. "I fear for him, too. Since Larena's death, he has not been thinking clearly. If Faxon knows he is out there, Quinn may be in more danger than the *Magellan*. Find him."

She nodded and tapped her access code into the lock. Her heart fluttered when the lock clicked shut behind her. Going out there alone was crazy, but somebody had to save Sayre from himself.

With careful steps, she made her way to the dock, the misty moors filling her with terror. There was no telling who remained in this camp to finish her and the others off. As she crept down the compound path, a blue blast of laser fire seared the muddy ground.

She careened left, bouncing off a tree trunk. Lurched forward.

Laser fire crackled. She stumbled again.

Dock boards creaked. Footsteps whispered. A volley of laser bolts charred the pier.

Dodging right, she threw herself into the nearest boat. Engines purred. Laser fire ripped across the bow.

Keeping her head down, she slammed the steering mechanism hard to the left and jammed the stick forward.

Engines roared.

The boat slid forward, leaving a wake of blue-black water and laser fire.

In a short time, the whirring of another boat stuttered behind her and the laser fire began again.

She was already going too fast through the moors.

The fog had grown thicker since she'd left the dock, but it didn't seem to bother her pursuers. There were times when the craft felt airborne and she feared she'd collide with a tree, but she kept up her dizzying speed, sliding in and out of causeways, praying she wouldn't dead-end somewhere.

A laser blast nicked her arm, singed her sleeve.

She winced and pounded on the burning fabric until the fire disappeared. Already, the skin underneath throbbed.

Ahead, fog spun wildly as she slammed the stick to the left.

Fire raked across the port side of the boat.

She veered left again, bogged down in a muddier channel, and finally backwashed into another smaller channel. The boat nearly flipped, but she held on, not letting up her grip on the stick.

The sound of the other boat had softened some. She smiled. They were losing her bearings.

She ripped through the fog and into a wide causeway, veering right at her first opportunity. The motor sounds grew softer until they faded away into the night.

When she heard only the night around her, Tarateal collapsed against the water shield, the pain in her arm throbbing into her throat. She felt feverish.

Cutting the motor, she reached for a cold pack from her medical kit. Carefully, using forceps and a glow stick, she pulled the fabric bits away from the burned skin. After cutting away her sleeve, she affixed the cold pack on the blistered skin and tried to find her bearings.

Glancing down at the map unit attached to the control panel, she found a jumble of melted wires and metal shards. Terror welled cold in her stomach. She had no way to get back to the compound. She was lost! And there was no way to contact the ship.

Besides, Faxon would be waiting for her to send a distress message. It would be a homing device for those laser-toting killers. Her only hope lay in finding the Shikari camp.

For a long time, she rode the channels until the fuel tank was almost empty. Finally, she ran the craft aground on a solid strip of land and began hiking.

She tried to recreate the route she remembered from her first trip, the one she and Sayre had first taken. Could she find the Shikari camp before she ran out of food and water? Settling her field pack onto her good shoulder, she set out to give it her best shot.

SEVENTEEN

QUINN TRAVELED the moors all day and half the night trying to find the Chiriga breeding grounds. Larena's notes were sketchy, but he refused to give up the breeding grounds as lost. The government had to know about the sanctuary and whatever purpose it served for Nearra and the Shikari's. If he laid claim to it in the *Magellan's* name, maybe he could protect it from Faxon?

And the other privateers.

Larena had spent many hours calculating oxygen/carbon dioxide ratios and analyzing air composition. The mist seemed to trap the moor gases, creating pockets of death. She'd alluded to details given to her by one of the chemists, who died before Larena, that these complex moor gases inhibited respiration. He skipped over all the useless technical details because Larena had summed it up in one frightening sentence:

The gases made the body forget how to breathe.

If Larena's calculations were correct, then the plant sanctuary had to be protected at all costs. The Chirigas processed the dangerous gases into harmless by-products and oxygen. If the

Chirigas died, then the moor gases would eventually consume the planet and turn Nearra into a noxious wasteland.

Humans were famous for creating those back on earth.

All of the causeways looked alike and Quinn didn't know what he was looking for—even if he found it. He'd traveled a long way past Haven and even beyond Faxon's slave camps. Now, the moors fanned out into a wild, mist-drawn lake. He couldn't see the other side of it.

Bluish-brown grasses hugged the lake's edge, dark gnarled trees framing the banks. The trees created a canopy of dusk above him, holding in the coolness and the mist. He pulled his blue jacket tighter around him. It would be cold tonight, the warmer air unable to settle over the chilly moor waters.

Ominous birdlike calls pealed and twittered around him. Insects chirred. Unseen things clicked. Far off to his right, a heavy branch snapped and cracked against the ground.

Birds took flight. Treetops rustled.

The mist hugged him. He shivered in the sharp air.

The deep, bass droning of something in the distance trembled through his bones, the eerie sound making his skin crawl. He dropped his speed back, softening the motor to a whisper and listened. It reminded him of a tribal chant. A single bass note carried aloft in the air, sinking through the tree canopy and into the mist. It hung in the air, the sound enveloping him, and then dissipating amidst the insect rumbles.

Ahead, the left bank jutted out into a narrow strip across the lake.

Quinn steered right, trying not to scrape the shallow edges, and skirted the shoreline. As he slipped around the point, he noticed a small channel that seemed to lead nowhere. Glancing at his map, he found an obscure channel that Larena had marked. He was getting close. There'd be one more point and a cove after this causeway. The channel beyond that led to the breeding grounds.

Abruptly, the left bank curved inward, forming a kidney-shaped inlet. Blue-black mud glistened on the murky banks as his boat slipped past. When he cleared the inlet, he saw the narrow causeway snake through the thick grass. It would be a tight squeeze with this craft, but he would take the chance. Dropping the speed down to nearly a stall, he edged forward through the thick water and into the channel.

Grass snapped and raked across both sides as he steered through the tight turns and dense brush.

No wonder no one had ever found these grounds. No one was dumb enough to follow this channel unless certain it led to some sort of reward.

Several times, Quinn had to crouch on the boat's floor and steer underneath low-hanging branches. The channel seemed to go on endlessly, losing him deeper in the Nearran moors. After having his arms scraped raw from branches raking across the boat, he almost backed out, but he thought about Roberts and all the pain she'd gone through and forced himself forward.

He even thought of Larena. The image of her execution remained an afterimage in his head. For her, he'd see this through. It was the last thing he could ever do for her.

A cove rose from the mist as his boat scraped past a boulder. Crawling through skeins of thorny vines that slashed at his face, Quinn steered the chugging boat into the cove. He tied off on a moss-covered tree, tossed his field pack down, and jumped onto the bank. As he turned, he noticed an iridescent sheen glimmering off the blue-black water and bent down to examine it. The smell overpowered him—engine fuel.

He groaned when he saw the small hole in the fuel tank. Trails of clear, rainbowed fluid swirled through the swamp. The hole was high on the tank. Maybe there was some fuel left? His worst fears were confirmed when he climbed back into the boat and started the engine.

Click, click, wheeze.

In a moment, the engine sputtered. He flicked off the starter mechanism. Damn. The gauge barely acknowledged the fuel in its tanks. Most of it had leaked into the moors now. Maybe there was still enough to propel him back into the main causeway, but he couldn't be sure.

After cursing the boat and himself for being stupid, Quinn picked up his pack. He still needed to document the Chiriga breeding grounds. Getting back would be his next problem; for now, the first was finding the Chirigas.

Beyond the bank lay a footpath that disappeared off to the left. All around the path grew massive trees, their triangular bases like podiums. They gave the moors a foreboding look. He trudged up the bank and followed the footpath into the woods, the warble of birds sounding ominous now. After winding through the forest, he reached a wider path that led toward an open, wooden gate. Reluctantly, he approached, but when he passed through the gate, the sight made him freeze.

A dozen or more plants, over two meters tall, appeared in the misty forest. The main stalk of the closest plant displayed five ridged, yellow blossoms, each one nearly the size of a man. The blossoms undulated with a soft rattle. The writhing plant reminded him of a Hydra. Blossom stems attached to the main stalk that disappeared into a bushy network of purple-veined leaves, and something beneath those leaves quivered.

He shuddered. Chirigas.

For the second time today, that eerie low-pitched note rumbled through him. He realized that it had come from the Chirigas. One plant rubbed its vines together until it produced a bass hum that vibrated through Quinn's jaw and into his rib cage. He watched as one of the yellow blossoms fluttered opened, spewing blue powder into the air. A thick, overpowering sweetness touched his nostrils, the scent vaguely reminding him of gardenias. Every year for her birthday, Tarateal's mother sent her gardenias. Here, the air smelled like thousands of them.

He gagged. The air shimmered blue, dusting a nearby Chiriga. Its blossoms unfolded, catching the blue powder on the petals and inside.

Farther down the path, he noticed what looked like blue feathers rise up in the wind. The feathery things drifted toward him. Some of them fell to the ground near his feet. He plucked a couple from the ground and examined them, turning them over in his palm.

Seeds? They reminded him of fishing lures.

He carefully released them back into the air. The others swirled aimlessly around his shoes, so he scooped them up and cast them into the wind. A sudden updraft caught the lagging seeds and carried them above the treetops with the rest.

Abruptly, the humming sound stopped. Tendrils stretched across the ground from the nearest plant. They moved toward him, making a fierce scritching sound, but stopped short of his legs.

Quinn froze. "I mean you no harm," he said in a calm voice.

What the hell was he doing? He was talking to plants.

Abruptly, the scritching sound stopped again and the tendrils rolled back toward the Chiriga. A shiver slid through him. Had they somehow understood him?

Sentient plants? It sounded absurd. On Earth, it was impossible.

When he returned to the *Magellan*, he'd have Sanji do some research—if these plants didn't kill him first. Sweat collected on his upper lip and brow. He brushed it away with a shaky hand.

The rustling leaves began again, this time, all the Chirigas participating. They seemed agitated, as if—was it possible—they felt his fear? He closed his eyes and thought of something pleasant.

He thought about Tarateal Roberts. The feel of her silky hair against his face, the soft soapy scent of her skin, the warmth of rediscovering her. Soon after, he felt the calm relax his muscles, which in turn softened the rustling Chirigas. They seemed calmer.

"I won't harm you." He stepped closer to the nearest plant and slid the optical camera out of his field pack. "I came here to protect you. Some people on this planet want to steal your pollen. I'm here to stop them, but I need to take images of you. So, my people will understand."

Slowly, he turned the lens toward the Chirigas and depressed the capture button. He expected the *zzzzzt* of the camera to agitate them, but the grove remained silent.

Quinn walked gently through the plants, capturing images to upload to the Deep Space Exploration Bureau. Toward the back of the grove, he heard that bass rumbling and steadied his hand to capture their pollination on optics. The other plants, apparently sensing no danger, also returned to pollinating. Blue dust flecked in his hair, on his arms, and collected on his clothing as he switched the camera to video capture.

He barely realized it when dusk fell over the moors. It would turn colder soon. He needed to leave now.

With cautious steps, he made his way through the grove and toward the path. As he reached the gate, he stopped, remembering what awaited him out in the moors. A near-empty fuel tank. Faxon and his First Contact goons. Sleeping on the boat could be dangerous —even if Faxon wasn't out there somewhere. And cold. Wind off the water would chill him faster.

He set down his pack and slid out his pallet. The gate might be a safe place to sleep. It was well inland from the boat and a good distance from the nearest Chiriga. He spread out his pallet.

His stomach rumbled as he opened his field pack to stow his camera. The rations were dry, but he finished them off and sat in the growing darkness to watch the Chirigas. It grew cold quickly and he soon found himself shivering. Quickly, he retreated into his pallet, but the insulated material did little to protect him from the rising winds.

As darkness fell, he noticed that the plants almost gleamed in the darkness. The Chirigas seemed more active at night. By the time the twin moons rose, the chirring Chirigas had overpowered the other wild sounds.

Until the wind rose.

The pallet no longer held out the chill. He huddled deeper into the capsule, but cold still trembled through him. His fingers were beginning to turn numb, the cold ache still throbbing deep into his bones. He felt the stiffness of his face and lips, the trembling intensifying. His teeth clacked together despite his attempts to quiet them.

A tendril from the nearest plant shot toward him. He was afraid to move as the vine slid across his chest, around his neck, and across his face. It seemed to be probing, as if trying to measure him. Study him. Fear tried to surface, but he swallowed it back and allowed the Chiriga to coil around his shivering body, across his chilled arms, and down his shaking legs to his ankles.

In what seemed an eternity, the tendril finally withdrew. Quinn let out a relieved sigh, teeth still chattering, and settled deeper into his pallet, folding his arms beneath him. His breath fogged the air. Shivering violently, he brought his legs against his chest, hoping that morning would come soon. But it was just too cold. He couldn't stay here. He'd have to chance a run in the boat.

A thicker vine snapped around his feet and jerked him backward. Toward the Chiriga.

Everything he'd ever learned told him to fight back, but his instinct whispered, *wait*. From somewhere deep inside, he gathered his courage as the vine pulled him underneath the first blossom.

The petals spread wide. Too late.

He flung a hand over his face and screamed as the petals enveloped him.

EIGHTEEN

GAGE HELPED Taka Yawakani set up the infirmary. As he stacked medicines in the cabinet, he couldn't help but notice her unease. The petite young woman was upset and nervous. He couldn't blame her. She had never faced a situation like this before and she was trying to go about her job like a professional. He admired that. Taka had always been reliable, even as an ensign. She'd been one of his favorites in class and he'd been thrilled when Taka signed aboard the *Augustine.* And she reminded him of the happier days—before Matt died.

"Taka, it's okay to feel out of sorts," he said. "You're in the Rim. You're only the second team to set foot on this world. It's going to be okay."

She stopped sanitizing instruments and walked over to him. "I hope you're right, sir," she said. "Before, on the Augustine, there were procedures to follow in times of crises. But here—all the rules have changed. We're easy targets in here. Didn't you hear all that laser fire? I hope Tarateal's all right."

Gage sighed. He needed to ask her about Sayre's story. All he had was Sayre and Shahir's word and the garbled log disc. He still wanted to hate Sayre—he needed to hate someone for Matt's death—but found he couldn't do it anymore. Deep down, he knew Sayre wasn't to blame now. He'd wasted five years blaming the wrong man. He moved closer to her.

"Taka...that night aboard the Augustine—what happened?"

Her expression softened. "I'll never forget that night. None of us will." She bowed her head. "I could have cleared him, but he wouldn't let me."

"Why?" Gage demanded.

"Because it would have ruined Sanji's career and Quinn refused to allow that. Sir, Quinn was with me that night. The three of us were in the infirmary when that message was sent."

Dale Park hurried in and laid some supplies on the nearest table. "Have you seen Mr. Shahir, Taka?" he asked, interrupting.

Taka shrugged. "Last time I saw him he was in Nav with Kuruk."

"I'll check there, thanks," he said. Casting an uneasy glance at Gage, he slipped back into the hallway.

Dale Park. That chatterbox medtech. Something about that boy nagged at Gage like a toothache. Yesterday, Park seemed surprised that he and Kuruk had survived the explosion. And after everyone else had gone to find Sayre, Park returned to the infirmary. Shortly after, Taka reported the explosion in the storage room. Coincidence? He scoffed. It was deliberate...and recent. Park seemed disappointed —almost angry—that the infirmary was still intact.

At first, Gage had attributed Park's actions to a green medtech with little discipline and a short attention span. According to the young loudmouth, this was his first commission, but Gage suspected now that it wasn't.

"Taka," Gage said, limping toward the computer, "is the backup computer still working?"

"Sure, it's fine, but the main system's a memory, so don't lose anything."

He pointed to the console. "Then I should still be able to access all the records we've amassed, correct?"

She nodded and walked over to the console. "Of course. Is there something in particular you want to know?"

Who killed his son for starters? "A few things. If I tell you what I want, can you find it for me?"

"I'll do my best," she answered, and turned on the computer. She stood stiff, her fingers poised over the keys. "Ready whenever you are."

He glanced around, making sure Park hadn't slithered into the infirmary without him noticing. "Without exception, all personnel are required to undergo a complete physical prior to a deep space mission, correct?"

"Correct, sir."

"Then I'd like to do a simple comparison of medical records."

Taka pressed several sequences of keystrokes and then paused. "All right, what do you want to use for the main comparison? A specific pattern, a location?"

"I want to compare Dale Park's medical records with the entire crew commissioned aboard the Augustine. You should have all the Augustine records. I uploaded them the day I came aboard ship."

"Dale Park?" She frowned. "Why him? He's only a kid. This was his first trip out."

A good question. It made no logical sense, but all he had was a gut feeling. He had to follow it or risk dying in this alien wilderness. He refused to die until he found Matt's killer.

"Please, Taka, just run the comparison. I'll explain everything when you're finished."

Nodding, Taka returned her attention to the console and entered a short series of commands. Finally, she leaned against the panel, waiting on results.

"The comparison will take a while to run, sir."

"Fine, I'll wait."

Gage paced as much as his injured leg and wounded side would allow him. It was a wild hunch, but he had to play it out. Something seemed wrong with Park. Something very wrong.

Several minutes passed until the information dumped to the screen.

"This can't be right," Taka mumbled, squinting.

Gage hurried back to the console. "What does it say?"

"There is an *Augustine* crew member that matches Dale Park's blood type, and height and weight are very close." She gasped and turned her gaze toward him. "A crewman named Dale Bridges, sir. He died in the privateer attack. Both files indicate that Bridges and Quinn were stationed aboard the Augustine about the same time—"

He squeezed her arm. "That's exactly what I was looking for! Thank you."

She shook her head, her gaze still on the screen. "What does all of this mean, sir?"

Gage smiled. "That Dale Bridges didn't die aboard the Augustine like the records show, Taka. He's aboard this ship—only he's changed his name."

"But, sir, the fingerprints are different. And he looks too young," Taka added.

"Taka, you and I both know that plastic surgery and rejuvenation treatments could take years off his appearance," said Gage.

Taka nodded.

Maybe that long-ago government experiment hadn't been a waste of time after all. If Park had an implant, it would be enough evidence to convict him.

"I think I've found Matt's killer, but I need one more piece of information. Could you save the links to that information so I can access it from what's left of my quarters?"

Taka nodded.

He hurried toward the door. That last piece of information needed to be gleaned from Faxon's computer system.

"What piece of information?" Taka called.

He paused by the door. "The reason that Bridges, now Park, was aboard the Augustine and now the *Magellan*."

"How do you expect to answer that question?"

"I don't," he said. "But Faxon will—or rather his computer will."

Gage hobbled into the corridor and down to his quarters. He turned on his datapad and tapped in his Level 5 security codes. He smiled. Faxon probably didn't realize that he had Level 5 clearance.

Only use them in an emergency, he was told, but Gage knew that Faxon's position as First Contact team commander awarded him a similar set of Level 5 codes. Those codes were the only way to override system passwords and other safeguards. Faxon used those codes to cover his tracks, to hide the deaths of anyone who opposed his drug-running scheme—like Sayre's wife.

For the first time, Gage felt sorry for Sayre. He understood the pain of losing a loved one, but he also knew that extra agony that dug down deep and gnawed through bones and muscle at the news they were murdered.

Scrolling through Faxon's system, Gage poked around in every crevice he could unearth until finally he located Faxon's most personal data. Shipping schedules for his new business, lists of privateers involved in the exporting scheme, it was all here.

For a long time, he searched through the files for information about anyone named Dale. Dale Bridges and Dale Park were the same person, but both names were place markers for someone else. Gage would know who very soon.

NINETEEN

TARATEAL'S BREATH pulsed in icy blooms as she trampled through thorny brush in the twilight. Her boots sank into mud halfway up her calves and filled with sludge. Her knee twisted as she tried to pull free of the blue-black mud, but sank back again. Finally, she yanked her foot free and hobbled away.

A bird screeched past. She wheeled. A furry, grey creature streaked through the tall grasses and brushed against her leg. Terrified, she threw herself backward, tumbling down a stark bank and into a soupy mix of mud and dead grass.

Reaching out for a skeletal tree limb, her hand landed on something sticky. She drew back her hand and flashed a glow stick at the limb. Slimy residue clung to the branch, oozing like sap down the rotting tree.

Her hand burned. She tried to stagger away from the cesspool, but her knees shook, her hand and palm on fire. She sucked in thin gasps of air.

Air thickened. Lungs burned. Chest ached.

She struggled to breathe, her whole body feeling numb. Drugged. She made a desperate effort to breathe, but everything seemed muddled, out of focus. She had to concentrate on breathing, but her lungs refused to obey.

Slowly, the realization touched her. Moor gas.

With half-dead fingers, she clawed at the mask in her pocket and sank to the ground, her legs buckling. It took effort and concentration to slide the mask over her head.

In a few moments, she could breathe again.

Slowly, feeling returned. Her lungs expanded and contracted, but her hand still burned. Hoping to extinguish the hot pain throbbing through her hand, she wandered away from the cesspool, her legs wobbling, and dropped down at the edge of the swamp. Quickly, she thrust her hand into the muck. Relieved by the coolness, she paused there, the intense burning pain dissipating. After the fire left her palm and fingers, she pulled her hand out of the mud and staggered away from the dead spot. Her best chance lay through the grasslands toward higher ground.

Twin moons hung directly overhead as she staggered through fields of blue grass. Her boot connected with a rock and she stumbled, field pack tangling around her arms as she rolled down a hill and into the swamp.

Swamp mud bubbled, thick waters sucking on her pack and clothes. Tarateal clawed at the chilly water, her hands turning numb again.

Something splashed nearby.

She struggled against the quicksand-like hold on her pack, but finally had to slide her half-frozen limbs out of the straps and let the moors take it.

Something gurgled and swished past her feet.

Fighting, she threw herself forward, kicking her aching legs toward the bank until finally her throbbing hands closed around a dangling tree root. Using the root as an anchor, she dragged herself back to the bank. The mask slipped off her face and settled into the ooze. Panting and shaking, she collapsed. The air chilled her skin. She groaned, feeling the pain in her hand again. Already, a feeling of lightheadedness had set in, but she fought it. For as long as she could.

In the end, her eyes closed and she slept in the tall grasses.

When morning came, she found herself without tools and—most importantly—water. Sitting up took great effort and she cursed herself for not being more careful last night. If she hadn't lost her pack, she'd at least have those tasteless rations to munch on instead of dry grass. She brought her hand to her muddy face; the blue-black goo had dried, drawing her face into a taut mask. That's when she saw the swelling. Her hand had swelled to twice its size. Cradling it against her dirty shirt, Tarateal forced her stiff legs to carry her away from the edge of the moors. The highlands couldn't be far. If she could find them, then maybe she could find the Shikari's.

Wind howled across the moors, cutting through her damp clothing. She thought about Sayre, wondering if he was still out here somewhere. Had Faxon already killed him? Fear shivered down her spine. She wondered if she'd ever see him again. She gritted her teeth. No, she wouldn't think like that! She'd come this far. She wouldn't give up now.

Faxon hadn't won yet.

Tarateal stumbled over a piece of dead wood, but caught herself and veered toward a stand of trees in the distance. They would protect her from this wind.

For the first time, she understood her own fear. At last, it made sense. She hated being out of her element. Out in the Rim, she hadn't known what to expect and that unknown terrified her. When it came to treating minor injuries, she could do that in her sleep, but out here? Out here, she had no experience and she was so tired of constantly having to prove herself. She was tired of questioning her every action, wondering if it was the right one.

Still...what if she made the wrong decision?

On FS-314, there was always backup for those situations, but out here—the wrong decision could kill the whole team. The unfamiliar terrain, strange equipment—it all made her uncomfortable with herself, a feeling she hated. In the Rim, the fear of death no longer figured into the equation. It was a regular occurrence.

Sighing, she knew exactly what it was now—she feared her own failure. She didn't want Anderson and Hernandez to be right. Facing this rediscovery mission and failing, she couldn't bear the thought. On Salice Minor, she didn't want to go out to the Rim with Sayre and fail. She couldn't let him see her fail. The same thing with Connor. And her not wanting to leave FS-314.

But in the moors, she'd fallen into every situation as if she'd been born to it and she hadn't failed. Even so, that didn't matter anymore. Because she knew that, for the first time, giving her best effort was enough. She wished Sayre had been around for her to tell him that. Maybe she'd be able to tell him soon?

The trees provided slightly more warmth than the grasslands, but the scent of musty leaves and decay made her sick. She held a hand over her nose, trying to mask the rotten stench, and hobbled through the dead trees and swampy grass. The trees were spindly, their trunks thin and tall—black and straight. Through this forest, she saw all the way to the other side. Her heart sank when she saw the causeway slithering into a tiny bay on the far side. She set a diagonal course, hoping to find a steep upgrade beyond these trees and swamp. Her hand still throbbed from touching that sticky goo.

She glanced down at her hand. The reddish-purple flushing had spread past her wrist along with the swelling. She had a bad feeling about this. The swelling, the discoloration, her weakness...all signs of some sort of poisoning.

Stepping up her pace, Tarateal weaved through the trees until she emerged on the other side of the forest. More marshlands. She groaned.

She wanted to collapse and go to sleep, but she shoved away her fatigue and followed the water's perimeter. The causeway ambled along for several kilometers, and Tarateal followed it until her knees buckled.

Cradling her hand against her body, she kept moving.

When the shoreline swerved right and opened into a narrow causeway, she dropped to her knees, exhausted. Her cheek smashed against the muddy ground. She shook off the dizziness and turned toward the moonlight. Broken columns littering a narrow strip of land across the causeway cast thick shadows into the moors. Beyond the columns stood a small stone building.

Tapping the remains of her strength, she plunged into the water, flailing, and kicking until she clawed herself onto the far bank. Wind pierced her soaked clothes. She trembled, her feet barely responding. As she staggered through the rubble, she wondered what had caused the columns to topple like this? Was the destruction recent? Had Faxon done this? Like the abandoned buildings she and Sayre had found? Faxon seemed to be driving the Shikari's deeper and deeper into the moors.

The pain in her hand had increased along with the discoloration and the swelling. She needed something to draw out the poison. But what? Her first aid kit was lost in the moors. Mud would have to do. She scooped up handfuls of mud until her hand was covered in it.

Ahead, the building was dark, but it felt safe somehow. After peering inside and seeing nothing moving, she stumbled through the threshold and collapsed on the dusty stone floor. The wind shrieked as it surged across the dark building. With her good hand, she fished a glow stick out of her shirt pocket and gripped it. It felt warmer inside the building, the wind not able to bite into her wet clothing and gooseflesh. For a long while, she curled up against the wall, fighting the enveloping cold and waiting for the mud to dry. When she felt comfortable enough to sit up, she thrust the glow stick in front of her and studied the chamber.

Beyond this first chamber—empty except for the layer of silt on the floor—was a narrow hallway. Slowly, fighting exhaustion, Tarateal hobbled to her feet and staggered down to the other chamber. A square slab of polished onyx gleamed on the wall, so shiny that she could use it as a mirror. She wondered if the Shikari's or some other native race used this as a temple. Did they prophesize here? She'd seen scrying stones in some cultures, stones that shamans and priests looked into to tell of future events.

Unable to stand any longer, Tarateal slid to the dusty floor, her glow stick's eerie blue light enveloping the onyx square. The stone looked almost magical, with its bluish tint and the howling wind outside. Its surface reminded her of the swamp water. She saw her dismal reflection rippling across the surface. There was startling depth to the square, almost tunnel-like.

What lay beyond this layer of onyx?

Her head bobbed as the cold drummed its fingers down her spine. This inner chamber was only a little warmer than the outer one, but it felt safer. Something about this chamber was comforting. She wondered if that was due to the influence of this strange onyx square. Her head bobbed again. She'd try to build a fire later. For now, she'd sleep a little while.

TWENTY

THE INSIDE of the blossom felt like wool. Quinn had expected gum-like fluids holding him immobile while acids dissolved his body, but the warm blossom floor was soft, the pollen cottony. He sank into the powder, his pallet still hugging his frame, and curled up in the warmth. In a short while, he stopped shivering and he felt his toes inside his boots again. Fingers tingled. Bones ached. But he was comfortable. Somehow this plant had sensed his distress and rescued him.

In the dark, warm safety of the blossom, Quinn slept.

He awoke to sunlight. The blossom had reopened with the morning light. Nothing tried to consume him and no nightmares disturbed him. Even his nighttime walks through the astral had not happened. Sometimes it took half the day to lose that grey cast that came from walking in that place, but today, his skin looked healthy. He hadn't walked; it was that simple. And for once, he was grateful. It was the best night's sleep he'd had in a long time.

Stretching gently, he slipped out of the pallet and gently slid out of the blossom. His field pack lay untouched near the gate. As he reached for it, he heard the hum of pollination in the grove.

After some water and a ration or two, he shook the pollen off his clothes. He surveyed the grove. It was badly overgrown and needed some attention. Faxon had taken the Shikari's away from their tending duties. Rolling up his sleeves, Quinn began to clear away thorny vines that had slithered into the Chiriga grove. He broke the vines with his boots and carefully removed them. After he had cleared the vines from the grove, he turned to other things that looked like weeds. Back in Oklahoma, his mother had spent half her Sundays pulling weeds from her garden. She refused to use sprays or dusts, saying that two hands were the best technology available. He smiled. What she wouldn't give to see him hand-weeding like this.

The Chirigas seemed to understand his careful tending and left him alone. If only they knew how terrible he was with plants. The dead cactus on his desk was a grim reminder of his way with plants. And people.

Using a stick, he dug a small hole in the ground behind the nearest grouping of Chirigas and planted a seed he'd found caught on a tree limb. The whole grove scritched and chirred as he carried some of the moor water to the seed. Remembering how cold the nights got in the moors, he scattered a few handfuls of grass and dead leaves over the seed.

Using vines, he tied a bundle of limbs together and raked away some tangles of dead leaves and dry grass that had collected around the some of the Chirigas. That's when he noticed a dusty irrigation trench. The Shikari's must have dug this trench. Smaller trenches diverged from the main one and stopped at each Chiriga grouping. Going back to the boat, he retrieved a small bucket and carried back several buckets full of water from the moors. He filled the trench with water and watched the trench branch out into little dusty eddies toward each of the Chiriga groupings.

By nightfall, the seed had sprouted.

Amazed, Quinn could only stare at the fragile purple seedling. He smiled. This from a man who killed cactuses? One of the three Chirigas in the grouping spread open a blossom and enveloped the seedling to keep it warm. It opened another blossom for Quinn to huddle into and he gratefully accepted the warm place to sleep. Exhausted, he gathered his pallet around him, climbed into the blossom, and slept.

———

QUINN LOST count of the days he'd spent caring for the Chirigas. There was so much to do here. Faxon had kept the Shikari's away for some time, judging by the conditions here.

When he wasn't tending the grounds, he spent his time capturing images of the Chirigas protecting the new seedling and completing cycles of pollination. The care of the seedling (and him) would provide the government with more proof that the Chirigas were sentient. As another day ended, the humming sounds suddenly dissipated until the Chirigas seemed to fall dormant and silent.

When dusk started to fall and no warm blossom opened to protect him from the harsh winds, Quinn understood that it was time for him to leave the grove. He'd have to try his luck with the last of the boat's fuel; he couldn't delay it any longer. Still, he wondered why they wanted him to leave. There had been no warning.

Had he somehow done something wrong? He chuckled. Maybe they found out about his dead cactus?

Removing the optical disc from the camera, he wrapped it tightly in plastic and tucked it into a pocket inside his left boot. Insurance in case Faxon found the camera. After spreading more dried grass around the small Chiriga seedling, he hiked back to the boat. Quinn slid over the side and clamored through leaves and twigs that had collected on the boat's floor.

He closed his eyes as he depressed the engage button. *Come on, baby—start!*

Click-click-click.

Sighing, he reached for the manual fuel injector and sent some fuel into the engine. Again, he pressed the engage button.

Click-click kachunk kachunk...

It still had some life in it! Holding his breath, he pressed it again and the engine fell into a nearly silent purr.

Back to camp—if he could make it that far. With the route mapped in his head and the optical images in hand, Quinn knew that Faxon could never touch these breeding grounds. That gave a little meaning to Larena's death, and for that, she'd have been happy. He smiled. And he'd go through all of this again, if it meant another chance to be with Tarateal.

Maneuvering the boat back through the serpentine turns took all his concentration. The winds swept across the moors, rocking the small boat as he made his way toward the First Contact compound. He'd traveled a long way since Haven. It'd take some time to traverse the causeways and channels to get back. He hoped he had enough rations—not to mention fuel. If he could get past Haven and Faxon's slave camp, then he could send out a distress beacon to the *Magellan*. To hell with Faxon.

Nearra's moons gave him enough silvery light to navigate the moors. He steered around rotting trees, protruding rocks, and red-eyed creatures that floated past in the murk. As the boat slid over the silky black water, his thoughts journeyed back to the Chirigas. The wind bit through his jacket and he wondered if the seedling was warm enough tonight. How long would that irrigation trench provide them with water?

Shivering, he remembered the warmth of the Chiriga blossom. He couldn't help but wonder what he'd done to make the Chirigas cast him out. For the first time in his life, he understood Larena's fascination with plants. To be part of a First Contact team like this and come across the Chirigas! Studying newly discovered sentient species was the experience of a lifetime. Even he wanted to study the Chirigas now. After all of this was over and Faxon was in custody, he'd petition the government to authorize another mission to Nearra —to rediscover the Chirigas...if Gage didn't have him hanged first. He'd dedicate the study to the people who died here.

As morning loomed frosty and grey above the blue blackness, Quinn, half-asleep, slipped past Haven, the fuel gauge quivering toward zero. The little cay looked serene in the foggy predawn silence, roof and column shadows hanging over the moors. There was still something soothing about this place. Probably being so close to the astralscape.

He let Haven fade off to his right as the boat's fuel carried him beyond. Maybe it would get him back to the compound? He'd refuel, check on Tarateal and his crew, and then go back out.

Rotting trees slid past on all sides, high-pitched bird trills echoing on the wind as the sun rose pale in the sky. The mist obscured most of its warmth, but it took some of the edge off the wind. He thought about the bottle of amara tucked in the bottom drawer of his desk. Even a swig or two of that swill would be welcome now. He thought about steaming cups of coffee and bowls of thick beef stew. And black cherry ale. He smiled. When he got back, he'd have that long talk with Roberts. He wouldn't make the same mistake twice.

Up ahead, another boat emerged from the fog. Squinting, he tried to recognize who was at the helm, but the distance was too great. Had some of his crew come out after him? Gage, maybe?

As his boat drew closer, he saw Faxon steering his boat toward him. Quinn groaned. Sanji must have sent him out here. After all, it had been several days. The whole crew was probably up in arms about his sudden, unannounced departure. He waved at the other boat and dropped his speed in half, the engine sputtering. Faxon steered his boat up against Quinn's as Quinn set the stick to idle.

"Sayre, your crew is quite distraught over your disappearance," said Faxon in a buttery voice. He ran a gloved hand over the steering mechanism and smiled at the two First Contact team members in the back of his boat. They shifted closer to the side, making Quinn uneasy.

"Sanji," said Quinn with a groan. "I told him I'd be all right, but he never accepts that."

"Mr. Shahir waited a few days before he came to my office, Sayre.

Said you came out here alone to find some sort of breeding ground." Faxon paused, his thin lips pinched. "Did you find it?"

Quinn studied Faxon for a moment, noting his suddenly taut grip on the steering mechanism, the tense facial expression, and the stares of the men in the back of the boat. He hadn't told Sanji about the breeding grounds. He hadn't told anyone.

Quinn shook his head. "Sorry. Didn't find it. Without a map, it's impossible."

Faxon gazed over the side of his boat and into Quinn's craft. The man was looking for evidence, but he hadn't brought anything back to link him to the Chirigas. He traced Faxon's gaze over the leaves and debris until it reached his field pack. Blue sparkles danced over it in the sunlight.

He cringed. Chiriga pollen.

Faxon glanced up from the boat and back at Quinn.

"It's a shame that you had to venture out here alone, with your wife dead and all. Mr. Shahir had good reason to worry." He nodded toward the two men in the back of his boat and they rose to their feet. "Especially after you've been gone for five days. Too bad you never came back."

The men leaped onto the boat and grabbed Quinn's arms. "Such a tragedy that you and your wife both died on Nearra." He clicked disapprovingly. "First contact missions are much too dangerous for civilians."

Quinn slammed his elbow into one man's ribs. The man yelped and doubled over, clutching his side. Quinn shoved the other man over a seat and leaped into the moors.

"You won't get far, Sayre. Larena didn't."

"You bastard!" Sayre shouted, and fought against the soupy black water. "There was no need to kill her! You could have kept your drug-running out here in the moors and she'd never been the wiser."

Faxon steered the boat toward him. "Leaving that sort of loose end is dangerous in my business, Sayre. Just too dangerous."

Quinn heard the motor moving toward him and kicked harder.

Off to his right was a clump of reeds. Enough to tangle a boat. He pulled at the water with his arms, swimming toward the blue reeds.

"I need him alive, so don't damage him too badly," Faxon said to the other team members.

A laser blast sizzled in the water beside his arm. Quinn slipped underneath the water. It was like swimming through ink, but he kept under the surface, zigzagging so they wouldn't know where he'd come up. When he finally broke surface, the crackle of laser fire exploded in his water-filled ears. Steam rose from the swamp water as he plunged beneath the surface again.

He overshot the reeds and had to double back, but Faxon's boat was edging closer to him. Every time he surfaced, laser fire ripped through the water. A black shadow floated over his head and he fought to hold his breath as Faxon's boat drifted past. He waited until the sunlight appeared before he resurfaced. Off to his left was a thin line of trees and a muddy bank. If he could reach that bank, they'd never catch him. He swam toward the bank, legs pumping, arms flailing. Behind him, he heard a shout and the whir of the boat. Again, laser fire crackled.

Something sharp gouged into his side and his movement was impaired. He screamed, the pain so intense that he momentarily blacked out. When his vision cleared, he discovered the finger-sized barb that was embedded in his side from a fishing net wrapping tightly around his body. Even the slight movement of the water caused him excruciating pain.

"Reel him in," ordered Faxon, "but carefully. I need him alive."

With every tug of the net, Quinn fought back a scream, the hot gnawing of the barb excruciatingly painful. In moments, like the catch of the day, he floated against the edge of the boat, tangled tightly in the net. All three men took hold of him and pulled him into Faxon's boat. They rolled him onto a tarp on his stomach. He felt hands on his back and hands grasping the net. In a blinding moment of agony, Faxon removed the barb.

Quinn screamed, the pain rippling through him. Then he fell into darkness.

QUINN AWOKE to the thumping and scraping of boots. When he opened his eyes, he saw hilly terrain and a footpath that cut through it. His boots dragged the ground. He felt the ache in his shoulders and the fiery pain pounding through his side. Nausea rose in his throat from his churning stomach. Despite his agony, he knew this place. It was all too familiar. He and Roberts had been here before. His heart sank.

Faxon was taking him to the slave camp. To kill him no doubt.

Larena had walked this very same path, Faxon forcing her to harvest pollen with the others. Until she escaped and he killed her. The bastard would do the same thing to him now.

He felt the terrain rise then fall. He strained his eyes to catch a glimpse of what lay ahead. Rows of wire pens, dry grass lining them. There were nearly a dozen Shikari's huddled in the pens. They dragged him across the dirt toward the nearest pen. He heard the gate creak open. They shoved him inside and closed the gate.

Agony rippled through him when he hit the ground. He swallowed the scream wrenching up from his gut. Through the throbbing waves of pain, he saw three Shikari faces swimming around him. One wore a mask. He gasped.

"Peetrek!"

Sayre's stomach lurched until he coughed up blood.

Peetrek laid a hand on his shoulder and the great turquoise and cream mask nodded toward him in acknowledgement. Hands shuffled across his clothing, tearing at the jacket and shirt until they found his wound. Someone pressed a cup of cold water to his mouth and he sucked greedily at the water. A hand pressed on the wound and he cried out. Another hand pressed against his head and stroked softly, soothingly. His muscles relaxed.

Peetrek held a sage-colored powder in his hand. The priest wet the powder with water from a pail, working it into a paste. The Shikari gently pressed it to the wound and covered it with Quinn's shirt. Finally, he laid his hands over Quinn's eyes until Quinn closed them. And he slept.

Until midnight. He awoke shivering to a silvery wash of moonlight directly overhead and the rattle of chains. One of the First Contact team members unlocked the door and dragged Peetrek and the other Shikari's from the pen.

"You'll be with them soon, Sayre," said a voice out of the darkness. "As soon as you're well enough to stand. Faxon will get what he needs out of you. You can be assured of that."

Not this time, thought Quinn as his cheek touched the dirt.

He wouldn't tell Faxon the location of the breeding grounds. No matter how much Faxon tortured him. He wouldn't give that bastard the location.

For hours, he suffered through bouts of fever and pain. Flashbacks of the barb being pulled from his side rushed back and he shuddered, feeling the burning pain in his side and the ache of fever. During a few moments of lucidness, he remembered poor Peetrek and the others and he wondered what they faced beyond the camp.

Backbreaking labor? Threatened by whips? Beaten for not working fast enough?

He remembered the pollination cycle of the Chirigas and wondered how anyone attempted to harvest the pollen. Lots of Shikari's had already been killed. How many more would die before this was over?

When morning came, Peetrek and the other Shikari's trudged back to the camp, arms limp against their bodies, backs hunched. They collapsed onto the dry grass and slept. Quinn slipped in and out of consciousness, his fever still erratic. Toward evening, he felt calloused hands against his face and shoulders. Slowly, he opened his eyes.

Peetrek.

"Peetrek," he murmured. "The breeding grounds—"

Peetrek snapped a hand to Quinn's mouth before he could finish his sentence and shook his head. Quinn nodded his understanding. Peetrek already knew that he'd found the sacred breeding grounds and didn't want to risk his saying it aloud. Peetrek made another poultice, using part of their allotted drinking water, and packed it around the puffy wound. He heard the whisper of a chant on Peetrek's lips. He wished he was strong enough to reach the astralscape tonight, to talk to Peetrek, but Quinn knew he was too weak to attempt it. For now, he'd endure Peetrek's silence until he regained his strength.

In two days, Quinn's wound had mended enough for him to sit up. He watched Peetrek and the others sleep. Aside from one team member guarding the camp entrance and one watching the pens, the camp seemed deserted. They were no doubt processing more Visiondust. Faxon had probably gone back to the compound with hideous stories of his demise. Probably the same story he told the government about Larena. His chest ached at the thought.

But Roberts would know Faxon was lying.

Toward late afternoon, Faxon appeared at the pen. Quinn lifted his head from the dry grass and glared. Faxon seemed shorter, slicked-back hair thinner, greyer than he remembered, beady eyes more animated. Flickers of sunlight dancing over the hillside sent Faxon's stocky shadow hovering across the pen. The corners of his mouth twitched, a smile slithering across his wide face.

"We lost one of the Shikari's last night," said Faxon with a smile. "That means I need one more man on my midnight harvest detail, Sayre. If you'd like to tell me where the breeding grounds are located, I can make sure that man isn't you."

"Go to hell, Faxon."

"Be very sure about this. There isn't anything sacred about an angry Chiriga slowly devouring a man. If you don't want that to be your fate, I suggest you reveal the grounds."

Quinn smiled. "If you let the Chiriga devour me, then you lose the location, Faxon. Sounds like you need me more than you need to feed the Chiriga."

The smile left Faxon's face, replaced by a frown. "You'll go on the midnight detail. Afterward, we'll see how willing you are to talk to me." Faxon turned away, striding toward a small building.

Quinn didn't know what an enraged Chiriga could be like, but he remembered the gentleness of the ones he'd encountered.

It may cost him his life, but he'd find out tonight.

TWENTY-ONE

ASH SCENT—DRY, musky—hung in the air. Warmth crackled. Softness covered her, supporting her weight.

Tarateal opened her eyes.

A doe-eyed Shikari, creamy hide streaking down its chest, laid a silky hand against Tarateal's face. Amber light flickered across its face, making the Shikari native look concerned and gentle. Tarateal felt moisture clinging to her cheeks and upper lip. A soft cloth mopped it away. Her hand throbbed and she moaned.

"How did I get here?" she muttered, her voice raspy with fever.

"Rest," said the Shikari in a meek voice. "Nuriel bring you late in last night."

"You know my language! But I was told that only your priests spoke."

The Shikari snorted disapprovingly. "Telled by *milakos*. Since they come here, it has been our custom not to speak to *milakos*."

"You mean the First Contact team?"

The Shikari flung its head back.

"Is that an affirmative?"

"Affirmative. They walk with their shadow souls and we fear

them. They seek to destroy us. So many times, they try take our eye souls, but we resist them best as we can. They have goned too far now. There no middle ground. When time right, we save Shikari's and the Chirigas."

Tarateal raised an eyebrow. "Chirigas?"

Again, the Shikari tilted its head back. "They guardians to the waters, of our world. They protect our eye souls and rid the air and water of shadow soul. *Milakos* walk without eye souls. The Chirigas suffer. We suffer."

"What is an eye soul?"

The Shikari's head bobbed uncertainly. "Eye soul is—Shikari...is Chiriga...is Quinn Sayre and you."

Tarateal sat up from the mat and grabbed the Shikari's arm. "Sayre? Have you seen Sayre? I came out here to find him, but they chased me—tried to kill me. I fear he's dead now."

A crippling burst of pain exploded through her hand and up into her arm. She gasped, the pain sapping her breath. The Shikari forced Tarateal back down against the grass mat and wrapped a warm cloth around her hand. When the pain subsided, she smelled a pungent odor from the cloth.

"What is this?" Tarateal asked, pointing at the cloth.

"Paste...to ward off the shadow soul until Nuriel returns."

"Nuriel?"

"Nuriel hunts. When he returns, we care for this wound. Your eye soul poisoned."

Tarateal glanced down at her arm and saw the flush of reddish-purple reaching past her elbow. She vaguely remembered the substance that had burned her in the moors. Her heart fluttered and her breath grew ragged, painful. It felt as if a rock had been dropped on her chest. She fought it, trying to gather enough voice to ask about Sayre. For days, she'd felt like something had happened to him.

"Who are you?" she whispered.

"Lomasi," came the fluid answer.

"Please, Lomasi—Sayre...what happened—to...Sayre."

"Much," Lomasi answered. "But not until you are well. Nuriel hunt for a light net and when we lay it, you healed. Until then, rest. You need strength, for your eye soul to fight poison shadows. Rest, Tarateal Roberts."

"Is Quinn alive!" she demanded, but she felt herself spiraling away. "Please!"

"Rest, Tarateal Roberts."

Amber replaced blackness again and again until the hazy image of the fire and Lomasi returned to her. Another Shikari, stockier and without any cream coloring, sat beside her, their gazes intense. The yellow-white twinkle of light against Tarateal's chest caught her attention. She glanced down at her olive tank top, long-sleeved shirt gone, and saw silky thin weavings intertwining and gleaming across her chest. The pattern reminded her of a Native American dreamcatcher woven with fiber optics. Light danced across the delicate fibers that formed a net across her body. She marveled at it. It was unlike anything she had ever seen.

She gazed over at Nuriel and saw that the Shikari nursed his left arm against his body, a thick white cloth shrouding it. Peeking out from the fabric were flickers of light. A small, glittery net had been draped across his wounded arm.

"Where—did it come from?" Tarateal asked, her voice weak and barely above a whisper.

"Light net? Comed from Chirigas," Nuriel answered, his tone louder and fierce compared to Lomasi's gentle voice.

Lomasi flicked her head back. "The Chirigas not tolerate pain in others. They weaved light nets to heal."

Nuriel's ears flattened. "And the *milakos* hurted the Chirigas, enraged them into a blindness. Until they lashed out even at the Shikari's." He snorted, raking a foot across the ground. "All *milakos* evil."

"No, Nuriel," said Lomasi, her tone chastising. "Peetrek says that Quinn Sayre not a *milako.* Says he use his eye soul. That she have one, too."

"For that reason, I harvest light net—hoped she help Peetrek."

"Please, is he all right?" Tarateal cried. "I need to know."

Tarateal felt her body tingle, the pain clouding. A black haze pooled like ink around her elbow and dripped down to her fingertips. It was as if the light net had culled out the poison from her hand. She watched the blackness spread until the light net drew it into its framework.

"See, it drawed out poison's shadow," said Lomasi softly.

The light net flickered like a candle in a draft and then recovered its pale yellow hue. It seemed to be absorbing the poison from her wound. Through all of this, Tarateal drifted in and out of consciousness, losing track of the time. It felt like days, but she sensed that only a few hours had passed. That scared her. In the back of her mind, she'd stored the fear of what had happened to Sayre, but it was trickling forward again. She knew that the Shikari's had information about him and if she remained patient, they would tell her what she needed to know.

In time, Lomasi returned to Tarateal's side, this time with a bowl of aromatic grains. The Shikari woman held a crudely carved wooden spoon to Tarateal's dry lips and she gratefully ate. The unfamiliar spices gave the grains a buttery, basil-like flavor. The warm meal felt good in her stomach.

"You eat well, Tarateal Roberts," Lomasi cried, and set down the empty bowl.

"I feel much better thanks to the light net." Then she noticed that the netting was gone.

"We apply final one last night." Lomasi softly raised Tarateal's hand, displaying only a slight puffiness and purplish haze. "Poison shadows goned from your eye soul. You safe again."

"Now can you tell me if Sayre is safe?" she asked with a sigh, and forced herself into a sitting position. Her legs ached from immobility and she rubbed them.

"He is not safe. The *milakos* hold him prisoner. They want him to betray the Chirigas, but so far, he say no. *Milakos* plan hurt to him."

Tarateal scrambled up from the ground. "I've got to find him, to help him if I can!"

"This why I wait to telled you." Lomasi pressed her hands against Tarateal's shoulders, forcing her back against the mat. "Quinn Sayre unprepared when he face *milakos*. That land him in his situation. If you do same thing, no one be to help. They hold our priest. He tries to help the Shikari's already taken, but he, too, goed unprepared. Whoever follows the harvest must prepare for all crops."

"But Faxon will kill them!" Tarateal shouted.

"And if you follow Quinn Sayre, the *milakos* take your eye soul. You think same way as Quinn Sayre and Peetrek."

Tarateal shook her head. "All I care about is helping Sayre and your priest."

Lomasi jerked her head up and stared at Tarateal. "And the Chiriga. Help also the Chiriga. *Milakos* kill not Quinn Sayre he know of sacred breeding grounds. *Milakos* know Peetrek never will them tell. They think they maked Quinn Sayre tell."

"All right, then Sayre's just stalling for time. We have to figure out a way to rescue them."

"No, we must find way save to the Chiriga."

Tarateal frowned. "How do we save the Chiriga?"

"Destroy *milakos*."

Destroy the *milakos*? Tarateal shivered. Kill Faxon and his team? The thought of killing someone made her dizzy. She'd sworn an oath to save lives, not take them. Even though she knew Faxon cold-bloodedly killed Larena Sayre and dispatched the other five First Contact team members—no, he executed them—she didn't have it in her to kill him. She'd leave that to the authorities. It went against everything she believed.

"I can't kill my own people," she said softly.

"You not understand," said Lomasi in an urgent voice. Her eyes darkened as she seemed to struggle with her words. "To destroy taked away what *milakos* crave most. *Milakos* crave Chiriga pollen. Trade for wealth. It must be taked from them. To destroy them."

She grinned. "I get it. You want to bust up their drug ring so they can't sell Visiondust on the black market." That fit well into her belief system.

"Your words make no sense to me."

"You want to make Faxon's harvesting of Chiriga pollen come to an end. That way, he won't have anything to trade for *wealth* and since this is what he cares most for, it will destroy him."

Lomasi snapped her head up. "Yes, Tarateal Roberts, that how is we destroy *milakos*."

Frowning, Tarateal laid a hand to her chin. "But to do that, we have to get the government involved. The *Magellan* will have to offer proof to the government that Faxon killed Sayre's wife and five other team members. Or attempted to kill Sayre and myself for asking too many questions."

"What happened then?" Lomasi asked.

She sighed. The first mention of Visiondust would cause mass extermination of the Chiriga. She remembered Sayre saying that the Chiriga kept the swamp gases from becoming lethal, but even the whisper of Visiondust would wipe out the planet. Faxon could easily turn the situation against them. The only way to protect the Shikari's and the Chirigas was to ensure that Faxon and his accomplices were convicted for the murders of his team members. If the *Magellan* crew submitted a report concerning the fragile environment here on Nearra, then the government would prohibit travel here...she groaned...by anyone except trained First Contact personnel. That meant Faxon could eventually return, buying the Chiriga a little more time at best.

"The government would destroy the Chiriga," said Tarateal, "so we'll have to figure out another way."

"We thinked on this as Nuriel trained you harvest Chiriga light nets. As long as Quinn Sayre refused *milakos*, we have time. We act. To save Quinn Sayre and Peetrek, then you learned ways of light netting."

TARATEAL HAD to wait one more day before Lomasi took her outside the Shikari hut. She was surprised to see the line of wooden structures built into the side of the hill. A natural valley had been scoured deeper so the buildings would not be visible at eye level. The tall grasses provided even more seclusion. But the wooden buildings looked almost new. Judging from the placement of the Shikari's' campfire, it seemed to be the center of activity.

Several of the natives worked around the fire. Some used sticks to weave a coarse, grey cottonlike material into clothing. One Shikari pulled the wet cottonlike matter into thick strands and rolled it onto a small wooden spindle. He had about four full spindles beside his feet. Others crushed grains using rocks, filling grey sacks stacked in a building nearest the fire. Two Shikari's took turns seasoning a pot of grain that cooked on the campfire. No one seemed to be playing. All the natives worked cheerfully and quietly at their tasks. She wondered if the abduction of their priest had caused a shift in mood or if this was the Shikari's' normal routine.

"Lomasi, has this place always been your home?" she asked, remembering the deserted places in the moors.

Lomasi shook her head, her nostrils flaring. "As long *milakos* hered, Shikari's have no place. For now, it safe."

"In the moors, we found many stone buildings," said Tarateal. "Did Faxon drive you out?"

A sadness filled Lomasi's eyes. "*Milakos* come in night, take Shikari's from homes and into the channels. Their eye souls slipped through Haven now." Her gaze left Tarateal's face, drifting toward the horizon. "Again and again, they come until we fear shadow souls that walk the night. So, we take everything we carry and leave our homes."

Tarateal's chest tightened. What horrible things had Faxon done to the Shikari's?

Lomasi's face brightened. "Is all right here. We safe." She tugged on Tarateal's arm. "Follow me." Lomasi led her toward the building where they stacked grain.

As she neared the structure, a pale yellow glimmer filled the doorway and spilled onto the sacks of grain. Draped on hooks in the back of the structure were two light nets. They clung to the back wall, the fibers reminding her of strings of glowing pearls.

"Nuriel bring in the harvest a few days ago. So far, you only one in village to have need their healing. They will be gone by morning if not used."

Tarateal reached out and ran a finger across the strands. "They are so beautiful. And the Chirigas create them?"

"You soon see. Nuriel go to Chiriga with blade wound he inflict on himself to get you light net."

She felt terrible now.

"The Chiriga senses injury in you that follow eye souls and weaved it healing net. Nuriel showed injury to get one. Harvest hard. Take time. Care for Chiriga to get. This what we wished to teached you. You free Quinn Sayre, you need light net."

"How will a light net free Sayre?"

Lomasi turned, her massive equine head drooping. "It not free him. It keep his eye soul in his body when Chiriga kills him."

Tarateal felt the blood drain from her face. "Kills him?"

"Chiriga lashed out at creatures who walk with shadow soul and any creature trying to steal its dust. Used the light net at the right moment keeped his eye soul in his body."

Keep his eye soul in his body?

It sounded like a bad magtape movie. *Curse of the Soul Snatchers* with Greysen Pierce and Monica Maine. She'd seen it four times and had never quite understood how the Alpha Centaurians had managed to steal the Martian girl's soul.

"No offense, Lomasi, but this sounds crazy to me. As a certified medtech —at this point, certifiable—I recognize the obvious healing properties of these fibers. They are quite capable of detoxing the body and restoring electrolyte balances..."

Her voice trailed off as she remembered Sayre's accident. Suddenly, the light nets made sense. They most likely served as a sort of equalizer, preventing the heart rate from falling or rising excessively and creating a sort of safe zone until the patient could receive further medical care. And all of this resulting from plant fibers! No wonder Faxon wanted their pollen.

"It not crazy, Tarateal Roberts," Lomasi insisted, her tone calm. "It truth and you will see."

Tarateal nodded. "All right, I think I'm beginning to understand this better. I'll learn to harvest them, but do we have the time? Faxon won't put up with Sayre's silence for long."

"What choice he haved but wait?" Lomasi asked. "All *milakos* haved time. They wait. To find the breeding grounds is to control all the dust."

"Control it?"

"All seeds released from sacred breeding grounds. If *milakos* taked seeds for planting, they no go out into waters to searched for new groves."

"Seeds come from only one location?" Tarateal raised an eyebrow.

"Only Chirigas in breeding grounds produce seed that scattered to the winds and across the waters. *Milakos* knowed this. They hunt nightly for grounds. They have plenty time."

"But Sayre and your priest don't," said Tarateal. "What happens to them when Faxon finds this sacred place?"

"Peetrek and Quinn Sayre will lose their eye souls."

Tarateal winced and Lomasi laid a silky hand against her arm.

"It won't take Nuriel long to show you what be doned. The rest take place on milako land."

She shrugged. "But I still don't know how to stop Faxon, Lomasi." What they needed was a plan.

"Perhaps Peetrek have answer? Or Quinn Sayre? We save them from *milakos*."

WHEN DAWN LIT the sky above the moors, Nuriel shook Tarateal's arm until her eyes opened and she nodded at him. She slipped her boots on quickly and filed out of the hut, leaving Lomasi sleeping soundly on a grass mat near a small fire pit. Nuriel led her behind the camp and across the damp grasslands. Moisture seeped into her khaki pants and olive shirt. Grass blades swished against her boots, the sound reminding her of taffeta. Up ahead loomed a misty grove of trees, and Nuriel seemed to be heading in that direction. She wondered if they'd encounter a Chiriga there.

As they neared the grove, she heard a fierce rattle and feared they'd stumbled onto water snakes. Her gaze snapped to the ground, searching for slithering creatures or something coiled and ready to strike.

"What is it?" she whispered.

"The Chirigas. Do no fear them. They gentle to those who care for them."

Tarateal swallowed back her fear and followed Nuriel into the grove. Through the tangles of vines and thick leaves, shadows swayed. Her heartbeat matched the beat of her boots against the muddy footpath that wound closer to the writhing shadows. Had Sayre already faced these creatures and died? Somehow, Nuriel sensed her fear and whirled around, gripping her by the shoulders.

"They do not send shadow souls to walk land unless it gooded reason. Do no reason, Tarateal Roberts. Respect them. Treat them with kindness. They'd reciprocate."

She nodded and motioned him forward. As the mist faded, the three huge plants, taller than Nuriel, undulated beneath a canopy of tall, leafy trees. Large yellow blossoms opened to catch the dew, the petals framed by purple leaves. The air smelled like potpourri. All three plants thrummed in a low pitch.

"Amazing," Tarateal cried, her voice barely above a whisper.

The three plants formed a triangle, and in between them, sparkling golden strands had been woven into a net. She glanced up at the misty canopy of trees, noting the sparkle of light nets covering the branches and leaves. So that's how Faxon located their groves; he looked for the light nets.

She watched Nuriel gently approach the light net in between the Chirigas. After a moment's pause, he laid his hand on the net and raised his chin into the air. A soft, throaty chant rose up in the silence. Tarateal realized that he was singing. The notes were clear and bright, but in the lower ranges of his voice. As he sang, the light net twinkled until light pulsed across the net toward him, moving in waves. As his voice drifted into silence, the lights continued to pulse toward him. He held his hand immobile; he seemed to be absorbing the light.

After a few moments of silence, Nuriel sang again, the notes louder this time. The Chirigas waited until Nuriel's voice was loud before they resumed their low hum. He kept almost a harmony with them, matching their low notes as best as he could. Finally, the humming subsided and the light net stopped pulsing. When the light remained constant, Nuriel pulled his hand from the net. Gently, he dipped his hand into the nearest blossom and scooped out two handfuls of pollen that he placed in a pouch at his side.

"How do you harvest the net?" she whispered.

"I show you after you speak to them."

She frowned. Speak to them?

Nuriel nudged her toward the net and she reluctantly gave into his prodding. The blossoms twitched, swishing back and forth like the tail of an agitated cat. Carefully, she laid her hand against the light net and heard the muffled pluck of the taut strands. They felt stronger than she imagined. Immediately, she felt the minute vibration rippling across the net. She closed her eyes, listening for the low-pitched *ohm* to vibrate through her fingertips. It coursed through her fingers, up her wrists, and into her shoulders, spiraling across ribs and breastbone until it quivered down her legs to her calves. She felt as if a cord had slipped through her hands and threaded its way into her feet. Never had she felt so centered—so grounded...so sure.

Something about the vibration sent her thoughts soaring. She remembered bits and pieces of broken pasts, things she had shoved deep into the recesses of her memory. She felt herself standing outside the shuttle wreckage on Lunar Colony, the fear draining down her body and through her feet. Moments of embraces with Sayre back on Salice Minor, the fear of deep space that had separated them now flowing from her body like water. Her muscles went slack, the low notes buzzing in her ears, in her vocal cords.

Without realizing it, she was humming the same note that emanated from the light net. She felt a brightness inside her, a clarity she'd never known before. And she welcomed it. The note blossomed in her throat and she let the harmony soar. Seeing the lights pulsing toward her brought waves of satisfaction.

With every pulse of light came a deeper understanding of herself and a bond with the Chiriga. There were no words, just understanding. They only wanted to serve those who served them, to comfort the mind and dissolve fears.

Soon, she grew tired and her voice softened, signaling an end to the pulses of light. When her voice faded into the chirring wilds, the waves of light disappeared. Slowly, Tarateal removed her hand. Nuriel steered her toward a blossom and showed her how to gather the pollen.

"Your visions produce this pollen," said Nuriel softly. He held out another pouch to her and she filled it with pollen. "The Chiriga changed shadows into dust."

"Why do you need this—this dust?"

Nuriel gazed at her strangely. "It sacred. Used by priest. He journey beyond dreamscape with his eye soul. It is sacred journey undertaken to strengthen our people, to plan for the coming seasons, and to seek whatever come our way. Peetrek founded Quinn Sayre in this way. It also a place to send eye souls on their last journey."

"I'm not sure I understand about the dreamscape. Perhaps I'll have Sayre explain it to me some time. Now, how do I harvest a light net? And what do I do with it once I have it?"

Nuriel flipped shaggy brown locks out of his equine face and moved back toward the light net. He pointed to three connection points, one on each Chiriga. "You harvest a net by twisting each point until it falls away from the plant."

Gently, Nuriel reached out to a cluster of clear fibers and twisted them until they came off in his hand. With his other hand, he twisted the second and third bunch of fibers and lifted the net away from the plants. He held out the twinkling net. "It is not difficult," he said, and folded the strands into a manageable bundle.

Almost immediately, the Chirigas began to create a new net. Tarateal watched the framework slowly build, strands forming and extending to the other plants.

"How long will it take to generate another net?" Tarateal asked.

"By sunrise, a new one will be ready to harvest. When night falled, nets glow like fire, but when sun rise again, a harvested net dissolves. Nets don't have healing light until we ask for it."

"So, I won't have much time," Tarateal mumbled as she reached out to touch the net.

Nuriel jerked his head up. "Only a short time to harvest it and the *milakos* won't let you try twice. Once the light touches them, they slowly disintegrate. By the time light replaces night, this one will be gone." He reached out and clutched her hand. "But be warned, Tarateal Roberts, just as the nets separate shadow souls, so can they join eye souls."

She frowned, unsure what he meant by that, but at least she had a way to save Sayre now. She didn't know what to do with Faxon, but the light net was more than she'd hoped for. Perhaps the Shikari priest would know what to do? As she followed Nuriel out of the grove, she prayed that Sayre would be alive when she reached the camp.

TWENTY-TWO

GAGE HAD DOZED off at the desk when the query stopped running. The datapad beeped an acknowledgement at him, rousing him from the half-sleep. Bleary-eyed, he stabbed at the screen and sent the results to it. In moments, the results cycled out in a stream of data. Gage leaned forward and perused the results. One match. Gage held his breath.

Anthony Dale Faxon.

Stunned, he stared at the screen, ignoring the rest of the data. Dale Park was Derek Faxon's son.

Anger flooded his veins and Gage struck the desktop with his fist. Faxon destroyed the *Augustine* and was directly responsible for killing his son. Gage thought back to the evidence that had mounted against Sayre, like the detection of the combat enhancement at the comm board shortly before the attack. No one could even tell Sayre he had it, yet it had been used against him in court. Dale Bridges had been the other ensign from that group to be signed aboard the *Augustine.* He carried a combat enhancement, too. It *must* have been him at the comm board. Only two of that batch of twelve recruits had been aboard ship. He doubted Sayre's and Dale Bridges' paths had ever crossed aboard the *Augustine*. Now, he just needed to prove that Dale Faxon was Bridges aka Park.

Guilt stabbed Gage in the stomach. Sayre had hid Shahir's indiscretion under a lie of his responsibility for the comm shift. But Sayre hadn't been present in the comm room at all when Dale Bridges sent that communiqué to...Gage shuddered. To his father's ship.

Derek Faxon led the privateers who destroyed the *Augustine* that night. Gage was certain of it. And now, after years of privateering, he was about to relaunch an insidious drug like Visiondust. Infusing that stuff into unsuspecting colonies would allow his privateers to swoop in and pillage whatever they liked.

As Gage accessed the links Yawakani had set up for him, he thought back to the awful government experiment that had put implants in the heads of those new ensigns. All twelve of those recruits had received combat enhancement implants that were to be tested without their knowledge. Sayre still carried his combat enhancement—and he was betting Dale Faxon did, too. That device had been lodged somewhere in Sayre's brain for years, doing who knew what kind of harm. The guilt burned in his stomach.

Looking through the *Magellan's* records, Gage studied records for all *Magellan* personnel. Sayre had finished flight school at twenty-three and was assigned to the *Augustine*. He'd been a little older than many of the ensigns and it showed in his maturity.

If Park had an implant, Gage could tie him to the *Augustine* and Faxon. It would be all the proof that Gage needed. A calibrated scan would reveal the device and it would place Park on the *Augustine* that night. Combined with the matching records and string of aliases, it would be enough to convict Dale Faxon.

The Faxons would be finished.

Gage worked feverishly to capture data into a file. When he finally gathered everything, he mailed the file to his office at the Lunar Colony and labeled it urgent. If the message arrived, his administrative assistant would process the message immediately. If it ever arrived at all. At this moment, he was certain about nothing. For now, he needed to alert the *Magellan* crew. They had to know that Dale Park was dangerous.

———

GAGE GRABBED a datapad and displayed a summary of the data. With it in hand, he hurried down to the infirmary. Taka Yawakani sat on the floor stowing the cleaned and sanitized instruments and the meager remains of their supplies.

"Taka!" he called.

Taka leaned out from the cabinet door. "Yes, sir?"

"Could I speak with you for a moment?"

She stood up, brushing off her knees, and walked over to him.

"Did you find what you were looking for, sir?"

He nodded. "I found one match to Dale Park's medical records in Faxon's computer."

"In Faxon's computer?" she asked, surprised.

"Yes, and it belongs to Dale Faxon. Derek Faxon's son."

Taka's face paled. "Faxon's son? Are you sure?"

"Their records are identical."

She sat down hard on the edge of a sickbed. "What would Faxon gain by having his son aboard the *Magellan*?"

"A way to get rid of the *Magellan* before it ever arrived. With him safely in an escape pod, no one would know what happened to the ship."

Her gaze jerked up from the floor and she stared at Gage. "Of course! The first engine room explosion."

Gage nodded. "Thanks to Sayre's meddling, he rerouted part of the overload. That caused a smaller explosion than intended, one that only destroyed the main engine instead of the entire ship. Then Dale set another charge to destroy the ship. Sayre must be poking his nose in the wrong places. Must have gotten Faxon nervous enough to make sure we couldn't leave the planet with our suspicions." He sighed. "Or our lives."

"Unless Kuruk can perform miracles," said Taka, "the only way off this planet now is by rescue ship."

"Taka!" shouted Kuruk from the hallway.

"In here, Kuruk!"

The Vardissian rushed into the infirmary. "Satlinks are down again. We can't send any more transmissions."

"How convenient," Taka muttered, and hurried over to the computer. She typed in a bunch of commands. "Medlinks are down, too." She turned around, her face pale. "What do we do now?"

Gage moved toward the computer. "He's completely cut us off now. What we have to do is gather hard evidence against Faxon to convict him of drug-running and murder."

"Where's Park?" Taka asked suddenly.

"He went with Mr. Shahir," said Kuruk.

"Went where?" Gage demanded.

"Into the moors. To look for Captain Sayre. Mr. Shahir was so worried."

Taka spun Kuruk around. "Tell me everything you heard, Kuruk. Everything!" She cast a frightened look at Gage.

"Mr. Shahir was asking me about scanning equipment and being able to scan for Captain Sayre. Park spoke up, telling Mr. Shahir that Faxon had left one of the boats behind. He said he'd be happy to go out with him to search."

"We've got to find Sanji, sir! There's no telling what Faxon or Park might do to him." She sighed. "Why would Faxon want Sanji?"

Gage's brow furrowed. What reason would Faxon possibly have for taking Shahir? Then he knew. "To use him as leverage against Sayre."

"You think Faxon's got Sayre?"

"I'm certain of it," he answered, and turned to Kuruk. "Kuruk, I'm going to need a special type of scanner."

Kuruk nodded. "If you give me the proper data, I can put together something for you."

"Taka, gather together some gear—including weapons. Kuruk, come with me."

Taka hurried out the door toward the storage bins, and Gage, with Kuruk in tow, moved toward his quarters.

TWENTY-THREE

MIDNIGHT CREPT like death into the harvesting camp. Startled awake by a frightened cry, Quinn jerked up from the dirt. He rubbed his eyes as the pen's gate squeaked open, two of the First Contact team members in the threshold, rifles slung over their shoulders. He recognized the first one immediately—Ian Veider. Quinn glared at him. The other man, thin and short, poked one of the Shikari's with the barrel.

"Get up," he snapped, poking until a shrill yelp punctured the stillness. "I said get up."

Faxon sauntered over to the pen and watched from the gate. With his hands clasped behind his back, he surveyed them, an amused smile on his face.

"I'll take three from this pen."

Sayre rose on his hands and scowled at Faxon. The guy probably knew exactly how many shifts it would take before he died out there. He rubbed his hand across his dry mouth, the memory of Tarateal half-dead in his arms cutting through him. His chest ached. If he could have one thing before he died, he wanted five minutes alone with Faxon.

The shorter man displayed a cowering Shikari to Faxon, who nodded his approval as if he had just chosen a ripe melon from the market. As the shorter man led the trembling Shikari out the pen, Faxon pointed at Peetrek.

"You'll add this one to the detail as well."

"The priest?" mumbled the man.

"And Sayre."

"Sayre?"

Faxon whirled around. "What are you, a damned parrot? You heard me. The priest and Sayre. Don't make me say it again or you'll be the seventh member of this harvest detail."

Nodding quickly, the man scurried toward Peetrek and yanked him to his feet. Peetrek displayed no fear as he endured the man's rough handling and joined his terrified kinsman outside the pen.

Reluctantly, Veider approached Quinn, a hand resting against the stock of his rifle. When Veider was in front of him, Quinn knocked him off his feet with a kick to the shins. As Veider hit the dirt, Quinn stripped the rifle from him and wheeled, hoping to squeeze off a shot at Faxon. A rifle butt slammed into his shoulder. He crumpled under the blow, dazed. He glanced up, seeing Faxon's leering face wavering above him, rifle in hand. Veider ripped the rifle from his hands and kicked him in the side. Quinn stifled a cry of pain as he struggled to his knees.

"Afraid of the Chiriga, Sayre?" Faxon needled.

"No," he snarled. "I didn't want to lose the opportunity to blow your head off your shoulders—like you did to my wife."

Veider winced. Faxon's mouth twitched as puzzlement twisted his features. Sayre smiled grimly. The man no doubt wondered how he knew that, and he'd be damned if he'd give that bastard even a moment's peace of mind. Somehow, Faxon would pay for what he did to the Shikari's and his own kind.

"Get him out there—now!"

The shorter man headed into the pen behind Veider, and both men dragged out Quinn. They shoved him behind Peetrek and marched them into line with three other prisoners, who headed out of the gates toward the marshlands. Faxon and the others followed behind in a small, slow-moving terrain vehicle. Quinn trekked through calf-deep mud and water, through ragged grasses, and across muddy footpaths until the detail reached a hazy grove of trees. Quinn felt a cold chill shiver through him. This encounter with the Chirigas would not be like the one in the breeding grounds.

Faxon climbed out of the vehicle and stepped in front of it, the frightened detail at least a meter away. Faxon glared at Quinn, who stood at the end of the line.

"Sayre!" he shouted. "Now would be a good time to reveal the breeding grounds' location. It would save your Shikari *friends* a lot of pain."

"Go to hell, Faxon. You know I'll never tell you."

"Have it your way, Sayre." He motioned to one of the team members, who nudged the detail forward.

Already, Quinn heard the fierce rattle emanating from the grove. It was an angry rattle that made his skin crawl. One of the Shikari's shrieked and bolted down the path. The shorter man shouted for him to stop, but Faxon raised his rifle and fired off two short bursts to the native's chest. The Shikari collapsed on the pathway in front of him, the scent of burned hide making Quinn sick.

He turned away. Images of Roberts gasping for breath in his arms ran over and over behind his eyes. Faxon blithely shouldered his rifle and stepped over the body.

"One last chance, Sayre," said Faxon as he walked past the detail to stand in front of it. "All I want is the location of the breeding grounds. Tell me that and all of you can go free."

Sayre looked him in the eye and scowled.

"No?" Faxon smiled and let his gaze wander to the three Chiriga plants clustered ahead, the rattle rising to a frenzied pitch. "Then let the games begin."

The First Contact team members poked Quinn in the back with a rifle and he reluctantly walked toward the grove. He knew that the

Shikari's had never seen the Chirigas so enraged before. Even Peetrek seemed frightened and unwilling to proceed. It took a lot of prodding to get them within viewing distance of the Chirigas. They looked like Hydras with their furiously waving blossoms, rattling vines, and rustling leaves. Quinn had no wish to approach them, but he knew that Faxon would force each of them at rifle point.

The well-guarded pollen meant disaster for his world. If he refused to harvest it, would Faxon back down? The man desperately wanted the location of the breeding grounds. Knowing that Quinn had the answer annoyed Faxon, and Faxon would keep him alive until he got that answer. Maybe that would keep all of them safe until the *Magellan* could rescue them? He knew that Sanji would be doing something about this from his end. If he could stall long enough, maybe they'd survive?

But there would be no more stalling.

The first Shikari who approached the Chirigas discovered what lay beneath those rustling purple leaves. Barbed vines shot forward like tentacles and clamped around the native's ankles. He screamed, fighting against the powerful vines as they dragged him toward the leaves. Quinn glanced over at Faxon. The man's eyes were glazed with intrigue, his gaze locked on the Chirigas.

Quinn cringed. Faxon was enjoying this!

He scanned the ground for a weapon—a rock—anything. A tree branch lay nearby in the grass. Scooping it from the ground, Quinn rushed the Chirigas. He slammed the stick against one of the rattling vines, pounding it until it released the shrieking Shikari.

A laser blast exploded into the air, but Quinn ignored it, instead pummeling the other vine until it too shrank away from the man. As soon as the last vine recoiled, Quinn dragged the convulsing native to a safe distance. Already, red rings had stained the Shikari's thick hide.

"Sayre!"

He turned and the air exploded from his lungs as Faxon's rifle butt ground into his stomach. He collapsed, his stomach heaving until blood trickled from his mouth.

"This isn't a team effort," Faxon said with a growl. "If you don't want to watch them die, then you'll tell me the location of the breeding grounds." He swept a hand toward the Shikari's. "They would die before they told me anything, and when most of them go out there, they don't come back again, Sayre. I'll find the grounds eventually, so save some lives and tell me what I want to know."

"I'd rather die than help you with anything, Faxon."

Faxon shoved him backward into the dirt. "You'll tell me, Sayre. I'll make you tell me." He motioned for the next Shikari to approach the Chirigas.

By the time the moons had sunk behind the moors, only Quinn and Peetrek remained. Quinn knew it was intentional, but he was too sick inside to care. Peetrek would die tomorrow unless he figured out a way to stop it. For tonight, though, he could do nothing.

His body ached as Faxon marched him and Peetrek all the way back to the camp. By the time he reached the pen, his body was collapsing. He crumpled just inside the gate, the dirt cold beneath him, and his eyes closed.

Shortly before sunrise, Quinn walked out of his body.

He walked through the pen, the familiar trappings fading into dreamscape and then blurring into astral. Stars dotted the blackness, paving his path as he called out to Peetrek. Abruptly the priest appeared beside him, on hands and knees, the mask shattered on the starry path. Shards of turquoise and yellow wood lay everywhere, Peetrek's raspy cry cutting through him. His face was long and angled, gentle equine-like features taut with distress.

"Peetrek," Quinn cried, and dropped beside him. "What's happened?"

"The sacred mask has shattered, Quinn Sayre," said Peetrek, his back still to Quinn. "What shatters in astral is a message to the physical. I fear it means I will die tonight. I do not want to die and leave my shadow soul to walk the land."

Quinn laid a hand against Peetrek's trembling shoulder. "You can't know that, Peetrek. And I thought only men like Faxon had shadow souls."

"No, Quinn Sayre, all of us have both. What the *milakos* are forcing us to do is wrong and clouds our eye souls. That will allow our shadow souls to slip free when we die. I cursed Faxon's name for what he has done to my people and the Chiriga. His shadow soul will slip free when he dies, too."

Peetrek rose from the ground, turning to face Quinn. For the first time, Quinn saw into Peetrek's eyes. Brilliant teal irises gazed back at him with determination, equine face animated with anger. His nostrils flared as he gripped Quinn's arms. "You must not tell Faxon where to find the breeding grounds, Quinn Sayre. Even if it means the roaming of your shadow soul, you must not tell."

"I won't, Peetrek, I won't. I give you my word."

A brightness appeared in Peetrek's eyes. "I was not wrong about you. My people will see that you are not milako. We may both die tomorrow, Quinn Sayre. I regret that."

Quinn winked at him. "Maybe we can take Faxon with us?"

Abruptly, Quinn felt the weariness in his body. He let himself sink through the pathway of stars, Peetrek's form fading into the dreamscape. When the trappings of the harvesting camp materialized again, Quinn stepped back through the gate and into his exhausted frame sprawled on the ground.

He felt nothing until one of the First Contact team dug the toe of his boot into his rib cage and kicked. Fire swelled through his torso and he fought his exhaustion to rise. They had already moved Peetrek outside the pen and into the line of waiting Shikari's. What Quinn wasn't prepared for was the sight of Sanji Shahir leading the way. He turned his bruised, bloodied face toward Quinn in relief.

"Quinn! They said you were alive, but I did not believe them," said Sanji, his voice muffled by the swollen lip. "We've been so worried."

"Sanji, what are you doing here?" Quinn saw Faxon approach

from the storage building, a curt smile on his face. Quinn wanted to smear that smug little smile all over the ground.

"My son brought him here."

Dale Park stepped out of the storage building and moved toward the pen.

"Park! What the hell's going on?"

Faxon laughed. "Park, Faxon, Bridges—they're all the same really."

Quinn shook his head. "What are you talking about?"

"It appears that my son has been causing you trouble for a long time, Sayre."

"Make some sense!" Quinn shouted.

"I'm the one who called in the privateers that night aboard the *Augustine*, Sayre," said Park, his voice loud and smug. "I'd already stolen someone's access code and was prepared to enter it into the comm board, but some dolt had already entered his code and left his post. You made it too easy, Sayre." Park laughed, the sound shrill.

Quinn's rage ignited and he lunged for Park, but Peetrek held him back. Quinn turned to Sanji. "Sanji, why? Why'd you let him con you into coming out here?"

Sanji bowed his head. "I was afraid something had happened to you."

Faxon grinned. "All Dale had to do was tell Shahir you were in trouble and he willingly accompanied him here. I wanted him to bring that mouse-of-a-medtech instead since you've obviously fallen for her. Too bad there was nothing to bring back."

Quinn's insides screamed. "You bastard!" He lunged at Faxon. When his fist connected with flesh, he tore and gouged until the others finally jerked him back again.

"I think Roberts would have been better, but all we have is Mr. Shahir. We'll make do." Faxon motioned toward the detail leader, who started the line of prisoners moving over the hill. He turned to Dale. "Son, you wait here. We won't be long." He patted the young man on the shoulder. "Good work."

Faxon climbed into the front of the terrain vehicle. In moments, the vehicle whirred softly behind them.

All Quinn could think of now was Roberts. What had those bastards done to her? He clenched his hands into fists. If she was dead, he'd kill Faxon slowly. Very slowly. He squeezed his eyes closed.

Then he realized that if Faxon brought Sanji out here, that meant he couldn't get to Roberts. She'd escaped him. Faxon would do anything to make him talk—including lying about Roberts. He wouldn't fall for his lies. She'd be there waiting for him when he and Sanji got out of this mess.

Quinn winced as he passed the shallow grave of the Shikari's killed yesterday. The detail slowed to a stop near the Chiriga grove. Flickers of pale yellow lit the surrounding trees that twinkled as if filled with fireflies. And that horrible rattling had begun.

Faxon parked his vehicle and climbed out. Without pausing, Faxon sent the first Shikari into the grove. She never came back. Sanji's face paled at the sight of the Chirigas. Quinn slipped through the line until he was standing behind Sanji.

"Don't worry, Sanj. I'm right beside you. You won't die on my shift."

Sanji set his jaw. "I hope you are right, Quinn. We've already lost Sheryl. There was an accident after you left."

"What? Sanji, no—"

"Planning to escape, Sayre," Faxon hissed, and moved toward him. "I suppose Mr. Shahir has informed you that your pilot was killed. You see, there was a little adjustment problem aboard the *Magellan*. A minor overload."

"Is he lying, Sanji?"

"No, Quinn. All of it is true." He glared. "And Dale Faxon set all the blasts."

Quinn gripped his arms. "Roberts? Where is she?"

"Unknown. She slipped out to search for you and never came back."

His heart wrenched. Dammit, Faxon hadn't been lying about Roberts either. He turned his heated gaze back to Faxon.

"I'd think very carefully about what you do next, Sayre," said Faxon. "You don't want your best friend to die, too, do you? You seem to have a problem with people around you dying." He leaned against his vehicle, smirking, and motioned for another Shikari to be sent into the grove.

Wincing, Quinn watched as the Shikari edged toward the nearest Chiriga, a small pail in hand. Spiked vines whipped back and forth across the ground, daring anyone to approach. The Shikari fumbled for a stick and poked the vines out of his way as he hurried around to the opposite side, rushing toward the rotting tree trunk near the Chiriga. Vines darted out from the purple leaves and slashed at the thin legs, but the Shikari reached the tree. He stood there, trying to catch his breath, but the sting of barbs clamping around his thigh forced him to the ground.

Clumsily, the Shikari stabbed at the vine and punctured it until a clear fluid bubbled up. The barbed thing fell away as three more vines wriggled toward him. The Shikari threw himself backward and crawled away from the plant. When he had regained his strength, the Shikari fought off the vines long enough to scoop pollen from a low-hanging blossom. He returned victorious to the line of prisoners.

"Damn your wife, Sayre!" Faxon shouted. "She tampered with the seedlings in this grove. Made them so vicious that no one can get near them. She did that to all the closest groves, but when I obtain the breeding grounds, this strain will be destroyed."

Sayre laughed. Larena had gotten the upper hand on Faxon after all.

"Send in Shahir," Faxon ordered, his gaze not leaving Quinn's face.

Quinn stopped laughing, and his face contorted as he watched them shove Sanji toward the writhing plant. He had to do something or Sanji would die.

The comm specialist fought their prodding, but was unable to stop them from moving him closer to the plants. A vine zipped across the ground and wrapped around Sanji's left ankle. The pail fell from his hands as he slammed against the ground. Spike after spike drove into his thigh and he screamed. Slowly, the vine dragged him across the ground. Sanji clawed at the grass and kicked at the vine, trying to escape, but he was losing.

Quinn rushed toward him, but Faxon tripped him. One of the team members pressed the barrel of a rifle to his temple.

He'd made a promise not to tell Faxon. Quinn's whole body shook, watching Sanji dragged nearer to the Chiriga. He promised Peetrek...but he couldn't let Sanji die. He couldn't.

"Stop it, Faxon! Stop it!"

"Only for the location, Sayre. That was the deal."

Quinn looked away from Peetrek. "All right! Just let Sanji go!"

Faxon fired a blast toward the Chiriga. Instantly, the vines retracted, releasing Sanji. Quinn scrambled to his feet and rushed forward, pulling the bleeding man out of the Chiriga's reach. Sanji was in shock, eyes staring straight ahead, skin clammy.

Quinn clutched his arms. "C'mon, Sanj, you've gotta pull through, buddy. Hang on, okay? Hang on."

Through his labored breathing, Sanji muttered, "I'll try."

Faxon moved the detail back toward the path. As Peetrek passed Quinn, he spit on the ground at Quinn's feet. "You milako after all."

Two of the First Contact team members picked Sanji up from the ground and carried him to the terrain vehicle. Quinn rode beside the badly injured man, trying to figure a way out. He knew he couldn't reveal the breeding grounds, but he couldn't sit back and watch Sanji die either. There had to be some middle ground and it was up to him to find it. Quickly.

"I'll have to show you the location of the breeding grounds," Quinn muttered to Faxon as the vehicle lurched forward. "It's too complicated to explain."

Faxon turned. "Of course, you will. And Mr. Shahir will accompany us. If you are lying, he'll be killed on the spot. I told you to proceed carefully, Sayre, and I meant it. We leave tomorrow afternoon. I want to reach the grounds by nightfall."

"Why nightfall?" Quinn asked.

"The Chirigas are more docile at night."

When the vehicle reached the camp, Faxon threw Quinn out in front of the pens. Despite his protests, they forced him back into the pen. He pressed his face against the wire frame.

"What about Sanji?" he asked, watching them unload the shivering man from the vehicle.

One of the team members gripped Sanji under the arms, the other carrying his legs. Faxon moved toward the nearest building. He opened the door for the men to carry Sanji inside.

"My team will treat him inside," Faxon announced. "And he'll be kept under armed guard. That way, you won't think about escaping in the wee hours of the morning. Sleep well, Sayre."

Sick, Quinn slid down the wire fence and collapsed in the corner. Sanji could still die, and now Peetrek thought Quinn was a traitor.

How could he ever make any of this right again?

He glanced over at Peetrek. The masked priest kept his body turned away from Quinn. Quinn couldn't blame him, but he had to stall Faxon for time. Now, he'd lost an ally. Quinn thrust his head in his hands and waited for morning.

TWENTY-FOUR

SHORTLY BEFORE SUNRISE, Tarateal reached the harvesting camp. Nuriel led her there and waited in a rowboat. Cloaked in darkness, Tarateal crept down the hillside toward the camp. None of Faxon's people were visible. At first, she thought it was a trap, but after watching for some time, she realized that Faxon thought everything was secure. The camp was dark, only Nearra's two moons providing blue slivers of light.

Moving as silently as possible, she crept behind a line of brush parallel to the pens. She peered into each wire pen until she finally saw Sayre curled up against the fence, eyes closed, face haggard.

Her heart hammered against her chest. Sayre! She longed to go to him. She crawled toward the fence and reached through, shaking his shoulder. Slowly, his eyes rolled open.

For a moment, he just gawked at her, his eyes turning watery, his mouth gaping, but then he grabbed her hands and pressed them to his lips, kissing them.

"Roberts, you're alive!" His voice cracked. "Oh, God, I thought I'd lost you. Faxon said you were dead."

She sighed. There was no telling what lies Faxon had told him.

"That filthy liar tried to kill me," she whispered, "but I got away. Sayre, I've been looking for you everywhere. When Lomasi told me you'd been captured, I didn't know what to do!"

"Lomasi?"

"One of the Shikari's. Listen, we don't have much time." She let go of his hands and reached into the pouch at her side. From it, she produced a rusty pair of wire cutters. "Nuriel is waiting nearby in a boat. Once you're out, we can release Peetrek."

Sayre bowed his head. "It's too late. Faxon took Sanji hostage."

"No! Oh, Sayre, how'd he get Sanji?"

"Dale Park lured him out here. The little creep is really Faxon's son."

Tarateal gaped at him. "What? His son?"

Sayre nodded. "When he couldn't destroy my crew, he lured Sanji out here. Probably told him I was out here dying. You know Sanji. The man worries about me like I was his kid brother. He was probably frantic—never even suspected it was a trap. Sanji's a much better judge of character than this. Dale must have been very convincing."

Tarateal gazed around the camp, wondering where Faxon would be holding the comm specialist. "Where did they take him, Sayre?"

He pointed toward the dark building across from the pen. "In there. He's being well-guarded—in case I decide to try something. If I don't lead him to the breeding grounds tomorrow night, he'll kill Sanji. He already tried once to feed Sanj to the Chirigas."

"Faxon can't destroy those breeding grounds," she whispered, her voice shrill. "If he destroys the breeding grounds, he'll destroy the ecological balance here. The moor poisons would kill everything. You can't take him there."

"Don't you think I know that? But I don't know how to get out of it without killing Sanji in the process." He gripped her arms again. "I can't let him die, Tarateal. I can't!"

She smiled when he called her Tarateal instead of Roberts. She hadn't heard him say her name in a long time. "It's okay," she murmured. "We'll free him, Quinn. We'll free him."

She pulled his shaking hands to her mouth and gently kissed the bruised, cut fingers. Sayre leaned forward and kissed her through the fence. She pressed her face against the fence, wanting desperately to be in his arms. Letting his hands slip from hers, she closed her eyes as his fingers traced the outline of her chin and neck. He stroked her hair.

"I think I love you, Sayre," she murmured.

He drew back, surprise in his smoldering gaze. "Damn. What I would've given to hear that on Salice Minor. You know I loved you back then, but you'd never say it back to me. Because you couldn't see past the Rim. What happened to us, Tarateal?"

She bowed her head, embarrassed. He didn't feel the same anymore.

Gently, he reached out and lifted her chin. "Being here with you now, I discovered that I love you more than I ever did on Salice Minor."

Her eyes welled with tears. She'd have given up twenty assignments on Earth to hear him say that. Through the fence, she reached for him again, just needing to feel him beside her. He pressed his face against hers, the cold metal separating her from his warm skin.

Finally, she sat up. "If we're ever going to do anything about this, we're going to have to take care of Faxon first."

"Glad you agree," he answered, "because I have a plan. It's flimsy, but it's the only way to stop him."

She sat back on her haunches and nodded for him to continue.

"If I can lure Faxon close enough to the Chirigas in the breeding grounds, maybe I can let them take care of Faxon. While I have Faxon busy, you can free Sanji and Peetrek. Unfortunately, getting him that close might get me killed, too."

She sighed. That wasn't a very good plan. "Sayre, that's not exactly what I was hoping for. Isn't there something else we can try? A diversion? Anything?"

He was silent for a moment, his gaze drifting to the ground. Finally, he looked up, hopeful. "You have a better plan?"

"No," she answered finally.

"The only option we have is to take Faxon into a Chiriga grove," said Sayre, sighing, "but it has to be the breeding grounds."

"Why?"

"Because those Chirigas hate the First Contact team, especially Faxon, but they know me. I—uh—spent a little time there. They might spare me."

She studied his eyes, how their honeyed hue burned in the moons' light. He knew he was risking his life. But Lomasi said the light net would keep Sayre's eye soul in his body. Still, Sayre was right. Even she knew that forcing Faxon to face the Chirigas was the only way. Maybe the light net would save Sayre?

"All right," said Tarateal. "I don't want to risk your life, but the grounds are our only chance." She smiled. "I have a little ammunition to play with, too, but in order to use it, we'll need to convince Faxon that the light nets let him communicate with the Chirigas."

Sayre waved a hand at her. "Wait a minute, wait a minute—what light nets?"

"The Chirigas spin them. They heal wounds and let others communicate with them. It's incredible, Sayre. Just incredible!"

Sayre leaned against the fence again, his face wrinkling in thought. "Then what?"

She rose on her knees, moving closer to him again. "After you demonstrate a light net, you must communicate the danger to the Chirigas. Most likely, they'll lash out at both of you, but the extra light net that I carry might prevent you from dying."

He gazed up at her, a sadness she hadn't seen since he'd learned about his wife's death. "Whatever happens," he said softly, urgently, "you and I have to stay alive. Do you hear me?"

She nodded.

"I know what I lost on Salice Minor now, but you and I have a second chance, Tarateal—I can't give that up. Not twice."

What if he died? She shivered. Her stomach sank into her knees and the tears stung her eyes.

"I won't throw away what we have here." He slid closer to her and gripped her shoulders. She felt his hot breath on her face. "No matter what, we have to come out of this thing alive." He reached up and cupped her chin in his hand. "Tarateal, promise me that you'll hang on, that you'll be there when this mission is over. Promise me. But if something happens and we're not together, you'll meet me on Salice Minor."

"At the Silver Orca Pub?" she asked in a small voice.

"Yeah," he said, laughing nervously, "our first date. I remember."

Tears slid down her face and he wiped them away with his index finger.

"I promise, Quinn," she said, and leaned toward him again.

"No matter what happens, go there and I'll find you," he said. "Wherever you are, I'll find you again."

She kissed him urgently on the lips. His touch simmered across her skin.

When she saw a light snap on in one of the nearby windows, she knew it was time to leave. Reluctantly, she let him go.

"I'll wait for you at the breeding grounds. Stall here as long as you can. Remember, you need to convince Faxon that he can communicate with the Chirigas using the light nets." She moved toward the hillside, and Sayre followed inside the pen, hurrying along the back of it.

"Roberts, how do I do that?"

"Chirigas group in threes," she answered in a half-whisper. "Between the grouping will be a light net. Place your hand on the light net and feel the vibrations. When you touch it, you'll know what to do. You'll feel it, Sayre."

"Where will you be?"

She smiled. "Right at your side. I'll make sure you come out of that grove alive."

"Be careful, Roberts," he called. "You're not leaving this planet without me."

"Not a chance, Sayre," she answered, and hurried up the hill toward the footpath.

TARATEAL FOLLOWED the ruts left by some sort of terrain vehicle. They gouged into the grasslands and snaked into the moors. When she found the path leading back to Nuriel's rowboat, she abandoned the ruts and hurried toward the shoreline. Nuriel stood up when he saw her approach.

"Where are they?" he demanded.

"There's a problem, Nuriel," she said, and climbed into the boat. "Faxon has taken one of Sayre's crew hostage. If Sayre doesn't lead Faxon to the breeding grounds, then he'll kill Sanji."

"No," Nuriel growled. "Quinn Sayre will kill all of us if he takes Faxon to our sacred grounds!"

"Listen to me!" she shouted above his angry voice. "We have a plan. By using the light nets, the Chirigas can see a person's eye soul, right?"

Nuriel snapped his head up.

"Sayre will communicate with the Chirigas first and receive pollen. This will tempt Faxon into trying to communicate with them. When he tries to communicate through a light net, the Chirigas will sense his shadow soul."

"And kill him," said Nuriel. "This plan good. Perhaps good Chiriga face *milakos*?"

She settled down into the boat as Nuriel swiveled the oars into the black water. "You and I will be nearby. You'll rescue Peetrek and Sanji, and I'll stand by with a light net in case the Chirigas attack Sayre."

"We will journey to the sacred Shikari lands and await the

milakos. But be careful, Tarateal Roberts. A shadow soul separated from its body is a dangerous thing. It can take your eye soul and your body if it so desires. Such is the curse that Faxon carries. Stay far away from Faxon when he dies."

The thought of taking another life made her queasy. Even though Faxon killed seven of his own crew and over a dozen Shikari's—and now, one of the *Magellan* crew. Still, she wished there was another way. She hated sending Sayre into the trap alongside Faxon. What if something went wrong? She couldn't lose him again.

She wouldn't.

Nuriel's muscles tensed as he dug the oars into the water. "Journey to sacred grounds complicated. Waters hide much. How Quinn Sayre find it?"

Tarateal wondered how Sayre found the grounds. He couldn't have gotten lucky. Perhaps his wife wrote down the route and he stumbled on it? If so, he probably had it mapped out somehow.

"He'll get through," she answered, and gazed out at the grey haze settling over top of the blackness.

Morning would come soon. And hopefully an end to Faxon's grip on the Shikari's. She hoped that when it was all over, the government would label Nearra a critical sanctuary. That would keep out everyone who didn't receive advanced clearance from the government. When she and Sayre got finished with him, that label would also keep out Faxon, if he managed to survive. She hoped to see him convicted of murder and spending the rest of his days in a mining prison like Arnstead. He deserved no less than that.

"We stop at Haven so I speak to my people...and Peetrek. To know what we do."

Tarateal frowned. "Haven?"

"Another sacred place. You see."

Tarateal leaned back and watched the slave camp slip away on the brightening horizon. Sayre would be okay. She'd see to it.

WHEN NURIEL EDGED the boat toward the cay ahead, Tarateal remembered the onyx square inside the stone building. When the boat nudged the blue-black soil, Nuriel hopped out and tied the boat onto one of the broken columns. Tarateal followed him down the path and into the dark building. He passed through the outer chamber and into the inner chamber with the onyx square. Nuriel faced the onyx square in silence, his back to her. After a few moments of bowed head and mumbled words, Nuriel slipped his hand into the pollen pouch at his side and scooped out a handful. He pressed the powder to his face and inhaled sharply. His whole body jolted, muscles rippling and tensing. With a final shudder, he fell forward, hands pressed against the square.

Tarateal stepped away as Nuriel's body lurched forward and passed through the onyx square.

"Nuriel?" she called.

Lightly, she touched the onyx square, which remained rigid to her touch.

Anxious, she paced around the interior chamber, watching the sunlight stream into the outer chamber. Still, Nuriel remained beyond the square. She waited for a while and finally wandered outside to wait in the boat. The sun slipped slowly across the sky. When it gleamed directly overhead, Nuriel emerged from the building. His chestnut hide had paled, almost tinged grey. She rushed over to him and steered him into the boat. He collapsed, draping himself over the seat.

"Nuriel, what happened?"

"Walking astral new for me—still hurted. Peetrek understand. Help Quinn Sayre lead Faxon to Chirigas. When time, he steer Sanji Shahir for us."

"You should rest a while," she said, and picked up the oars. "I'll row and you direct." Nuriel snorted and started to rise, but she pressed him back against the seat. He resisted for a moment, but finally gave in to her insistence.

"Follow cay...away from light."

She nodded and pumped the oars into the water. The wood rasped her palms with every stroke. She ignored the burning, concentrating on the murky sky ahead. The trees seemed darker and wilder in this direction, the air misty and the grass thicker. Even the bird cries and other creatures sounded more ominous the farther away she moved from Haven.

Somewhere off toward sunrise, Faxon was probably interrogating Sayre for the breeding grounds' location. They were probably already gearing up for the journey. She needed to hurry.

NURIEL'S DIRECTIONS WERE PRECISE, and she found the boat moving effortlessly from causeway to causeway. Eventually, the tall trees formed a ceiling overhead, obscuring the sun with mist and branches. She felt the temperature change, but the heat from rowing kept her from feeling cold. Even in the twisting channels that seemed to lead nowhere, she felt warm and safe. The air smelled clean and cool.

Finally, they reached the mouth of the channel, marked by sharp vines and a boulder. Nuriel motioned her forward. She complied, whipping the oars through the water. The boat squeezed past and glided toward a small bay ahead.

"We here, Tarateal Roberts," said Nuriel.

He sat up as the boat's prow slid into the soft ground. She climbed out, her arms burning and rubbery, and tied the boat off on a tree. Her palms and fingers burned, blistered from the rough wood.

Nuriel dragged the boat into the brush and covered it. When the boat was hidden, he led her down a footpath that widened into a larger path. Up ahead stood a wooden gate. It was propped open. She heard the bass hum as they moved closer.

Chirigas.

"Walk slow. Certain, Tarateal Roberts," said Nuriel. "They not fear Shikari's, but *milakos* make them uneasy."

She nodded and continued her pace behind him. In the gate's threshold, she marveled at all the Chiriga groupings, but the first grouping stood out. A fourth Chiriga plant, much smaller than the rest, undulated behind the other three.

"There are four here," she said in a soft voice. "Is that typical?"

Nuriel approached the grouping cautiously and gazed at the fourth plant. After studying them for a moment, he turned back to her. "A grouping of four is unusual, but not unlikely." He pointed toward the light net in the second grouping. "Approach with care and request harvest the light net."

She nodded, and with determined but careful steps, she approached the second grouping. Almost instantly, the rattling began. She tried not to let the sound unnerve her and continued her pace. The Chiriga vines skittered past her feet, brushing over her boots. She was careful not to step on them, realizing that she was being summed up. Finally, she paused in front of the light net that stretched and glimmered between the grouping. A vine slid around her shoulders, winding around her waist and down to her legs. It slipped to her ankles and withdrew. When the vine left her body, her muscles relaxed. The light net pulsed. She reached out to it.

In her mind, she spoke words of friendship and of a need to heal. She sent the word *help* soaring through her thoughts and watched the ripple it cast roll across the light net. The low-pitched hum began, trembling up through her feet and into her shoulders. She matched the sound until it died away, allowing her to retrieve the light net.

"Remember, Tarateal Roberts," said Nuriel, " light net fade with sun's rise. Use before then."

She nodded and folded it gently. "Now what?"

He motioned her behind the first grouping of Chirigas. A thick clump of brush stood a short distance from the grouping. "We hide here. Wait *milakos.*"

Her heart sank as she slipped behind the brush and sat down. All she could do now was wait. She had no idea what would happen when Faxon arrived.

TWENTY-FIVE

HERDED out of his pen at midmorning, Quinn was forced at rifle point toward the camp building. Inside the sparse, dusty building, Sanji lay on the floor, his wounds bandaged. He rolled onto his side and stared bleary-eyed at Quinn.

"Sleep well, Sayre?" Faxon asked with a grin.

Quinn set his jaw. "What game are we playing now, Faxon?"

Faxon motioned to the crude wooden chair against the wall. When Quinn didn't move toward it, Faxon shoved him forward. "Sit. We need to talk."

"I prefer to stand," he answered.

Faxon nodded at one of his team members, who kicked the legs out from underneath him. He slammed against the floor as a second kick caught him in the gut.

After a moment or two of gasping for air, he could breathe again. He clutched his stomach. It was on fire. Again, Faxon pointed to the chair. It took most of Quinn's restraint to climb into the chair. He glared at Faxon.

"Now then, Sayre," Faxon said, and paced in front of him. "The route to the breeding grounds has eluded my team for months. How is it that you've been here only a short time and you've managed to find it effortlessly?"

"I found it in Larena's things. She knew enough to protect the information so you wouldn't get it."

For a moment, the world exploded into a red haze. When his senses returned, he felt something damp on his face. Blood. Rough wood scraped against his cheeks and he realized that Faxon had kicked him out of the chair. Slowly, he rose from the floor, but two team members grabbed him and shoved him back into the chair.

"Now, Sayre, you're going to give me that route."

He shook his head. "All I can do is show you the way. Larena's e-planner was lost in the moors thanks to you and your goons."

Faxon slammed his fist into Quinn's face. He felt blood spray. Pain surged into an intense ache. His swollen lip throbbed. Faxon grabbed him by the shirt and twisted until he felt the air recede.

"I'm only going to say this once, so you'd better hear me the first time. If you make one wrong move, even as an accident, I'll blast Shahir right in front of your eyes. One stupid mistake, Sayre, and Shahir is ashes. Do you understand me?"

Quinn nodded.

Smiling, Faxon released him.

Bastard thought he was in control of everything, that he'd won. In a short while, Faxon's control would be in *his* hands. He counted the moments.

"All right, Sayre, we're taking along your little Shikari friend, too. In case you get us lost. It's your job to get us to the breeding grounds. If you don't, Shahir and the priest will be killed." He turned to his team members. "Prepare the supplies and pull out the priest. Take him and Shahir to the boat. Sayre and I will be waiting."

Helpless, Quinn watched them lift Sanji from the mat and walk him outside the building. Then they motioned Quinn outside. His steps were shaky and he hurt with every step. He paused to fight down a wave of nausea. Faxon immediately drew his laser pistol and ground it into his back.

"Move, Sayre, and don't be stupid."

Quinn walked out the door and plodded toward the camp gates, the barrel of the pistol painful against his spine. Faxon forced him onto the path created by Faxon's terrain vehicle. Quinn stumbled over the muddy ruts until the shoreline bled into the grass. He walked across the spongy ground and toward a small white boat tethered to some brush. Faxon pressed him toward the ladder and into the boat. Once aboard, he was shoved into a seat and his right wrist was tied to the rigging.

In a short time, three of Faxon's team members and Dale Park arrived at the boat. Dale carried supplies while the other three led Sanji and Peetrek toward the boat. Peetrek's mask was dirty and tinged with blood as he climbed into the boat and sat as far away from him as possible.

Quinn winced at Peetrek's distancing. He sighed. To Peetrek, he must look like a traitor. Sanji collapsed in a seat beside him. His stomach burned, the nausea rising in his throat. Must have been the beating he'd taken from Faxon. His stomach lurched and he leaned over the side of the boat, tasting the salty warmth of blood in his mouth. The amara was catching up to him. He spat out the blood and turned back around.

"Sanj, you look like hell."

"So do you," Sanji answered in a weary voice. "Are they going to kill us?"

Quinn shook his head. "Not until they find the Chiriga breeding grounds." He smiled grimly and patted Sanji on the shoulder. "Don't worry, we're not dead yet. It just feels like it."

QUINN'S DIRECTIONS were sketchy and several times, they got lost. He took a few punches from Faxon before he finally got the route straight. The throbbing in his face and the pounding in his head didn't help to hone his directional skills, but he managed to get them to the channel.

One of the team members shook his head. Quinn scowled. Veider.

"Sir, we'll never get through that channel. Sayre's probably lying, hoping we'll get stuck so he can ambush us."

Angry, Faxon stormed over to Sanji, slid his pistol from its holster, and pressed it to Sanji's temple.

"Is this the correct route, Sayre? If we reach the end of it and there are no breeding grounds, I will shoot Shahir."

Sayre rose to his feet, but the rope binding his wrist prevented him from moving far. "There's a cove at the end of the channel! From the cove, we take a path that leads into the breeding grounds. They can't be seen from the moors."

Faxon's finger moved to the trigger.

"No! I'm telling you the truth, dammit!"

Faxon turned to the man at the helm and motioned him forward.

Quinn's muscles corded. He gritted his teeth as the boat pitched forward. The minutes dragged by as the boat barely squeezed through the channel. Brush scraped the port side. Limbs raked across the stern. Still, Faxon pressed the laser to Sanji's temple. A boulder scoured the side of the boat, but it managed to slip past.

Quinn felt his body go slack, relieved to see the mist-shrouded cove ahead. He nodded toward the cove. "See, I told you it was here."

As one team member secured the boat to a tree, Faxon, Dale, and the other team members herded Quinn, Sanji, and Peetrek out of the boat and onto the sandy, blue-black soil. Quinn rubbed his wrist where the rope had cut him.

Faxon kept a firm grip on Sanji, pistol still pressed against his head, and ordered Sayre in front. He led them down the path, onto a wider path, and finally to the gate.

The rattle of Chirigas made Faxon anxious, but Dale hung back. Faxon released Sanji and shoved past to stand by Sayre.

"It does exist," Faxon half-whispered, his eyes wide.

Quinn wondered if the man had ever seen this many Chirigas in one place.

Faxon's eyes glazed. "All the seeds I'll ever need and more pollen than I dared dream about! We'll have enough to ship out after all."

"If you can extract it," Sayre replied.

"Of course, I can extract it. I'll force those Shikari fools into harvesting it. I have their priest. They won't refuse."

Sayre wanted to pound the life out of Faxon, but he knew the Chirigas would take care of that for him. His job was to get Faxon close enough. Nothing more.

"The Chirigas in the breeding grounds are much stronger than the groves you've dealt with, Faxon." He pointed to the nearest plant. "They'd annihilate the entire tribe and then where would you be?"

Faxon rubbed his chin, his gaze not leaving the Chirigas. Their vines whipped across the ground, yellow blossoms trembling. Quinn felt their rage, but Faxon was too greedy to notice. "Perhaps you're right," Faxon muttered.

"What if I told you there was a better way?"

Faxon turned his gaze to Quinn, his brows furrowing. "Better way? What are you saying?"

Peetrek lunged at Quinn. "*Vishta! Enowah!*"

It took two of the team members to subdue the angry priest. Quinn felt his heart wrench. It was a dirty trick to play on Peetrek, but there was no other way.

Grinning, Faxon put an arm around Quinn's shoulder. He felt his body recoil from the touch. Hands that had dragged Larena out of Haven. Eyes that had leered at her as he threw her to the ground. Fingers that had apathetically pulled the trigger. He wanted to break each one of those fingers off and shove them down Faxon's throat.

"And tell me, Sayre, what better way is there to harvest Chiriga pollen?"

He fought back his revulsion. "By asking for it."

The hair on his neck bristled as Faxon burst into a fit of insane laughter. The Chirigas' rattling intensified into a fevered pitch. "Go ahead, Sayre," he said finally, wiping back tears. "I'd like to see that."

When Faxon let go, Quinn stepped forward, a little afraid to approach them. He knew they sensed Faxon's evil presence, but they had to also sense that he was trying to help them.

"Enowah! Enowah!"

Again, Peetrek's desperate, raspy voice shrieked that agonizing word. It cut through Quinn. Peetrek thought he was selling them out.

The first Chiriga plant lashed out at him with purple vines that sliced gashes into his arms.

He held up a hand. "I won't hurt you. I give you my word."

Again, the vines snapped around him, but they no longer struck his flesh. The Chiriga grouping allowed him to stand close enough to see the glistening light net between them. The entire time he'd spent with them, he'd never seen a light net.

Had his caring for the grove brought them out of a hibernation state?

With slow, careful movements, he stretched his right hand toward the net.

A vine dropped down from the Chiriga to his right and coiled around his palm, the thorns gouging.

He winced and continued his slow movement toward the light net.

"Bosh'natan, Quinn Sayre! *Bosh'natan!"*

The pain and desperation in Peetrek's voice tore through him, but he didn't have a choice. Only by luring Faxon in could he save the grove.

One of the team members slammed a rifle butt into Peetrek's stomach.

Quinn shuddered, his whole body jerking from the strangled sound that bubbled up from Peetrek's throat.

His hand began to shake as he drew it closer to the light net. When his fingers lay against the taut strands, the vine receded. In his mind, he replayed scenes from the harvesting camp, allowing the

Chirigas to feel his pain at watching Shikari's die, his pain at seeing sentient creatures tortured. He let them see Faxon killing Larena and shooting Tarateal.

Then the bass humming began, deeper and more jarring than he remembered.

The vibrations hurt his bones and caused his muscles to ache. It brought tears of pain to his eyes as he fought to maintain contact. The humming turned into a coarse lament as his agony over Larena's betrayal surfaced in a hoarse wail.

His hands trembled, knees quivered. Stomach burned.

From underneath the light net, the new Chiriga plant that Quinn planted slid a thick vine toward him. It coiled around his legs, up around his waist, and across his shoulders.

The contact was comforting, holding him up.

He matched the humming sound, his throat aching. Gold lights danced across the net, rays sliding up and down the strands from every angle. It was a symphony of patterns, parallel strands pulsing, successive cross-strands flashing.

As if someone plucked them to create the music.

Still, the young Chiriga vine held him in place. He maintained the hum and only let it slip away when the vibrations began to dissipate. When the light net returned to its glimmery form, the young Chiriga's vine unfurled and slithered back underneath the net.

Abruptly, the blossom nearest Quinn unfolded, several handfuls of blue pollen dust twinkling inside. Gently, Quinn scooped out the pollen and carried it back to Faxon.

Faxon gaped at Quinn. "How did you do that?"

"I discovered that the light nets allow communication with the Chirigas. That's how the Shikari's serve them. All you have to do is place your hand on the light net and ask for the pollen. After the humming subsides, they offer their pollen."

Peetrek lashed out at Quinn, barely clipping his shoulder. The Shikari fought viciously against his captors, snarling and hissing Shikari words at Quinn and Faxon.

This seemed to delight Faxon.

"Well done, Sayre. It would appear that all I need to harvest their pollen is you."

"What?" His mouth gaped. "You'd risk your entire operation on one man?"

Dammit, that wasn't supposed to happen!

"It appears I have no choice. You've got the touch and I risk nothing. We'll load you up with painkillers and antibiotics to keep you on your feet."

Faxon wasn't stupid. The man had no intentions of going out there, not when he had Quinn to go for him. Dammit! He rubbed his face. How could he tempt Faxon into going himself?

"You could harvest the pollen yourself. All you have to do is touch the light net and ask. Unless you aren't man enough to do it yourself. You don't strike me as someone who'd depend on others for your operation."

Faxon grabbed Quinn's arm. "You're right, Sayre. I wouldn't, but you're going to accompany me out there just the same."

"Don't trust me, Faxon?" he asked with a dangerous grin.

"Not at all," Faxon answered, and shoved Quinn ahead of him into the grove.

The rattle of the Chirigas began again, the sound fierce. It was angrier than Quinn had ever heard.

He took a deep breath and walked toward the first Chiriga grouping. Faxon walked a comfortable distance behind him. The man wasn't stupid. He'd give him that much. He hoped the Chirigas would allow Faxon close enough to safely touch the light net before they attacked.

The sound seemed amplified, but he didn't let his apprehension show.

As he stepped toward the light net, he wondered if Roberts watched nearby. She'd better keep that extra light net close at hand or he wouldn't survive this thing.

He felt the Chirigas fighting to restrain the razor-sharp vines. To him, it looked like a trap. Would Faxon sense his betrayal?

Quinn reached out to the light net and pressed his palm into the framework.

"It reacts to your thoughts and communicates them to the plants. Close your eyes and ask for pollen."

Faxon reached out and grabbed Quinn's arm, holding his hand against the light net. With his other hand, Faxon reluctantly pressed it against the light net.

Quinn hung his head, knowing there was no other way to stop Faxon—and no way for him to escape this attack either.

The hum that reverberated through him was a feral growl filled with fury. Faxon would soon pay for what he'd done to Nearra. Quinn braced himself for the puncture of thorns about to riddle his body.

A bird squawked. Chirigas chirred. One of the team members coughed.

The humming quaked through him. He glanced down at the light net, watching the pulse of lights begin.

Brush rustled. His hand ached.

Like a catapult, spiked vines snapped toward him and Faxon.

The first vine struck Faxon in the chest, piercing his flesh, and pinning him against the second Chiriga plant.

Razors dug into Quinn's flesh, but he kept his hand against the light net. The Chirigas had to know that he'd brought Faxon to them. He closed his eyes, the pain radiating in arcs through his shuddering frame.

A rustling sound from beneath the light net drew his attention.

The young Chiriga's vine wrapped around his torso and pulled him underneath the light net.

He screamed, his skin raking the ground, but in moments, he found himself out of the middle of the attack.

A light net fell over him. He gazed toward the brush.

Roberts crouched there, relief mixing with the pain in her eyes. He saw in her eyes that she wanted to go to him.

"Dad!" Dale screamed. "Dad!"

Again, Faxon screamed, but the vines wrapped like ropes around him, dragging him toward the purple leaves. One of the Chiriga blossoms opened wide and engulfed him. Sanji and Peetrek leaped at the three First Contact team members.

Laser fire punctuated the horrible rattling that filled the grove. One man fell.

Another series of blasts burned through the grove.

Someone shouted. More laser fire. Two people went down. Dale ran.

One last time, Faxon shrieked, but the muffled sound quickly dissipated into silence. All of the vines retracted and the rattling sound stopped.

After a few agonizing moments of silence, the Chiriga blossom opened, dumping the lifeless body of Commander Derek Faxon onto the ground.

"It's over," Quinn muttered.

The soothing energy of the light net pulsed over his skin. The pain lessened. He gazed up at the motionless young Chiriga beside him. It saved his life—that and the light net. He reached out and lightly touched its stalk.

Roberts fell down beside him, a hand against his torn and bloody face. "Sayre, you did it! And you didn't get yourself killed!" She leaned down and kissed him.

His lips urgently met hers and he let her cradle his head in her lap.

"Thanks to you and this Chiriga plant."

She smoothed the hair out of his eyes and stroked his face. "Faxon finally got what he deserved."

He nodded. "Now I have to see to it that the government has all the data on what he did here. We'd better get back and uplink that report."

Roberts helped him to his feet and he hobbled beside her to the gate. Nuriel and Peetrek trained rifles on the remaining First Contact team member, who cowered on the ground at their feet. Veider lay dead on the ground. Quinn's heart wrenched when he saw Sanji lying in the brush.

"Sanji!" he shouted, and limped over to him. Searching frantically for a pulse, Quinn found none.

Gently, Roberts moved him out of the way and examined Sanji. The scorch marks of a laser discharge burned into Sanji's tunic on the right side of his chest. His pupils were fixed and dilated.

She tilted Sanji's head up and attempted to resuscitate him. After a few minutes, there was still no life in Sanji's eyes. Roberts kept trying, but out here with no equipment, Quinn knew there was little else she could do.

"I'm sorry, Sayre," she said finally. "I've got a very weak pulse, but it's fading. It won't be long."

"No!" he shouted, and frantically shook the man's shoulders. "Sanji, get up! Don't do this to me, get up!"

One more time, he shook Sanji, the tears streaking down his face. "Aw, dammit, Sanj. I told you not to come out here alone. Why'd ya have to come after me?" His voice cracked and he fought to hold back his sorrow. "Keep trying! Maybe we can get him back to the *Magellan* and get him on life support?"

She kept her vigil of breaths and compressions. "There's not much else we can do for him, Sayre."

Roberts's words were red-hot pokers drilled into his chest. He stood up and turned away. Sanji shouldn't have been out here. He'd told him to stay with the *Magellan*. Why'd he fall for Dale's line of shit? Dead like Larena. Would he walk with Sanji on the astralscape like he had Larena? Cursed by that stupid accident to have his dreams haunted by ghosts.

He winced. People he couldn't save.

Finally, Nuriel knelt beside Sanji, and from his pouch, he

retrieved a light net. He laid it across Sanji's wound and pressed his hands against it.

"Hold eye soul in," Nuriel said softly. "Maybe no time for Haven?"

Wait, Haven? What did he mean by that? He'd always wondered what Haven meant to the Shikari's, but there had never been time to ask.

"What does that mean?" Quinn demanded, moving toward the Shikari.

Nuriel gazed searchingly at him for a moment. "It many things, but at end, all Shikari's pass through Haven. To better life."

Like Larena. He stared at the light net stretched across Sanji's chest. Was there some way—any way—to stop Sanji from crossing through? Or had he finally lost his mind and believed these alien superstitions?

He gazed at Sanji's still frame and the emptiness in his best friend's eyes. He clenched his hand into a fist. He had to go to Haven and try. Maybe it wasn't too late for Sanji?

He whirled around, gripping Roberts' shoulders. "I'm going after him."

"Going after who?" she asked.

He let go of her and ran down the path toward the boat. His ankle throbbed, but he gritted his teeth and kept moving.

"Sayre, wait! Where are you going? Sayre!"

"He goes to Haven," said Peetrek softly.

Sayre rushed through the gate and onto the pathway. Brush blurred on both sides until he reached the cove. Faxon's boat was still tethered there, so he scrambled into it. He fired up the engines, zipping into the clogged, serpentine channel at breakneck speed. In moments, the voices calling after him had died away.

They'd understand when he brought Sanji back. With the Chiriga pollen, he'd be able to walk through Haven for real, not just in his dreams.

This time, it would be enough.

TWENTY-SIX

COMMANDER GAGE, accompanied by Taka and Kuruk, landed at the Chiriga breeding grounds moments before the laser fire started. Using Kuruk's scanner, they traced Sayre to the cove. Gage expected trouble, but not so soon.

He ducked against the boat's engine housing and grabbed a pistol from his belt.

Scanning the line of trees, Kuruk pointed at a pathway leading into the wilds.

"The scanner has located two implants," said Kuruk, his voice low. "They have the same signatures."

Gage smiled. His gamble paid off. Anthony Dale Faxon *had* been aboard the *Augustine* that night. The scanner proved it.

As abruptly as it began, the laser fire ceased. Only the click of insects and sound of water undulating against the boat filled the silence. A faint, burnt scent hung in the air. Gage rose from a crouch and motioned Taka and Kuruk behind him as he climbed onto the bank.

Something crashed through the brush. Gage whirled.

Dale Faxon rushed past, nearly knocking Gage down.

Gage gritted his teeth, his grip tightening on the pistol. Young Faxon would pay for the destruction of the *Augustine*—and for killing Matt.

He would see to it.

"Kuruk, give me that scanner."

Kuruk handed him the slim, black device.

"Both of you—find Sayre. I'll retrieve Park."

Taka started to protest, but Gage turned away, hurrying after Park.

The brush was thick and Gage fought his way through it as he closed the gap behind young Faxon.

Ahead, the moors loomed. Dale skidded to a stop and turned. His face was white as Gage moved toward him.

"You almost got away with it—Faxon," said Gage, pistol pointed toward the young man's chest. "But the government gets the last laugh."

Dale sneered at him. "You have no proof of anything, Gage. You can't even place me aboard the Augustine that night."

He took a step forward, but Gage thrust the pistol against his chest.

Dale stopped. A sheen of sweat glistened on his upper lip.

"Remember the shuttle accident you experienced en route to the Augustine?"

"Of course, I remember it! I was in the hospital for a week after that. Like everybody else aboard that shuttle."

Gage sucked in a breath of air. "It was staged. You were used as a test subject for a neural combat implant. It's in your head right now, Faxon."

"What?" His mouth gaped.

"It's true. Have a scan done and you'll find it. We had a scan done five years ago—at the comm station. The one on the Augustine." Gage smiled knowingly at him. "But you probably didn't know that, did you?"

Dale's face scrunched into a pained expression as he considered his situation. Finally, the smirk returned. "I don't care what's there, Gage. You can't prove I sent that message."

He smiled. "But I can. Sayre also had an implant. Two of you from that shuttle were assigned to the Augustine. And Sayre has an airtight alibi."

"Sayre has nothing."

"I have the video sequence placing Sayre in the engine room when that message was sent. Scans registered a combat implant near the comm station. By elimination, that can only be you, Dale."

"But there were still two of us from that shuttle aboard the Augustine. And everyone knows that those log files were damaged. You can't prove anything."

Gage set his jaw. He had one last card to play.

Dale didn't seem shaken. He paced around the edge of the moors. "Give it up, old man," he snarled. "With two exact implants aboard, you still can't prove I sent that message. You've got nothing, old man!"

Gage reached into his pocket and slid out the small, flat scanner. He held it out to Dale and a series of red lights twitched across the display along with an alphanumeric number.

"According to this display, you have a neural implant in your head. It's an exact match to those combat implants. Each one has a unique serial number and yours matches the implant registered at the comm board that night."

Dale's mouth fell open.

"I ought to know. I designed them."

Gage stepped closer. "Anthony Dale Faxon, you're under arrest for the destruction of the Augustine, for murder, and privateering."

For an instant, their gazes met, the smug expression long gone from Dale's face. His shock quickly turned to fury.

Dale lunged for the pistol, but Gage pivoted and Dale slammed into the ground. Gage pounced on him, forcing Dale's arm behind his back. He ground the barrel of the pistol into Dale's side.

"I'd love to shoot you right here, but the pleasure of seeing you interrogated and imprisoned far outweighs the instant gratification of shooting you."

Gage jerked him up from the ground and shoved him forward. Then they started back for the boat.

For the first time in five years, Gage's shoulders felt lighter. Some good finally came from those disastrous implants. They found Matt's killer and the crew of the *Augustine* had been vindicated.

He sighed. And so had Sayre. He owed the man a debt and an apology.

TWENTY-SEVEN

"WHY WOULD SAYRE GO TO HAVEN?" Tarateal asked Peetrek.

Why would Sayre want to go back there? Had he finally lost it? What possible reason could he have to go there, especially with Sanji barely clinging to life?

She checked Sanji's pulse again. Thready. The light net across his chest pulsed with a steady, vibrant light.

Was it keeping this whisper-of-a-pulse in Sanji's body?

Peetrek finished tying a knot in the vine binding the First Contact team members' hands behind their backs. Peetrek stood up, flexing his arms, and then turned toward Tarateal. "Quinn Sayre enters astral."

"Astral?" Had there been some sort of chamber that she hadn't noticed? Somewhere the Shikari's laid his wife to rest?

"Where *milako* ghosts journey alongside Shikari eye souls. Their eye souls cross Haven on endless journey. Quinn Sayre go there. See wife before she...go on. He go now...try send friend back."

Astral...her thoughts reached backward, trying to remember what Sayre had been talking about. He'd mentioned it before. He'd been talking a little crazy about it, called it *walking the astral*. He'd said that his accident gave him some bizarre ability.

Suddenly, it hit her and she gasped. Visiondust.

Faxon's sole reason for wanting the pollen in the first place. She'd never tried Visiondust, but she'd heard of its wild visions. People claimed to see mythical worlds, past civilizations, and even Heaven. Maybe, just maybe there was a grain of truth in those visions, some sort of commonality to it?

She shuddered. Sayre was going to use the Visiondust, thinking he could somehow help Sanji with it. It didn't take much Visiondust to cause an overdose in humans. Heart failure, coma—the list was long and terrifying.

"Peetrek!" she cried, taking hold of his arm. "Sayre's in trouble. He'll kill himself out there. We've got to stop him. Please! Is there a faster route to Haven?"

He snapped his head up. "I take you."

"Nuriel, will you stay with Sanji?"

Nuriel's head snapped up as he laid a second light net across Sanji's face.

Peetrek motioned her through the Chiriga grove and she followed.

She paused when they reached Faxon's body. Even a beast like Faxon deserved a proper burial. Perhaps they'd bury him when Sayre was safe?

Peetrek waved her onto a path and she ran toward it.

Out the corner of her eye, something dark wavered. She turned.

A massive, opaque shadow coiled up from Faxon's body, expanding as it rose. Shrill chirring pierced the calm, the Chirigas suddenly frantic.

Tarateal's blood chilled as the thing loomed over her like a black phantom. Even the Chirigas were frightened.

"*Mazanaur!*" Peetrek screamed. "Curse rise!"

Tarateal ran toward the priest. "What is it?"

"Shadow soul!" shouted Peetrek. "It consume us!"

The lithe priest rushed away from the grove, Tarateal running behind him.

The ground shook. She stumbled. Tree limbs ripped across her arms.

Peetrek veered right.

From somewhere behind her, branches cracked. A rushing sound built in the silence. She sucked in a hot breath of air, Peetrek's frenzied pace difficult to match.

The path snaked over a hilltop. She pounded over the top, her feet aching. The wind rose. Rushing toward them.

Peetrek yanked her to the ground as the beastlike shadow leaped at them. It rolled down the hillside, a bitter cry echoing through the trees.

She scurried to her feet and dashed down a side path toward the narrow strip of land that connected another moor island.

Again, the soft padding of a pantheresque shadow whispered behind them, speed gaining, air rushing.

Somewhere on the string of moor islands, Tarateal realized that Peetrek was no longer beside her. She raced across a swampy clearing, waist-high grasses crunching beneath her waterlogged, mud-heavy boots.

A ghostly yowl bellowed through the wilds.

She ran, realizing she'd been here before. Familiar paths and thin flagpole trees rose ahead.

From somewhere behind, the padding of ghost feet echoed again, slowly picking up speed.

She ran harder, her throat hot and raw, breath ragged.

Ahead, the mist hung heavy over the swampy land, the hue like ash. It smelled hot and rotten with sulfur and toxins. She held a hand over her mouth.

Toxins? Lomasi had said that the poison shadows would kill her people.

Would they also kill Faxon's shadow soul? It was her best chance.

She veered left, slipping around a dying tree that hung decaying limbs over the moors.

It was her only chance.

The shadow panther's pule raked across her spine.

She pushed harder through a stretch of dead trees, the mist burning her eyes. The rush of air drowned out her hearing.

Ghost claws slashed across her shoulder. She stumbled. Mist swirled.

Pain burned like a fuse down her arm.

Another hoarse cry, shadow panther legs springing.

She fell and darkness enveloped her. Mist choked her, vapor clogging her lungs. She gasped for air as the shadow soul tore at her torso. With a wrenching shriek, the massive shadow reared up, ghost claws unsheathed, plunging.

She turned her head. "Forgive me, Quinn," she whispered.

Shadows slithered up from the poisoned ground, wrapping tendrils around Faxon's shadow soul, immobilizing it.

She pounded on the ones binding her wrists and ankles until they dissolved. As the other shadows ripped and tore at Faxon's shadow soul, the pantherlike thing screeched and fought to escape.

Tarateal lunged forward and rolled away.

She crawled through the grasses, poisons filling her lungs. It took most of her strength to drag herself out of the poison and into clean air. She collapsed headfirst into the swamp water, clawing desperately to reach the cay at the end of the moor island chain.

When the columns rose ahead, she burst into tears of relief as she crawled onto the bank and hugged the ground. Her lungs burned with every breath. She struggled to her feet when she saw Peetrek rush out of Haven.

"Tarateal Roberts!" he cried. His hand pressed to her throat. He shook his head. "The shadows have poisoned you."

She nodded, pulling away, and staggered toward the building, summoning the remnants of her voice. "Sayre."

Peetrek silently took her arm, steering her inside and toward the onyx square. He pointed. "Quinn Sayre went through here."

Her legs turned rubbery. She crumpled against the wall, weakness washing over her body. For a moment, she closed her eyes and concentrated on standing. No good. She wheezed, the rawness stretching white hot fingers down her throat and into her chest.

She'd wait for him here. She'd be here when he came back. No matter what, she'd be here.

"Peetrek." She gripped his arm. "Don't let—Sayre—die in there. Please." Another painful breath rippled through her chest. "I need him. Please, Peetrek. Don't let him—die. If something happens...and we're separated, tell him to—go to Silver Orca."

The priest smoothed the hair from her eyes and nodded. "Rest, Tarateal Roberts. We must banish the poison shadows or they will claim your eye soul."

She shook her head. It was more than that. So much more than that. It would take away hers and Quinn's last chance to be together. Sayre was in trouble—maybe dying—and she couldn't move.

Swallowing her own spit sent furrows of razor-sharp pain throbbing down her throat. Wincing, she glanced up at the onyx square on the wall.

Come home, Quinn. I'll stay here as long as I can. Just come back.

She hoped she could last long enough for Sayre to hold her in his arms again. Maybe Taka would find them? Maybe the poison could be stopped in time?

"Salice Minor, Peetrek," she said, her voice strained and hoarse. "Remember for me. I'm begging you."

TWENTY-EIGHT

AFTER INHALING THE CHIRIGA POLLEN, Sayre walked through the onyx square. His heart pounded wildly as he tried to keep his thoughts centered on Sanji. He moved quickly through the now-familiar astralscape, indigo ribbons of star fields beneath his feet.

Already, he felt the life pulsating across the strange landscape. Stars and planets lit the horizon in all directions. It felt like he'd reached some sort of crossroad. It reminded him of Las Vegas back on Earth. All gaudy, flashing lights outlining desert mirages of *what-ifs*.

His life was filled with so many what-ifs. What if he'd stayed with Tarateal? What if he'd saved Matt Gage? What if he'd stayed in the military? Here he was, throwing away his life for that one big chance at fame in the Rim. Gambling away his friends and the bits and pieces of his life in this vast desert of uninhabited worlds for a mirage.

What should have been a fascinating case study of sentient plant species and their humanoid caretakers had turned into cheap drug-running where lots of people died. He had to ensure that no one picked up where Faxon left off on Nearra.

Already, his skin had lost its healthy cast and his stomach burned deep with fire. It was much worse than ever and he didn't have his pills. A flicker of weakness shot through his knees, but he kept moving in search of ghosts. He had to find Sanji—somehow.

Would his grief cause Sanji to linger in this astralscape—like Larena had, waiting for him for so long?

He kept his thoughts centered on Sanji as he passed through an icy alcove of stars and into the frantic rush of lights. Chills rolled across his arms and he drew them against his torso, watching stars shoot across the indigo darkness.

Endless streams of lights flitted around him and he wondered what they were—more ghosts? Was Sanji somehow among those flutters of lights? Or was the Visiondust making him hallucinate?

Following every surging light was impossible, so he concentrated on Sanji until the comm specialist's image rose up from the ribbon of stars beneath his feet. His stomach hurt so badly.

"Quinn, I should have listened to you," said Sanji, behind him, his voice sad. "I did not see the laser rifle until it was too late."

Quinn turned. "I know. It's all right."

Sanji squinted at him. "You have not perished, too, I hope?"

"No, Sanj," he answered, fighting down the quiver in his voice. "I followed you into this—this astralscape or whatever the hell it is. Now, I'm going to get you out of here."

"How? How do I leave this place?"

"I—I don't know, but we've gotta try, okay?"

Sanji nodded.

"Follow me."

Sanji walked along beside Quinn. All around them stars trailed across the darkness in streaks of blue and gold. Along the path, pearls of white light scattered at their feet, dissolving into glimmers then disappearing.

The whole universe seemed to stretch before them. It was all he'd ever wanted, but now, all he wanted lay within a few meters of him. On the other side of that onyx square.

Ahead, Quinn saw the alcove he'd passed earlier. They were

getting close. He glanced at Sanji. Faint grid lines shimmered across his face and chest.

Quinn smiled, recognizing the pattern. The light nets! They were working! If he could just reach Haven again, then maybe Sanji would pull through? Then he'd take Tarateal Roberts in his arms again.

For real. For good.

Every step made his stomach throb, each one harder and harder to take. Finally, he hunched over, the pain sharp as a razor. He gritted his teeth.

No, not here. Not now!

"Are we going home to Jammu?" Sanji asked.

Quinn flashed him a weak smile. "Don't worry about that now. Let's concentrate on getting out of here. Keep your eyes on the ribbon of stars and don't leave it. No matter what, okay?"

Sanji kept moving, talking about Faxon's death and what would happen to the *Magellan* and Nearra.

Good, Sanji needed the distraction.

He let the lanky man babble, knowing they were moving closer and closer to the onyx square. He didn't know how much time they had. If he could just get Sanji through to the other side of Haven, everything would be okay. They were almost safe.

Maybe, just this once, his luck would hold?

"Will you and the *Magellan* leave Nearra now that Faxon is dead?"

Quinn nodded. "No worries, Sanj." His voice was tight with pain. "You'll be right there when we do."

Sanji didn't seem to have heard Quinn, or if he did, he didn't respond. His distraction was increasing and his form seemed more ghostlike as they moved toward the alcove.

Just a few more steps ahead. They could make it.

The closer Sanji got to the onyx square, the more transparent his form became, dissipating as he talked.

Quinn's heart hammered against his chest as they reached the alcove.

Now. They had to go through now.

Red-hot pain exploded through Sayre's middle, knocking him to his knees. He clutched his stomach as the nausea rose in his throat. Salty blood mixed with sourness. He gagged. No! Not now!

Sanji stopped walking. They were running out of time!

"Go, Sanji! Quickly!"

Fighting the agony in his gut, he scrambled forward, shoving Sanji into the blackness ahead.

A piercing pain gripped his chest and Quinn sank to his knees, unable to move. His lips were wet with blood as his gut pulsed with fire.

A cold emptiness shivered through him. And he knew. He wasn't going to make it back to Haven.

He thought of Tarateal and he cursed. She was the best thing that had ever happened to him. Twice.

Why'd he have to rediscover that now? Now—when it was too late?

His heart pounded in his ears and rattled through his head like the marching of soldiers. He gasped for air.

Too much Visiondust. His muscles corded and he fought to breathe.

Dying alone.

He'd never wanted to die alone. Now, he understood Tarateal's fear. Even her fear of deep space.

That empty feeling clutched his chest now and he dreaded that final moment of consciousness.

He thought about the Nearran moors. The mist that had collected on Tarateal's eyelids and cheeks, glistening against her skin, and dampening her hair into ringlets. He could almost see her waiting on the other side of Haven for him, fingers pressed against that onyx square, her smile anxious, oval face bright. He swallowed hard. He wanted nothing more than to meet her there.

He thought about the biosphere where he grew up. Of the first ship he'd ever flown. Teaming up with Sanji on the *Augustine* and then again in Jammu. Matt Gage. He winced. At least the young man hadn't died alone. That was a comfort now.

Quinn wanted to close his eyes and wake up aboard his own ship surrounded by his crew, Tarateal beside him.

But it was just too far away.

"Tarateal!" he shouted at the square.

Frantically, he rolled onto his stomach and dragged himself across the ribbon of stars. If he concentrated, he could follow Sanji through.

Pain wrenched his gut and he held in a shout, dragging himself forward again, agony gnawing through his torso.

Softly, his consciousness began to blend into the alcove's darkness. Shooting stars whispered around him, the sounds reminding him of the surf against Sancian beaches. He closed his eyes, imagining the rosy-colored water and green-flecked beaches. Tarateal's smile in twilight. He was adrift in that rosy-colored surf, the darkness closing in around him.

He felt his resolve breaking down. He couldn't fight the pain any longer.

A gold, latticelike flicker brushed across him. Only then, did he let go.

TWENTY-NINE

LIGHT AND SHADOWS intertwined and released in the faint glow of the onyx square. Tarateal lifted her cheek from the stone wall and stared directly into the square's swirling blackness. Her heart raced.

Sayre! He was returning with Sanji.

Forcing the remains of her strength into aching muscles, she sat up, managing a smile for him. Was he hurt, maybe critical? What if he was in cardiac arrest from that horrible Visiondust? There was no telling what had happened inside that thing.

The hand that plunged through the watery substance startled her as it clawed for a handhold. Peetrek grabbed hold and pulled.

The man plummeted from the square and cracked against the stone floor. She strained to see his face while he lay groaning.

"Sayre!" she cried, the syllables clawing into her scorched throat. "Oh, God, Quinn! You scared me to death!"

He had to be all right. He had to be. She reached for him, his skin warm to her touch.

When he looked up, eyes sad, face long, it took her several

moments to realize it was Sanji Shahir who lay on Haven's stone floor. Not Sayre. Her heart wrenched.

Frantic, Tarateal turned back to the square, waiting for Sayre to follow him through.

"C'mon, Sayre!" she shouted. Too much had already happened. "Sayre, where are you?"

The moments dragged by and Sayre still hadn't emerged.

Her heart plummeted into her stomach. No, he had to come back. Her chest burned as she scraped across the floor toward Sanji.

"Where's Sayre!" she demanded, grabbing Sanji's arm.

He shook his head, disoriented, and could only stare at her in confusion.

"Quinn Sayre," she cried, tears threading down her face. She shook him. "He went in...after you. Where is he?"

His gaze wandered. "I—I don't remember. Everything is jumbled. I remember seeing Quinn...but it seems so long ago. Or maybe a dream?" He pointed toward the doorway, one of the columns barely visible through the outer threshold. "I remember that doorway," he answered slowly. "And a grove. Then darkness." He cast a lengthy stare at the onyx square. "I heard his voice. He spoke to me. There were moments of nothing and then his voice. I do not remember leaving him." Suddenly surprised, his gaze traveled around the dimly lit room. "Why am I here? Where is Faxon?" His voice trailed off when he saw Tarateal's panicked expression. "Is Quinn all right?"

"Faxon's dead," she said, and sucked in a weak breath. "Didn't you see Sayre—in there? Anywhere?"

Maybe he'd been too weak to leave that place? She dragged herself toward the square and clawed at it, trying to find some way to go beyond it. He needed help. She was certain of it.

The square remained rigid to her touch. Her frantic gaze fell to Peetrek.

"Please," she hissed. "Go in after him! Please."

Peetrek jerked his head upward and reached to the pouch at his side. From it, he retrieved a small handful of Chiriga pollen. He pressed his hand over his nose and inhaled. For a long time, he stood there, eyes closed, blue dust twinkling across the chestnut hide of his face. Finally, he walked toward the square. Extending both arms, he pressed his hands against the square. It parted like water and he plunged through the opening.

Again, Tarateal sank against the stone wall, her breaths coming in gasps now. Sweat from a fever coated her face like a mask. She closed her eyes, fearing she may not be here when Sayre came through. The poison she'd led that shadow monster through had done its work on her, too. There hadn't been any other way to destroy it.

Poison gnawed away at her system. It was moving fast. Her eyelids drooped and she hugged the wall, the cool stone soothing.

In the distance, she heard voices. Footfalls against stone. They seemed so far away. Had it come from the onyx square? Or was it just the fever?

Another voice rasped against the silence. Taka?

"Taka, I'm here!" she shouted.

She listened again for the footsteps, for Taka's voice, until suddenly, Peetrek was there beside her, crouching, a hand against her shoulder. She braced herself, feeling his apprehension. He stiffened.

"I no find Quinn Sayre," he said in a whisper. "No flesh or eye soul walks the astral or beyond. All is quiet."

"No! You're wrong, Peetrek!" She dragged herself toward the square again, pain shooting steel rods through her legs. "Sayre! Sayre, please!"

She pounded the square with her fists, beating on the rigid surface, but she couldn't reach inside. Sobs wracked her body.

"Damn you, Sayre! Damn you for doing this to me again!"

She couldn't go in there after him. Hot tears flowed down her cheeks. Only then did she realize that she'd never see him again.

Peetrek gently pulled her back and she collapsed, the ceiling spinning. She touched Peetrek's arm, feeling lost. It didn't matter. Nothing mattered now.

"Please, Peetrek—go back in—find him." It was such an effort to squeeze out the words from her nearly paralyzed vocal cords.

Hands took hold of her legs and gripped her shoulders. Voices mixed with the rushing sound in her ears. Faces she didn't recognize hovered over her.

"They heard our distress signal," said a voice—Taka? It sounded so tinny and far away. She couldn't make out the jumble of words.

Something about a hospital ship.

"Leaving—your...world now. Peetrek. Find. Him."

The last thing she felt before the onyx darkness enveloped her was Peetrek taking her hand.

"I do best, Tarateal Roberts," he whispered into her ear.

She clutched at the moments of comfort his words brought as consciousness slipped from her grasp.

THIRTY

TARATEAL REGAINED CONSCIOUSNESS. Terrified, she stared at the medtechs through the remnants of deep sleep, her last memory surging through her head. She'd been lying in a dark chamber, that ominous onyx square against her fingertips, calling for Sayre. She'd begged Peetrek to find him.

Where was she?

She glanced wildly around. The bright whiteness of the room blinded her. Where were the others? Did they find Sayre? Her breath caught, her stomach sinking.

What if Sayre never came back?

Her whole body felt stiff and unresponsive, fingers clutching the soft white bedsheets she'd twisted around her in the narrow hospital room bed. She'd spent a lifetime around hospital beds, syringes, and scanners. The cool air smelled tart, almost lemony as she pulled in a deep breath. What had they done to her and where was the rest of the crew?

Finally, she noticed the blue curtain drawn around her bed, flashes of the small white room beyond. And the dull ache in her hand as she reached toward the curtains and peeled them open. Bright shiny white. Soft green and yellow flashes from the vital signs monitor on the wall.

She was in a hospital.

A walnut-haired medtech in a blue lab coat and white scrubs slid the curtain open. Humming softly, she moved toward the bed. Tarateal grabbed at her coattail and missed as the woman's hand scanner gurgled and beeped as it touched pressure points on Tarateal's body.

Tarateal sighed. She wasn't used to being on this side of the fence.

The medtech gently pressed Tarateal's hand back against the bed. Her arms felt leaden, and any movement at all was difficult.

"WhereamI," she mumbled, the words slurring together from the numbness in her tongue.

"You're in hospital on Salice Minor, Ms. Roberts," said the woman as she laid a pale green blanket across Tarateal's shivering frame. "Your motor skills will improve quite a bit over the next twenty-four hours." The woman set down her scanner. "The poison that almost killed you was very complex, so it took some time to find an antidote. As the toxins dissipate, so will the paralysis, so don't try to do too much until you feel like yourself again."

Herself? What did it even feel like to be herself? She didn't know anymore. Childhood memories of Douglas firs and waterfalls, rainy afternoons and hot chamomile tea mixed with flights to the Rim, misty moors—moonlight and stars in Sayre's arms. Her eyes welled with tears.

"Where," she said, concentrating on every word. "Are. The. Others?"

The woman shook her head. "You need to rest. We can talk about those things later."

"No!" Tarateal shouted, the tears slipping down her cheeks. "Have to. Know. Now." Her hands were too heavy and clumsy to wipe them away.

The medtech sighed as she pulled a white rolling stool over beside the bed. She leaned forward, her hands clasped together.

"The information we have is sketchy. Two private vessels heard the *Magellan's* distress signal and came to your assistance. They called in other support vessels, including a hospital ship. Several of the injured were transported off-world to nearby medical facilities for treatment."

The medtech laid her hand against Tarateal's arm. She felt a sharp ache, her heart thumping against her chest.

"Your condition was the most serious, Ms. Roberts, requiring a med evac stasis to stabilize you. You were only moved to Salice Minor yesterday."

"Was. Everyone. Rescued?"

Tarateal sighed in frustration, wanting to blurt out a hundred questions. But there was an urgent one on her lips. *Sayre! Did you find Sayre?*

The medtech shook her head. "I'm sorry, no."

"No?" Tarateal stiffened. The ache in her chest began to throb, her heart racing as the medtech gripped Tarateal's arm tighter.

"Three people are still listed as missing."

"Show me," Tarateal said in a strained voice. "Names. Sayre?"

Already the woman was nodding. "I'm sorry. That name wasn't listed among the injured."

Stunned, Tarateal turned away. No. This wasn't happening. She bit back a strangled sob and pressed her face into the pillow.

"I know all of this is a shock to you, but the search and rescue mission is still underway as of this morning. They may still find your missing crew members. I'll keep checking on this for you. What was the name again?"

"Quinn. Sayre," she said in a tight voice, struggling against the ache in her chest.

"As soon as your motor skills improve, you'll move to a transition room where you can access data and contact your crew members.

They're spread out from here to the Rim outposts, but we'll get you in contact with them."

Spread out from here to Haven. Maybe Peetrek found Sayre alive and brought him back to the Shikari camp? As soon as she was well enough to travel, she'd return to Nearra.

She had to find Quinn.

"Thank—you," she answered. "I'd like. That."

"We're gathering all the information available, including data from the *Magellan*'s records. It might help you reconnect with the crew. We should have it all for you by tomorrow."

She nodded. Anything that would get her back to the Rim.

AS THE DAY WORE ON, Tarateal felt in control again, her fingers and toes responsive as the heavy stiffness faded away. By evening, she was able to hold a spoon and eat a little soup on her own. Satisfied with her progress, the medtechs wheeled her into a transition room.

Small and boxy, it was still stark and shiny white against the dull nickel bed frame. A light green recliner sat beside a small round window that let in the stars. The faint scent of fried fish hung above the lemony smell as she noticed the orange duffel bag on the floor beside the bed. It looked brand new. A pair of navy blue sweats was stacked neatly inside the bag. A small datapad lying on top. Its silver frame and screen were dented and scratched, the touch surface already beginning to repair the damage as a green light winked back at her.

She smiled. Her datapad. From the *Magellan*.

Moments after the medtechs left her alone, she picked up her datapad and sat down in the recliner by the window. She touched the datapad's screen and it flickered on, information retrievals in process. Right now, she'd take anything she could get about the *Magellan* and what had happened after she left Haven.

For hours, she studied the data trails, stumbling over bits and pieces of her own safe and secure past as she searched. A copy of her certifications, her first commission on Lunar Colony. The shuttle crash that had nearly killed her. The images and clips from that crash made her shiver, but what frightened her more was the pattern that stared back her.

She traced her path of retreat far away from her sense of wonder and back to the safe, secure life that bored her to tears. Assignments near Earth. Lost promotions after turning down deep space missions. Reassignment to something worse followed, something very, very safe. By the time she reached FS-314, she was underexperienced and apparently overcompensated (according to her colleagues)

Always the same pattern. Every. Single. Time. Why hadn't she done something sooner? Taken a risk. A chance.

She turned her attention to the Magellan and Sayre, searching for medical reports, raw news footage, anything about Nearra, but nothing had reached the nets yet. How was that possible? If someone even farted on a first contact mission, it was all over the aggregate streams.

Maybe Gage had kept all of this quiet somehow?

Nearra. It all seemed like a bad dream now. How did she end up in the Rim this time? Breaking her pattern. Leaving her comfort zone. The thought of that journey terrified her more now than it had the day she left.

Had she really gone out there? With Sayre?

When her eyes began crossing from the exertion and the massive info dumps, she lay back in the bed. None of the information helped. She had more questions now than she did this morning.

The room's lighting was dim, simulating twilight. She rose and unsteadily moved to the wall, staring at the closed vertical blinds.

"Sunset," she said. "Behind Mount Baker."

The blinds clattered open, revealing a view of snow-capped Mount Baker shrouded in a fiery sky. Seeing the time-lapse vid made

Salice Minor feel familiar. Sometimes those Washington sunsets were a dull ache in her bones only lessened by the smell of pine and sea. Out here, she even missed the winter drizzle.

"Lights off," she spoke softly, her voice feeling more like her own now. "Backlight the sunset."

The sunset was luminous in the darkness, Mount Baker so close she could almost reach out and touch it. But even going home couldn't ease her pain.

She sat down on the bed and removed her slippers, her eyes turning watery. She would find him. Somehow. The medtechs promised her clothes in the morning. After stretching her arms and legs, she lay down, her churning thoughts dissipating. The sunset calmed her enough to finally close her eyes. But she knew that sleep would not come easily tonight.

And when it finally came, so did the dreams.

She dreamed she was flying, soaring high above a forest of gigantic trees. Massive cedars and firs. Washington State. Her body felt weightless despite the heavy white robe.

Until the mist rolled in.

At first, it only obscured the horizon, but soon it clumped around her like foam so thick it forced her back to the ground. When her feet touched, she sank into mud up to her knees. She fought the blue-black muck, raising her feet high until she found solid ground. Her muscles burned from the effort, but she managed to pull herself out of the bog.

All around her, mist shrouded gnarled, bent trees, the conical bases swelled and covered in blue moss. Creatures screeched and chirred around her, the noise nearly drowning out the gurgle of the moors. She wandered away from the water and collided with a tall, masked creature.

Peetrek—but the mask looked so foreboding. Not like she remembered him at all.

The creature's satiny chestnut sheen reminded her of a well-groomed quarter horse. His body was lithe and sinewy, muscles defined but not bulging. But his umber and red mask, striped white, terrified her.

"Peetrek—is that you?" she asked, backing away.

"Yes—help you remember, Tarateal Roberts."

She shook her head. "I have nothing to remember."

The creature reached out to her and she stumbled backward, fleeing. Trees rushed past, brush nicking her bare legs. When her feet hit the mud and began to sink, she screamed. The muck rose to her chest and bubbled up beneath her chin.

"Ms. Roberts, wake up. Ms. Roberts! You're having a nightmare."

Through the haze of sleep, she stared fearfully at a medtech standing over her bed, a hand on her arm. It had all been so real. The mud, the water...Peetrek. She shivered. Had she screamed out loud? Her whole body felt stiff now, especially her neck.

"I dreamed of water and strange creatures." Had that really been Peetrek?

The medtech eased her back against her pillow. "The poison has left you very weak and extremely disoriented. Sleep disturbances are common, but they rarely last over a few days." She pressed a hypodermic needle to Tarateal's arm. "This should help you get a good night's rest."

In a few moments, a calm washed over her and her eyelids began to droop. Peetrek and the moors tried to touch her dreams again. She tried to reach out to Peetrek and call Sayre's name, but she was slipping deeper into a dreamless sleep.

The medtech crept toward the door, snapping off the lights and whispering close to the blinds before she left.

One last time, Peetrek flitted on the edge of her memory and Tarateal tried to speak, but she was falling. Suddenly, she was flying above the treetops again, the Washington State drizzle tapping against her cheeks, scent of pine tingling against her nose. From the silence, someone whispered *silver orca* in her ear.

MORNING CAME TOO SOON, the call to breakfast nauseating. She rolled over, burying her face in the pillow. It felt like she'd battled an army last night. Her eyes burned and her muscles felt stiff. She ignored the breakfast and caught a few extra moments of warm sleep. Later, she would contact private charter ships. One that would take her as far as the Rim.

A few moments later, she bolted up from the bed. Silver Orca!

Sayre made her a promise that if they got separated, they'd each go to the Silver Orca Pub. Where they had their first date. Maybe he was there now? Waiting for her?

Hope trembled through her now as she struggled to rise from the bed. She hurried into the shower and let the warm water run over her body. The warmth felt good against her skin. She stood there, chin up, eyes closed, and let the steaming water blanket her body. Maybe he'd left a note for her there? Telling her where to find him.

She shut off the water and wrapped her shoulder-length hair in a towel. She slipped into a soft white robe, but when she reentered the transition room, she found a tan flight suit and white t-shirt on the bed. Quickly, she put them on along with loose-fitting black chukkas and towel-dried her hair.

She tried to sign herself out, but the medtechs refused. They agreed to consider her release in the morning pending the results of her blood test. She asked for comm access and agreed—in the morning.

Trying to occupy her mind and calm her anxiousness, Tarateal spent the morning on the computer, studying the routes of various charter vessels, choosing the best possibilities, and saving them into her mobile. Several charters journeyed to the Rim, but the Silver Orca Pub nagged at her. She needed to go there and if nothing else, leave a message for him.

THAT AFTERNOON, she met with a reassignment counselor, as required by her government contract. They would try to shuffle her back into service quickly, especially now that she had deep space experience. The dark-skinned woman was pleasant and reassuring as she ushered Tarateal into her office. Tarateal marveled at the smooth, ageless appearance of the woman's maple syrup complexion.

"I'm glad you're feeling better, Ms. Roberts," said the woman cheerfully. Her hair hung in sable triangular curls around her face. Her bobbed hair angled out on the right side, curving into a smooth C around her left ear. She folded her hands in front of her and led Tarateal into the black and white office.

"Thank you," she answered softly.

The carpet looked like raw granite. Desk and chairs looked like pressed sand, the texture raspy against Tarateal's hand as she touched the back of one. She noticed a faint blush of pink in the chairs. A black and white speckled cushion wrapped around the seat of the chair. Reluctantly, she sat down, her gaze shifting to the room. The walls had a faint grey color to them, drapes matching the speckled cushions. Seashells and rough rose quartz pieces dotted the tables and the counselor's desk. The woman sat down behind the desk and called up her console. A screen winked on in the middle of the woman's desk.

"Access Tarateal Roberts' file. This will be your fourth commission. That's not a lot of commissions, my dear. You've been very careful in your career."

Tarateal nodded. "I always tried to stay close to Earth. Before the Rim, FS-314 was as far as I wanted to go." Now, she'd give anything to be out in the Rim. To find him. Again, she gazed around the room, anxious to leave the hospital.

"According to my records, you're a medical technician with a class rating of one. We shouldn't have a problem placing you within any of our various government facilities."

"Good," Tarateal answered in a soft voice, distracted. "I'm glad that I'll have a choice this time around." Right now, though, she couldn't care less.

The woman picked up a pen and leaned back in her chair. "Your handling of this recent contract has proven your ability to adapt to a variety of situations. And they show that you learn quickly. Employers will notice that, Tarateal, especially the time you spent out in the Rim."

Tarateal sighed. It was all she'd ever wanted, a chance to go home. But now—honestly—she didn't care anymore. Everything felt so wrong now. The time she'd spent on Nearra had been the best moments in her life.

"Look," she began, her gaze not meeting the counselor's face, "I'm feeling very disoriented. I'm in no condition to decide on a commission right now. Can we reschedule this for another day?"

The smile disappeared from the woman's face. "Of course, Tarateal. Take as much time as you need. Choosing a commission can be very stressful. Take two or three days to rest, and in the meantime, we'll find something to suit you." The counselor leaned down and Tarateal heard a drawer scrape open. The counselor motioned toward the mobile in Tarateal's pocket and it beeped. "I sent you a list of commissions, about ten screens full. Think about the choices listed there, and if you see one that appeals to you, I'll put a hold on it. You can talk to me about it in a few days."

"Thank you for giving me more time," said Tarateal. She rose from the chair. "I'll be in touch."

As soon as I return from the Rim.

"Oh, I almost forgot," said the counselor with a polite smile. "A medtech left a file folder for you. She said it was additional information from the *Magellan*."

"Thank you," Tarateal mumbled, accepting the folder.

Tucking the folder under her arm, she hurried out of the office. Heaviness sat on her chest and she felt like she couldn't breathe. This place was making her feel claustrophobic.

She dashed down the hallway, weaving around carts and medtechs and visitors until she reached the main lobby. Holos of plants, simulated wood on the walls, streaming sound of water filling the vaulted space, the front all glass. Beyond the glass walls, Salice Minor's dark streets glimmered with LED lights, reminding her of old strands of neon that once lit up the night on Earth. Still, the heaviness on her chest persisted. She sucked in a thin breath of air. As she moved toward the row of doors, she collided with a man.

Papers went flying.

The dark-haired man bent over and collected the pages for her as she shuffled the sheets back into the folder.

"Sayre?" she asked.

The man looked up, confused. "What?"

"I'm terribly sorry," said Tarateal, tucking the folder underneath her arm. "I thought you were someone else."

"No harm done," said the man, and handed her the rest of the pages. He squinted at her. "Are you all right?"

"Fine," she answered, and fumbled with the papers and the folder.

He paused for a moment and finally moved toward the hallway.

"Miss," said a voice from behind.

Startled, she whirled around, nearly dropping the papers again. The voice seemed almost familiar, but the young man in the teal sweater didn't. He smiled at her and pointed at her wrist. "Do you have the time?"

She shook her head. "Sorry, I don't have a watch." She wasn't about to pull out her mobile and drop it. She was too unsteady.

"Thanks anyway," he said, and moved toward the exit.

The exit sign winked green at her. A smile slid onto her face. The way out at last.

Her whole body screamed, demanding to be free of all this technology and confusion. She brushed past a clerk and the doors parted in front of her, a soft whirring sound humming in her ears. She dashed outside, the spaceport's dry, stale air making her nose itch, and paused at the top of a gently sloping set of stairs.

People hurried past her, filtering into the hospital. Even the staleness of the recirculated air was comforting. If she closed her eyes, it felt like she was back aboard the *Magellan* again. Her heart fluttered.

And Sayre would be just down the hall.

The three flights of stairs, each one separated by a landing, ended near a bustling shuttle stop. People milled around the green awning that hung just beside the shuttle track. A shuttle glided down the track like a stream of molten metal. The sound was like an ocean swell as it slid to a stop in front of the awning. People rose from their seats and filed off the shuttle. Other passengers rushed onto the shuttle through doors in the back.

She smiled. The shuttle would take her into the city—to the Silver Orca. She needed to get away from this hospital for a while. Pick up some clothes, some food, her life—her place in time. It all felt so jumbled and out of order. Without looking back, Tarateal plunged down the stairs toward the shuttle stop.

The flow of people coming up the stairs nearly bowled her over. She tried to sidestep them, pushing through the wave that threatened to carry her back toward the station, but she shoved through to the first landing.

"Tarateal?" a voice cried. "Tarateal Roberts?"

She turned, glancing around for the face with the voice.

When a young couple with a baby surged past, there on the landing stood a man, his sable hair brushing the top of his jacket collar.

She held her breath.

He smiled, honey-colored eyes glowing, bruised face shadowed with stubble. Her heart bounced into her throat. The folder slid out of her hands, papers fluttering down the stairs.

"Quinn?"

His eyes were glassy as he held out a hand to her.

For a moment, she could only stare at him, afraid that if she moved, he would disappear forever.

She took a step toward him. Another. Blinked.

He was still there.

His brow furrowed, anguish in his eyes. "They told me you'd been poisoned," he said, his voice soft and aching. "I was so afraid you wouldn't be here...but I came anyway."

Her steps quickened until she was running. She fell into his arms and buried her face against his neck. His soft, cedary cologne wrapped around her like wool. His arms were tight against her, holding on for dear life.

"I thought I'd lost you forever, Quinn!"

She felt his tears hot against her cheek. "Peetrek said our eye souls were bound together, one forever looking for the other." His voice cracked. "Ever since I left Nearra, I've felt like I've been blinded in one eye, Tarateal."

His kisses simmered against her neck, burned on her lips. She stroked his hair, running her fingers across the wonderful curves of his face. She blazed a trail of kisses across his smooth jawline, down his neck.

"I'll follow you anywhere, Quinn."

He held her tighter as he laid his forehead against hers a moment. Then he let go, still gripping her hands.

"I waited for you to come back through," said Tarateal, squeezing his hands. "But it got later and later. I tried to hang on, but the poison—"

"It's okay," he said, his arms enfolding her again. "I tried to come back through, but I was too sick. Nuriel's light net kept me from dying."

She held him tighter. "Where's your crew?"

"Sanji's still in the hospital on Ramantra. He won't be out for a week or so. Poor guy almost died. They had to rebuild his rib cage after that laser blast, but he's doing fine. Kuruk and Taka are fine. Gage, too."

He let her go again. "The *Magellan* was hauled away as slag. With my share of the contract money and the salvage payment, I bought a new ship, the *Magellan II*. She's a little nicer this time. When Sanji's ready to travel, I'm shipping out again."

"What?" She gasped. "You're shipping out?"

He nodded. "Back to the Rim. I'm leading a new rediscovery mission to Nearra. After Dale Faxon and the others were arrested, the government officially listed Nearra's ecosystem as fragile. I've been given research clearance to return there."

Tarateal frowned at him, a wary look in her eye. "By the way, how many medtechs do you have for this mission?" she asked.

"Two," he said, laughing. "Because this research mission only requires two." He reached out and cupped her chin. "But I need you at my side, no matter what the mission."

His smile widened into a grin as he grabbed her hands and pulled her down the stairs toward the shuttle.

"Wait! My papers!"

"Leave 'em," he said with a grin. "They're ancient history. Let's take a ride!"

Quinn was right. All that mattered now was what lay ahead. She ran through the stack of papers, scattering them anew.

He pulled her into the back of the shuttle and into his arms. As the shuttle raced down the track, he settled in beside her and told her about his time in the Shikari camp and what he wanted to do there.

When the shuttle slid to a stop back at the hospital, they disembarked. A tall, lanky man waited at the stop. His brown hair was mottled grey and his face seemed sad. It was former commander Gage.

"Sayre, I need to talk to you," said Gage, his voice soft.

Stiffening, Sayre walked toward the man, and Tarateal followed. "Good to see you, sir."

"I heard they'd finally found you on Nearra. I tried to catch up to you, but was told you were en route to Salice Minor." He smiled at Tarateal. "So, I figured I'd find Tarateal here, too."

Smiling, Sayre slid his arm around her waist. "Couldn't get here fast enough."

Gage handed a paper to Sayre, who frowned and studied the document. "What's this?" he asked.

"That is the official communiqué clearing you of any wrongdoing aboard the Augustine," said Gage. "I asked to deliver it personally." Gage paused. "I did you a great injustice, Sayre. Forgive me. I know it's been a long time coming, but your name is finally clear. My son would have wanted it that way."

"Thank you, sir," said Sayre.

Gage held out his hand and Sayre shook it, surprise evident on his face.

"What about Dale?" Tarateal asked.

"Dale Faxon and the others were tried and convicted on several counts of drug trafficking," said Gage. "They were sent to a deep space prison facility. I made sure that all the Visiondust was seized and destroyed." He paused, smiling. "The source of the drug is listed as unknown."

Sayre's face brightened. "Thank you, sir. That means a lot to me."

Gage smiled and glanced at Tarateal. "Good luck to both of you," he said, and turned away.

Tarateal watched him disappear into the crowd surging up the stairs. Then she turned to Sayre. He grinned and took her in his arms, spinning her around. Her lips met his, his embrace warm and safe. She wanted to melt into his arms. She burned for his touch, longing to rediscover the curves of his body.

"It's been so long, Tarateal," he whispered into her ear, kissing it gently, sipping her skin.

A lifetime, she thought.

Arm in arm, they walked toward the shuttle track again, this time to the Silver Orca Pub.

"Tell me more about this new trip to the Rim," she said with a wry smile. "And don't leave out the good parts."

He grinned and held her close again as they stepped back onto the shuttle.

A week later, Tarateal was in his arms at the shuttle port, boarding the *Magellan II*, and bound for the Rim. Again.

And she couldn't wait to get there—with Quinn Sayre at her side.

***The End of* REDISCOVERY**

Want more of Lisa's science fiction? Check out

RECOMBINANT, Book 1: Experiencing True Purple

A Genetic-Engineering Military Alien Invasion War Saga

They stole his memories. Deleted his dreams.

Because he was government property.

They gave him one year to live. At an alien war front.

To save a world he'll never see.

Programmed to fight and kill…He just wants to live.

NOVELS BY L. S. SILVERTHORNE

Standalones:

REDISCOVERY

Experiencing True Purple series:

RECOMBINANT, Book 1

HELIX, Book 2

FORTHCOMING!

Experiencing True Purple series:

Splice, Book 3

Cipher, Book 4

Renascence, Book 5

OTHER NOVELS

Writing as Lisa Silverthorne
Paranormal Romance & Romantic Suspense

A Game of Lost Souls series:
THE CINDERELLA HOUR
THE PRINCE CHARMING HOUR
THE EVER AFTER HOUR
THE FALLEN HEARTS SEASON
THE RISING SPIRITS SEASON
THE ETERNAL SOULS SEASON
THE ROYAL WEDDING HOUR
THE HEAVENLY HONEYMOON HOUR

Standalones:
ISABEL'S TEARS
LANDFALL
PACIFIC BLUE TATTOO

Haunted Portraits series:
BEAUTY: CAPTURED AND FRAMED

FORTHCOMING!

Writing as Lisa Silverthorne
Paranormal Romance & Romantic Suspense

A Game of Lost Souls series:

The Divine Newlyweds Show, Book Nine **(Nov 2021)**

The Celestial Couples Show, Book Ten

The Enochian Apocalypse Show, Book Eleven

The Angelic Anniversary Hour, Book Twelve

A Game of Lost Souls—Angelic Hearts:

Muriel's Spark

Kesien's Fire

Anahera's Flame

Azrael's Embers

ABOUT THE AUTHOR

LISA SILVERTHORNE, writing as L.S. SILVERTHORNE, has published sixteen novels and over 100 short stories and novelettes in many genres. Her short fiction has appeared in professional publications that include: DAW Books, Roc Books, Prime Books, *Pulphouse Magazine,* and *Fiction River.* She lives in Las Vegas, Nevada.

Before you go, you are invited to please leave a **review of this book**!

Reviews are a wonderful way to help an author. They are also an exciting opportunity to share your honest thoughts with other readers, so **please post yours,** in as many places as possible!